HADRIAN'S FLIGHT

J. DANIEL SAWYER

Hadrian's Flight

A Science Fiction Adventure

AWP Fantasty, a division of ArtisticWhispers Productions, Inc.
Copyright © 2016 J. Daniel Sawyer
All Rights Reserved

Book Design by ArtisticWhispers
Cover art *Hadrian's Repose* © 2016 Kitty NicIaian
All rights reserved. Used with permission.

DEDICATION

For Miles, Graham, and Emerson

Whose adventures are just beginning

DEDICATION

CONTENTS

Skyguard

FROM HIS VANTAGE atop the long thermal column at the bottom edge of the ag dome, Haddy Jin scoped the hundreds-meter depth below him through his blink-lenses. Flicks of his fingers tweaked the primaries on his wings, allowing him to cut a grand circle in his designated airspace, sandwiched between a hard ceiling at the entrance to the ag dome and the top level commercial space of the Gallery.

Two fast blinks zoomed him in by a factor of ten. It made the image jittery, but it let him focus right down to the bottom of his zone where the Gallery shaft met the opening of Reservoir Cave.

No trouble down there, either. Nobody straying too close to the caged tracks where the massive lifts—with their on-board refreshment shops—ran from the bottom to the top of the Gallery at all four corners.

The fledgers—easy to spot with their wings marked by green stripes and blinking lights at their wing-tips—weren't allowed into the cave, where they'd have room to really get in trouble. They had to get the basics down first—the circling rise, the circling descent, the deliberate stall, the hard dive, the flattening recovery. The space in the Gallery wasn't exactly *ideal* for it—after training more fledgers than he could count, Haddy was of the firm opinion that the Gallery could stand being about four times its current size, in order to give the fledgers some horizontal latitude.

But not letting them go too horizontal was the point, according to the skymaster. First they had to get used to having wings, to trusting that the wings would carry them, then they had to get used to dealing with the z-axis as if it was a normal thing. Height was safe—the higher you flew, the more time you had to recover from a problem.

But, given the option, most fledgers would stick right near the ground, where they had no margin for error. Because they thought that falling was something to be afraid of. Which, apparently, was "normal."

Haddy didn't believe it for a minute. "Normal" couldn't be that stupid, or humans wouldn't have ever made it out of that awful gravity well where they'd started off.

Besides, Haddy *knew* it wasn't normal to be scared of heights—after all, he'd taken his share of tumbles, and broken a few bones, but not once since he could remember did he look over a ledge and get any kind of flutters other than the excited kind.

Heights were for soaring on. And on Luna, terminal velocity was only thirty-three kph for a flat fall anyway. A hard fall wouldn't do more than bang you up a little bit, unless you were mush-brained enough to fall on your wing (and get stabbed by a broken strut) or on your head (and maybe break your neck even if you were wearing your helmet).

Anyone who was that stupid kind of deserved to spend a month or two in the hospital getting themselves rebuilt.

But, he had to admit, most people he'd trained over the years had been more than a little defective in the brain-meat. They *did* get woozy at heights, and they kept trying to do acrobatics before they knew how the gear worked.

And then there were the wannabe dog fighters. They *never* waited until they were ready before they cut loose.

Not that there was anything in the world better than dogfighting. Snap your gaming goggles on, dive down to Reservoir Cave, and go at it team-on-team until everyone on the opposing team was dead—then go again. High-bank turns, hard flaps and peregrine dives and Herbsts and Cobras, enough to leave even Haddy's head spinning and his chest heaving for oxy.

Haddy side-slipped out of the thermal and descended for a bit. He didn't want to stray too high. If he broke the beam grate at the ceiling, well, that would mean a fine that would eat up half his bonus for skyguarding, and it would bump him down on the performance charts, too, and that would keep him out of a Reservoir Cave post.

That's where the primo assignments were. Two solid klicks long, half a klick wide, plenty of room to fly, with ducts at both ends to keep the air moving. Two major waterfalls coming off the condensation towers to swing round. It was the best place on the colony to fly, except for the race course, but that wasn't open to fliers except during competition and practice. Down in the cave you weren't keeping an eye on fledgers, you were making sure the dog fighters and advanced fliers behaved themselves—especially that they didn't break the hard-deck.

That was always a problem. More common than near-misses. When you were soaring up three hundred meters in the top of the cave by the condensation towers, and you saw all the naked people swimming and laying out on the rock beaches and generally running around like ants, it was pretty hard to resist the urge to swoop down and spook them. You did that over the water and they all dove down to get clear. Do it over the land and they scattered like gazelles running from a lion. It wasn't very nice, but it never stopped being fun.

But if the skyguard caught you, you'd get a *big* fine. Haddy'd gotten caught doing that enough times that it hurt his bank account just thinking about it. And if you got caught doing it too often, you'd get grounded, sometimes for months.

That had been the worst six months of Haddy's life—manning the booth renting out the wings, never allowed to put them on himself, looking at all that glorious air just *aching* to get flown in, and not able to do anything about it.

He'd been flying since his arms had been strong enough to handle the weight-load of the orn-suits his family had designed and manufactured for the last forty years, ever since they'd immigrated. Not being allowed to fly was like not being allowed to walk. He'd have liked it better if they'd just shoved him in a closet for a few weeks—at least then, he wouldn't have spent all his time looking at the one thing he couldn't do.

That had been the last time Haddy had ever even thought about swooping at the bathers.

And now, since he'd just turned sixteen, he'd graduated from training tourists how to fly to being a mobile air-traffic controller. Now he got to enforce the rules, instead of getting them enforced at him. Those hundred-or-so fliers working in the training space below him were depending on him to keep them safe.

Once upon a time, there had been roads back on Earth where people operated their own high-speed rovers that weighed enough to mow a grown man down and not even notice it. Haddy had actually seen some in person in a museum display in a place called Reno, where his uncle Jorah had taken him for a suffocating high gravity vacation a couple years ago. They looked like retro-future sculptures to him—the kind of thing you might see hanging from the ceiling at the Juno—it had taken some convincing and a full documentary for him to believe they'd actually been designed to move people around.

The documentary showed people moving around in them, though, with an amazing degree of order and a minimum of carnage. It was as if everyone had somehow agreed to drive one direction on one side of the road, and another direction on the other side, then gone on to make customs for sorting out whose turn it was to move at an intersection, and conventions for dealing with people who were foolish enough to go walking next to those hulking metal machines.

He'd been quite gobsmacked, at least until Jorah pointed out that the sky had the same kind of rules:

You couldn't pass within two meters of another flier unless you were flying in formation.

You had to stay four meters minimum from a wall, unless you were heading in for a perch or a landing.

You circled counterclockwise to climb, clockwise to descend.

In the Gallery, up and down right-of-ways were controlled less by rules than by air flow—the heat from the ag dome above, and from the climate-control radiators at the bottom of the shaft created a natural thermal that hugged the south face.

A little red dot flashed in Haddy's blink-lens display. Five minutes left in his shift, and everyone had been depressingly well-behaved. He hadn't gotten to write a citation all week.

What happens when you're enforcing rules that nobody's breaking?

You get paid to mill around in big circles trying to look at girl's butts with the zoom on your blink-lenses—which never worked, because from the top, under the wing rigs, you could barely see anyone's butt, let alone figure out the sex of the person who was wearing it.

Oh well. He needed to get in, scrub down, and put on his other suit so that he could pick up some training clients. His account was already almost all recovered from the coin he dropped buying Josie last semester—the faster he could bring it back up to parity, the sooner he'd be able to lay off the extra work and spend more time up on the surface, working on his novel. He'd built himself a cave out of loose stones a little ways north of the crater, where he'd stashed himself a private dictation setup.

Haddy descended lazily, barely paying attention to what was going on around him, moving slowly, finding a groove in the tourist-clogged descent lane as if he were negotiating rush hour at the tram station.

Then, without knowing why, he dipped his left wing. An automatic reflex.

A soft gecko boot blasted just over the dipped wingtip, missing him by only a few centimeters. He barely had time to feel a blast of lemon-scented air on his face before his wings surged, pushed him up, and stalled hard.

Haddy swore as he found himself in a sideways tumble. Falling slowly, then more quickly, as one level, then two, then four rolled past him in an endless handful of seconds. He reflexively pulled his wings in, which increased his spin speed. He pulled his toes in toward his body and bent double into a jack-knife, canting his faux tail feathers down flat against his hamstrings, then straightened out again pointed straight down.

He speared down like a peregrine falcon, spinning corkscrew-fashion with the angular tumble he'd picked up from the stumblebum tourist's wake. Then, once he was in a more-or-less stable dive, he pulled his toes in again, but this time he didn't bend at the waist. Instead, he pushed his wings out, crooked at the elbows, and curled his fists in.

The wing-tips and tail-feathers bit the air, steadying his spin and pulling him into a swoop.

An instant later he was climbing again, pushing straight up with his momentum, scanning every-which-way for the creep that had bum-rushed him.

There. Almost at the top, flapping hard, zipping in and out of the lanes, trying to push up through the ceiling into the ag dome. He blinked twice, zoomed in, got a bead on the wings and the flyer. They were solid blue wings, with no fledger stripes. Whoever was doing that had been out at least once before, and should have known better.

They were strapped to a girl, maybe a couple years older than him, who didn't seem to give a good goddamn who she knocked out of the sky.

Well, she would soon. Nobody pulled that kind of stunt and got away with it. Not in his sky. Haddy burned with the righteous rage of his office. Oh, he was gonna get to throw the book at her. In five minutes, he'd make good and sure she was a lot poorer, and maybe grounded for a few weeks.

But he had to get her before she busted the ceiling, or he'd get it right in the neck for letting her get up where she could interfere with the city's food supply. If she crashed in the triticale, or god-forbid the corn, she'd cause enough damage that the farmers would start agitating to get the fliers banned from the Gallery. It had happened before, and they'd always lost, but that didn't mean they'd lose next time—and if they did win, Haddy's whole family would be screwed.

The thermal was clear for most of the way up. Haddy flapped hard, goosing his speed, banking into the thermal, using the rising column of air to help push him faster.

He dodged out into dead air as he caught up to the soaring fledgers, then back into the thermal before he stalled out.

"Hey!" he shouted. "You in the blue! Stop!"

She kept right on soaring up like she hadn't even heard him. She was crossing into the skyguard's nest now. Another twenty meters, and she'd bust that ceiling like it wasn't even there.

Haddy pulled against the air like a champion rower, pushing vertical faster than he'd been falling before his dive.

He was gaining on her.

He hauled and pushed. He had to resist the urge to kick his legs—if he did, his tail feathers would cant back and forth and drag him down, queer his vector, and lose him the chase.

"You in the blue!" He shouted between panting, loud enough to make himself hoarse. "Up top! Can you hear me?"

She looked down. He was close enough to see her head bend toward him. She made eye contact.

She could hear him.

"You're nicked!"

"What?" She wasn't pushing against the air anymore, but she was still riding the thermal up.

It wasn't a surrender, but it was enough. Haddy took the opportunity presented, exhausted himself completely fast-climbing the rest of the way up, closing the distance before she busted the ceiling.

"Stop now! Don't climb any further!" he shouted. "You bust that ceiling and you're grounded for life."

"And who exactly do you think you are?"

Of course she couldn't see the badge-patches on his wings from this angle. He was only five meters below her now, so he canted his wings horizontal, letting them catch the full force of the thermal. Soaring instead of flapping.

Now she saw the badge-patches on his wings. He knew she did. Though he had to crane his neck to see it, she got *that* look. The one he'd given skyguards a dozen times before, the one where you roll your eyes and your face goes slack because you know you're completely, totally screwed.

"S'crats," she swore.

"You're nicked," he said again. He wasn't sure she heard him—he was breathing so hard he could barely get his teeth around anything resembling a word. "Follow me down. No showboating."

She shook her head—not like she was saying "no," but more like she was kicking herself for being stupid enough to get caught.

Then she slid sideways out of the thermal and glided to the other side of the gallery, and started a deliberately-slow I'm-not-going-to-do-anything-more-you-can-cite-me-for descent.

Haddy formed up above and behind her, and descended with her.

"Head for the roost on the west wall, level eight." The level numbers were painted in giant, unmistakable numbers on each wall, so that the fliers wouldn't get lost on the way home.

The prisoner—okay, she wasn't really a prisoner, but thinking of her that way made him feel very official, and he liked that—behaved herself perfectly. Now that he'd caught her, he didn't have a good gust of anger blowing him forward for the stunt she'd pulled, and he was secretly hoping she'd do a few more things on the way down that he could cite her for.

But she didn't.

And that really pissed him off.

Actually, come to think of it, she couldn't have done anything more calculated to annoy Haddy.

Oh, she was gonna get it, for sure.

Right in the middle of the gallery's seventeen main levels—which were sandwiched between the overlevels and the sublevels—a little neon orange platform stuck out about three meters from the marble-faced concrete half-wall. The tongue-launch for the first ever orn-suit flying operation in the whole history of the solar system: Bob and Ginny's Flying Lessons.

Haddy's grandpa had started it. He said he'd gotten the idea from a story he'd read when he was seven or eight years old, and he named the shop after the guy that wrote the story.

The oldest, and still the best. They'd even named the deck: Ginny's Perch. Haddy got a little sparkle of pride every time he set down on it. Now for the first time, he was using it in an official capacity, that sparkle was more like a private fireworks display.

The girl swooped in for a fast landing, then pulled up vertical at the last possible moment, scooping the air with her wings, then flapping hard twice at exactly the right time, putting herself in a vertical stall, and dropped ten centimeters to the deck.

Textbook perfect. And not an easy landing to do. It had taken Haddy until he was eight years old to pull that landing off, which was almost half his flying life.

Okay, a third, but who was counting?

Not to be outdone, Haddy swooped in low, then pulled back so he rocketed upward, and wrapped his wings around himself. He stalled out a full level-and-a-half above the deck—not bad since the levels were ten meters high once you factored in the thickness of the floors and ceilings, where all the wiring and ventilation ran—and let himself fall straight back down almost all the way to the deck.

When he reckoned he had less than two meters to go, he spread his wings out and flapped once with all his strength, and his feet lightly touched the deck.

He immediately found himself enveloped in a cloud of lemon perfume. It hadn't smelled half bad when he'd gotten a whiff of it blasting past him on the wing—up close, though, it smelled like whoever-she-was bathed in the stuff.

Haddy tried to not-breathe as much as possible while he took the PPD from his belt and deployed the stylus.

"All right," he said as he turned to her, "you're no fledger, so just what do you think you were..."

He ground to a halt as she turned to face him, and, for a moment, forgot what language he was supposed to be speaking—which was the least of his problems, considering that he also forgot what grammar was, the name he'd answered to since he was born, and how to supply his brain with oxygen.

She had blue eyes. *Real* blue eyes. Not pale blue,

but the kind that looked like someone had run lightning through the oceans on Earth to give them an extra sizzle, and then popped the result into someone's head. He'd seen great eyes before, sure. Everyone had. He even knew a place where you could buy them. But you couldn't buy eyes like these, not before you were eighteen, and if you did you'd never put them in a face like *that*.

It was the kind of face he'd seen in the bas reliefs in the Capital Dome down in Petra at the heart of Luna City. Round eyes, high cheeks, light bones as if she'd been built by a Gothic architect.

And that skin. Toasty brown. Indian, almost. But not quite. And no pimples either, and no freckles, and no makeup, and girls her age always had one of the three.

He figured her for about seventeen. Maybe nineteen. No older than that. And blonde. And stuck up, too, judging by the way she looked at him as if she wanted to laugh at the way he couldn't remember how speech worked.

And oh, boy, he'd better start talking before he looked like a complete derp.

"Is there a problem, *officer*?" She said "officer," but the way she said it made it sound an awful lot like "jerk off".

Okay, too late to avoid looking like a derp. But he could still throw the book at her.

"Hold still please." He tapped the "Citation" button on the PPD screen, and got an instruction in his blink-lenses that said "Facial Identification Required."

Right. He had to look her in the face again. This was official business, though. He could do this.

Haddy looked up, and focused his blink-lenses on her face. This time it didn't feel like she was looking at him—more like he was looking through a camera at her. Which was, in fact, what he was doing.

"What's the idea buzzing people like that? That's a proximity violation, and then there was a traffic pattern violation, and you almost busted the ceiling."

"Oh, tosh, I didn't even get *close* to hitting you. A girl tries to have a little fun..."

He tapped the PPD screen again, so the system would record her face. "Fun's fine. Endangering other peoples lives, especially fledgers, is not." Haddy recited, almost verbatim. "How long have you been flying?"

She shrugged. "I don't know. A few years, I guess."

"Then, I'm sorry," the PPD pinged. It had identified her, so he could assign the citation. He looked down as he continued his sentence, "but I'm going to have to recommend you be suspended. With that much experience there's no excuse for...what the hell?"

The ID field on the screen leapt out at him.

Charis Jin.

He looked up at her again.

"You're..."

She smiled like she'd just won some kind of prize.

"Hi cuz," she said. "Long time no see."

HARD NEWS

CHARIS JIN. HIS cousin, who he hadn't seen since he was about five. Oh, she could fly all right.

She'd taught him how to fly.

She'd also moved away with her parents ten years ago, and he'd been too busy to even see a picture of her in three or four years.

If he'd known she looked like *that* now, and could still fly like that? He'd have kept in touch for sure. She might have a friend she could introduce him to. It occurred to him he ought to be nice to her.

But that was personal. He had a job to do. Just because she'd taught him to fly didn't mean he couldn't cite her anyway, so he did.

"You're kidding me, right. You're gonna write me a ticket?"

"Already did." Haddy sent the citation. "And, that's my shift done."

"So...?" She was giving him the big eyes. He tried looking away while still looking at her, but that didn't work very well. Every time he did, he was reminded that she was as much girl as she was cousin.

"So what?"

"So did you request a grounding?"

"No. Not this time." Haddy was feeling pretty good about this one. He was all prickles and he was pretty sure he was blushing up to his ear-tips, but he'd kept his voice steady and official.

To add a nice flourish and end his citation in style, he smartly slid the stylus back into its docking port on the PPD.

At least, that's what he intended to do.

He discovered that he hadn't, in fact, been successful in finding the port when the stylus shot forward past Charis and into the open air of the Gallery.

So much for throwing the book at her.

"Um. You'll get your fine in your inbox..."

"Yeah," she said. "I know how it works."

"What are you doing here anyway?" He'd meant it to sound friendly, but it came out of his mouth sounding a lot more like *Who do you think you are coming to my city like this* than it did *I'm so happy to see you again.*

Charis noticed.

"My life just wasn't complete without a chance to ruin yours." She rolled her eyes. "Why do you *think* I got dragged here?"

Haddy put a knowing expression on his face, because the last thing he wanted to look was clueless. "Oh, right. Of course. Well, uh, look, I've gotta get out of the official gear and get back to work..."

"When do you get off?"

"I don't know. Whenever the traffic dies down. Nineteen or Twenty-hundred maybe?"

"Have you *been* out there?"

"Where?"

Charis waggled a wing-tip in the direction of the Gallery Bazaar, the large open-plan shopping district filled with artisans who made everything from hand-knit shrugs to custom cannabis strains to snow cones. It stretched along level 8 and then sloped down into the spaceport about half-klick to the south.

"I *do* live here, you know."

"There's enough people crammed in there to keep you busy till the next Solstice," she said.

She did have a point. The Bazaar was always crowded, but it had its rhythm—by zero hour, most of the day's rush had died down, and what merchants stayed open through the slack shift would keep themselves busy cleaning out their booths, dealing with stock shipments, and training new employees.

Haddy's family didn't bother to keep someone in their booth for the slack shift. They stayed open during the hours when people were most likely to fly, and spent the rest of the time on the "family" side of "family business." Which, in Haddy's case, meant a lot of school work, an annoying little brother, and late dinners with everybody home and around the same table, to facilitate "family togetherness."

Which seemed screwy to him, but he never could find excuses good enough to get out of them.

And Dad was a good enough cook that Haddy didn't usually try very hard. Even if he did have to eat at the same table with The Monster Brat.

But things in the Gallery had gone strange in the last few weeks. People weren't going home for slack shift. A lot of new—and illegal—booths had gone up, and the Security Service didn't seem to care, which annoyed Dad and the other regular merchants to no end. They were always talking about it when the customers were out of earshot, and around the dinner table, enough that Haddy had begun to wonder if he shouldn't worry—except that he didn't know what he might worry about.

And it wasn't just the booths. There had been a string of attacks over the last year, and no one knew who to blame. The news said it was Loonie radicals, the Loonies said it was the government back on Earth. And everyone was seriously riled up. There were stages in the Bazaar, now, all the way down near the entrance to the spaceport, where people stood with bullhorns and screamed about revolution, and fighting-for-our-rights.

Haddy didn't pretend to understand any of it. He wasn't a politically-minded guy. One of the advantages of living out on the frontier is that you didn't have to be political the way people on Earth were. You could just do what you want, and nobody got in your way unless you got in theirs first.

But things were changing.

And Charis was right—that crowd wasn't going to shrink during slack-shift.

"How 'bout this," Haddy said, "If it doesn't let up, I'll quit at twenty-two thirty. Where do I meet you?"

"Meet me at your place."

"My place?" Haddy's family didn't even live in the same district they did when Charis had last been around.

"We're staying there."

"We?" The family apartment was barely enough for the four-people-plus-Josie who lived there. How many more were cramming in?

"Me and Dad and Pop and Arn."

Four?

That meant they were gonna make him share his room with someone. Or several someones. Haddy clenched his jaw, and did his best to maintain composure.

"All of you but...where's your mom?"

A shadow crossed Charis's face. "Long story."

She shrugged, then pushed past him and leapt off the end of the deck, probably headed down to Reservoir Cave.

Haddy stared after her and worked himself up into a real lather. One thing was for sure, he wasn't *about* to share his room with anyone without being asked first. That went *way* beyond rude.

BUT THAT WASN'T the way his father saw things.

Haddy collared him after he'd shucked his skyguard wings, and was as reasonable as anyone could ask. He explained carefully how it wasn't right to make him accept a bunkmate without even asking his permission. The Constitution said you can't quarter troops without the permission of the property owner, and surely that basic principle extended to this situation. There were people out in the streets screaming because their rights weren't being respected, and Haddy wasn't even raising his voice. He ought to get credit for that.

"When you're paying the rent around here, young man, you can decide who comes and goes." His father said in the kind of tone that said *talk back at your peril.* "Until then, you can be polite, or you can work slack-shift. Your choice."

Haddy bit back a snarl. Most of the time, Dad would lean in to a good fight, and sometime he'd even concede when it wasn't possible to escape the tentacles of logic. But there was a look in his eyes that said *not this time.*

And, like all the strangeness in the Bazaar, Haddy didn't like it a bit. He had that feeling, like something awful was about to come at him from his port-side aft, and he wouldn't see it until it was too late to dodge, and it knocked him out of the sky.

HADDY LEFT WORK after that—it was half an hour earlier than he'd planned to, but if he was going to have to share his room with Charis's snoring brother—or worse, her fathers—he was going to get some time to himself.

The smells of the Bazaar crowded around him like the people clogging the hallways. The sweet-caramel smell of garlic'd ostrich meat, the sweaty gym-socks whiff of goat skewers, flowers from greenhouses all over the city, the metallic coconut smell of body paint, the musky yeasty funk of sweaty unshowered naked people—there were always naked people in Luna City, but the ones haunting the Bazaar had given up even *trying* to smell like they wanted to be sociable—and, like anywhere in the city at peak times, the skunky uriney undercurrent of hash oil and blunts.

Perfumes, soaps, bare feet, dirty hair, linens and silks and oils of all kinds. A veritable cornucopia of nauseating nasal-numbing noxiousness.

Any of the smells on their own, even any twelve of them together, probably would have been okay. They were all smells he liked, more or less. And in spite of what people on the nets said back on Earth, Luna City didn't smell like a locker room. It had good, clean, very efficient air recycling. No smells of any kind hung around for long, except the faint whiff of ozone from the first stage air cleaners.

It was just that, having all it blend together in one place made his nose feel like it was swimming in brown sludge from the back-end of some failed genetics experiment. If Haddy hadn't already been seething it would have turned his stomach inside out.

Nor did the foods on display, or the flesh, or the hand-icrafts hold his attention. He looked at them all because it was polite to do so, and because it gave him time (in between nodding and making the correct "ooh" and "ah" sounds) to try to sort things out. Try to figure out why he felt like the world was about to take a left turn.

He felt it as much here in the crowd as he had back talking to his father—maybe even more. It was as if some primitive part of his brain was screaming *Danger! Danger! Tiger attack imminent!* but the rest of him didn't understand the language it was speaking.

And that scared him. Really frightened him in a way he'd never been frightened before. It wasn't the heady rush of fear he got from careening headlong toward a wall after having a close shave during competition, and it wasn't the flush of humiliation he got when he was on the verge of losing an argument. This felt more like the domes that kept the air in might crack and explode at any time, and there wasn't a thing he could do about it except wait around to die.

Haddy dawdled as much as he thought he could get away with—even tried do get down to the Terminal to hop a tram to the lock where he kept his pressure suit, and go out to that cave he'd built. Some time alone to think would be just the thing.

But the trams weren't running. Too many people on the tracks. It would take him an hour just to push through the crowds and get to the lock, let alone the time he'd spend walking to and from his rock-hut.

Haddy elbowed his way through the press of people for an hour, and never found the end of it. He eventually remembered the PPD he wore on his hip—his personal one this time, as he'd left the skyguarding one in his locker at the office.

He waded into the fountain that marked the entrance

to the main concourse between terminals B and C. There were a dozen or so people of all ages and sexes sitting in it, enjoying the water and the break from the crowd. One woman who was old enough to look like a leather satchel with nipples was actually soaping herself down, the rest of the bathers were sitting around, talking with each other, except for a boy and a girl the age of the Monster Brat chasing each other around, splashing and squealing.

It was an everyday sight for Luna City, although it was more common to find skinny dippers further up in the city (or in Reservoir Cave) than in the spaceport where it might frighten the tourists. Tourism was the big cash industry up here.

Haddy had been living and breathing tourists since he could learned to walk. He lived right on the border between "Loonie" and "Tourist," so he had a diplomat's finely-honed sense of decorum. He never called the Terrans "Groundhogs" (even though they were), and he never insulted them to their face (no matter how richly they deserved it). His job, whether he was at work or not, was to make the newcomers feel comfortable enough to stay a while, learn to fly, and go back home to tell their friends.

It came as naturally to him as breathing.

After a few taps, the screen on his PPD displayed the Grissom Space Port Information Page. He tapped on the flashing red bar at the top.

Travel advisories:

1400 hrs.

Be advised that due to citizen activity in terminals B and C, all traffic is currently being re-routed through Terminals A and D. Shuttles from Ring Alpha are being directed toward the outer pad and serviced by mobile terminals. Expect travel delays of up to five hours on some inbound and all outbound flights.

So much for getting anywhere useful. And now he was too turned around to get home without finding another way to navigate.

He looked up at the ceiling. Every Loonie knew that the spaceport hugged the base of the cliff at the north end of Mare Tranquilitatis, which meant it ran basically east-to-west. The booth was around five or six hundred meters north and up from the spaceport, and then around a couple small corners. The passage leading to the booth was a few dozen meters wide, stretching all the way between two enormous ribbing struts in the spaceport ceiling.

They were easy to remember, because they both hosted art installations that changed from time to time.

If he could find one of those struts, follow it to the corner, and then make his way back up either of the walls, he could duck into a side passage and get home without having to wade all the way back to the main gallery and take a shop-lift.

& TONIC WAS stenciled proudly across the deep green door to the Jin household. Haddy had stenciled it there as a joke when they'd moved in five years ago, and his Mom had insisted it stay as "A testament to the drunken insanity that obtains within."

When the door slid aside, the noise that blasted him in the face made him think, not for the first time, that she'd been on to something.

The door opened in to a fairly spacious living room, as Lunar apartments went. In a city built underground, the private spaces were pretty cozy unless you lived in a unit with a window. Otherwise, the cloistered feeling drove most people outside. Home was a place you came back to for privacy, not a place where you spent all your time.

The sixty-five square meters of hollowed-out granite that made up the Jin homestead managed to cram in a living area large enough to seat nine people comfortably around a small active surface coffee table. It was a good space for games or study or reading, and it doubled as a dining room with the open kitchen built in along a wall at the back of the space.

Four modest bedrooms led off at even spacing down each side wall—one for his parents, one for the business office, and one each for himself and The Monster Brat. These were each barely big enough for a queen bed, but the family needed nothing more, and Vin—Haddy's father—had long proved immune to his son's pleas to move to a more fashionable district.

"Dad, we've got the money to live anywhere we want," Haddy had said (over and over).

"And if we spend it on something we don't need, we won't have it any more, will we?"

Because of this conversation and many others like it with both his parents, Haddy had developed the conviction that parenthood caused brain damage, rendering its victims unable to see plain sense or have any care whatsoever for their social standing. If Haddy ever got the itch to become a scientist, he could make a good name for himself finding the cure.

The small space was filled to bursting. Haddy's mother Nita stood at the stove against the back wall, stirring something in the wok that depended heavily on a ginger-soy glaze—Haddy could tell because the smell hit him along with the wall of noise rushing out through the open door. She wasn't normally the one that cooked; she didn't enjoy it like Vin did, nor did she have the flair for it. But ginger glaze was her specialty, and a treat Haddy didn't get often enough.

The black ostrich-leather sofas were occupied by everyone else in the galaxy. Charis was sitting on one of the two matching armchairs—the one with its back to him. His uncles were on the sofa to the left. Charis's little brother Arn, about eleven years old, sat with Haddy's father and The Monster Brat—his little brother Ulmar—on the sectional built into the right wall that separated the sitting area from the cooking space. They were all shouting at a holographic display rising up out of the coffee table. *Resnikopf's Reach*. Haddy recognized the game—last year's big obsession. He'd lost a fair amount lot of coin to the betting pool before he'd written it off as not-his-thing.

The only occupant of the household who appeared to notice him was Josie, who'd been laying just-at-the-border between the living space and the kitchen, hoping to demonstrate that she was a good dog and really did deserve a scrap of the chicken (or whatever) that was swishing around in the wok.

She bounded down the narrow aisle behind the left sofa and the carved-in shelves as if she meant to knock him over, but at the last moment she stopped, sat, and lifted her right paw.

It had taken Haddy four months to teach her that greeting. It hadn't been easy for her, not with the kind of energy she had, not before she'd even turned a year old. Four months well spent—she'd learned the house rules and avoided the fate of previous dogs that had failed to live up to his father's standards of "civilized behavior for members of this household" which he held to regardless of species.

Haddy squatted down and deliberately took her paw in his hand, gave it a firm shake, and smiled.

"Good girl," he said, then scruffed her back and forth up her black-brindled sides until he'd come to the point of her Dutch Shepherd ears. "Yes, yes, I'm home. Yes, it's good to see you too." His fingers found a fresh scratch behind her left ear. It was swelling a little, he'd have to keep an eye on it to see that it didn't develop an infection. "Another one, girl? Really? What happened? You been chasing cats again? You gotta be careful, girl, they'll take your eyes out."

Josie laid her ears back and turned in a whirlwind-tight circle between his two outstretched arms, whining just a little, then sat with her back to him, her tail thumping the floor as if she were trying to alert everyone on the lower levels to the fact that he'd *finally* come home again and all was right with the world.

She was the best thing about coming home. The best coin block—a full six hundred LOX—he'd ever dropped on anything.

Josie let out two sharp barks to announce his homecoming.

Normally this would have drawn a "Bad dog" or similar from his father, or a shush from his mother, or an "uh-oh, you're gonna get it" from Ulmar.

Tonight, Josie's bark shut everyone up, as if she'd bumped the light switch. As a unit, every head in the place turned to look at Haddy.

They were all looking at him as if he'd died, and hadn't noticed it, and was shambling around with half his head missing or something.

Haddy looked back. And for three hundred years of

the most uncomfortable two-and-a-half seconds he'd ever experienced, he didn't say anything either.

"What?" He meant to just say it, but it sounded like a shout when it bounced back to him off the polished granite walls, as if the acoustical panels hadn't even been mounted yet.

Vin sighed. "You'd better come in, Hadrian."

S'crats. Dad only calls me Hadrian when I'm really in trouble.

Haddy couldn't fathom what had everyone looking so grim. It wasn't like he'd offended a client today—every one he'd taught had given him a good tip, and they never did that if they intended to complain. And he hadn't made anyone pregnant—he was sure about that one because he'd hadn't even ever *kissed* a girl yet, but he wasn't going to use that as a defense unless he absolutely had to.

Come to think of it, there was nothing he could call to mind that he'd done to merit the full witch-trial treatment. Not in the last six weeks, anyway. And especially not that they could have found out about.

Haddy cautiously slunk forward a couple steps, then remembered that the best way not to get into trouble was not to look guilty. He squared off his shoulders, looked down at Josie, and said "Josie, couch," then pointed to the wide chair where he intended to sit.

To Josie, there were only two kinds of furniture: "couch" and "bed."

Josie bounded before him, hopped on the chair, sat down and waited for Haddy as he made his way with a confident posture through the narrow spaces between relative-legs and table until he could sit down opposite Charis. He tried to make as if he were a sultan on a throne, sharing it with his loyal tame wolf, holding court over supplicants whose dour expressions were due entirely to their fear of his awesome power.

It didn't work, and not just because his thin grasp of Terran history hid from him the implausibility of his imagined scene.

Vin, seated on the long couch to Haddy's left, rubbed his hands together as if he were rolling a pencil between them. Then he interlaced his fingers, leaned forward, propped his elbows on his knees, and pressed the bridge of his nose to his tented index fingers.

"Ulmar," Vin said to the Monster Brat, "Take Arn and go to your room please. I'll call you for dinner."

"Aww, Daaaad..."

"NOW!" Vin snapped like Haddy had only heard him snap a handful of times in his entire life.

Ulmar's face went from toasted-rice to bleached basmati, then flushed red. He stood up on the couch, leapt over the table and the opposing couch in one bound, and ducked into his room. The door slammed behind him.

Arn followed more carefully, avoiding eye contact with Haddy or anyone else, and slipped through the door silently.

"Dad, what the hell is going..."

"Shut up." Vin's voice was sharp. He closed his eyes, and continued with a softer voice. "Just...hold your horses, son. This...this gets complicated."

"What gets complicated?"

"You've seen what's going on down in the Bazaar."

"Yeah," Haddy shrugged. "It's like a party got out of control."

"It's not a party. It's a protest."

"Okay..." Living on the moon as he did, Haddy had *heard* of protests—when studying history to pass his CORE exams. But as a practical matter, the concept was meaningless to him. Nobody on Earth cared what happened on the moon. Nobody in Washington ever paid them the slightest attention, and that's the way everybody liked it. "So, what, is that a bad thing?"

"Normally, no. But there isn't anything normal about this. Has it occurred to you to wonder where your Aunt Min is?"

Charis's mother. Vin's sister. She was usually the scout leading the exploration party around the solar system. She had abandoned the moon when Haddy was five. Min had sold off her share of the flying business to Vin and packed her whole family into a second-hand freighter and gone off to see the solar system. Her husbands Mike (the one Charis called "Dad") and Amit (the one Charis called "Pop") were big-deal habitat designers, so there was always a new station to consult on or a new ship concept to evaluate. It kept the family on the move.

"Well, I mean yeah. I asked Charis about it earlier and she didn't give me a straight answer."

"I'll give you one," Uncle Mike said. "She's been disappeared."

"What, like a magician?"

"Not vanished," Vin said. "She's 'been disappeared.'"

"I don't get it," Haddy said.

"It's a term for when a government or a corporation kidnaps someone and takes them off the grid. Away from any surveillance. Away from anyone who could identify them or communicate them. And they...question them. Roughly. Usually they don't come back."

"Wait, wait, you're saying she just vanished, and you

think it's cause someone wanted to torture and kill her? What possible reason would anyone have to do that?"

"Pick one," Uncle Mike snorted.

"What's that supposed to mean?"

"It means," Vin said, "that there are a lot of people that might have wanted a look inside her head."

"Or use her as leverage," Uncle Amit graveled.

Before Haddy could ask why, Vin cut in again.

"Don't ask why. The less you know the better."

"The day before she...disappeared, we were at Sidon," Charis said. "And she was up in the docking ring, and she saw Marines."

"What? Why?"

"Because," Vin said, "They're coming to suppress the rebellion."

Haddy's head was spinning. He didn't know what to make of anything he was hearing. Was Aunt Min dead? Why was the government sending Marines to break up a party in the Gallery? And what the hell did any of this have to do with him?

A hand touched Haddy's shoulder. Haddy looked up to see his mother's sharp green eyes, rimmed red and raw and bloodshot like she'd been hot-boxing bad hash, staring down into him.

"I'm afraid you're going to have to grow up quicker than any of us would like," she said.

Uncle Amit nodded, his big brown Indian eyes studying Haddy with concern.

"Don't worry, Had," he graveled. A touch of his family's Punjabi accent still flavored the edges of his speech. "We'll get you out of harm's way."

Haddy reeled again. "*Me?* What do I have to do with any of this?"

"You're sixteen years old, and male, and in a city that's about to go to war. You're going to get drafted," his mother said.

"Drafted?" That was a word Haddy had only ever heard in a sports-related context before.

"Forced to fight, whether you want to or not," she said.

"This will blow over in a year," Vin said. "Maybe less. But until then, we have to get you out of the line of fire."

"Dad..." Haddy's lungs were trembling. The dread he'd been flirting with earlier had bloomed into full-blown terror. But he'd be damned if he backed down from a fight. It was an old, primitive urge that ran deeper and older than humanity itself: the imperative to protect one's home and family from the enemy. "If people are coming to attack us, and I can do something..."

"You're not going to get that chance, son. I'm not going to lose you to some damn fool skirmish. These things happen from time to time, and the people who die are mostly the people too stupid to keep their own heads down." Vin took a big breath, and made a face as if he was searching for the right words. "For now, you need to follow your uncles."

"Where?"

Charis smiled at him, just a little bit. "Nineveh. You're going to love it."

A Bumpy Embarkation

"*NINEVEH?*" NINEVEH WAS a transfer station that orbited the sun between Earth and Mars. "Dad, *nobody* lives out there. Nobody that matters. I'll be on the far side of the sun for, like..." Haddy tried to remember his orbital positioning calendar, "The next four *years*. Or longer."

"You'll fly back long before that. Like I said, these things have a way of settling themselves if you have enough sense to stay out of them."

"What about you, and Mom, and the Monst...um...Ulmar?"

"We have to stay here and run the shop," his mother said. "Don't worry, we're not going to be in any danger. None of us are political, Ulmar's too young to be of any use to anybody..."

Well there's the understatement of the month.

"...and he still will be when this is all done."

"War imposes its burden on young males," Vin said. "Everyone else is exempt, unless they want to volunteer."

"I am *not* going to puss out on..."

"We're saving your life, son. And we'll be okay. You would be too if you were five years younger or ten years older. It's just bad luck."

Haddy swallowed hard. His cheeks were wet. His sight was blurring. He didn't want to go to the ass-end of nowhere and hide on some spinning tin can while his home got smashed up by military thugs.

Josie, who'd done a champion's job sitting quietly

through all the excitement, laid her head on his lap and looked up at him with infinitely sad yellow-brown eyes, as if she could tell that Haddy's whole world was spinning out of control and headed straight for the cavern wall.

"It's okay, girl," Haddy mumbled. "We're gonna be okay. It's just a little trip, is all. Like here, but with smaller halls. We'll find somewhere for you to run, I promise."

Uncle Mike coughed. Haddy looked up to see strain lines carving canyons into his father's neck and jaw. His eyes were leaking.

"Hadrian," he croaked. "You'll all be shipping out on the *Buchman*. She's an ITN ship."

Haddy blinked. The ITN was the Interplanetary Transport Network, spacer slang for the gravitational grooves in the solar system that didn't require thrust to travel. You nudged into the groove, then floated for *years*.

"You said I'd be back in a year."

"She doesn't spend the whole time on the ITN," Uncle Amit said. "But she's a smaller ship. She doesn't carry enough fuel to torch the whole way."

"But what about your ship? I mean, you guys design ships. The *Rising*, she can make the push, right?"

Uncle Mike shook his head. "We can't take her. She'd be recognized making port."

"What does..."

"Forget it," Vin said. "The less you know, the safer you are. You three will give me your word," he said, looking not just to Uncles Mike and Amit, but to Charis as well, "that you will not bring him in on *anything* that could put him in danger."

They all swore, in succession. Which meant Haddy was gonna get stuck in the dark.

"Anyway, what does it matter that we're going on this ITN ship?"

"Sweetheart," his mother said, as if she weren't throwing a dinosaur-killing asteroid through his last airlock, "Josie can't go with you. She won't survive the trip, not in free fall."

Haddy felt as if his heart had just been yanked out of his chest. Dogs didn't do well in free fall unless they were one of the specially engineered breeds, but normal dogs could still do okay if they were introduced in the first four months or so. If they weren't, they'd get motion sick and puke their guts out. Literally. The strain caused heart failure in most dogs in a day or two.

He couldn't take Josie.

He couldn't take Josie.

HADDY DIDN'T EAT dinner. He didn't even try to pretend. He went to his room, and laid in his bunk, curled around Josie, trying to remember how to breathe in between fits of sobbing.

Josie whined and licked his face. She had no way to know it was the last night she'd get to spend with him, maybe ever. She just wanted to take care of him, because he was everything she depended on.

He and Josie had the place to themselves. All the guests slept in the living room, except for Arn, who slept with Ulmar. His mother had come in to tell him they were doing it so that he could have a last night in his own room. Some privacy. Time to get used to things.

Haddy suspected it was so that he couldn't take Josie and slip out the front door. If they hadn't been sleeping between him and the front door, he could have done that just as easily as he could get up to use the bathroom. But now he was under guard.

No choice, unless he wanted to bum-rush the door and try to get lost on the lower levels, where the life support machinery screwed up tracking and there wasn't any good surveillance.

The thought crossed his mind several times. All he had to do was get up. Josie could follow as long as he waved for her to heel. He could tiptoe to the front door, key the unlock, and then run like hell.

Around 0200, he made a sortie out to the bathroom, taking a good squint in the dark at how the guests were arrayed.

The Uncles were each sleeping on a couch. Charis was in the chair nearest the door, with her feet propped up on the table.

He could actually make it.

He returned to his room to find Josie laying on her back, full-asleep, on his bed. Her paws were twitching in the air as she chased a ball, or a rat, or some other thing in her sleep. A light snore jogged occasionally as the prey in her dreams dodged this way and that—Haddy could tell by the way she twitched and twisted when she did.

He leaned against the wall above his bunk-cubby and watched the sleeping pup. He couldn't leave her here. He *couldn't*. Who would take care of her? She'd go crazy without him, worse than she did when he had to leave her here during the shifts when he was skyguarding. He had to get her up and make a run for it.

But he didn't quite have the heart to wake her up in the middle of a dream, especially one that looked that good, so he waited, soaking in every last second while he did, until he was too tired to stand.

He *had* to sleep. Just a quick nap. That was all he

needed. Then he could make a run for it.

He set the alarm on his PPD to wake him up in ninety minutes, then slipped into bed next to Josie. He turned his back to her, laying on his side. She immediately curled up in the crook of his legs—her favorite sleeping position—and was back to gentle snoring and twitching inside two minutes.

Haddy fell asleep soon after.

"HADDY?" A SMALL voice came from behind him.

Haddy felt himself shaking. Small hands were on his arm, rolling him this way and that.

"Haddy."

That was Ulmar's voice.

"What...hey, get out of my room."

"It's time to get up." Ulmar wasn't sneering, or hectoring, or doing any of the Monster Brat things he normally...

Haddy flipped over and opened his eyes.

Ulmar's face was looking down at him, hazel eyes wide and wet. As soon as Haddy was looking at him, Ulmar threw his arms out and enveloped him in a bear hug.

Josie, not willing to tolerate being left out of the action, dove in, nose-to-faces, and started licking as if they were both covered in peanut butter.

Haddy pushed Josie off, sat up, saw his PPD stuck to the wall that served as his headboard.

He lunged for it. He'd set the alarm clock so that he'd get up at 0330...

...on Thursday. Not Tuesday.

Haddy pressed his eyes tight together. If he'd had a club handy, he'd have beat himself with it. Since he didn't, he knocked his head against the wall.

It was full morning. He'd missed his chance. If he wanted to run and hide now, he'd have to ditch his uncles and cousins in the space port, and then how would he get back to get Josie?

"Haddy?" Ulmar's voice was cracking around the edges.

"What? Oh. Nothing. I thought I had a message." Haddy hugged his brother, and Josie, and then got up and started to pack a bag.

Halfway through, he stuck his head out into the living room to ask what his mass allowance was, then he returned to his room to re-pack.

He did have enough allowance for a thumbnail with as much data as he cared to store—and he cared to store it all. He loaded everything he could think of. His music, his manuscripts, his favorite vids, and then it dawned on him he couldn't bring his wings, so he logged into the company server and stole all the top secret design files. He could build himself a set at the other end. Nineveh was an O'Neil cylinder, so it had a sky he could fly in if he found the right launch point.

He couldn't imagine living anywhere without being able to fly.

Then again, he couldn't imagine living anywhere other than Luna City, or going to sleep without Josie curled up in the small of his back.

Haddy brushed the corner of his eye. He didn't have time for this right now.

He'd need a PPD, of course, and a couple changes of clothes.

There wasn't any room for personal keepsakes, but he slipped Josie's collar off anyway and strapped it around his left bicep.

"I'll get this back to you, girl. Just gotta borrow it for a while."

For the rest, he took pictures of everything he thought he might want to look at when he got lonely.

Pictures of his flight trophies, pictures of a crappy painting he'd done in an art class, pictures of a sculpture he'd modeled once, and lots and lots of pictures and vids of Josie.

He didn't stop, except to pet her or play with her, until his door opened and his father informed him it was time to go.

Haddy nodded. He finished his digital business, then shoved the thumbnail in the bag. Then he touched Josie on the head, right between her enormous erect ears, and said the hardest word he'd ever had to say in his life:

"Stay."

LIKE A FUNERAL procession, the whole family trekked down to Grissom space port. They had to take the long way around, walking a full klick west through their residential level, then down into Terminal A where the skiffs and shuttles were running up to Ring Alpha, where the larger deep-range vessels docked.

Haddy said goodbye to his parents and brother as quickly as he could. If there was no way to get out of going, he didn't want to hang around until he couldn't stop himself from breaking down and making a complete mess of himself. He didn't want to leave Luna City looking like a complete wimp—and he *really* didn't want to be moving through airlock after airlock with clogged sinuses.

That was the kind of agony the Inquisition used to use to torture people. Okay, they didn't have airlocks back then, but they would have if they had.

Despite his noblest efforts, though, by the time he got into the mobile lounge that ran him and his cousins and uncles out to the shuttle, his eyes were red, and his nose was dripping, and his sinuses were stabbing him with knitting needles under his eyes.

Charis sat down next to him, looked around furtively, then reached her right hand into the zip-collar of her top—like most habitual flyers, including himself, she wore stretchy athletic clothes that gave her good temp regulation and freedom of movement, even when she wasn't flying. A moment later, she produced a little pack of tissues, and it was only then that Haddy realized she must have been carrying them in a bra-pocket under her left arm.

She slipped them between his left elbow and his body and whispered "Your mom gave me these, just in case."

Haddy thanked her, and she hung around for another few seconds, but Haddy ignored her, and she got the idea that he didn't want to talk to anybody right now, and mercifully left him alone.

VIN AND NITA Jin hadn't been the only ones eager to get some or all of their family out of harm's way. The outbound shuttles were packed with tourists evacuating back to Earth and Loonies heading out to Nineveh and Mars—anywhere they might be out of the line of fire.

Haddy noticed the chatter as he leaned his head disconsolately on a shuttle porthole window. The rattle of the thrusters beat the glass against his head in a steady thrum. The noise and buzz kept him from thinking too hard about everything he'd miss, or from dwelling on the the beautiful, rugged gray-brown landscape dropping away beneath him, or the fact that he might never see it again.

Oh, sure, they said he'd be back soon. It would all blow over. It was just temporary.

But somehow, deep in his bones, Haddy *knew* this was his goodbye to Luna. Everyone would change while he was gone. He was going to be one of those sad sacks he sometimes gave lessons to—the ones who grew up in LC, and moved away to get married, or take a job, or just to see the solar system, and then came back ten, twenty, forty years later.

He could spot them from a hundred meters, looking around with that sad sparkle in their eyes, wondering why everything looked *almost* like they remembered it. They looked lost, like the world stopped fitting. They talked about the old days, when the city was less crowded, less Terran, quieter, nicer.

That was going to be him. He wasn't ever going to see his home again. Not really. Even if he came back to Luna City to stay.

RING ALPHA WASN'T your classic space-minimizing modular inflatable transfer station, such as you got in Earth orbit, or dotting the Lunar surface, or saw in just about every movie the Terrans put out about life in the great untamed solar system.

It had a water-jacketed, solid-state superstructure bounded by struts and decorated with long, spiraling radiator tower-loops. It stretched for two kilometers in a long, barely-detectable arc, with spinning sections jutting above and below to house anyone who needed to stay for more than the few hours of wait time that was typical of most flights in and out of the station. The exterior was covered in bright patches of red and green and yellow, making it stand out from the surrounding blackness like a piñata.

Haddy's shuttle slid its port-side sideways into a clamp-dock with the long, narrow Lunar-facing edge of the station. On approach, through his porthole he could see massive interplanetary liners of all shapes docking on its far side—the fat edge that permanently faced Earth.

Further still, a handful of moving stars marked the location of the ghost ships ponied up for cargo transfer. Some carried passengers, most did not. All were long-haul ITN ships. most piloted by AI, destined for long multi-month and multi-year journeys between ports of call, pushing the ore and manufactured goods and biostocks that let the machinery of the inner solar system run as smoothly as it did.

If the *Buchman* was an ITN ship, she was probably one of those lights.

The *PRS Buchman* was part of something called the "Phobos Reserve Fleet." Uncle Mike told him that Phobos was flag-of-convenience for shipping companies—like Mannix Spaceways, which owned the *Buchman*—wishing to stay as far from Terrestrial politics as possible.

Haddy couldn't say as he blamed them. He'd never heard of a Terran government doing anything sensible, at least not on this side of the gravity well. Groundhogs just didn't understand the first thing about real life. They had free air and more land than they knew what to do with—they had so much land that they could give over an area greater than the entire Lunar surface *just* for unmodified plants and animals to run around being...well, plants and animals.

They called it the "Terrestrial Darwin Preserve" and

justified the waste by calling it a "natural experiment"—a concept utterly alien to a boy who'd grown up only knowing artificially engineered environments. Seemed like a pretty useless idea to him.

That the Terrans had enough room to feed ten billion people and *still* set aside that much land to be decorative proved that they didn't know a thing about how the universe really worked, and they sure as vacuum didn't have any business trying to set the rules for people who had to make their own air, and their own water, and their own land using machines they built themselves, and grow their own food using plants and animals they designed themselves.

The docking clamps engaged. The ship jolted as it was dragged a few centimeters into direct metal-to-metal contact with the electromagnetic docking clamps.

The passengers disembarked. Haddy joined the crowd a few bodies ahead of Uncle Amit's short-cropped black hair. Once clear of the hatch, he found a sign set up to catch the eye of the disembarking passengers that said "Connections" and listed the outbound flight roster, and where the departure gates were.

The shuttle to the *PRS Buchman* lay, according to the sign, about a hundred meters along a rung-walk to his right, down the long axis of the station.

Because it was a free fall environment, Ring Alpha didn't have much in the way of clear vision from one part of the station to the next. There were large open areas periodically, strictly for the mental health of its occupants, but in the interests of avoiding traffic jams and minimizing major injuries, passengers were routed along paths made of two-meter wide rungs mounted in the walls.

The center of the terminal was marked by ropes stretched at odd intervals, like a loosely-woven spider web, so that people who came unmoored might arrest their trajectories rather than smashing hard into the opposite wall (or other people) or floating aimlessly down the long axis, missing their flights, and complaining to management.

Haddy kept his eyes on the road, so to speak, and didn't really take in anything else around him.

Normally he'd be excited to be here. He liked new experiences, he liked exploring. But he'd seen Ring Alpha before, just last year outbound to Earth and then back again. It couldn't have changed that much.

If Haddy hadn't been staring blankly at his hands as he palm-walked along the rung path into the main terminal area—the the free fall equivalent of shuffling along with his eyes on the ground—he might have noticed all the little changes.

Like how much busier it was than it had been last time.

Or how much of that traffic was outbound.

Or how many interesting characters there were hanging around.

Or how many of those interesting characters were dressed in uniforms that were seldom visible this side of the gravity well.

"Attention passengers," said an authoritative female voice, "Due to recent terrorist activities, some ports of call have been designated as 'areas of special concern.' If you are destined for an 'area of special concern,' be advised that you are obliged to go through a customs inspection before departure from Ring Alpha, as well as subject to whatever customs procedures your port of call might require. Attention passengers, due to recent terrorist activities..."

Haddy heard the words, but he couldn't imagine why anyone would do customs inspections on *departing* travelers. Customs were for making sure people didn't bring the wrong diseases into the colony. Sometimes the wrong tech. Space stations, for example, didn't like projectile weapons or explosives—things that could rupture the hull or damage the infrastructure—but Haddy wasn't carrying anything that would violate customs rules in any port he'd ever heard of, so, upon consideration, he figured it wasn't something he needed to worry about.

A few more meters along, Haddy came to an official-looking woman, but he didn't recognize the uniform she wore. Navy blue beret cap and shoulder pads, rank insignia over her left breast, pale blue button-up shirt, black slacks. Definitely the kind of outfit a groundhog would wear.

She waved him to a stop. "You're for the *Buchman*?"

Haddy nodded. "Uh-huh."

"Passport, please?"

"Passport?" Haddy said. He hadn't heard that word anywhere except... "Oh. Sure."

He produced his ticket, and handed it over.

"This isn't a passport."

"What...like an..."

Someone tapped on his foot. Haddy looked "down" to see a Korean woman in a dress—who must have been a groundhog, because nobody in their right mind wore an open-crotch lower garment in free fall—staring at him with a reproving look on her face.

"She means your OxyCode," the woman said in a tone that suggested that his stupidity was a major personal burden for her.

For a second he looked blankly at her, not sure whether to thank her for the help or kick her for her attitude. She wouldn't have gotten far in Luna City with that kind of mean streak, that was for sure.

"Oh!" he said finally. "Thanks."

Haddy fumbled with his bags, unable to let go either the rung or the bags due to fear of losing something floating away himself. He wound up sandwiching his bag between his body and the bulkhead, holding onto the rung with one hand, and using the other to slip into one of the bag's two end-pockets. There, between his socks and his underwear, he found his OxyCode, the pass-card Loonies used for authenticating contracts and payment of the breathing bill, and handed it over.

The official clicked the card into a handheld reader.

"Are you carrying any biologically active samples, infected with any engineered viruses, or in possession of any weapons at this time?"

"No."

"Are you in possession of any information retrieval or storage device?"

Haddy thought of his thumbnail and PPD. He shrugged. "Yes."

The official gave a curt nod, and returned his card.

"Step over here for secondary inspection please." She pointed off to the left, toward the center of the station. A small cube-shaped plastic room had been pitched in the middle of a tangle of ropes.

Haddy stowed his card, grabbed his bag, and aimed. His flying experience helped him line up the shot. He pushed himself off gently, giving him a good thirty seconds to work up a healthy sense of indignation.

Last year when he came through, there wasn't any

of this rigmarole. He'd gotten off his shuttle, and onto his ship, and he'd done customs at the destination port. That's the way it was supposed to be. That was the only way customs made sense. He didn't much fancy getting pushed around by people in uniforms, especially when he didn't know what it was all about.

The announcement was still on a loop. *Due to recent terrorist attacks...*

But those attacks had been attacks on Luna City infrastructure, and on Space Station Sidon which orbited Earth. Why check people going for the outer territories where there wasn't any *reason* to do terrorist things? Nineveh and Mars were too far out there for anyone to even bother with. Only crazy people and prospectors lived that far out.

Or people on the run.

Haddy was on the run.

Were they trying to catch someone else who was on the run?

Haddy held out his left hand as he approached the gray cube. He used it to brake his acceleration, rolling his wrist to his elbow to his back with practiced ease, settling in with a small hollow *thump* against the hard plastic door jamb.

Before he could bounce off, he got his fingers into a pad-eye next to the door and used the grip to swing himself in.

He found himself in a brightly lit annex with cubby at one end, backed by a mirror.

The door rolled shut behind him, leaving him in a seamless white world.

"Um, hello?"

"Thank you for your cooperation." came a voice from the air, "Please place all of your electronic items, weapons, and bioactive compounds in the inspection tube above. Our scanners indicate that you are carrying two such potentially dangerous items."

Not even the courtesy to face him when they tried to steal the only things he cared about.

Aunt Min was missing, probably dead—okay, he wasn't all that close to her, but he did love her and he didn't want her to be *dead*—he'd lost his home and the only thing he really loved doing besides writing, he'd abandoned Josie, and now they were going to rob him of all his stories and all his wing designs and everything he was counting on to keep himself sane in this stupid-long passage on this god-forsaken ship to the ass end of nowhere.

Haddy didn't know whether to cry, or scream in frustration, or throw up.

But it wasn't like there was a lot he could do. They wouldn't let him out of here till he did what they said—why else would they close the door on him like that? And even if he could, if he turned around and went home, his parents would just force him back onto the next shuttle, and his uncles and Charis and Arn would go nuts trying to figure out why they'd lost him when the *Buchman* took off without him aboard.

They'd feel responsible.

So he couldn't do that to them. Even if this was all kind of their fault. Besides, he didn't like running away from the big scary might-be-drafted thing because he didn't like running away, period. People who ran away got squashed. Haddy wanted to be the kind of man who stood his ground.

Even if that meant that, this time, he had to give in.

Chin wobbling, he took a breath, fished his electronics out of his pockets, and let them go in the cubby. They tumbled enthusiastically as his fingers pulled away.

When his hands were clear, the cubby closed. He heard a tone beeping about once a second for twenty seconds, then a light came on next to the cubby.

"Your carry-on items have been verified safe. Please retrieve them and continue to your vessel."

The door on the cubby opened, and his thumbnail and PPD were both floating in it as if nothing had happened—except they had less spin on them than when he'd let them go. Some robotic arm had touched them, maybe—otherwise, they'd have gone on tumbling at the same speed they had when they rolled off his fingers.

Haddy pocketed them and got out of the room as quick as he could, in case they changed his mind and wanted to screw around with him some more.

He left out another door which appeared to come out of nowhere. It led through a long, curved tube to where it re-joined the queue for the shuttle to the *Buchman* on the far side of the uniformed security woman who'd checked his OxyCode earlier. He wound up close to the end of the line, but not quite at the end of it.

Three or four people trailed aboard after him into a shuttle that was, by any human standard, overloaded. Two rows of seats on the floor, two on each wall, two on the ceiling, all were filled with people. A further dozen were hanging onto ring holds on one of the four poles that ran the length of the cabin.

Haddy took a ring near the airlock where he'd come in and started scanning for Charis—and not just because she was fun to look at. She had that *thing* that some people do that makes them stand out in a crowd even when they're dressed identically to everyone else.

"Attention passengers," a companionable male voice came over the intercom, "we are closing the gangway. This shuttle is outbound for the PRS *Buchman* with partial ITN service to Space Station Nineveh, Phobos Station, with return service to Space Station Sidon and Ring Alpha. This is a one-way shuttle. If you are not bound for Nineveh or Phobos Station, you must disembark now."

Haddy felt a thrill in his chest. A point of no return. It was unthinkable that someone got aboard by accident, seeing as how they scanned your ticket as you came on, and they had sensors tracking all entrances and exits, but he supposed there must be a way for it to happen if they warned you like that.

He resisted the urge to make a beeline for the door and find a shuttle back to the Lunar surface, but it wasn't an easy thing.

The announcer continued while Haddy kept up his search for familiar faces:

"Our travel time to the *Buchman* will be fifteen minutes, with embarkation to Nineveh within the hour. We'll be accelerating at one-quarter gravity for brief burns on either end of our journey today, so if you're not strapped in we'll want you holding on tight to your belongings and your roost ring. If you believe you've gotten on the wrong shuttle, please press the red button next to your seat or roost ring. This shuttle will not be returning to Ring Alpha. Thank you."

The airlock sealed. There was a high pitched sucking sound as the seals settled.

Haddy didn't pay attention. He'd finished looking at the faces below him, and had come up empty.

Nothing to worry about, he thought. *Everyone has their heads down, half the people have their backs to you. And a lot of them are upside down. You can't really see faces when they're upside-down.*

The shuttle shuddered as the docking clamps disengaged.

Haddy swallowed the lump of panic rising in his throat, and turned upside down, and looked over the faces on the opposite side of the shuttle.

Then he hand-over-handed along a little so he could see the people with their backs to him.

He didn't see Charis.

He didn't see Mike or Amit.

He didn't see Arn.

He was alone on the shuttle.

Under Boost

THE SHUTTLE SETTLED into its burn, pressing Haddy backwards so that he was effectively hanging from his ring, albeit weighing all of eighteen kilos while he did so, baggage included. A little more weight than he was used to supporting when he was on the wing, but not much, not by a long shot.

The burn lasted only a few seconds.

Haddy barely noticed. His gaze darted around the compartment. The walls seemed to be racing away and closing in at the same time. He was trapped here, trapped in for the long haul. The next time this shuttle made port, it would be at Nineveh on the far side of the sun.

It's okay, Haddy told himself. *Don't panic. The* Buchman *is an interplanetary long-hauler. They'll have the capacity for a lot of passengers, probably enough for more than one shuttle this size.*

That was it. He must have gotten on the second shuttle out because he was signaled out for a random inspection. There were some *big* interplanetary vessels, and slow-boat passenger liners were usually the really big ones that carted cargo as well as passengers. Passengers commanded higher prices and were only marginally more expensive to haul, as long as they were willing to sit through a longer passage.

Fuel was the big expense, and the ITN was a fuel-free route, more or less.

He couldn't check his PPD. Robot shuttles didn't have net relay. A security feature, to prevent remote hijacking.

Haddy's heart thumped like someone had connected it to an industrial pump. His chest twitched beneath his shirt. His heart was going to break his ribs from the inside, he just knew it.

He checked the faces over again, and another time.

They weren't here.

They'd disappeared.

No. They'd *been* disappeared.

Don't tell him anything that could put him in danger.

Haddy's father's words rang in his ears like a gunshot.

What had they all known that they weren't telling him?

And if Dad had known enough to insist they not tell Haddy, did he know?

He had to. That meant he was marked too.

Haddy's stomach hardened into a cold knot of dread, a knot that wouldn't come undone for a long, long time.

INSTEAD OF HAVING an interior laid out for free fall, *PRS Buchman* was rigged with a floor, complete with strap-in seats for acceleration turns and flips.

But while it did accelerate and flip during the normal course of operation, it wasn't a nimble vessel. Four hundred meters from stem-to-stern, and squat round in its habitable section, it looked like a turnip that had been welded to a rocket drive.

Two triangular gantries projected into the void from her port side and starboard side, at the point where the passenger area met the engine. A dozen ISO vacuum-safe shipping containers clustered around each gantry. The welcome video explained that the loads were carefully balanced to within a gram of one another, and that the ship itself rotated around the pivot provided by the cargo arms so that it could boost and brake without having to negotiate the complexities of a skew-flip maneuver.

Haddy watched the video after being shown to his stateroom, as he was directed to, because he'd never been on an ITN liner before. It was an economy room—no outside view, which Haddy found a relief. He hadn't fancied watching home shrink to just another pinpoint of light.

In addition to the video, the smallish space sported bunks for five, a private head, two micrograv treadmills, a set of cooler drawers, a microwave, and a pressurized drinks station. It was painted in swaths of bright, soft green against deep and maroon backing, and touched with chrome and gold and faux-wood accents to give it a sense of occasion.

And it was empty.

Haddy waited.

Nobody came.

He called the concierge to ask if his party had come aboard, but the concierge was busy with pre-flight and would get back to him shortly. In the mean time, would he please stay in his cabin for his own safety and that of his shipmates until the voyage was underway?

The answering service thanked him for flying Mannix Spaceways *PRS Buchman*, the jewel of the night skies.

When Haddy hung up, the screen offered him a selection of viewing related to the history of Mannix Spaceways, the *Buchman*, and the human colonization of the solar system. Or, if he wasn't interested in that, he could watch the TGN news feed, or enjoy any one of a selection of thousands of complimentary films and serials on demand from the shipboard media servers.

Haddy turned off the screen, stowed his bag next to one of the strap-chairs, strapped himself in, dove into his PPD and prayed furiously that his family would show up before boost.

He hooked his right forefinger through Josie's collar on his left arm.

And, very quickly, he found his eyes closing of their own accord.

BEEP BEEP BEEP

A soft-but-persistent pager sound roused Haddy out of his sleep. He felt heavier than normal—just enough extra weight to be a little uncomfortable, not enough to be oppressive. More like he was weighed down with three large sacks of flour. In Earth-normal terms, he now weighed sixteen and a half kilos, where he was used to weighing just under eleven. If he hadn't been a regular flier, he'd have found it much more difficult than he did.

It made him think, though. Nineveh ran mostly at full earth-normal gravity. All the spinning space stations did. Some of them—he couldn't remember which ones—had some spinning sections for weak-grav transition, but all the interesting stuff lived in the Earth-normal districts. For "health reasons", even though Loonies, as a rule, didn't have health problems. It was another one of those things Terrans did—they assumed that *just* because humans evolved on Earth, that must mean Earth is the best possible environment.

You couldn't fly on Earth. That made it an automatic loser in Haddy's book.

But if he was going to be staying on Nineveh for more than a few days, he was going to have to get into high-grav shape. His cardio system and leg muscles, not to mention his bones, wouldn't do well when he weighed six times his normal weight. He remembered how hard he'd had to work to be able to deal with his visit to Earth last year. Three months of centrifuge treatments and weight belts and all sorts of stuff.

Maybe that's why they'd booked him on an ITN ship. It gave him time to get in shape for high gravity. Assuming there was any way to do that on a ship that spent most of its time in free fall.

When he reached the screen, Haddy found the face of a young man, maybe twenty years old, on the other end.

Well, he *looked* twenty, anyway. Looks didn't mean much for telling age once you got done with puberty. More than once Haddy had discovered that a cute twenty-three looking client was actually fifty and fresh off rejuvenation therapy. It was one of the things that made him gun-shy about dating.

The young man on the screen introduced himself as the concierge.

Haddy breathed a sigh of relief. Finally he'd get some answers. He'd find out that Charis and her family really did make it aboard.

He gave their names. Explained how they got separated at the surprise customs checkpoint.

The concierge dithered, saying that he wasn't at liberty to disclose passenger names. Those were a passenger's personal business. This was a long voyage, and people valued their privacy, and he was sorry, but there wasn't anything he could do. He was sure Haddy was mature enough to understand these things and how they worked.

Haddy was. And even though he didn't want to let go of any cash when he didn't know what kind of fix he was in, he slipped his credit jack into the port and authorized a ten LOX transfer to the concierge.

"Thank you sir. Let me see if I can help you," the concierge said. "Yes, your party is on the passenger manifest. They were assigned to stateroom G-72."

"That's my stateroom. They're not here."

"Ah, I see, one moment. Yes, I found your problem. Your party did not make final check-in."

"What does that mean?"

"It means they never made it aboard the shuttle, sir. That's all I know."

Haddy thanked him, and signed off.

He looked at his PPD. He knew he wouldn't be in real-time range of the nets for long, but if he hadn't slept too long, he might just be able to send something back home. Maybe his parents had heard something?

He did find the Luna City net, so they weren't fire-walling him.

Now, what time? 1400. Everyone should be manning the store right now, so he tried to call in.

He got voice mail. He left a message telling them he'd made it safely aboard. He almost said more, but he stopped before he got past "there's something I needed..."

It occurred to him that someone might be listening. The same someone, or someones, that made Aunt Min disappear. That probably made Uncle Amit and Uncle Mike and Charis and Arn all disappear too.

Maybe he shouldn't say anything where it would be recorded.

"...something I forgot to do before I left. Could you call me back when you get a free minute?"

And when they did, what would he say? If he told them what happened, would that put them in more danger than they already were from knowing whatever-it-was that they didn't want him to know about?

Could he trust that nobody was listening in?

He decided to send a note. He could send a note securely. There was a provision for it on the business server. He'd heard his Dad talking about it—Vin was a man who cared about the privacy of his business, and he reviewed it every six months.

Haddy found the company's reservation system. There was a public drop for customers who had questions before they booked lessons. Haddy wrote a note:

> *Mom and Dad-*
>
> *I hope you're still the only ones who check this box.*
>
> *I made it safely to the* Buchman, *and we're under-way. Some people in uniform searched me before they let me on. Like a customs inspection, but I think they were looking for something.*
>
> *Charis and Mike and Amit and Arn didn't make it to the ship. Don't know what happened to them. Do you know what happened? Did they call you?*
>
> *Please let me know.*
>
> *-Haddy*

He hesitated a moment when he finished. There was so much more he wanted to say, but he couldn't tell them how scared he was. They'd be worried enough already.

And he had two months in front of him to worry about how he was going to handle things when he got to Nineveh.

LONG HAUL FLIGHTS on the ITN have four major hazards: meteorites, piracy, sabotage, and boredom.

Of the four, boredom is the most likely, and the most realistically dangerous. A restive passenger compliment can do more than annoy the crew—any time you pack a few hundred humans into close quarters for an extended period of time, you run the risk of violence.

People get tired of each other. Faces get old. Tempers get short. Somewhere, down deep, people start to blame the people around them for their own boredom.

NASA's early moon missions were all run by people who had been trained to handle isolation and close quarters, as were the early space stations. NASA astronauts were ex-military, and later civilians who'd gone through years of training. What little violence erupted among them happened on the ground, not in the sky.

But the earliest Mars mission put the world on notice. The ship had been too small, the demands on the crew too large, and the mix of personalities too volatile. There had been a series of murders, and a near disaster at the far end. There were other complicating factors as well that were not discussed much in history books in the curriculum for Haddy's age group, but the basic thrust came through loud and clear:

If you're on a long-haul space ship, you'd better keep yourself occupied.

Haddy lasted almost a full day on his own in his quarters. Mostly he ate from the prepackaged meals in the cooler drawers, and slept as his body got used to the heavier boost.

By day number two, he was going stir crazy, and ventured forth in search of adventure—or at least amusement.

A high-boost ship accelerating at one full gravity outbound from Luna could make port at Nineveh in anywhere from a few days to a few weeks depending on the orbital alignment. That kind of trip would mean a couple weeks in a high boost, complete misery while his body adjusted, too busy to do anything but read and write. Haddy reckoned a ship like that would be a slimmed down liner, like you got on the Earth/Luna runs, and he wasn't far wrong.

But it hadn't occurred to him that the slower ships would, by necessity, be outfitted more like cruise ships on Earth.

The *PRS Buchman* was a compact, mobile city in space. It had twelve restaurants, each serving a different range of cuisines and catering to a different range of dietary preferences. Kosher and halal in one, Mediterranean in another, and then one each devoted to Far Eastern, Luna City fusion, Indian, North African, West African, North American, Central American, fine dining, barbecue of all sorts, and a pizza place, each with kitchen able to produce food that was safe to eat in free fall as well as under boost—no mean trick, as crumbs and droplets are both a health hazard in free fall.

There were gathering areas and social spaces, of course. Places for games suitable for boost and larger areas for games suited for free fall.

But its centerpiece was an enormous, nearly-spherical zero-gravity gym.

Of course, while under boost, only the floor area was usable, but the space was so big it could fit the entire passenger compliment without making anyone feel crowded, at least during free fall.

Like the large interior of Ring Alpha, it had areas of

spider-webbing from time to time—unlike Ring Alpha, it left most of the space free and open.

Haddy had not spent much of his life in free fall, so his understanding of zero-g sports was limited to what he'd happened to encounter in vids or reading up on other things. Despite his devotion to the family business and the sport it had more-or-less invented, sports *per se* weren't his thing. He preferred *doing* to *watching*.

Because of this, he couldn't quite figure out what all the knobby features on the walls could be. They looked like bollards that someone had welded to the bulkheads. They gave large sections of the roughly-spherical space the look of the inside of an iron maiden, if all the spikes were tipped with sponge rubber.

The equipment attached to the floor, on the other hand, he recognized. It was littered with resistance machines for weight work that didn't depend on gravity to function properly, and tether-line treadmills for loaded cardio work, all arrayed around the centerpiece of the gym, the thing that would be key to staying healthy once the ship went into free fall:

A centrifuge.

This one was sixty meters across. Wide enough that you could lie on your back against a wall, get spun up to a gravity or two, and relax for half an hour. With a slow enough spin up and a slow enough return, it wouldn't make you motion sick, or even dizzy. After a few treatments, you'd move to sitting position. Take a couple treatments per week, and after a couple months your internal systems would all be acclimated to a full gravity, or even more.

The human body is an anti-fragile system, Haddy's mom had explained when he asked her why people paid to ride centrifuges back in Luna City. *When you stress it, it gets stronger. A lot of things are like that—the human mind is like that too. Stress it regularly, make it uncomfortable, and it learns and gets tougher. If you want to be strong, you have to be brave and seek out difficult things. When something frightens you, jump into it with both feet. Sometimes you'll get hurt, but you'll always wind up better off, in the long run.*

He'd been six years old when she told him that, and it was the first time he remembered thinking she was about eight shades of crazy. Haddy couldn't imagine, at the time, how anyone in their right mind would *invite* trouble. The whole idea sounded nutty.

But then he started teaching, and there wasn't a day that went by when his mom's words didn't ring in his ears.

They were ringing extra loud today.

Haddy was just about to go looking for a crew member or a terminal to ask about all the bollards when he heard a sing-songy rough-edged tenor beside him.

"Hell of a 'fuge, dontchathink?"

Haddy looked left to see a man a little shorter than him, and a lot stockier, with a brush-style mustache and unusually pale skin—well, unusual for Luna City, anyway.

"I've never seen a bigger one, anyway," Haddy said.

"Well, I betcha it'll keep us in the strong bones so's we don't break before we're hitting the bricks at Nineveh." The man turned the full force of a solar-intensity smile on him. "You're a Loonie boy, ain'tcha?"

"Uh...yeah, I guess." Haddy wasn't used to this much friendliness. Politeness, sure. Directness, absolutely. But nobody smiled that big upon meeting a stranger, at least not in Luna City.

"Hadrian Jin. From Luna City." Haddy extended his hand.

"Well, ain't that the thing? Malcolm Rushti, from back in Minnesota, up near Brainerd if you know where that is."

Haddy shook his head. "Can't say I ever heard of it."

"Well, it don't matter now, really. What brings you out from the tunnels and out among these here stars out here?"

"I uh..." Haddy stumbled as it occurred to him that he probably ought not talk about his troubles to anyone. It seemed to be the kind of trouble that was contagious. The less anyone else knew, the safer they were. It seemed to have saved his skin so far...though he had to admit to himself that he would have traded a little safety to know what the hell was going on. "My family owns an orn-suit shop, and now we're expanding. I'm going to Nineveh to try to get people interested, and maybe open a franchise out there."

"Oh, a young man going out into the world to make his fortune. I like that. Gonna jin up the interest and shoot for the big bucks, eh? I might have to follow you around, dontchaknow."

Haddy scowled. "Why would you want to do that?"

"I'm up here researching my dissertation, dontchaknow..."

Haddy almost said *No, I don't know, or I wouldn't have asked*, but Malcolm kept right on talking. The whole "dontchaknow" thing had to be some kind of verbal tick, the way surfers said "dude" and Californians said "fuck" and Irish people said "jaysis."

Anyway, he didn't have any time to answer, because Malcolm was still talking.

"...gathering data on the economic habits of *homo solaris*."

"Homo solaris?"

"Space-born folk, dontchaknow. The way that money

and trade works up here, I've got good reasons to think it's different than the ways it works back home, and it's an angle nobody's studied yet. The whole fight heating up between your people and my people, it's all because my people think your people think the same way my people do. I reckon if we could find a way to understand all of you better it might save a lot of lives and make for a brighter future for all of us, dontchaknow."

"Sounds good to me. But why *homo solaris*? I thought we were all *homo sapiens*."

"Well, it's like this...come to think of it, you hungry?"

"Sure."

MALCOLM SUGGESTED THEY avail themselves of chili and chips at the North American restaurant, since things that shatter and things that have a lot of droplets associated with them would be hard to come by, or impossible, once the trip went into free fall.

"Eat now what you can't get your teeth around later," he said.

It seemed a good enough philosophy to Haddy, and he'd never had chili.

He got his first taste at a round table that sat off to the side of a wide hall on the entertainment deck, only a little ways from the exit of the zero-g gymnasium.

He found it reminded him vaguely of begue wot, but there was something darker about it. Not exactly grimier. Dirtier, maybe, but not in a bad way—or at least, it wasn't altogether unpleasant. But it was certainly different than anything he'd tasted before, and he wasn't quite sure he liked it.

But it grew on him with every bite. And the conversation didn't hurt, either.

Malcolm had a theory that growing up in reduced gravity, and especially in artificial environments, fundamentally changed human nature. He talked about the different kinds of things groundhogs—he called them "Earthlings," which sounded odd to Haddy's ear—valued and traded with.

"It's like back in the age of conquest and discovery on Earth, dontchaknow. The Europeans, they valued the gold the natives just had hanging around, cause the Europeans used it for money and the Indians used it for religious things, and jewelry..."

"What does India have to do with it?" Haddy asked.

"Oh, sorry, sorry, no that's my fault. It's an old joke. A mistake that...anyway it would take too long to explain. I meant the natives, my lad, don't worry about India, they're not really involved in the story at all. Anyway, the natives used it for jewelry, but not for money. It wasn't rare or useful to them that way. But the natives, well you know they didn't have anything like glass or iron, and the Europeans had tons of it. So early on—before they started going on about conquest and all that—the Europeans, they'd trade, like, nails for gold, and glass beads for big pieces of land, and they were getting it all at a steal."

Malcolm stopped for a moment to take a bite of chili.

"Mmm. They do done did this up just right. Better'n any hotdish, dontchaknow."

"Huh?"

Malcolm chuckled. "Call it another one of my midwesterly related disabilities, my weakness for hotdish. Skip it. But you up here," he said, finding the main topic again, "you have to pay for everything that we get for free down there. But then there's everything you get for free, or for free enough it doesn't matter."

"Like what?"

"Food. Power. Any kind of material or consumer good."

"We pay for things..."

"Really?" He held up his spoon. "How much would you pay for this?"

It was a carbon fullerine composite—light and strong, virtually indestructible. The same stuff that came out of any household printer with a bog-standard feedstock cartridge.

"I don't know. Maybe a couple LOX for the design file."

"How much is that in dollars these days?"

Haddy had to think for a second. LOX was an informal currency that Loonies used. Major stuff was all dollars, and tourists paid in dollars, but he was used to thinking in LOX.

"About one? Maybe a buck ten?"

"And then for the actual spoon?"

Haddy smiled. "I can't count that low."

"You know what a set of four of these costs in Brainerd?"

Haddy shrugged.

"Five bucks."

"You're...serious?"

"Dead serious. We breathe free. We drink almost free. But our material goods and our feedstocks are where we put our money. You know most people don't even have a household printer?"

"What? Why?" Everyone had a printer. You had to be able to fabricate all manner of things, on demand, on the fly, just to keep a home in good repair.

Malcolm chuckled. "It would take too long to explain. Just...trust me. It's actually easier for most people to order what they need."

Haddy shook his head. He couldn't imagine a place where there was so much space that it was practical to send people this way and that to every residence, clogging up the passageways with traffic and drones and who-knew-what-else. Especially when it was *so* much easier just to decide what you want, buy the design file, modify it if you needed to, then print it out.

He couldn't imagine how life would be possible without the ability to do that—and, in fact, he was correct. In space, it wouldn't have been.

"This is what I...Oh! Sil! Come on and join us!" Malcolm waved at someone behind Haddy.

Haddy turned to see a woman with hips that seemed to expand and shrink with every step, dressed in billowing trousers that met a loose white pirate shirt at a wide black leather belt. Haddy had never seen loose clothes make someone look like *that*.

In the three seconds between when he saw her and when he managed a halfhearted wave, Haddy realized he would do anything just for the privilege of teaching her how to climb a thermal. He could probably spend the rest of his life watching the way her short brown hair swept across her Chinese face, and the way her light brown eyes turned almost yellow when she looked just the right way at the light, and listening to her talk about the most boring things he could imagine—like politics, or maybe parenting.

And he hadn't even heard her talk yet.

She smiled a polite smile, but as far as Haddy was concerned it was the deepest, most genuine smile he'd ever seen. He found himself looking at the ground sheepishly without really knowing why.

Then, suddenly, she was on other side of the table, where Malcolm was.

"I was wondering where I'd see you," she said.

And then she kissed him.

Just a quick little kiss, but it was enough. Haddy's stomach sank. Heat rose in his cheeks, and he wanted all at once to disappear completely and to punch Malcolm in the face.

"Smells good," she said, pointing at the chili. "Is it?"

"Yeah, pretty good. You think so, Had?"

"Um. Sure. Yeah. I guess so."

"Sil, this is Had, just come up here from Luna City. Had, this is my friend Sil, here, dontchaknow. Ow." He rubbed his arm where Sil punched him. "Okay, my *good* friend Sil. Better?"

Sil regarded Malcolm with narrow, suspicious eyes. "I'll tolerate it."

It occurred to Haddy that he hadn't even had a chance to say "hi." But whatever chance he'd had, had passed. Malcolm was talking again.

"I was just telling Had here about my thesis. About the economics thing."

"Oh? Yeah. You interested in economics?" She looked at Haddy.

Haddy looked at his half-dead chili.

"Uh...not really."

"Well don't *bore* him." She made it sound like boring someone was the most terrible crime a person could commit.

"Actually," Malcolm said, "Had here's heading out to Nineveh to start a flying franchise dontchaknow."

"Flying?"

So, Haddy re-iterated his franchise story, making like he was a couple years older than he really was. He finished his chili while he talked, and then had some coffee, and he talked more than he'd talked to anyone. He told them about Josie, and about having to go leave for Nineveh because he didn't want to get caught up in the war.

About halfway through the tale he remembered his cover story about opening up a franchise on Nineveh, so he worked back around to it and embroidered in some details, but he felt guilty about it. He didn't like lying to his new friends, and now that he'd had some rest and some food and some good company, he didn't feel like it was possible that he could be "next in line" to disappear.

He figured that his uncles and cousins had to be detained at that bogus security search he'd been diverted to. They'd been searched, just like him, but where he'd been let go, they'd had to stay.

It scared him, sure. It petrified him all the way down to his bones. It pissed him off. He knew he'd have to find a way to help them somehow, if he could.

But he didn't need to worry about himself. He was between planets now. There wasn't anyone back on Luna or on Earth that could even get close to him for months, and it wasn't like anybody on Nineveh would care what anyone on Earth wanted. *Everyone* knew that Nineveh was where all the anarchists and losers went.

Still, the last thing he wanted to do was come off looking like a liar. And starting a franchise wasn't a bad idea. He was going to need to make a living when he got to Nineveh, and he did have the company designs on his thumbnail. He could open a new shop. By the time he came home again, it would be going great guns. He could sell it. Or give it to his brother to run. Or...

Well, he didn't know yet. But the future was long. That was it's job. He'd figure things out when he got to Nineveh.

One hour rolled into another. Coffee turned into more coffee, which turned into polite vapor huffing on some hash oil, courtesy of Malcolm's private stash. That turned into dancing in a dance hall with them both at first, and then with just Sil, for hours.

And even though he knew it was just dancing, for a little while he could pretend it was something more. A little slice of paradise where they were the only two people in a world full of music.

Haddy didn't last as long as he wanted. His body still wasn't used to the acceleration, and after only about six hours of being up and about he was so tired he could barely drag himself back to his stateroom.

So he traded berth numbers with Sil and Malcolm, and promised to look them up again tomorrow after he'd had some good rest.

When he reached his quarters, he laid himself down on a bunk and tried to sleep, but couldn't, so he found his PPD where he'd left it on the strap-chair and put on some soft music from his personal library.

There was a message on his PPD. Haddy opened it up and found a note from his father.

> *Don't communicate again. Not safe. Will keep watch here. Check for message when you dock.*
>
> *Don't trust anyone.*
>
> *-Dad*

A Long Passage

THE EXTRA GRAVITY made even the soft stateroom beds uncomfortable. He was used to one-sixth g, and they were boosting at one quarter—not a huge difference, but everything weighed half again as much as it should. Not just his body, but his lungs, and his hair, all the little things that little muscles work to keep balanced all the time. It didn't matter that his main slow-twitch muscles were well developed from the constant flying, his body still wasn't used to the low level, constant pressure, and the net effect was exhausting.

It wasn't just that, though. It was worse. Way worse.

Not having Josie curled up at the small of his back made him feel unmoored, somehow. As if everything that had happened in the last day and a half wasn't quite real, and he might wake up from his fitful anti-sleep and discover it had all been a bad dream.

His father's words rolled over and over in his head. *Don't trust anyone.*

He wanted to ignore it. In fact, he had. Haddy closed the message thinking that his Dad was being paranoid and maybe it was a good thing that he was going to Nineveh after all—but that thought was chased up not half-a-second later by the sinking-stomach realization that Charis and her family *had* disappeared, and Dad was too afraid to talk about it.

So Dad was afraid of someone listening in, and

maybe...what? Arresting him? Arresting Haddy? Killing them?   Haddy had no way to judge, he didn't know anything that was going on, so his mind swam with vague, half-formed possibilities cobbled together from movies and books, none of which he had any reason to suspect accurately depicted real things that people really did, but all of which were enough to make his stomach try to crawl up into his rib cage to hide from the men with the knives and the cattle prods and the ropes and the *it's just my job* explanations.

Don't trust anyone.

How could a person live like that?   You *had* to trust people to get by.   That was the only way life existed out here where things were civilized.   Because person A trusted person B not to poison the air, and person B trusted person C to provide good quality food, because person A made the water for person C, in exchange for the food, and person B ran the oxygen cracker that let person A and person C breathe, so they each gave person B the food and water he needed to live.

That was what civilization *was*.   You couldn't just expect the universe to provide for you, you had to make something or do something, and then you could trade that for other things you needed.

And how was he supposed to know how to do that when he didn't know who it was that his Dad was afraid of, or wanted him to be careful of?

It felt like hours between laying down and finally falling asleep.   Haddy couldn't quite tell when the night faded to dreams, and he couldn't remember the nightmares afterwards, but he did remember waking up sobbing and shaking, at least once, feeling certain, somehow, that everyone he'd ever cared about was dead.

HADDY WROTE FIRST thing in the morning, intending to make it a habit. He had seven half-finished stories on his stack. He wasn't going to be able to fly for the next he-didn't-now-how-long, and he'd always thought of himself as a flyer before and after everything else. Well, up here, at least for a while, he needed something else to be. Writing was his next favorite thing, and if he could actually manage to finish a story, he could tell people he was a writer, so he wouldn't have to keep thinking about how much he missed flying every time he introduced himself to someone.

And, if he could finish one, it might even turn out to be good.

So he wrote, before he even grabbed breakfast. It gave him a chance to work out the mass of feelings that were swirling around inside him, and, after some initial fighting, he gave up trying to control what the stories were doing.

The one he was concentrating on, which had been a comedy, started turning dark almost as soon as he attacked it again. His confused feelings about Sil bled through the words. So did his creeping dread about who to trust, and what might have happened to Charis and her family.

The nightmares, too, bled into the story.

But he wrote anyway. It was all he had that seemed to matter right now. The only thing he could do that didn't make him feel completely helpless. Because, as far as he was concerned, stories were special.

In the world he knew, things were really only worth anything if they were personal, somehow. The trinkets people sold in the Gallery Bazaar were worth selling because some piece of them was hand made. Each one was unique in the universe.

Stories were like that. So were flights on the wing. And since he wouldn't be able to fly until he'd gotten to Nineveh and built himself a new suit...

After his writing and a bit of breakfast—and a shower—he made his way up to the gym and took his first centrifuge treatment.

Once the ship was in free fall, treatments in the centrifuge would progress toward walking around, then doing calisthenics and weight-bearing exercise on the walls of the spinning room.

That wasn't practical while the ship was under acceleration. For now, his treatments were very like what he went through on Luna before his visit to Earth—he stepped into a cylindrical room, found a spot along the wall, and leaned up against it. When all passengers were loaded, the room began rotating at a gentle rate that gradually intensified until a full gravity was pressing down on him.

But where the centrifuges in Luna City were a scant fifteen meters across and bare of wall, this one was padded, soft, and immense.

His first time inside, Haddy wondered at the difference, but a single trip in it explained it all. Small centrifuges were more likely to make their occupants motion sick, and bare walls were easier to clean than white padding. But when you had the extra size, and the lower risk of motion sickness, the padding made all the difference.

This treatment didn't even make Haddy dizzy—just exhausted from the weight bearing down on him, pushing his bones and organs to adapt to greater pressure.

After a full hour of gradually increasing weight up to a full gravity and then stepping down to half, then cycling back up to full before beginning a very gradual deceleration that took a full ten minutes, Haddy was ready for a nap.

So he returned to his stateroom to do just that.

Then some lunch, and a wander around to take in more of the ship. He subconsciously marked all the doors where he wasn't allowed to go, and wondered how he might get around them to find out how things worked behind the scenes.

He ran into Sil in the afternoon, and found himself talking to her like he'd talked to her and Malcolm yesterday. Haddy was beginning to wonder if he was going to run out of interesting stories to tell, especially as they paled next to the weird stories from the bottom of the gravity well—from American colleges and freeways, campgrounds and beaches and forests and other utterly alien things that he'd only heard of or seen in vids.

It became a matter of normal routine for the most of the remainder of his time under acceleration (which, granted, was only about a week and a half). Write, eat, gym, sleep, wander around, meet people, maybe spend an evening with them.

The evenings always went well. Haddy's customer service practice served him in good stead. At one point he met some businesspeople outbound from Earth who had transferred at Ring Alpha. They were headed for Phobos to do an in-person inspection on some kind of big geoengineering project they had in mind, and intended to put in a bid. It sounded to Haddy like they wanted to turn Phobos—the moon—into a rotating space station.

"The material's all there," the project lead said as she sipped at her cappuccino, "Well, more or less. It's just a matter of rearranging it in the right order."

Her partner showed Haddy some of the concept renderings, Haddy had been duly appreciative, and that had been a good evening's meal.

During 'fuge treatment the next day, he'd met a family he'd taken to immediately. They were all conservatively dressed, with three mothers, a father, and six children, three of whom were his age and a little younger.

He spotted them when he entered, and, since there weren't a lot of people his age on the ship, he'd gravitated toward them and asked if he could lay on the wall with them during the treatment.

They were, he discovered quickly, a family of True Saints of the Latter Day from the Mormon compound near Tycho base. He'd heard about the New Zion colony before, mostly because their prophet was always in the news, but he'd never actually *met* people from there before. He always figured it was because New Zion was eighteen hundred kilometers to the south of Luna City, and they had Firsttown down there that they could trade with.

While the spin was on, he lay between one of the mothers and a daughter his own age, and they told him about their plans to start a satellite colony in one of the underused domes on Mars. They were heading to Nineveh first, rather than the quicker journey straight to Mars, in order to meet up with some other brethren that hadn't had good luck in establishing a mission there.

"You shouldn't wish to stay there, you know," said the strawberry-haired girl named Hannah Young, who was about his own age. "It's a wicked, godless place."

"Oh, I don't," he assured her. "I'll be going back to Luna City as soon as I can save the money."

"Luna City?" she gasped. "That's almost worse!"

Haddy asked why, but didn't get an answer he could understand, and Hannah's mother quickly changed the subject.

They were a very polite family, and Haddy found it a great relief to spend time with people his own age, even when their parents were around. But over the course of the treatment, and then a lunch, Haddy noticed that the mother he'd lain next to in the centrifuge was nudging him, over and over, to interact with her daughter Elle, who was thirteen. More than that, she exhibited an air of disapproval when Haddy got too engaged with Hannah or the other girl his age, Sarah.

Still, it didn't bother him too much. He enjoyed spending time with them, and they invited him back to their stateroom for board games and a reading circle, where they read from their holy book and then from a novel that they passed around, each person reading one page aloud while everyone else listened.

It felt good to be part of a family again, even if their traditions and entertainments were different from his, and even though there wasn't much work to do. Haddy had always loved working with his family—in his mind, that's what family was: people you did interesting work with, and still liked enough to share a home with.

But his lack of interest in Elle evidently did not sit well with his hosts, and the next day he found that they had changed to a different centrifuge time slot and were busy when he asked after them. For the remainder of the flight, he caught only brief glimpses of them. They never did invite him around for a second night as they promised they would.

On his seventh day aboard the *Buchman*, he met some Persians who were taking in a diplomatic survey on behalf of the Naderi Throne and didn't seem at all secretive about it, which surprised him. Haddy remembered hearing big news recently that the Persians had just launched a new fleet of warships into the inner solar system, and it had the whole solar system on tenterhooks.

Fearsome reputation aside, though, these Persians weren't even a little bit posturing or superior. He found them in one of the games rooms, and shared a few rounds of billiards while they told him about the history of the Persian Empire and some of the interesting things they'd learned on their trip.

Toward the end of the game, Malcolm showed up and kept playing with him long after the Persians left.

A familiar face was a good face, and Haddy found himself regurgitating everything he'd heard from the Persians, and the Mormons, and everyone else he'd gotten to know aboard ship over the last couple days, and then, after Sil showed up, talking more about life back home.

When the lighting changed at 2300, Sil invited him across the games room to the little dance floor, and taught him how to find the groove in the music, and move against her like he and she were two parts of the same song.

After that, evenings with Malcolm and Sil became his regular routine. He found he needed the company of familiar faces, and a lot of the things they talked about jived well with how Haddy saw the world—especially Malcolm.

Malcolm reminded Haddy, a little, of his dad. At least the way his dad had gotten paranoid right before sending him away. Malcolm talked about the coming war, a lot, and how it would mean that decent people were going to get squeezed to do things they wouldn't like. Hearing that kind of talk didn't make Haddy feel any better, but it did make him feel like maybe Dad wasn't crazy, and maybe it had been a good thing to come along after all.

But it didn't make him miss Josie any less. Especially at night.

On the last boost day, two weeks into the trip, Haddy shifted his schedule around so that he did his centrifuge treatments first thing in the morning. When he went to the zero-g gymnasium, he found a parkour group using the exercise equipment and some of the big soft bollards on the floor as obstacles.

It looked like the closest he'd get to flying under gravity this heavy, and he wished he'd picked his new centrifuge slot on the second day so that he'd have had time to learn how to run up walls—but, he realized, his bones would probably crack under the kind of punishment they'd get during free running in a quarter-g field.

At least, they would now. On the far side of free fall, he'd be strong enough to join in. He just had to keep up with the conditioning until then.

WITH THE EXCEPTION of gravity disappearing, life continued as normal when the ship went into free fall.

Well, mostly as normal. The zero g sporting arena opened up.

The bollards, it turned out, were deployable obstacles. The vast space in the center of the turnip that was the *Buchman* turned into a massive, sub-dividable arena suitable for free fall polo, all manner of laser tag games, hide-and-seek games, and a team sport that struck Haddy like a blend of hockey and orn-suit flying, except that the participants rode compressed air rockets to lob two different kinds of balls through goal nets while a little gold drone zipped around everywhere causing havoc. He never quite could get his head around it—the rules didn't seem to make any sense to him—but the ship hosted an intramural league with sign up sheets and everything, and it seemed like Haddy was the only male under thirty who wasn't interested in playing it.

The games were a good place to meet the other teens on the ship, though. Haddy took to bringing his writing into the gym with him and anchoring to a wall and working on his stories where he could watch people and poach them for character fodder.

He found, though, that he didn't have much of a knack for making friends with his peers. While he'd never been the most popular kid on the block, he'd never had trouble making friends before—well, when he wasn't working, at least.

But now, even with the handful of other kids from Luna City, something was...different.

As if he didn't come from the same world anymore. He looked at them, and talked to them, and they felt *young* to him. Young like the Monster Brat.

The only friends that stuck, really, were Malcolm and Sil. He'd never had an older brother before, being the oldest himself. He wondered if this was what it might feel like.

And he'd never had a friend like Sil. He didn't even know how to think of her. He just knew that he felt a little motion sick whenever she was around, and he ached anytime she came close enough to touch him, but didn't. He didn't think he could be in love. Love was supposed to be a tender thing, like he felt for Josie, but with sex involved somehow.

This was different. Something he didn't have a name for. It scared him half to death, the way stepping off the perch in the Gallery terrified the fledgers. Anytime it seized him, he just wanted it to stop.

But when she wasn't around, he found himself wondering where she was. What she was up to.

By his third week aboard, he was standing and walking around during his 'fuge treatments. They weren't burdensome anymore. They did take away the delicious freedom of free fall, but it was a problem he was willing to deal with. They didn't exhaust him anymore, almost didn't make him tired, which meant he needed to start adding weights to the treatments.

He filled the extra time with laser tag, mostly. When all else failed, good hard competition cleared his head and helped keep his mind off the ache in his heart.

BACK WHEN ENGLAND was a going concern, it had a national holiday called Guy Fawkes day, where the whole country turned out to celebrate a foiled terrorist attack by staging mock shellings of their homeland. The Americans who came after them gradually lost the tradition—it wasn't really part of the American consciousness, so the Americans eventually remixed the idea to celebrate their independence from England, by staging mock shellings of all their own cities.

Christmas was like that for Loonies. Of the things about Christmas that made it special to Americans—the scent of winter in the air, the songs about coming home again, the legend about God coming to Earth as a baby to bring peace and love to the whole world—very few of them made any sense to a native-born Loonie.

Loonies didn't have seasons, so they couldn't know

what winter smelled like. They didn't have a home to return to, since everything they knew as home could be walked to over the course of a long day. Even the other domes were a quick jump away, rarely more than a couple hours, and one compartment cut into the rock was very much like another. Home was the city itself and the people you loved, not the house you'd built, because nobody built houses in Luna City. And Loonies didn't have much Christianity running around, because the sorts of people who'd colonized first were not the kinds of people who were inclined to it, and the sorts that came later on were more likely to adopt or create religions that had a Lunar flavor. To the Loonie way of thinking, coming to Earth to save the world was all well and good, but that was a story about Earth. It didn't have the visceral appeal to someone who grew up with Earth hanging like a Christmas decoration in the sky.

So, in Haddy's world, Christmas was mainly a time to hang some decorations around the shop, offer two-for-one flying lessons, and, a couple days before Christmas proper, head out to the spaceport, or to the surface, and watch the year's major fireworks display in the silence of the vacuum over Tranquility basin.

Nonetheless, a month into the trip, Christmas came, and the groundhogs went nuts over it. Carols sounded all over the ship. The crew cranked up the air conditioning in one of the dance halls—which didn't see much traffic when the ship was in free fall—and turned it into a zero-g snowball arena. The ship's chaplain announced that there would be services at 1700 on Christmas Eve in the zero-g gym for anyone who wished to attend.

The festive spirit on board, with its emphasis on family and merry-making, seemed to draw a line around the empty pit in the center of Haddy's soul. After taking a go or two at the snowball arena, and sampling some of the "holiday food" that he found floating around—literally, in this case, as it was delivered on a refreshment tray by a meandering drone—he decided to hide in his stateroom for the duration and write.

It was a plan that lasted about a day before Malcolm showed up to ask him to come to services with him and Sil. Haddy hemmed and hawed and eventually caved to assuage the loneliness that the shipboard festivities seemed to bring.

When it came time to go, he went to the pizza restaurant where they usually met, only to find Sil waiting there alone for him. She was dressed in a shimmering white bodysuit with black highlights running down the sides, which drew his eyes right to her hips. Well, more than usual. The green tendrils of a diaphanous scarf wound around her arms like a vine, and red splashes of glitter across her breasts and shoulders somehow tied her in with all the holiday decorations, and at the same time made her stand out utterly apart from everything else he'd ever seen.

When she saw him, she smiled. Haddy felt himself blushing from his toes to his ear-tips. He'd made the mistake of wearing a bog-standard flight suit—the *Buchman* supplied them free of charge to its passengers—and without any underwear. Now he had to make sure, somehow, that he kept his crotch out of her line of sight without making it *look* like he was trying to hide what her smile did to him.

Well, her smile, and her outfit, and that unbearable ginger-vanilla scent that was wafting off her, just at the edge of smelling.

"Where's Malcolm?" Haddy felt proud that he didn't stammer.

Sil shook her head. "Ear infection."

"Oh, man." There weren't many things you could get in free fall that was worse than an ear infection. In a gravity field, ear pressure problems could make you dizzy and maybe a little nauseated. In no gravity, when your semi-circular canals went wonky, you were screwed. Treatment involved ketamine sedation and aggressive antibiotics to clear the infection. Without both things, a body could vomit itself to death in the space of a few hours. "He got...I mean, he's going to be all right, right?"

Sil shrugged. "As good as he ever is, once they wake him up tomorrow. Come on—we'll be late."

She stretched her hand toward Haddy, and Haddy took it. The two of them kicked off the floor, aiming for the open gymnasium door a few meters away.

"Are you okay?" she asked. "You're shaking."

Haddy blushed again, but at least she wasn't looking. He rummaged around for the most truthful lie he could find, and said "Just homesick. I wish my family was here."

Sil made a sympathetic noise, but then fell silent as they entered the gymnasium.

Instead of its usual flat, indirect lighting, the entire space was filled with little point lights, some of which held steady—the candle-flame colored ones—and some of which twinkled on and off at random in all colors of the spectrum.

The bollards were out, with ropes stretched between them so that people would have anchor points from which to watch. Haddy and Sil took their places at one near the door, facing inwards on a small blue sphere that seemed as if it were designed to serve as the focal point.

The service started with music. *A Capella* music coming from everywhere. Soft, growing voices, singing about bells, growing into a tinkling, pulsing terrorific intensity before fading off again into the soft darkness.

Then another song, and another, and another. Songs Haddy only vaguely recognized, if at all, but all of them shot through with wonder, and fragile hope, and plaintive longing.

It was the music of a refugee.

Haddy found himself struggling to keep his composure. His right hand, still attached to Sil's, was all electricity. Every time she adjusted her grip, or moved her thumb over the back of his hand, little thrills rushed up his spine to the back of his head, and up his legs to his whole midsection, and everything inside him fluttered and throbbed. His left hand, though, kept having to let go of the rope so that he could brush tears out of his eyes as the music sank straight through his chest and made everything in his heart ache.

WHEN IT WAS over, Sil accompanied him back to his quarters. She said he didn't look all that steady, and she was going to make sure he was okay before she headed back to check on Malcolm.

"Don't be a lunk," she said when he tried to beg off. "I can't have you getting sick, too."

"I'm not sick," he said.

And then he didn't say anything else for a few minutes, as they flew together out of the commercial area and up into the residential decks. Three decks forward and sixteen rooms along, they came to Haddy's hovel. It didn't *look* like a hovel, because you can't get away with not keeping tidy in free fall, but he was certain it *smelled* like one.

He couldn't tell, not really, because whatever his stateroom smelled like, he was used to smelling it. But if there was one constant, drum-beat refrain of his life since he'd turned twelve, it was his mother complaining that his room smelled foul. Locker room, sweat shop, bathroom, fermentation vat—she never seemed to run out of similes.

But Sil wasn't hearing any of it. She followed him inside, insisted on making coffee, and the two of them leaned up against velcro strips on the ceiling, and she cuddled up next to him while they sipped coffee from squeeze bottles.

Haddy's head was swimming. Compared to the boldly decorated stateroom, his consciousness was a technicolor kaleidoscope. Swirling, confusing hungers and longings, none of which made sense with each other. He wanted to go home, and he wanted to curl up with Sil, and to kiss her, and touch her, and he wanted to be alone.

He'd thought he was homesick in his first few days on board. But it was nothing like this. He'd thought he was the kind of guy who would rise to the occasion, make something of himself, return home to make the family proud.

But, the truth was, he just wanted to be somewhere he belonged.

He found himself pouring it all out to Sil as she wrapped her body around him like a lemur. She held him as he talked, and he found that it helped.

His heart slowed down. The blind panic and grief that were swirling around in his head quieted, even if they did not go away, and the plaintive, painful songs from the service faded into lullabies in his head.

He told her everything. About how his family had sent him away after his aunt had been disappeared, how his cousins and uncles vanished in the spaceport, how his father had told him not to trust anyone and kept implying that there was something terrible that might happen to him if he knew too much. And about Josie, and how he'd bought her, and how he'd been training her, and how he knew that she had to be going crazy right now even though he'd trained her to run on the treadmill when she was bored and lonely.

"Your family sounds like they really care about you," Sil said softly into his ear. She was wrapped around him from behind, her head resting on his left shoulder, their right shoulders both still stuck to the velcro strips on the wall.

"Yeah, well, I'd rather they told me the whole story and let me deal with it than keeping it all secret. I mean, if there's someone after us, wouldn't it be better to know?"

"But if they're right, it could get you killed."

Haddy thought about it through two more mouthfuls of coffee.

"No," he said. "I still want to know. Even if it means..." he gulped, realizing as he said it how reckless he sounded. And felt. "...well, even if it means the worst."

"That," she said, "is seriously sexy."

Haddy felt her breath on his ear, and then her lips, and suddenly his entire world shuddered.

Her mouth slipped over his ear. He felt her teeth on his earlobe.

He wanted to ask what she was doing. He turned, opened his mouth to speak, but he couldn't figure out how his tongue worked.

It didn't matter anyway. She covered his mouth with

hers and started working on trying to map out any problems with his tongue, using her own.

"Mrremamfff," Haddy said.

Sil tore free of the wall. She twisted herself around, climbing him like a rock wall, until her pelvis rested against his. But it didn't just rest, it rolled.

He felt panic rising in the back of his throat. He wasn't sure if he was going to vomit or have a heart attack or die of bliss.

"Armfrrum!" Haddy said.

Sil pulled away, her breath coming in heavy pants, hot against his face.

"What'd you say?"

"What...what...what are you doing?"

She chuckled. "What does it look like?"

"I...I..." His throat swelled shut again as she squeezed her legs around him, pressing her warmest parts against his, as if the simple insistence could tear the cloth layers between them away. He wished, more than anything in the world, he could blink his eyes and their clothes would disappear. But he couldn't. "I can...oh god..stop stop just...please..."

"What's wrong," she gasped.

"Malcolm. You and..."

"Oh baby, we're not monos, if that's what you're worried about. He approves of you."

Haddy swallowed hard. She was older than he was. She was sexier than anyone he'd ever met. She knew what she was doing.

But he didn't know how he'd be able to talk to Malcolm without dying of embarrassment. Knowing that every time Malcolm looked at him, he'd be thinking of Haddy naked and doing things with his...wife?

Girlfriend? Haddy realized he didn't even know what they were to each other.

He liked his friends. He was glad he had people he could trust. People he could talk to.

He couldn't have them thinking of him like *that*. It was bad enough that he thought about Sil that way.

Sil kissed him again. Haddy found himself touching her face, her small braless breasts through her suit, trying to push her away and only pushing against her hard enough to make himself want more.

When he came up for air again he said, "Sil, please. I really don't want to."

"This says you do." She ground against him again.

"This," he tapped his forehead, "Says I don't. Please."

"You're sure?"

"Yeah," Haddy gulped again. "Yeah I'm sure."

She kissed him softly. "Okay."

Sil's body floated away from his. She slipped out of the stateroom without so much as another word.

Oh great, now I've insulted her.

Haddy smacked the wall in frustration. The rebound knocked him loose and sent him in a long tumble across the room.

He spent the rest of the night icing his hand and feeling like an idiot.

IT STILL HURT in the morning, but his pride didn't. He actually felt more like himself than he had since he'd left Luna City.

As soon as Haddy woke up, he took a quick sponge-bath so he didn't stink more than absolutely necessary—staying clean in free fall took extra effort, since you couldn't shower without drowning—then settled himself in for a pre-breakfast writing shift. Something about last night had given him the itch to finish a story this morning.

It would give him something that was truly his. It would mean something. Make a difference somehow, he was sure of it.

Haddy was velcroed to the wall in his stateroom when his door beeped.

"Who's there?" Haddy tore his attention away from his PPD.

"It's Malcolm." His voice had an edge in it.

"Come on in." Haddy looked back at his PPD as the door latch popped. "Just...a....second here..." he said when Malcolm floated through the hatch. He finally had the ending of a story, and he wasn't going to let it get away before he finished keying it in. His blink-lenses created a keyboard in the air, which he manipulated while his PPD hung in the air in front of him on a thin swing-arm mounted in the wall.

"Had..."

"I know, I know. I'm sorry, I didn't mean to insult her just...just shut up a minute, okay?" Haddy said.

Malcolm waited loudly, clearing his throat, but Haddy was only a few words away...

There.

The End

Haddy let out a whoop of triumph. A year he'd been trying to finish a story—any story. Now he'd done it, and it was a long one, too. Almost thirty thousand words, and it made sense, at least to him. He was gonna celebrate tonight. He didn't know how, but he was going to find some way. Maybe Sil would be available to play laser tag...

Malcolm interrupted his thoughts with a grouchy:

"Well what in the world's got you so goddamn happy now?"

"I," Haddy said with a well-earned air of superiority, "Just finished my first ever story."

"Congrats, kid." Malcolm's voice was flat. His face wasn't looking very friendly either, with his eyes set hard and his stubble setting the down-turned edges of his mouth in deep scowl lines.

Kid? What is this?

Haddy felt his hackles rising. "Something wrong, buddy?" He growled the last word.

"Now haven't you heard the news?"

"What news?"

"It's started."

The tone in his voice left no doubt: "it" was "the war."

"What happened?"

"The Marines went in. Had...they killed thousands."

"What? Where?"

"Luna City."

NEW WINGS

BY THE TIME Malcolm came to tell him, the ship's news feeds were all blacked out. No off-ship communications, by order of the captain. A basic security measure, Malcolm explained, to prevent factioning among the passengers. Everyone on board was still stuck together for another month, and political arguments were right up there next to boredom for creating a situation that the crew of an ITN liner was ill-prepared to deal with.

Malcolm gave him the basic rundown that had come through on TGN before the nets were cut off. The big party in the Bazaar had grown enough that it was choking off spaceport traffic, so the security services had come in to try to do crowd control, and that had started a riot.

So the government sent the Marines. From what Haddy'd been led to believe, the Marines were a cross between a plague of death and angels of mercy, and woe betide the unrighteous man who set an unworthy foot on their path.

Malcolm didn't know how many died. Not exactly. The report only said "thousands dead." It didn't even say on which side.

Thousands.

Luna City only had sixty thousand.

Haddy was good enough at math to see instantly that he had at least a one in thirty chance of knowing someone who died there.

Except, he knew as his stomach sank as he processed the news, that it was much more likely than that. He knew a lot of the cops in Luna City—they stopped by the booth from time to time looking for lost tourists, checking in for neighborhood watch things, sometimes renting a pair of wings for themselves or bringing their own and using the locker room and the launch.

And the Bazaar was his part of town. It was where he'd grown up, where he'd spent every single day of his life that he'd actually been on Luna, near as he could remember.

They might all be dead. Everyone he knew. Everyone he'd ever known.

Haddy patrolled the ship for days trying to find news. He was hoping for some kind of solid numbers. Maybe a casualty list. Even a whisper. Anything that would let him know what happened.

But Malcolm was the only one with any information. He said he'd paid off the concierge to listen in on the forward decks, where the crew lived, and report back anything he found.

What information there was trickled in slowly. When Haddy asked, Malcolm would invariably say "We're just going to have to wait."

TIME PASSES SLOWLY on a long-haul transport.

It goes even more slowly when you're waiting for bad news.

Haddy settled back into his routine, but he lost the ability to write. Every time he tried, his mind seized up. All he could think of was how it used to feel when he'd noodle at stories in the Gallery, and how it all smelled of garlic and hibiscus and cannabis and lemons, and how now—at least in his mind—it was stacked with dead bodies and awash in blood and smelling like...well, he didn't know how any of that smelled, but he imagined it was at least as horrible as a broken sewage line.

So instead of writing, he spent two hours a day in the laser tag arena.

The problem with zero g laser tag was vectors. You couldn't dodge a shot. Every time you got out into the open to go for the opposing team's base, you got nabbed.

And, like any good game, getting hit gave you a decent high-voltage shock. It felt like being whacked in the chest with a cricket bat.

If you didn't want to get shot like a sitting duck, you had to use diversionary tactics, like sending half your team around one side to draw enemy fire while the other half made an end run at a base that is always protected by somebody.

Or you could try a protected formation—wrap yourself in teammates, and use their bodies to protect you. They all got killed off, but you still made it through to enemy base.

Haddy was bored after two days. More than that, he was offended. The best entertainment on the ship going, and it was a stupid sniper's game. It needed something more...more...

Something more Luna City.

Something like an orn-suit.

There wasn't anything in the arena rules against them, it's just that nobody thought of using them. Hell, Haddy hadn't even thought of using them—they were designed, like real bird's wings, to provide lift, and you didn't necessarily *want* lift if you were in free fall.

What he needed was a new design. Something suited for free fall.

If he could make that work, and find some printer time somewhere on board...now that would be something.

IT TURNED OUT HE needed more than a printer with the right feedstock (which, he discovered after making some inquiries of the cruise staff, might wind up being a problem). The demands of the project meant he couldn't actually design just from memory, or by modifying any of the company designs he'd brought with him.

The problem he faced—and didn't realize he faced it until he found himself chatting about work with his neighbor in the centrifuge—is that all the wings he'd ever touched, or read about, or studied, were designed to create lift.

In zero g, a wing that created lift would get in the way of everything that would make it interesting. It would mean a permanent bias in the direction of travel. What Haddy needed was a design that would give him the thrust and directional control of a good orn-suit, but without the lift. Instead of lift, he needed balanced, even drag with quick directional control across all three axes over seven hundred twenty degrees.

He needed wind tunnel software, which he hadn't brought with him and which he couldn't find on the ship. That meant he had to get out to the nets, and *that* meant he just might be able to get some news, maybe get a call in to his parents. Something.

He wound up splurging another fifty LOX—he was using up his LOX because they weren't negotiable currency on Nineveh, but the shipboard staff would take them quite gladly—to get a porter to get a coms officer to give him net access.

It almost worked. The coms officer happily accepted

his piece of the bribe, and downloaded the program for him and happily loaded it onto his PPD. But no matter how much Haddy cajoled, nobody in the chain would give him direct access to the net and wouldn't tell him anything about the situation in Luna City.

What was going on out there that was so bad that the crew didn't feel safe letting the passengers know about it? How many people had really died? And how many of them did he know?

He couldn't get any answers, and neither could anyone he talked to.

Oh, there were theories. There were more theories than he knew how to make sense of. One of them said that someone had discovered alien technology on Mars, and the Naderi Throne was in cahoots with the Loonies, conspiring to distract the Americans with a Lunar uprising while the Persians took their new fleet to conquer Mars and get exclusive control over the alien technology.

Because...the alien technology would let the Persians rule the solar system, evidently.

There was also a theory floating around about an international banking conspiracy. And another one about a secret alliance between the Persians and the Mormons at New Zion—Haddy hoped the Youngs hadn't heard that one—but the most involved story that Haddy sat through talked about how the Jews were using the Americans to prevent the Persians from taking the moon because they intended to set up a new Jerusalem in Agrippa crater.

There seemed to be a new one every time he got into the centrifuge or went to one of the restaurants to fetch a meal. He didn't know which one of them might be true, if any. They made for good stories to pass the time, though.

He mostly kept his head buried in the simulations. He was working on his avionics problem by trial-and-error, because he couldn't find any precedent in any of the avionics books he could access through the shipboard library.

He was getting close, but there was a piece he was missing, and he couldn't figure out what it was.

But it didn't seem to be doing any good. He felt like he was trying to reach through a cloud of static. Anything he touched afterwards felt artificial and numbing.

He decided that the reason he couldn't concentrate was the isolation. The stateroom was making him crazy. Curling around a PPD for hours on end with the the same blank six walls with their velcro strips and hand holds and screens staring back at him. It would make anyone crazy, wouldn't it?

IT WASN'T ANY BETTER better outside, though. The communications blackout hadn't just spurred the formation of one elaborate theory after another, it had actually started people breaking off into groups. Haddy could see it everywhere he flew—clusters of people sorted by port-of-origin. Mormons here. Americans there. Europeans clustering together. Australians off in a corner. Loonies looking over their shoulders as if they expected to be bum-rushed at any moment.

He tied himself up to an empty table in the Central American restaurant. It was between meal rushes, so he didn't expect any company. He ordered a sleeve of churros and settled into his simulations. Not easy to do on a small screen, and he'd left his blink-lenses back in his stateroom, but he settled in well enough anyway.

Malcolm tapped Haddy on the shoulder two hours later. It made Haddy jump—if he'd been sitting down,

J. DANIEL SAWYER   103

he'd have jumped out of his seat. Floating in free fall as he was, he just twitched like he was trying to throw off a swarm of bees.

"Hey, hey, settle down, buddy, what's wrong?"

Haddy found the control knob on his heart rate and ratcheted it down from "jackhammer" to "marching band."

"Nothing, I'm just...I don't know. Nothing's working." Haddy smacked his PPD as if that would fix anything.

"What isn't working?"

Haddy laid his problem on the table, going into the kind of overweening detail that would interest only an engineer and clearly didn't interest Malcolm in the slightest, politely feigned fascination notwithstanding. He found himself getting more angry as he talked, and he didn't know why, which made him more angry.

"You say you've been all up in the avionics, for sure?" Malcolm asked. "But have you gone and thought about ship design at all?"

"What? What are you talking about? You don't need to deal with any of this crap in vacuum. Look at this thing we're in..."

"No, no, no, not space ships. *Ships.* Sailing ships. Submarines especially, dontchaknow."

Haddy resisted asking *What's a submarine?* He could figure it out from the name.

"You're telling me there's a whole *class* of underwater pressure vessels?"

"Yeah, for sure. Goes back hundreds of years, too."

It hadn't before occurred to Haddy that underwater pressure vessels could be so common, let alone so old. He'd assumed, like any Loonie kid would, that Terrans stayed on the surface and sent drones down under the water when they needed to see something down there.

Instead, he focused on the truly ridiculous implication in the suggestion, and asked:

"Why would that have to do with..."

"Air and water are both fluids, right?"

Haddy bit off a nasty reply. He only wanted to poke Malcolm because he was angry already, and he didn't want to look like he was some dumb kid, even if he was *really* feeling it right now.

And, of course, Malcolm was right. Well, mathematically speaking, anyway. Air was just a thinner fluid than water—in math, fluids aren't liquids. Fluids are a larger class of materials that include anything that's not a pure solid. Gases, liquids, putties, plastics—anything that has a free surface and can't resist shear force, and flows when subjected to gradients of temperature, or of slope when under acceleration.

"Submarines, huh?"

"Guaran-damn-tee it, Had my lad. If there's an answer, that's the place to look, youbetcha."

Well, it was better than nothing. And the ship's library *did* have books on the subject.

He'd been on the right track. He needed the curve of the wings to match, top and bottom, and be as flat as possible, but seeing photos and drawings of conning tower stabilization wings made something tick over in his head.

It hadn't been a failure of conceptual imagination that was defeating him. It was a failure of geometry. So he tore down his wing models and started from scratch. Starting with an even cross-section, he built out in segments, so that each of the cross sections would remain even. Then, adding bones and joints, he tweaked the deformation properties so that the default lift characteristics wouldn't change at any degree of open or closed-ness.

Then he added the standard suite of vane controls to the wings, and duplicated the process for the tail, and spent the next several days testing and tweaking and testing and tweaking.

He stuck mostly to his stateroom, except when he had to go out for his 'fuge time or to get meals. The mood in the rest of the ship was turning uglier by the day. There had been reports of fist-fights in some of the common areas—Haddy was embarrassed, but not surprised, to learn that the fights had all been started by Loonies looking to take a piece out of the Americans on board for their loved ones who had died. Or, who they *imagined* had died, since there was no casualty list and no way to know which of the numbers running around the ship was the accurate one.

He didn't actually blame his compatriots for mixing it up. It wasn't as if he didn't have the urge himself. Only his years of dealing with stupid customers—and the fact that his only two friends on board were Americans—kept him from going out and helping to start a riot.

But even without his participation, tensions on the *Buchman* had risen so high that the captain was openly threatening to issue a general quarters alert for the remainder of the voyage. Haddy didn't see how the captain could enforce such an order—as far as he could tell, the crew compliment was too small to *force* the passengers to do anything—but he sure didn't want to find out the hard way.

In order to try to defuse tensions, the concierge had organized an intramural laser tag league with teams based

on port-of-origin or port-of-sympathy, and, at the opening match, had promised that the communications blackout would lift a week after acceleration resumed—which
Haddy found a great relief, though he couldn't fathom the
reasoning.

Sil, who was floating next to him when he heard the
news, said "Anyone can endure anything if they know
when it's going to end," as if that explained everything.

Haddy didn't have much time to think about it,
though, since Sil was joining the American team for the
game, and demanded a kiss for luck.

He liked kissing her. It just made him want things that
scared the hell out of him.

Haddy didn't see how the game went—he was on a
mission of his own. The wind tunnel tests were done, and
he needed to find a printer with the right feedstocks—in
sufficient quantity—to bring a little surprise to his own
match the day after tomorrow.

"SORRY, KID, YOU are not even supposed to be down
here," Makrov said. Haddy knew her name was "Makrov"
because it was sewn to her shipsuit above her improbably
large left breast. She was the engineering watch officer,
a round woman with angular features, and spoke with a
slight Russian accent. She gave him a half-sympathetic
shrug and turned away to face the big bank of screens that
made up her entire world.

And, judging by the undecorated state of the rest of the
room, they were interesting enough to her that she didn't
need any other stimulation. She tapped a control pad in
front of her, and the center screen switched from a reactor
temperature display to a medieval tactical simulator.

Haddy hadn't had much luck above decks. He figured

he might get more joy below decks. Engineers were people that liked to make things work, right?

"But have you *played* laser tag in the zero-g arena?"

She grunted. "Boring as *govno*."

"Exactly! And have you been up there? Have you *seen* what people are doing?"

"What, you mean the fights?" Her avatar on the screen—an enormous muscled barbarian—drew its sword. "People fight. Why is this a problem for me?"

"The captain..."

"Captain Fresnel is sort of man who'd need diapers to watch murder movie." She emphasized that she was not bothered by a little violence by casually lopping the heads off a few other sword-wielding barbarians.

"But if he doesn't have to worry because the laser tag games are suddenly *really* fun and people aren't fighting as much, doesn't that make your life easier?"

"Mmm...yes. He is not a pain in my ass, then, as much."

"I can make it happen."

"You think you can."

"I guarantee it."

"What you give me if you are not right about that?"

Haddy had to think for a minute. He didn't have a lot to trade. He could offer money, but he had to be frugal—he didn't know when he'd be able to get work, and he had to eat when he got to Nineveh. On the other hand, he'd probably have to bribe her to use the printer in the first place, so he'd be out his cash whether it was up front or on the back end.

Unless...unless he could think of something really creative.

He thought back over the shipboard politics he'd mapped out over the past few hours when he'd been looking for a suitable printer.

"When we're back under boost, I'll hit the concierge in the face with a whipped-cream balloon."

The engineer chuckled. Then the chuckle turned into a laugh. The laugh turned into a howl, and Haddy started to worry that she might forget how to breathe.

"That is the best idea I have heard in eight trips! You have a deal, kid. What kind of stock you need?"

"Carbon fiber, steel, silicon, high-stress abs, graphene, latex, nickel, and spider silk. Here." He shoved the PPD in front of her.

She took it, looked over the shopping list and the model.

"It is all what we have here for parts fabrication. I can do this. Will be ready in two days, will cost you two hundred dollars for materials."

It was more than he'd expected to pay, but Haddy took the deal on the grounds that he didn't think he could bear to *not* find out whether or not the prototype would work—and where would he ever get the chance to test a zero-g orn-suit again, anyway?

IT DID TAKE two days—but the first draft didn't work. Haddy could see it wouldn't as soon as he pulled it out of the printer. He'd overlooked the matter of fastenings on the wing surface, and didn't have a good sealed seam between the struts and the feathers.

Another two days and another two hundred dollars—Makrov refused to give him a core-charge refund for the materials on the failed rig—and he did have something that would work, even though it made his wallet hurt more than he cared to think about. On his second run through the printer, he'd designed in his personal flyer's logo into the stitching on the wings. If he was going to put his neck on the line testing them, he wanted to look memorable doing it.

There was, after all, a certain amount of style a flyer was obliged to, and Haddy wasn't going to puss out on style. It was a matter of family pride.

Even if, with the communications blackout, the chance of him getting any attention beyond the ship was basically zero.

Haddy strapped himself into it right there in the engineering fabrication room. It was, it turned out, much more complicated to attach all the rigging in free fall than it was in a grav field. He'd gotten used to dressing himself in free fall so he figured he should have the moves down. He hadn't banked on the fact that he'd been strapping himself into orn-suits for so long that his body thought it knew what to do—and all of that under lunar gravity

Haddy wound up in a tumble a half dozen times as he tried to get his straps tight.

As he was securing the last strap, he realized he hadn't thought to print himself up a proper suit. When you really wanted to bite the air, you used a full-body second-skin suit made of spider silk. Light, breathable, it was better than being naked because it kept all your bits tucked back, pulled in, and all the pesky little hairs flattened down so that your body became as good as it could possibly be for slipping through fluids like air. His official complimentary *PRS Buchman* shipsuit would flap and catch and create cavitation pockets, which would throw off the aerodynamic balance he'd been spending all his concentration on.

But, it couldn't be helped. And with the thin-ness of the air in the *Buchman* (while planetary stations like Solon on Mars or Luna City on Luna pressurized at a full atmosphere, ships and space stations preferred to pressurize at only two-thirds of an atmosphere. The reasons behind the divergence weren't something Haddy had ever been curious enough to look into), the performance difference between a second skin and a shipsuit was something only an experienced flyer would notice anyway.

"You look like a Christmas ornament," Makrov said with an air of amused derision.

"Why?"

"White suit, red and green wings. Looks like angel crashed into clearance sale."

Well, what did she know anyway?

Haddy twiddled his fingers, moving the control surfaces on his wings back and forth. Everything seemed in good order. He worked the treadle control, which pulled the very tips of the tail "feathers" down. It worked. He worked his legs together as a unit to control gross pitch on the tail—good job there too. Ditto for the twist-roll function when he swiveled his ankles each way.

"It might look silly," Haddy said, extending his arms above his head, "But look what it can do."

He flapped his wings, surged forward and almost smashed his head into the far wall.

He rolled sideways and bounced off with his back.

"Looks too hot to handle," Makrov said.

Haddy shook himself off out as he drifted across the room on the rebound.

"Nah, just used to flying in bigger rooms is all." He used the fine control surfaces to re-orient himself toward the open door. "Thanks a bundle, Makrov. See you around!"

"You remember our deal!"

"I remember."

Haddy flicked his wings, just a little bit. It gave him the right amount of momentum to sail lazily out the door—then he twisted his wrists to cant his wings back, and banked hard to make the ninety degree turn, picking up a nice little bit of acceleration on the whip-round.

His course was steady. He tried a corkscrew as he flew through the hall back to the hatch to the forward decks—where passengers were allowed to be—and found the controls a bit touchy, but workable. The next version, if he ever got around to making another version, would need to have different rigging ratios for the fine control surfaces. A tenth of a percent difference—maybe three tenths if he ever decided to make a spongy version for tourists.

The wings did have one little feature he was keen to try—something he'd never seen on an orn-suit. He'd made the primary wings foldable like a bat's wings. The hatch he was headed for would be the right place to give it a whirl.

He gave another half-hearted flap to build up just enough speed to be dangerous, then balled his wrists up into fists and jacked his arms sharply into his chest.

The wings folded against his body like a flying squirrel's skin flaps, the tail over his hamstrings snapped shut like a Chinese fan, and he was free to reach forward with both hands.

His feet stayed lashed together.

Of course they would.

Not having them available to brake his momentum against the hatch, he slammed against it with both palms and his chest.

The wind rushed out of him. He felt like he'd been hit in the chest with a cricket bat, but he couldn't shout about it, because his diaphragm wasn't breathing in and out.

Haddy hadn't knocked the wind out of himself since he was eight years old. It wasn't the kind of sensation he'd ever wanted to repeat.

He floated for a good thirty seconds, waving his arms like a puppet with cut strings, trying to remember how to breathe. Eventually he punched himself in the stomach to try to force something to start working, but it didn't help.

It took *years*.

Then, forty seconds after impact, his diaphragm started up again, and he remembered how nice it was to be able to breathe and made a mental note to himself never, never, never to go near an airlock without a breather unit, just in case he took a wrong turn and wound up in hard vacuum.

Not being able to suck air into his lungs...well, it didn't suck, because that was the whole point, but it did feel like the worst thing that could happen in the world.

Well, that's how you work out a design flaw.

With a bog-standard orn-suit, your feet moved together to control the tail feathers. The rigging connected each side of the tail to two foot harnesses that fit on underneath booties, and the booties had a catch to keep your feet together that you could un-do with a kick if you were coming in to roost. It took thought and practice, but when you were flying in a grav field, that wasn't a problem, since you never needed to have your feet move independently except when you were landing.

But in free fall, you needed your feet free all the time so you could bounce off walls without hurting yourself. This was a complication that hadn't occurred to him.

Haddy grabbed a hand hold recessed in the wall and pulled himself into a ball.

He looked at the attachment points on his ankles.

The post-and-slot attachment mechanism didn't detach quick enough for free fall, but you needed to be able to keep your feet together, and aligned, in order to control the rig properly.

Okay, so what if he used velcro instead?

How will I make velcro work up a precise alignment?

He thought about it for a moment. Maybe velcro wasn't the answer.

But what if he used magnets?

Decently strong neodymium impregnated into a slick-surface carbon fiber, but left soft and sewn into the booties—that would be self-aligning, but anyone could detach just by moving their legs apart scissor fashion, which was exactly the motion anyone instinctively used when they were jumping up into a climbing position, or catching themselves on a wall. They'd lead with their non-dominant foot, and a magnetic aligner wouldn't interfere with that, it would just keep the feet aligned exactly when they were together. It didn't take a lot to remind you to keep your feet still, after all.

With that matter sorted, he resolved not to fasten his feet together while flying here. When he got back to his quarters he'd find some kind of tool to remove the peg from the latching rig so that he didn't re-latch by accident.

Haddy took another moment to take stock of himself. He was going to have an interesting bruise, he was sure, but it wasn't hurting when he breathed now, so he didn't think he needed to find the infirmary.

Once more, and without latching his feet together,

Haddy deployed his wings with a modicum of trepidation, and then flapped gently to get himself sailing in the direction of the hatch, then he retracted his wings and grabbed onto the hatch, using all four limbs like a spider monkey clinging to a banyan tree. He re-oriented, pushed forward, then deployed his wings on the fly, and used them to steer himself through the connecting tunnel to the main deck.

He emerged at rush hour into the commercial area, and used his control surfaces to deftly dodge this way and that between his fellow passengers, being careful to keep his speed down so as not to alarm anyone. The last thing he wanted was an order from the hotelier to stow the orn-suit until disembarkation.

As he flew, Haddy noted other little improvements that he would want to make in the next iteration, then found a perch on the "ceiling" above the food concourse entrance to the zero-g gymnasium and punched all his notes into his PPD before he could forget them.

HE SPENT THE rest of the day shaking down the suit. He was scheduled for an intramural game in the morning, the final one before acceleration kicked in at 1245 tomorrow. He'd been playing all along, ever since the captain set up the league and made the games an officially "encouraged" activity. Haddy had discovered, when he tried to avoid playing because he had better things to do, that "encouraged" was a euphemism for "compulsory for all males between the ages of twelve and twenty-five."

He'd discovered this when one of the hotelier's assistants left a message on his stateroom screen instructing that he *would* be participating in the games or he would be confined to quarters during peak hours.

"Okay, look, this is what I want to know," he'd said to Malcolm over bratwursts with him and Sil. "Everyone is up about 'young males' lately. Dad wants me off Luna because 'young males are obligated to fight wars.' Now the captain wants all the 'young males' to wear themselves out with this *boring* ass game."

"It's the testosterone, dontchaknow," Malcolm said. "Peak years. Makes us aggressive type folks, makes us take risks. We're basically the junkies of the human set, and it's all coming down to our balls. They can strap a gun to us and send us into a fight, and we love it. And you know when they don't, we have to do something to compete, or we go crazy for sure. Do you know that more than three quarters of all violent crime is committed by males fifteen-to-twenty-five?"

"And seventy five percent of risky sex, too," Sil said with a sneaky smile on her face.

Haddy blushed.

Malcolm looked between them. "Wait, did you two..."

"Oh, not yet," Sil said.

Haddy shook his head at the same time. "Stop it."

Sil winked at him.

"So what?" Haddy wrenched the conversation back on track. "It doesn't mean *I* am going to commit a violent crime."

Malcolm shrugged. "It's what people with power do, Had my lad." he said. "They worry about groups, they don't care about people. It's a game of averages they play, you betcha."

"So I have to waste my time playing laser tag because the captain doesn't want anyone like me starting fights? I thought almost all the fights were between, well, middle-aged guys."

"Everyone loves a good scapegoat," Malcolm said.

SO, ON THE last day before acceleration resumed, Haddy reported for his intramural game in his new orn-suit.

He had read the rules very carefully in his quarters before he came. There was nothing in them that prohibited any unpowered flying aid, maneuvering aid, or anything like that. If the other players complained, the referees wouldn't be able to do anything.

And, once the game got under way, the other players did complain. Loudly, and with great creativity where their profanity was concerned—at least, the ones on the opposing team. His teammates didn't complain a bit, and his ability to actually dodge shots gave Team Luna City its best—and most dearly needed—victory of the very brief season.

Ten minutes after the game was done, a security officer informed Haddy that he was confined to quarters until acceleration by order of the captain.

Then, at 1300 hours, he was to report to the Captain Fresnel's office.

OLD NEWS IS BAD NEWS

"HADRIAN JIN," SAID the football-sized (and shaped) red drone that acted as the captain's gatekeeper and secretary, "Captain Fresnel will see you now."

Haddy pushed himself off the wall he'd been leaning against and trudged toward the wood-finished fullerine door at one end of the cramped anteroom.

Captain Fresnel's office felt to Haddy like something out of a children's book. The wall was decorated with pictures of party balloons and lollipops and little colored...horses, maybe? Haddy hadn't seen a lot of pictures of horses, and he'd certainly never seen any that had pink or yellow or orange hair, but he didn't know of any other animals that had those big manes growing out of long necks between little pointy ears.

The captain, stood behind his desk looking out a port-hole behind him. He cut a slight figure—short, narrow shoulders, not fat, but soft all over. A spaceman's body.

"Um. Captain?"

"You're the boy who disrupted the league game yesterday."

"No sir."

The captain turned his severe face on Haddy and took him in with a quick glance.

"Your name is Hadrian Jin. You came when summoned by that name. You look like the boy in Hadrian Jin's passenger manifest photo. The kid who disrupted the game was named Hadrian Jin and bore a remarkable resemblance to you."

The captain's dry sarcasm brought a rush of anger up Haddy's neck, but he bit down on it and eyeballed the captain. Sure, the captain could fine him, or confine him to quarters, or throw him into the brig, but that didn't mean Haddy had to knuckle under to his being a jerk.

"I certainly *played* yesterday. As ordered. And according to the rules." Haddy shrugged theatrically. "If that counts as a disruption, I guess it just goes to show that the groundhogs are sore losers that can't stand the heat in a fair fight."

The corners of the captain's mouth twitched.

"You brought new equipment to the match."

"I did. Nothing in the rules prohibited it."

"Why?"

"Have you ever *played* laser tag in free fall?"

"Yes."

"Do you *still* play?"

The captain shook his head. "My duties do not permit it."

"I don't blame you. If I was captain I wouldn't let my duties permit it either." Haddy smirked.

"Explain." It was an order, given by a man that might have been in the military once. Clearly he was accustomed to giving orders in any case.

So, Haddy launched in to a protracted explanation of the defects of the entire zero-g laser tag setup, and why it was the kind of game that only monkeys could ever enjoy, and ventured into speculative territory with regards to the average IQ of the Mannix Spaceways recreation design department employees.

"Don't get me wrong," he said, "the gym is great. And the 'fuge is the best I've ever seen. But if I had to play one more stupid game of laser tag I was going to just give up and punch a groundhog for invading my city, and that's a fact. So I figured that I'd find a way to improve the game instead, so I did."

The captain nodded gravely. "I see. What gave you the idea?"

Haddy couldn't see what it would hurt. *Don't trust anyone* didn't mean that he couldn't tell the captain about what his family did for a living.

Captain Fresnel's face opened as Haddy talked.

"Bob and Ginny's? I learned to fly there when I was a boy. Your family runs it? I though it was started by someone named Wallace or something."

"My grandmother, sure. Her maiden name. She started it with my grandfather. His name was Jin, and when they got married she took his name—I don't know why, she thought it was romantic or something. My dad is their son."

"I see." The captain pressed his lips together and nodded gravely, then turned his back on Haddy once again and returned to contemplating the cosmos beyond the porthole window. "Are you authorized to make deals on behalf of your company?"

Haddy had no idea what the captain had in mind, but his instincts told him that this wasn't the time to be throwing up obstacles. "I think so, yeah. I mean, unless you want to buy the company."

"How long would it take you to create and deliver four thousand units of your new design, along with training materials for new users?"

"Four *thousand*?"

"Recreation is a problem that deep-range ships never quite solve. It seems to me this little flying suit ..."

"Orn-suit."

"Huh?"

"Orn. Like ornithological. Like birds?"

"Oh, of course. Very clever. This orn-suit of yours could go a long way toward increasing our options. I've had a talk with my superiors, and I've been instructed to arrange a purchase order, if your price is reasonable."

Haddy thought it over. The suit still needed some refinements. And he sure didn't have any way to manufacture in that quantity. The business at home didn't either, but Dad knew how to set up big orders. He'd done it at least once that Haddy knew of, when someone tried to set up an orn-suit operation in Firsttown that time that Mom was in the middle of getting her spine rebuilt. Normally Dad would have offered to back it and set up a franchise, like he had with the competition circuit in Darkside, but that year there was just too much else on his plate.

There were a couple other options that he was vaguely aware of—licensing deals, for example, that might let Mannix Spaceways print suits on ships as they needed them. But that assumed they could afford to carry the spare feedstock they'd need to accommodate passenger demand.

Much as he wanted to make the deal himself and return home the conquering hero, Haddy was going to need to talk to his Dad before he made any commitments.

"Captain, sir, I'm not the one in the company that deals with large lots. But if you'll let me through the communications blackout, I can speak to our jobber and get our current costs, I think we can do a deal."

Captain Fresnel's back seemed to think things over for a moment. It must be a captainly trait, being able to communicate with posture like that. Haddy found he could tell the man's mood just by looking at the slope of his shoulders.

At length, the captain said:

"I'm willing to allow it, if you swear on your honor that you will not say a word to anyone aboard this ship about anything you might learn. I will not have rumors circulating any more than they already are. Do I have your word?"

"Yes, sir." Haddy said.

"If I find you've broken it, I will withdraw from this transaction."

Haddy swallowed hard. He felt as if an enormous weight had just settled on his shoulders.

"I understand."

"All right, then. Follow Girdie..."

"Girdie?"

The captain waved his hand dismissively. "The red drone that showed you in. Follow her, she'll take you to a private room where you can use the network. Girdie!"

The door to the captain's office rolled aside and the red drone buzzed in.

"Show Mister Jin here to the conference room."

"Yes, sir," the bot said in a tinny feminine voice. "This way, please, Mister Jin."

GIRDIE LEFT HIM alone in a largeish room with a wooden-trim table suitable for ten people. It wasn't very well-lit, and the darkness made him a little uncomfortable.

Raised as he had been in Luna City, he didn't really understand darkness—he knew you needed to have it dark when you slept, and that maintaining a consistent sleep schedule was essential to maintaining your health because your cells reacted to irregular light to give you pancreas problems, make you fat, and give you headaches, but that was just basic health-and-hygeine stuff, right up there with chewing your teeth-cleaning taffy every morning and evening. When the door closed, Haddy felt ghostly fingers fluttering up his spine.

It wasn't pitch black. It was worse than that. Mood lighting in little strips along the corners at the ceiling and floor junctions gave the whole room an eerie blue glow. It was meant to simulate moonlight for the mostly-Terran crew. A soothing environment that could be splashed with highlights as the occupants of the room desired—but Haddy knew none of that. All he knew was that he felt like someone was watching him, and he didn't like it.

The table surface winked to life.

"Welcome to Mannix Spaceways Communications Network." The computer spoke in a voice so soothing that it could have made a raging drunk settle down and think that maybe life wasn't so bad. "Please select your destination."

Haddy asked for a connection to the Luna City subnet, voice relay, and gave the address of the family business.

"Be advised," the computer said, "calls to Luna City are subject to a round-trip transmission delay of approximately six minutes."

"I understand." Haddy did a little mental math. He knew that Nineveh orbited the sun between Earth and Mars and was currently in a favorable position, but thinking about it in terms of light speed transmission delays drove home the vastness of the distance in a way mere kilometers never could.

In all his life, the only time he'd ever been more than a hundred kilometers from home was his trip to Earth. Now he was almost forty million kilometers away.

All that incredible emptiness separating him from his home. From his family. From Josie.

His heart twisted when he thought about Josie. As long as he didn't think about her, it was okay, but any time he even got near the word "dog" in his head, he wanted to break down crying. Haddy felt as if he were on a cliff over an endless gorge, and everything that mattered in the world were on the other side.

"Please record your initial message."

"Dad, this is Haddy. I've got an offer for four thousand orn-suits, for a new design I came up with to use in free fall. It's for Mannix Spaceways, completely legit. How do I put this together?"

Now he waited. Three minutes there. Then, if his father didn't answer, it would take a moment or five to fetch him. Then, when he did, it would be three minutes on the return.

That was a long time to be alone with his thoughts, jumbled as they were between his excitement over the deal, his homesickness, and the stack of worries in the back of his mind about his cousins, his uncles, and everyone he knew back home.

Eventually a message came back.

"Haddy? Thank the goddess! This is Uncle Mike." Uncle Mike's face filled the screen. Haddy was too shocked to process the strange expression on his face. "Your Dad can't come to the line, but I've got the corporate records right here..." Mike's brow furrowed as he tapped at something below the screen, "it looks like we can turn that kind of job around in about two weeks. Our costs for delivery to the Mannix corporate office are..." he shrugged, "...well, they're just down the ramp here, so not much. I'll make up a sheet here and drop it to your box. Is everything okay out there?"

"Yeah, yeah, it's great—I mean, boring, but...what happened to you? What happened there? We've been hearing these stories..." Haddy went ahead and spilled his guts on everything he'd heard. "What's really going on? Why did you all miss the flight? Is everyone okay?"

Haddy stopped talking when he realized that he would have to wait six minutes *after* he stopped speaking in order to get a reply.

They were the longest six minutes of his life. Longer than they might have been otherwise, because he used the time to read up on the news.

Luna City had been attacked—not just once, but twice. And it *had* been thousands that died.

Nine thousand.

Haddy's mind couldn't even process a number that big. He'd grown up in a world where murder never happened, where violent death came by accident or—in the last two years—by bombings targeting infrastructure. All two of them. Only a handful of people dead, but it had been enough to change the entire way Haddy saw the world.

But this. This was something else again.

Grissom Space Port Hosts Biggest Civilian Massacre since Hama Massacre of 1982

Haddy scrolled by the headlines, afraid to open them and find out the details.

The headlines told the whole story anyway.

Nine Thousand Dead in Christmas Massacre

Marines Defeated by Loonie Mob

White House Faces Congressional Inquiry Over War On American Citizens

Luna City And Associated Colonies Declare Independence

President Hale: "We Will Remind Them of The Lessons of the Civil War"

Haddy felt like he was going to throw up. He'd almost forgotten where he was or what he'd asked when Mike's voice came again.

His uncle's eyes were fixed and intense.

"It's bad. I can't talk about it now. Remember what your Dad told you. And take care of yourself, okay? Is there anything else I can do for you?"

"But...dammit. I...Josie isn't there, is she? Can I see her?"

Six more minutes. He waited, staring blankly at the headlines, trying to figure out what any of it meant.

He had to know what happened. If any of his friends had died. Not knowing was killing him, and he still had two weeks left on this ship where he didn't even have a project to keep him distracted.

He *had* to know. Knowing the worst was better than the sick dread in the pit of his stomach every night.

It had been weeks since the massacre now. There would be a casualty list publicly available. That's how these things worked, right? That's what the government did anytime there was a hurricane or an earthquake on Earth.

But would they do it with something like this?

Luna City Provisional Government Releases Preliminary Casualty List

There was a link. Haddy pulled it up and started scanning through.

It was long. Much longer than nine thousand. It contained not just the dead, but the injured. It would take a while. But he had four minutes left.

He scrolled alphabetically to his flying buddies. Garek Joyner was listed under "injured." Emily Bradshaw, too. Both expected to recover.

Another half dozen names he recognized from around the Gallery showed up on the injured list.

A few were among the dead. Jim Forkins, who did rug weaving. Indra and Tebo Olajuwans, who sold jewelry they made from Lunar impact glass.

"Sure. I brought her into work so she wouldn't have to be home alone." Mike's voice jolted Haddy like a cattle prod.

Haddy shifted his gaze from the window with the headlines to the one with his uncle's face.

It was filled with Josie's face. She was sniffing whatever device it was that Mike was talking on. "Here she is! Oh, yeah, girl, you see Haddy there?"

Josie licked at the camera. Her ears laid back against her skull. Her brown eyes yawned wide with recognition.

"Hi girl," Haddy said around the lump in his throat. "I miss you. I'm gonna come home soon, okay? Promise." *If it's the last thing I do*, he didn't say. "You're a good girl. Keep helping Uncle Mike." Haddy's eyes burned. His cheeks itched. He watched as long as he could bear to.

While the phone was still focused on Josie, Mike's voice gravely said: "Keep your head down, Haddy. Remember what your Dad told you."

"Thanks, Uncle Mike. I'll call when we reach port, I guess."

Haddy terminated the link. He took a deep breath, got his tears under control.

He needed to settle on a price. He opened another net window, logged in to his company mailbox back on Luna. Then he returned his attention to perusing the casualty lists while he waited the six minutes for his mail box to open and cache locally.

So many names. It seemed to take forever to go through them all.

Just as the console dinged, telling him that his email was ready, his eyes found another name he recognized.

Nita Jin.

FRIENDS FROM OUT OF TOWN

HADDY STAGGERED BACKWARDS. His chest caved in. He felt as if someone had just blown an airlock and everything breathable had left the room.

Mom.

He looked at the list again. But her name was still there.

Nita Jin: deceased.

The words swam in front of his eyes. They had to be in some kind of foreign language.

It would make more sense if they were in Russian.

Mom's...dead.

The whole universe wrenched and groaned, a noise so big that he couldn't believe that nobody else heard it. It ground to a halt. Stopped working. Everything that mattered seemed to evaporate all at once.

There *were* only three things in the universe that Haddy could be sure of: he needed to breathe, he needed to eat, and his parents existed.

They always had. As long as the universe had existed. As far as Haddy was concerned, there never had been a time when they hadn't been around.

He wasn't stupid. He knew their birthdates. He knew they'd been born. But those were just facts. Answers to trivia questions. He didn't *know* that his parents were mortal in the same way he knew that the ground was down and the stars were up.

Vin might have taught Haddy how to build a orn-suit,

and how to keep customers happy. But Nita had taught him how to see the world, how to think his way out of corners.

She'd been everything. The air he breathed.

And now...

He couldn't breathe anymore.

A century or so later, Haddy somehow got himself under control and managed to finish his business with the captain with mostly dry-eyes.

When the captain asked if he was okay, Haddy mentioned that he heard that some of his friends had died in the battle of Grissom—and then had to reassure the captain that he would not pick fights with any Americans, and that he did understand that citizens weren't responsible for the actions of their government, and yes, his promise still held: He wouldn't tell anybody about anything that he learned.

He walked out of the captain's office with a purchase order for four thousand units, deliverable to Mannix Spaceways in Luna City.

It was the hardest walk he ever took.

His commission, transferred straight to his credit jack by the captain, was enough to replenish everything he'd spent on bribes (or "tips" as the shipboard crew liked to call it) and R&D during this trip and then some, and the rest went to his family's account via direct transfer.

Items were deliverable in eight weeks, which gave Haddy two more weeks to get the design tweaked. He'd send the finals to his Dad as soon as they were done—Haddy didn't think he'd be up to finishing them before the coms blackout lifted in any case.

It was the kind of order that might have proved some-thing—that he was ready to become a full partner in the business, that his parents could retire for a while, when they wanted to.

Maybe. In another world. Another life. Another time.

Now, it felt like nothing. It tasted like ash. The entire world felt artificial.

Haddy locked himself in his stateroom and put on the loudest music he could find and listened until it felt like his ear drums were going to burst.

HADDY DIDN'T LEAVE his stateroom the rest of that day. He didn't move from his place on his bunk, except to use the head.

He missed a Chinese dinner with Sil and Malcolm, he missed the dance club visit.

He missed his 'fuge session the next day as well.

And lunch.

A little after 1500 the next day, a pounding at the door jolted him out of his catatonia.

And the bell ringing.

He shouted for whoever-it-was to go away, but they wouldn't, so he got up and trudge all the weary way to the door and opened it up, fully prepared to give his caller a fistful of knuckles.

"What what WHAT?!" He yelled as the door rolled aside to reveal Sil's face.

A face which blanched, then scrunched up and curled around itself like it had been drinking lemon juice.

Her arm snapped up, her hand grabbing his upper arm. She pushed him back inside the stateroom and hissed: "What the *hell* do you think you're doing?!"

"What?" Haddy yanked his arm away.

The door rolled shut as they cleared the jamb.

"Doing a deal with Mannix Spaceways!"

Haddy shook his head. How did she know? Why would she care? "What...what are you *talking* about?"

The door rolled open again.

"The company that owns this ship, Had my lad." Malcolm said. He walked in, let the door close behind him, and looked around. "So you been really hiding in here all this time now?"

"I'm...I'm busy. I don't want to talk, okay?"

"Tough," Sil said. "We've got a problem."

"We?" Haddy said, feeling his control slip like a dog lunching on a long leash. "*We?* They waltzed right into Grissom spaceport and killed *nine thousand* people." He realized he was screaming, but didn't care.

"Come on, now, just slow down there," Malcolm said.

But Haddy kept right on like he wasn't even there. "*We* don't have problems. What the hell do the two of you have to do with it anyway? Plonkin' tourists, the both of you, and who gives a damn anyway?"

"Haddy, please," Sil reached for him, but Haddy swatted her arms away.

"My mother is *dead!* My friends are *dead*! Who the *fuck* are you to come in here and push me around? Now get the hell out of here and leave me alone!"

Haddy pushed past Sil, nearly shoving her off her feet, and stomped across the stateroom to his bunk.

She didn't even protest.

Haddy sat down on his bed, back against the wall, and proceeded to stare at his feet.

"We can't, you know." Malcolm said. His voice was calm and quiet, almost dangerous, despite the familiar friendly lilt.

"Can't what?" Haddy growled.

Malcolm looked to Sil. Sil nodded at him. The kind of exchange of looks Haddy couldn't help but notice even though he was trying to focus firmly on the foot of his bunk.

"We can't leave," Sill crossed her arms an stood with her legs shoulder-width apart, making herself look a lot more solidly-built than she was.

"Because," Malcolm said, "We've been sent to keep you safe, for sure."

Haddy felt like he'd been swatted across the head with a sock full of rocks.

He looked at them through narrow, suspicious eyes.

"What...in the hell are you talking about?"

"We," Sil jerked her head toward Malcolm, "are with...well, we don't have a good name for it now that we're an independent country. The press calls it the 'Resistance.' We work for your Aunt Min."

"The Resistance?" Haddy had heard of them. Militant crazies who'd been scaring tourists and making business slow down.

Malcolm shrugged amiably. "Lay off Luna, dontcha-know."

Haddy sniffed and shook his head. "No, no. Min wouldn't have any part of those terrorists..."

"Not terrorists," Sil said. "We don't attack civilians."

Haddy's jaw clenched. "That's not what they say on the news."

"And since when have you heard of news telling the truth, Had my boy?"

"This is a lot bigger than any of us," Sil said. "The whole future of the solar system is on the line, and people are trying to get to you because of your Aunt, so she sent us to keep an eye on you."

"My uncles..."

"They never intended to get on board," Sil said. "Their job was to bring you here. Coming with you would have drawn attention."

"No, no..." Haddy shook his head. This was all wrong. It went against everything he knew about Mike and Min and Amit and Charis...though, he didn't know all that much about them, if he was honest with himself. Hadn't seen them for years and years, except for the day before he boarded the flight.

But his parents wouldn't lie to him like that. Not in any universe he'd ever heard of.

"Why would they do that?"

Sil and Malcolm shared another significant look. This time Malcolm shrugged, and they both sat down as if they were partners dancing—Malcolm on one of the boost seats, Sil on the bunk next to Haddy.

"Do you know," Sil asked, "Why your aunt left all those years ago?"

Haddy shrugged. "She was bored. She wanted to see the solar system."

Malcolm grunted. "That would be one way you could put it, I guess."

"Malcolm, please. Delicacy." Sil said. Then she turned to Haddy. "There's a lot going on that you don't know about, but you need to."

"Like...?"

"Just," Sil held a hand up, "Hold on. Ask questions when we're done."

Haddy shut up.

Sil talked.

Malcolm filled in details from time to time.

And between the two of them, they turned Haddy's world inside out.

"Your father doesn't care for politics," Sil said. She left it hanging as if it were a question, even though it didn't sound like one, so Haddy nodded. She continued: "Your aunt Min did. She got interested in political philosophy while she was away on Earth attending school, and she kept it up, as a sort of hobby."

Haddy shuddered, more of a reflex than anything. Politics was a game for bullies and delusional crusaders who wanted to fix other people's lives because they couldn't run their own—that was his father's attitude. Haddy had inherited it—growing up in Luna City, it was hard not to. The only time politics ever became even slightly relevant to every day life, other than Board and city council elections, was when Washington wanted to raise port taxes or institute a curfew or give LOXCOR more power over the air supply or some other thing that never turned out to be any good for Loonies.

Sil kept talking: "She kept it to herself until your grandparents retired to Mars, reading books and attending meetings for the organization that would grow into the Resistance. After a while, she didn't keep it to herself. After your father caught her talking politics with customers, they fell out. She sold her half of the business to him, and used the money to buy a ship."

"And you're telling me that's why she left?" A stone sank in the pit of Haddy's stomach. His parents had always told him that Aunt Min didn't have a head for business and had wanted to see the solar system in style.

"You betcha, yup," said Malcolm.

"And she just went and traveled. And raised my cousins..." Haddy ground to a halt.

Sil was pursing her lips and shaking her head, as if she thought he was terribly sweet to have swallowed such a story. "Revolutionary agitation. She was building a spy network."

"A spy network," Haddy repeated incredulously.

"Take a good look here, now," Malcolm said. "You want to make a successful war you gotta have supporters all over the place, right? So you build a network of people, and you organize it so that nobody can turn in more than three other people if they're caught. Think of it like a pyramid made out of triangles which only share a single point, and no sides."

Haddy tried to visualize it. Malcolm must have seen the confusion because he said:

"Don't worry about it. I'll make you a picture when I got the time okay?"

"And time is something we don't have right now," Sil said. "You have to stop the deal with Mannix Spaceways."

"You keep saying that." Haddy said, brushing it aside. He was still hung up on his Aunt being some kind of criminal mastermind. "What do you mean a spy network?"

"The Resistance," Sil said. "She made it what it is. Everything that's going on here? It's because of people she recruited. Eyes and ears all across the solar system. We were her cell in Minneapolis...well, we were part of it before things went wild..."

"We were supposed to meet your aunt on Sidon, dontchaknow" Malcolm said. "And she was supposed to give us—"

"—something vital to the future of the solar system," Sil cut Malcolm off. "We got a message from your uncle Amit that we were to meet you here, that you'd take us to your aunt."

"No, she's dead. They 'disappeared' her."

Malcolm shrugged. "That's what he told us, dontcha-know. There must be something you're supposed to do that will bring her out..."

"The bar," Sil said. "It's the bar."

"Bar?"

"Oh, yeah, right you are there. Course it is." Before Haddy could ask for an explanation, Malcolm said, "And we were supposed to keep you safe till you got there, Had my lad..."

"A job you have not made easy," Sil grumbled.

"...and make sure you reached the other end without causing any more problems..."

"Like making a deal with Mannix," Sil said.

"What? Why? What bar are you talking about?"

"Phalanx. Skip it. Not important. Had my lad, Mannix is part of the American government, dontchaknow," Malcolm said. "Well, near as dammit anyhow. And they're going to ride that contract straight into your family business and find out how to shut you down for being party to the terrorists, you betcha."

Haddy's stomach started shaking.

"They're gonna put your father up on the gibbet, that's for sure, and there's nothing we'll be able to do to stop it. You gotta back out before it's too late."

"But...but...the deal...it's already done." Haddy was shivering all over now. He just lost his mother, and he didn't know how to deal with it. Was he going to lose his father too? Had he really just handed them over to the Americans by making a deal for orn-suits?

Sil closed her eyes slowly, as if she were blocking out something unpleasant.

Malcolm swore. "I guess we're gonna have to deal with that one another way."

Sil and Malcolm started talking in language Haddy only half-understood. Contingency plans, operational protocols, all sorts of jargon he'd never heard before.

"You need to come back to your routine," Sil said. "Anyone who's watching needs to think that everything's okay."

"Everything's not okay."

"Nobody out there knows that, and they won't for a few more days," Sil said.

"And we'll stick close by, youbetcha. If someone on this boat is gunning for you, Had my lad, we'll get them before they get you."

"Don't worry," Sil said. "We've done this kind of thing before. Just pretend everything's normal until the news breaks, then hole up in here till we reach Nineveh. We'll keep you company."

"Thanks," Haddy said, rubbing his eyes. "I don't know what I'd do without you."

HADDY STUMBLED THROUGH the rest of his trip, coping as well as he could, trying to act normally. The talk with Malcolm and Sil had helped him re-focus, as did the nights in his stateroom with Malcolm on the top bunk, and Sil on his bunk, just to keep him company.

It wasn't the same kind of wonderful as Josie, but it helped. And the kisses were nice. They didn't scare him as much anymore. That was nice too.

In the precious few hours he got to himself, he managed to make the tweaks to the rig design for Mannix. He didn't think Sil and Malcolm could be right about a simple purchase order putting his family in danger, and he couldn't figure out any way to back out without causing more damage to the family name.

Besides, he'd signed the contract himself. Maybe the world Sil and Malcolm and his Aunt Min lived in was a world filled with lies, and maybe war meant he was gonna get sucked into it, but he didn't know about that when he signed the contract. He'd signed it meaning to follow through with it.

So as soon as the blackout lifted, he sent the plans off—but not without putting a warning in the comments. Dad and Uncle Mike were smart, maybe smarter than Haddy had ever given them credit for. They could make sure the family was safe from the Mannix corporation and whoever they were working with.

The news kept getting worse and worse.

The Americans had nuked Ring Alpha. Vaporised it, like it was nothing. This time, they'd had the decency to evacuate the civilian population. The Marines had stormed in and forced everyone onto available ships and shuttles, then evacuated themselves before blowing it up.

According to the news, it was a critical strategic piece of infrastructure, and its destruction would bring Luna to its knees. Ring Beta and Ring Gamma were still too small to handle the transfer traffic to economically sustain Luna City and the other colonies by themselves.

The ship was buzzing like a rock-saw, and he could feel it any time he ventured out even with the escort. Malcolm and Sil had made the trip bearable for him, but he was beginning to wish his family had played straight with him instead of plunging him into all the cloak and dagger.

Haddy was used to flying free on his own wings, with his own life in his hands, not walking everywhere with minders watching over him, making sure that he didn't get...mugged? Kidnapped? Robbed? Killed? He didn't see how any of those were possible in a contained environment like this. There was no way on or off the ship. He didn't know any secrets he could spill, except for Malcolm and Sil's involvement in the Resistance. But they were out in neutral space, so that couldn't hurt them out here.

He couldn't figure out what the danger was.

It should have made him relax. Made him feel like someone cared about him. Like the universe didn't have a big hole in it that nobody could ever fill again.

But it didn't. It just suffocated him, like they were wrapping a warm blanket around his face.

When they weren't tailing him, Sil and Malcolm drilled him on what they called "trade craft." How to spot a tail, how to read people, how to communicate with gestures and facial expressions.

His questions about why they were drilling him got shrugged off again and again, until the last day before docking.

He was in the gym, people-watching with Sil under cover of lifting. In another few days all of life would feel like a bad day in the centrifuge (Nineveh was, after all, a giant centrifuge), so he wanted to get in all the extra weight bearing activity that he could. Sil wouldn't let him go out alone, so she tagged along and drilled him.

"Keep your eyes on the bollard there. Don't close them." Sil said. "Now, describe the people around you."

Haddy squatted under a total load of six hundred kilos—his body weight combined with the band pressure on his shoulders, adding up to the equivalent of a hundred sixty-five kilos of Earth-normal weight —and ran through his recent memories without closing his eyes.

"Let's see, let's see. At three o'clock there's a Korean

girl in a pink workout suit with a black, um...hip harness..." it was the most genteel way he could put it, "...and red hair. At six there's a Nigerian woman with blonde hair, she's had a couple kids and not had a follow-up visit for cosmetics. At seven there's a kid with her, a little boy, looks like his father was Australian aborigine. There's a grandmother at nine with purple hair and a good tan, but the skin texture gives her away. Did I miss anything."

Sil snickered. "Yeah, you're sixteen."

"What?" Haddy pushed up against the weight and hooked the pressure bar over its rest.

Sil kept snickering.

"What? Come on, let me in on the joke!"

Sil looked at him, rolled her eyes, and stuck her index finger out pointing to Haddy's two-o'clock.

There was a very well-built man there, working at a bench press.

Sil poked her thumb over her shoulder, at Haddy's ten o'clock. A group of five teenage boys and a couple older men, maybe about Malcolm's age, were running on tread-mills.

Then Sil circled her finger.

All around them, there were men and boys that Haddy had completely failed to notice.

"You're hopeless, you know. You only see women."

"Well," Haddy shrugged, "They're the only ones worth looking at."

"And that will get you killed."

"Oh, come on. Killed?"

"Killed."

"Why would *anyone* want to kill me?"

Sil slipped closer to him and lowered her voice.

"You haven't figured it out yet?"

"What?"

"Whoever gets to you has a straight ride into the entire Resistance network. It will lose us the war."

"Huh? I'm just a flyer. What are you talking about?"

"I don't think they have your aunt. And neither do your uncles. But rescuing you from kidnappers is the one thing that might make your aunt come out of hiding. If they can get you, they'll get her. And if they get her...they get all of us."

Haddy swallowed hard.

And threw up.

THE TOWN THAT SWALLOWED JONAH

SPACE STATION NINEVEH was independent of any government in the system. Constructed by a crowd-funded consortium intent on selling it of piecemeal to its inhabitants, it existed outside of any law but its own.

Incorporated and governed like a condominium complex, property owners had a say in operational matters via their votes in the Owners Association, into which they paid annual dues and from which they drew bonuses in the form of overage from docking fees, station taxes, and graft. Its location in Solar orbit at 1.25AU made it a primary transfer point for cargo, passengers, and mining traffic moving between the Earth-Luna system and the outer colonies on Mars, Phobos, and the thinly scattered asteroid mining bases that had sprung up here and there over the course of the late twenty-first and early twenty-second centuries.

The six-kilometer O'Neil cylinder-style station sported an exterior docking ring and two interior cargo bays for ISO compliant freight, shuttles, and private yachts, and a large spindle-harness platform that ran the length of the spinning station and provided a parking area for large ships that were designed to load and unload while landed.

The *PRS Buchman* fit neither profile. As was the case at Ring Alpha, the *PRS Buchman* was too big to use any of Nineveh's docking facilities. Instead, she matched orbit with the station a hundred kilometers off her bow end and began to unload.

The ISO containers, being outfitted with proper autopilots and thrusters as per spec, detached from the *Buchman's* docking arms and nudged themselves toward the station, lining up in a long, brightly-colored rainbow parade in their hours-long fall toward the station's internal cargo bay.

As this patient ballet got underway, shuttles that had also been docked with the cargo units detached themselves and flew inward to the *Buchman's* two main docking ports.

The passengers—those not aboard for the round trip—loaded themselves onto the shuttles along with half of the crew, who were due for shore leave. They ordered themselves by staterooms, as Captain Fresnel preferred orderly queues to people elbowing each other this way and that for prime seating on the shuttle.

PRS Buchman would stay at Nineveh for two weeks, performing maintenance and letting its crew rest and recuperate in comfortable anonymity before it loaded up, aimed itself back at the Earth-Luna system, and got underway for Space Station Sidon in high Earth orbit. Round trip passengers would be allowed to come and go at their leisure during the stop—once the transport passengers were clear of the ship.

The shuttles docked themselves inside Nineveh's main cargo bay, at the center axis of the station, and the passengers—Haddy included—flew out of the main shuttle and into the vast mechanical superstructure of the space station.

Inside, Nineveh's docking area functioned very

like the zero-g area of Ring Alpha. Trains of people hand-walked along cables going from docking slips to entry ports, converging like ants from their various slips onto a passageway at the center of motion.

The spin created centrifugal force, pushing on the outer decks with the same force as a full Earth-normal gravity. The higher one climbed, though, the lower the acceleration. Up here near the center, Haddy weighed a fraction of a kilogram—little enough that he could keep himself suspended by a pinky finger.

Moving into passage, they queued up for customs. This time, there was just a cursory check for explosives—nearly invisible as the entire line moved through a ring of mechanical sniffers programmed to detect explosives residue and other nasties—and then to a verbal interview.

The purpose of his visit? Well, he couldn't say "I'm running for my life because some spies want to kidnap me to extort secrets from my aunt" so he just said "Personal."

Did he have anything to declare? Well, "Kill all the Americans" seemed a bit out of place, though it was what he was dying to scream at the top of his lungs ever since he'd read the news about his mother. But he knew they were really after anything on the "controlled items" list right next to the counter, because the sign there told him so.

The customs agent waved him through.

Haddy followed the throng down the white, brightly-lit tube as it sloped away from the center of the station, a direction that eventually became "down." A couple dozen meters after his feet touched the floor, the causeway opened into a broad platform. Traffic split to the left and right, most people shuffling along, keeping their hands on the guide wires, eyes mostly to the front, as if they didn't even notice what was right in front of them at the end of the platform.

Haddy did.

Beyond a half-height railing, the platform opened into a room the likes of which he'd never seen. A vast open space stretched for kilometers directly in front of him. Above his head, at the axis of the station, a long column ran from one end to the other. Along the column, every once-in-a-while, there were four spokes that jutted out and sank down like pylons into the cylinder walls, carpeted with green and gold and red plants the likes of which Haddy didn't think he'd ever seen before, all interspersed with irregular pools of shiny blue-green and clusters of high glass that looked like crop towers.

The room stretched and stretched until it ended in a blinding whiteness on the far side, as if someone had ripped a hole in the station and stuck a star in the far end.

The implications crashed over him, one after another.

A place like this had *free air*, as a side-effect of growing food. Or mostly free air. He'd have to actually do the numbers to figure it. There were lakes in the greenery in front of him, and if they were percolating the lakes they might be feeding kelp beds in there. They had to be.

And it had all this open space. Not just like the walking paths through the ag dome and the spaceport, but space that was really *open*.

It took his breath away, made him dizzy in a way that free fall never had.

But it was more than that. *This very spot* was the perfect place for to set up a booth and start a Nineveh franchise. True, he had some money to live on for a while thanks to the Mannix deal, but he was going to have to pay the bills somehow until he could get back home.

He'd expected Sil or Malcolm to find him here—they hadn't set a meeting, but Haddy'd had the good fortune to be near the front of the queue in his assigned shuttle. They *should* be coming through somewhere behind him...

Except they weren't.

He stayed there for twenty minutes, hanging around, watching the crowd, They hadn't shown up after twenty minutes. The view paled as the worry crawled up his throat.

He waited another twenty. The crowd thinned out, until eventually he was alone on the platform.

They weren't coming.

Well, then, he'd have to just carry on alone. He'd run into them again. If he'd learned anything from them in the last few weeks, it's that they knew how to find people and keep tabs on them.

Meantime, he was finally on Nineveh. He needed to find a place to sleep, get something to eat, and plan his next move.

Haddy shouldered his bag, which didn't weigh anything this close to the center of the station.

He shuffled toward the exit—he didn't pay attention which one it was, because he didn't know what the directions were called on this station. Some places used fore/aft/port/starboard, some used north/south/east/west, other places might use other schemes, he didn't know. He didn't care, either.

All that gorgeous space out there beyond the balcony suddenly felt as empty as his whole life.

He wondered if he would ever feel whole again. If he would ever fly again. If he'd ever see Josie again or go a whole day without missing his mom and wishing he could have coffee or go flying with her one more time.

That might make life feel like it was worth enduring. At least for a little while.

"Hadrian Jin? Excuse me! Are you Hadrian Jin?"

Haddy turned around to meet the unfamiliar voice behind him—too quickly, unfortunately, which sent him spinning in the light gravity.

He slid into a sideways tumble and then did a ridiculous high-stepping dance to correct himself.

When he got his footing again, he looked up to see a broadly-built pot-bellied man: two arms, two hands, two legs, two meters tall with a drab brown uniform two shades lighter than his skin and one shade lighter than his close-shaved woolly head. He was dressed like the customs agent.

"Yeah," Haddy said. "Yeah, that's me. Why?"

The man held out a hand. It contained a folded paper.

"Message for you."

"Uh...uh, thank you..." Haddy took the proffered hand. "I don't have any cash on me..."

"No charge for the message. And it wouldn't be proper for me to accept a tip."

"Right, right." Haddy nodded as the other man skipped lightly from the room in a gait that would have looked comical under any other circumstances—but Haddy didn't notice.

His focus was on the paper. He unfolded it and read it.

Apartment 2415, Level 4 Section B.

Entry code 2439243 + voiceprint

Burn after reading.

Well, now he at least knew where to find Malcolm and Sil.

Haddy didn't have a lighter on him. He'd never smoked, and didn't have many friends who did, and he didn't think he'd have been allowed to bring a lighter onto the *Buchman*—the gift shop on board only sold Safe-T-Heats—so he folded the paper double several times over and kept it in his left palm, pressed between a his middle and ring finger.

Resuming his walk, Haddy followed the passage he'd chosen as it ramped down to a bank of elevators—over a dozen of them arrayed around a kiosk.

The kiosk gave him directions to the address—turns out it was in the second section in from the docking area and the associated commercial districts, which held the forward position in Section A—and he followed them by taking an elevator up to the hub where he found a micrograv tram station.

There were no standing positions on this tram, and all the seats faced only one direction. The seats had generous arm space. Rather than being laid out in bench-banks with an aisle down the middle like was the custom on Lunar trams, these were laid out in evenly spaced rows with aisles between them—no chair touched another, or even came close, and each chair looked like an easy chair, with arm rests and generous padding.

As he took a seat in the front row center, Haddy mused that the Ninevites certainly lived up to their reputation of doing things with an absurd amount of style.

"Welcome to The Vine, your solution for all your Nineveh inter-district express travel needs. This is a complimentary service provided by the merchants and property owners on Nineveh station—please support the maintenance and operation of this express service by enjoying our wonderful retail, culinary, and entertainment establishments in Section A, or by taking advantage of the deluxe accommodations available throughout the station. You can find more by searching 'accommodations' on your Cetacean Networks Information Page. To prevent injury and death, please ensure that all your belongings are stowed in one of our available safety slots or secured with one of the complimentary safety harnesses. When your belongings are secure, press the white button on the left arm of your seat."

Haddy was the only person on board, and he didn't see why leaving his bag loose could result in "injury and death," but when one goes to another colony, one is obligated to behave as the people in that colony behave. It was basic good manners, and common sense—you didn't break rules you didn't understand, because until you did, you never knew which rules were there to keep you alive and which ones were just there to get in your way. He stowed his bag in the cubby below his seat and stretched the safety webbing across the opening, then pressed the button.

The doors closed along the length of the car, and the tram eased forward—but where in Luna City he would have expected a gentle acceleration followed by some coasting, here the acceleration pushed hard, sustaining a full g for a few seconds, then cutting entirely, leaving him in free fall while his chair rotated, then pushing again hard as the tram car braked into the next station.

"Entering Beta Terminal, servicing Section B. Residential and boutique commercial, hiking trails, swimming, and green space recreation. All passengers destined for Section B may now disembark."

The car slid to a gentle stop, a soft alert tone sounded, and the doors opened.

Haddy retrieved his belongings and exited the car, shouldering his way past a smattering of oncoming traffic.

The terminal was arrayed as a ring around the tracks—from here he could plainly see that there was track enough for four tram cars to run simultaneously—and there were modest banks of elevators jutting inwards at quarters around on the outside wall.

Haddy drifted toward the nearest elevator, sailed in through the open door, and rode it down. When he got off at Level 4, he found himself in an annex near a junction of two large passages. After some experimenting, he found that the halls leading down the long axis of the station were numbered sequentially as avenues, and the ones ringing the axis of the station numbered in ascending tens as streets.

A check of nearby house numbers told him that the streets created a co-ordinate grid, with the avenue number first and the street range second. That meant that apartment 2415 would be on Twenty-Fourth Avenue, between Tenth Street and Twentieth Street.

That was fifteen blocks *that* way.

He had to learn what to call directions around here, or he'd never be able to get anywh...

Haddy just about smacked himself in the head. He took his PPD from his belt and called up the local net.

There it was. The default welcome screen for Cetacean Networks contained a big, friendly "maps and navigation" button.

He touched it, wishing he'd put his blink-lenses in instead of carrying them in his toiletries kit. Without them, or a pair of glasses, he'd have to cope with the unforgivably small ten centimeter active-surface on his PPD.

Sure enough, the screen blinked, then showed his current location on a grid. He punched in the address he was looking for on his keypad.

"Go downstation one block," the computer said, "Then turn right. Proceed fifteen-point-five counterspin. Your destination will be on your left."

A little line on the screen helpfully showed him where to go. If he'd been wearing his blink-lenses, like any sane person would do upon reaching a new station, he'd be seeing it all laid over his vision—nice, private, and easy to see.

Oh well. Nobody was around to witness his humiliation. A little foot traffic milled about—a couple kids blew by on skateboards, and a woman about Sil's age out for a stroll, and a handful of other adults all wearing overcoats and hats—but not much in the way of actual crowds. The local time was a little after 1430, and this was a residential area, so everyone was probably at work or off in the entertainment district.

Nice area, though. In Luna City, the architects and engineers made virtue out of necessity by adorning the rock walls with all manner of bas relief sculptures, fountains, benches, and anything else they could think of to make life underground feel open and airy instead of confined and depressing.

Here, where the designers could have created a purely functional space out of modular pieces (like you could see happening with homesteaders and their habs on the Lunar surface), they had opted instead for striking stylistic choices that seemed to vary every few blocks. As he walked, Haddy passed through an area that felt like a VR simulation of ancient Egypt, another that had an ultra-modernist flare with straight lines, boxy ribbing, and bold geometric highlights, and yet another that was splashed with greens and browns and crawling with ivy.

Haddy found the transitions jarring, and not altogether pleasant, but the different themed areas themselves provided a kind of variety that Luna City didn't. He found that he liked it more than he found it off-putting—but only just.

The walk didn't take long. He'd been diligent during his time in the centrifuge, working as hard as he could bear under the acceleration so that he wouldn't collapse when faced with Nineveh's decidedly Terran attitudes about gravity. Now he was glad he had. He arrived at the apartment door at a brisk pace without so much as getting mildly winded.

Worlds different from the slogging agony he'd endured on his trip to Nevada a lifetime ago.

Apartment 2415, Level 4 Section B.

That's what the note said. That's where he was now. He switched off his PPD and clipped it to his belt once again, then he unfolded the paper he'd been keeping pressed in his left hand between his ring and middle fingers—which felt awkward without the paper, now that they'd grown used to it.

Entry code 2439243 + voiceprint

Haddy touched the dark glass on the right side of the door. It sprang to life with the image of a keypad. He punched the code in, and the keypad was replaced with text that said:

Read aloud: I'm a winged creature, and a perch is all I need.

"Um...okay." Haddy cleared his throat. "I'm a winged creature, and a perch is all I need."

The panel blanked. Haddy heard two short beeps.

The door slid away in front of him.

Haddy stepped through, and found himself in the sitting room of a modest apartment. Two doors lead out of the main room, both closed. One open arch lead into what looked like a kitchen. Most of the flat seemed to be taken up with the one room, and the space was bare of anything personal. Only some basic furnishings—a chair, a love seat, a fold-down table coming out of one of the wall near the door...

Haddy stopped.

There was a bra on the chair.

And a barrette on the table.

Was Sil here?

Sil doesn't wear a bra, stupid.

Thinking it made him blush, but it was true. Her breasts were too small for her to bother. Not that Haddy minded.

But that meant...

"What the hell is going on here?" he said.

Behind him, a familiar female voice said:

"I was wondering when you'd get in."

Haddy froze. Spiders crawled up his neck as he matched the voice to a name.

It couldn't be.

He turned on his heel, and looked. The sight of her made him forget how to grip. His bag thunked to the floor.

"Charis?!"

The Trouble With Zeros

SHE LOOKED AS if she'd aged five years in the last two months. Her blonde hair was done up in a bun with a stick through it. Her eyes had purple rings under them. She was wearing a fitted and collared t-shirt, a suede vest, and fitted blue jeans, which was miles away from the athletic-wear she'd preferred in Luna City. He wondered if it was a costume, or if it was just one of the dominant local styles.

The corner of her mouth was twitching, as if it couldn't decide whether to smile or disapprove.

"You remembered my name! Well, you just cost me fifty bucks."

"What?" Haddy blinked a couple times, caught up to the joke. "Oh, gee, thanks loads. How'd you get here?"

The door slid shut behind her.

"I took the *Rising*." She turned around and flipped a mechanical latch—a large, flat hook that swiveled from the door into a cavity in the jamb.

"The *Rising*?" That was their family ship. "You can't fly that on your own..."

"Of course I can. Doesn't mean I did."

"Uncle Amit is here?"

"Of course he isn't, what do you think I am?" she snapped at him, and walked past him to the seating area, where she started tidying up while she kept her voice sharp and pointy. "I hired a crew—work in exchange for passage. I *am* a qualified ship's master, you know."

"Hey!" Haddy snapped back. "I just got off a ship I've been stuck on for two months trying to figure out whether you and Arn and Mike and Amit were alive or dead—the only reason I know Mike's not is because I got special permission to call home. I didn't even get to *talk* to my family, because oh, right, Nita is dead! And who knows how many others..."

"I was there, you know," she snarled, "I *saw* what happened."

"...and then I hear that they blew up Ring Alpha and I don't know what the hell else is going on but I sure didn't...wait, what? You *saw*?" Haddy felt as if he'd gone from full run to slogging through syrup.

A cloud passed over her face. Her eyes welled, and she set her teeth against each other.

"I saw. I barely made it out alive."

"What happened?"

She turned away, headed for the kitchen. "Look, you want something to drink?"

"Uh, sure. You got any coffee?"

"Yeah. Yeah, I got some," she said from beyond the archway.

Haddy followed to find her bustling around in a little galley kitchen, around the corner to the left. To the right, a door stood open leading into a bathroom.

He ducked inside and availed himself, then returned to the smell of coffee brewing in the machine.

Charis was standing in front of it, arms crossed over her chest, watching the pot fill as if her scrutiny would make a difference to the quality of the finished product.

"You didn't tell me what happened."

"Oh," she said without looking up. "You know. People died."

"How?" It still didn't make sense—his mother hadn't been much for politics, even on her bad days.

"The shop is in the Bazaar. They came to the Bazaar," Charis shrugged, still staring into the hot black liquid gradually filling the carafe. "I was just suiting up when the noise started. People were running, we started throwing suits on everyone that would take one, and sending them over the edge to go hide in Reservoir Cave. Me and Pop and your mom. We ran out of suits, and people kept coming. There weren't enough spots on the lifts for everyone to get out. There were so many. I swear to god, the whole city was down there."

Haddy's mind filled with an image of people, like lemmings, bum-rushing the railings around the gallery. Flooding over the edge like corn cobs falling out of a combine. It filled him with a well of numbness, a vast emotional blanket shielding him from the sight of his mother's mangled corpse.

Charis kept talking:

"Your mom pushed me over the rail, screaming 'Fly! Fly! Get away while you can!' But I couldn't leave them, so I circled, waiting for her and Pop to come over. I thought I could grab them, take them down, you know? We would hit hard, but we'd survive. I could take one down and then come back for the other."

Haddy grunted as if he thought it was a good idea, though he didn't see how a plan like that could possibly work without a tandem harness.

"You know how you can see into the whole Bazaar from up there? From the right angle, all the way down to the spaceport?"

"Yeah."

"It was like watching an ocean. Everyone was packed

in like those square cigars in a box. I could see ripples moving all through, everyone pushing and pulling, some people trying to run, some people trying to get down to the fight. The whole room would just lurch ten meters this way, ten meters that way. I could see the thermal blasts and the projectile guns flashing and everything down in the concourse. The Marines were trying to push up into the Bazaar and..." she stopped talking, pressed her lips together, like she was trying to keep hold of herself.

"And...?" Haddy didn't know how much of the suspense he could take. He found himself wishing he'd been there, thinking he could have done something, and yet glad he'd missed the whole thing.

"Pop and your mom were trying to run for one of the side passages, to get back home. The crowd lurched sideways, and it just...crushed them. They just suffocated, right up against the wall. Nobody even noticed."

"Wait...Amit too?" Haddy didn't know how to understand what he was hearing.

The coffee maker spluttered. Charis switched it off and took a pair of mugs from under-shelf hooks above the coffee maker.

While she did, Haddy wiped his eyes and tried to sniff all the mucous back up his nose. His stomach turned as soon as it hit the back of his throat.

She poured two mugs, handed one to Haddy, and he greedily swallowed two large, searing gulps to help clear his throat and settle his stomach.

Charis used her empty hand to take the pot and gesture with it toward the sitting room.

Haddy led the way in silence. He sat down on the couch, and sipped at his coffee, and wished the whole world could feel as wonderful as the drink smelled, instead of being as dark as it looked.

Charis sat in the chair, her legs folded up under her.

At length, he said, "What about everybody else?"

"Everybody else is fine. Well, you know, as fine as you can be with...with all that."

"Yeah." Haddy sipped. He rolled the coffee around before swallowing it. Something about the sharp, bitter taste helped keep him grounded in the moment when everything inside him wanted to run away and hide. "What happened at Ring Alpha?"

"They nuked it. I got out just ahead of the attack, watched it in my rear-view."

"No, no, I heard about that. I meant when I was there. Why didn't you get on the *Buchman?*"

"Oh. You were ahead of us in line. When they pulled you out, we knew they'd pull us out. So we turned around and tried to leave." She shrugged. "They saw us. Of course they saw us. They arrested all of us on the spot."

Haddy cocked his head. "How did you get out?"

"Well, it was the Americans. They have rules about that—or, had rules. They were looking for Mom," Charis said.

Haddy mentally substituted "Aunt Min" for "Mom." Keeping his cool (at least, as well as he was able to keep it) was tiring him out enough that he needed to double-check with himself who Charis was talking about.

"They let me go after a few hours, and I flew back to your place with Arn, well, after we found a flight," she growled the last part. "Dad..."

That's Uncle Mike Haddy reminded himself.

"...showed up later that day. Pop didn't come back for a week. We thought they'd disappeared him like they did

Mom. So we were going to load up and head out here to meet you, and Pop showed back up. He came straight into Grissom, right before they shut it down. We were his first stop—at the booth, that day? He never made it home. But he told me we needed to get to Nineveh as quick as we could. And then the fighting started..."

"Yeah." Haddy grabbed around for a way to steer the conversation away from the battle. "But why Nineveh?"

"It's a...tradition, I guess you'd call it."

"Huh? What about Mike?"

"Your Dad couldn't cope. Mike had to stay. He said they'd be safe there for a while. There wouldn't be another battle in the city so soon. Congress would have to have its say,..." Charis trailed off, finishing her coffee to cover up the silence. She leaned forward to refill it, as if operating on autopilot. Haddy held out his cup for a top-off as well, and she swung over and poured without thinking a thing about it.

She was close enough that he could spot the smears of food on her collar, drips of grease on her shirt front.

"You're working as a waiter?" He blurted it out, then wished he could take it back. He wasn't supposed to let people know he'd been getting training in trade craft.

Her brow furrowed. "Yes. At Phalanx."

Phalanx? Haddy knew that name, but couldn't remember from where.

"It's a..." She hesitated, then continued with certainty., "It's a pub. How did you know?"

"I don't know. Just a feeling I guess."

She nodded, like she was conceding him the right to jump off the perch first.

Haddy looked for some clues in his coffee to what to say next. He wanted ask about the Resistance, but he realized he couldn't mention that, since he wasn't supposed to know about it.

Charis sighed. When she did, her shoulders sank like she'd been stabbed and all the air holding her up was whistling out, and would keep on whistling out until only her skin was left.

"I'm glad you made it," she said.

"Why wouldn't I?"

"I don't know." She shook her head. "Well, I don't know everything. What you can't know, you can't tell if they get their hands on you."

A chill went up Haddy's spine. But before he could press, she changed the subject:

"It's your first time here, right?"

"Yeah. I've only ever been to Earth before."

"Well," she raised an eyebrow and crooked a half smile, "We've got a whole station here. It's all ours. You'll have to do something for money—there aren't any LOXCOR dividends here..."

"We weren't ever stockholders."

"Oh. I didn't know whether grandpa got in the IPO or not. Well, anyway, there's no family business here either, so we'll have to get you a job, but the rent here's already paid for the next two weeks, so we can take a few days and see around..."

"What about your job?"

"Well, I can't go out during work, obviously, but I'm only doing four hours a day. What did you want to do?"

Haddy drank more coffee. He didn't want to look like he had no idea bout anything, not in front of Charis. So he made believe that the coffee was the source of all wisdom and lingered over it.

"I thought I'd set up a franchise here. There wasn't anyone out there flying. But if I can get the spot up just after customs—you know that spot with the big view where you can see down the whole station..."

"Yeah, but you'll never get in there. There might be a couple places I know though...but it won't work."

"Why not?"

"Have you felt your weight? This station spins up a full gravity, and the only reason we can fly in Luna City..."

"Oh, no no, I thought about that." Haddy grinned, forgetting his troubles for a moment. "I got it licked."

"How?"

"The station *spins*. It's just a big centrifuge, so there's no real gravity. As long as we don't *land* on the ground, and only land higher up where the acceleration is light, we're basically weightless, so all we need is my new wing design and..."

"New design?"

Haddy filled her in on what he'd been up to, and the order with Mannix Spaceways. He pulled out his PPD and showed her the designs, moving over next to her and sitting on the arm of the seat and the two of them hunched over the small screen as he walked her through the whole process.

"I've *got* to try one." She grabbed his arm with excitement. "I know a place we can take off from."

"Do you know where there's a printer that can handle it?"

"Yeah, my boss has one. I can get us a couple printed up. Can you tweak one for me?"

"Sure, I could do that tonight. I'll need your measurements. Stand up."

He slipped off the arm of the chair. She stood up, shucked her vest and pulled off her shirt, then stripped off her jeans and held her arms out.

Since Haddy was from from a culture where social nudity was a common phenomenon, he had been conditioned from birth to that most basic rule of politeness: "do not stare." According to the rules he knew, it was his responsibility not to make her feel immodest or exposed, rather than her responsibility not to distract or arouse him. If their positions had been reversed, he'd have expected the same from her.

So he didn't stare, even though part of him really wanted to. He just pulled up his biometrics sampler and pointed the PPD at her. It scanned her front-ways, she turned ninety degrees, and it scanned again, and again, and again for each of her four sides. Then he took scans of each of her hands, fingers splayed out as far as she could manage.

"Got it." It would take him probably ten minutes to create a design for her—most of that checking that the program didn't make any errors when it adapted the new rig design for her frame. Some of the default variables for a normal orn-suit might not map right onto the new rig. "I'll send you a copy before you go to work tomorrow."

"Hot damn!" She picked up her clothes and headed toward one of the two doors leading off the sitting room. From the other side, from what turned out to be her bedroom, she said: "You know, when I asked what you wanted to do I wasn't looking for a business plan."

"Oh." Haddy mentally kicked himself. "Sorry."

She came out again, this time dressed in a loose pirate shirt and a pair of baggy shorts, scooped up her coffee and sat on the sofa. She patted the seat next to her, and Haddy took the other end, facing her.

"So, what do you want to do?"

Haddy sighed. "Well, I've never been here. Could you, maybe show me around?"

She smiled a private smile.

"I'd love to." She sounded like she meant it, too. Then, as if she was moving on to other business, she slapped her knees and said: "Gods, I need a shower."

She stood up.

Haddy did the same, mostly as a reflex.

Charis stepped toward him and wrapped her arms around him. Haddy hadn't expected this, and for a moment wasn't sure what to do.

Then he felt her shaking, and before he knew it he was wrapped around her, spilling his grief all down her shoulders.

"I was so worried," she said, "I didn't know if you'd make it."

Haddy didn't even think to ask why. He was too wrapped up in his own relief. Touching someone real, someone who understood his loss, someone he cared about, someone who knew who he was—it was as if he'd been starving for so long that he forgot what hunger was, and then suddenly found himself at a banquet.

They stood there, clinging to each other, until each of them had grown so tired they could barely stand.

Haddy's tears ran dry, and still he clung to her until, by stages, he became acutely aware that he was holding a woman who smelled like lemons and felt like everything soft and wonderful in the universe.

He let go, a new flush of embarrassment creeping up his neck.

Charis let go too, and patted his chest.

"Thanks. I needed that," she said.

"Yeah. Um. Me too. Thanks." Haddy reached for his coffee to hide his face behind the mug.

He needn't have bothered. Charis wanted to shower before getting dressed—again—in something more appropriate for going out. She also demanded that he shower and get into his other set of clothes. She pointed him at the second door, behind which he found a small bedroom, and told him to unpack in there, and take the shower after her.

Twenty minutes later, fresh, washed, re-dressed, and having had a piece of teeth-cleaning taffy, Charis led Haddy out the door.

But when she stepped through, he suddenly didn't want to go out.

"Charis, wait," he said. "Before we go out..."

She backed up into the room and closed the door, turned around and leaned against it, her arms crossed over her chest.

"What is it now?"

"I can't handle this. I *have* to know. What's going on? As much as you know." When she cast about like she was trying to find a way around telling him, he said, "Look, I'm in this whether I want to be or not, right? I mean, someone took Aunt Min, and now I'm a citizen of this new Lunar state in exile, whatever they're going to call it. Dad and Mike told me not to trust anyone, and to be careful, like they expected something to happen to me. You can't leave me flying in the dark like this. What the hell is all of this about?"

Charis looked down. When she looked up again, her face was wet.

"What this is about...what it's about is we're in trouble."

"Yeah, I got that. *Why?*"

"Do you know what a zero-day exploit is?"

"I think so. It's, like, a back door that lets you attack a network, right?"

"Or a flaw in one that nobody knows about yet, so they haven't fixed it, yeah."

"Okay, what about them?"

"Well, gods, how far back do I go..." Charis filled him in on how Min was running a spy network, and how it was the reason she'd sold out of the family business. It was the same story that Sil told him, so he tried to act surprised and shocked in all the right places. "You know how Dad is, though."

"Dad is Mike, right?"

"Right. He can't play poker, so he never wanted to know exactly what was going on, because he didn't want anyone to see him acting suspicious. Me, though, well...I've been known to play a game of cards or two." Her eyes sparkled darkly. "Mom and Pop kept me in the loop most of the time, so that if anything happened to them I could at least tell Dad what happened. When we were on Sidon back in September, Pop bumped into a tourist from Dakar, and they started talking. Mom came by, and they all had a drink together, and then we went hiking in the greenbelt."

"Who was he—the guy from Dakar?"

"He was a man who had a friend who had a friend who worked for a subcontractor for the Persian Military command. He'd slipped Mom a thumbnail. Well, while we were walking, Mom did the thing Mom always did when she got a drop like that. She made a backup and handed it off to Pop. She had me keep Dad busy asking

him about the plants, since Dad's into botany and everything. And...well, that's when Mom disappeared. Just
vanished while we were walking, just like that. Pop went
full-on red alert, and we were on the ship and leaving port
less than an hour later. We went out to Gagarin and did
what we could to track her down, one of our sources told
Pop something that made him think she might be on Luna,
that's how we came to your house. We didn't find her
there, and our failsafe was always to meet back at Nineveh
if anything separated us."

"What was on the thumbnail?"

"You can't tell *anybody*."

"Of course I won't. What kind of a moron do you think
I am?"

Charis took a deep breath. "It's a remote zero-day
exploit for the central command module of the Persian
Destroyer class."

"It's...but that would let anyone steal a *whole destroyer*."
That one thing could win the entire war for the Loonies.
With Persian ships, they could go toe-to-toe with the
American ships, and keep them from landing troops, or
from orbiting Luna, or from blowing up any more space
stations. And it would keep the Persians from capturing
anything, too. For the first time in the whole war, Haddy
found himself getting really excited. "We could keep the
Terrans and their fights down on Earth. Charis, this is...it's
not big. It's everything!"

"Yes."

"So where is it?"

"Assuming that they didn't get it from Mom and patch
it already?"

"Yeah."

"Pop's the only one who knew about it. And he's

dead."

"And it wasn't on him when he died?"

Charis shook her head.

"They don't know that. They think one of us still has it."

"Yeah."

Haddy felt like he'd swallowed an anvil.

"Like I said," Charis grimaced, "We're in trouble."

A House is Not a Home

FOR THE FIRST TIME since he'd left home, Haddy felt like himself again. He was a man on a mission—to explore, to learn, to adapt, to find all the interesting little cracks and crevices that defined this world that was almost entirely new to him, at least by his own standards.

In truth, the strangeness in this world was more akin to that experienced by an American visiting Australia or Britain—just enough to be disorienting, but similar enough to feel comprehensible. Had he been visiting a station that spoke a different language, he might have felt like a true alien instead of just a distant relative, but there were no stations that did not use English as their lingua franca—not even Sidon, which had been built and operated by the Persians.

Outside of the multitudinous nations and city-states on Earth itself, only a few scattered bases on Luna and Mars had what Haddy would have considered truly foreign cultures, but they were notoriously unfriendly to visitors. Just as the oceans had created a filter to migration which only the most determined and malcontent ever passed through, so too did the edges of Earth's atmosphere, without coercion or emigration restrictions, serve as a barrier to all the "normal" members of the human race. As a rule, only the ambitious, the desperate, the deluded, or the extraordinarily adventurous ever made it out of the gravity well, and only a fraction of them stayed permanently.

But that didn't matter. To Haddy, it was all strange, and new, and well worth exploring. If he'd been used to a tremendous variety of people in Luna City, he was more astonished at this place. Not just at the variety of people—which was prodigious—but at the sorts of people he was seeing. More South Americans than Luna City, more Nigerians, and so many people of all colors and shapes dressed in overcoats and hats.

When Haddy asked Charis about this, she chuckled and said "It's an inside joke," but wouldn't elaborate. It was only later that Haddy learned that clothes that hid the face and gait were part of the local culture—a notional protest by a minority faction in the owners co-op against the extent of surveillance on the station.

Charis led the way upstation to the major commercial center, and to a bar. The one she worked at, as it turned out.

Phalanx felt lavish. Covered all in wood, or a very good simulation (at least to Haddy's untrained eye), it had signs boasting home brew beers to rival anything in the solar system, a special high-rollers drinks menu with liquors imported all the way from Earth, a poker room, and the kind of atmosphere Haddy might have expected from something in the middle ages in England, or the Klondike gold rush (two eras and cultures that seemed more-or-less identical from Haddy's perspective, despite their separation by seven centuries and one hemisphere).

And, now that he saw the inside, he knew why the name had sounded familiar. It had been all over the news he'd read on ship: *Investigation Into Bar Bombing Hits Dead End.*

Someone had bombed a poker tournament here,

though you wouldn't know it to look at the place now.

Haddy waited at the bar while Charis went in the back to look for her boss. He was at no risk for getting bored while he waited, but nonetheless, he didn't have to wait long.

"Good news!" Charis said as she emerged from the back room, "They've got all the feedstock and he's only going to charge me materials."

"Yeah, but what is that going to cost us?"

"Dollars or LOX?"

"They take LOX up here?"

"So far. Thirty dollars. Twice that for LOX."

Well, it was a better deal than he'd gotten on the *Buchman*.

THEY WALKED FOR a few hours—first around the entertainment districts, which were sectioned off between those which were "family friendly" and those which were "intended for adults."

The terms, Charis explained, were advisory. Anyone could go wherever they wanted, but it was just good business to label your entertainments. On Nineveh, the former category included theaters, restaurants, sports arenas of all sorts, arcades, museums, and gambling establishments, while the latter category included brothels (of both the virtual and flesh-bound varieties), paintball and laser tag arenas, shooting ranges, purveyors of recreational chemistry, and anything else that a tourist from one part or another might consider too morally compromising for their children to be exposed to.

"You know," he said, "Josie would *love* this."

"Josie," Charis said. "Your dog?"

"Yeah." Haddy felt his eyes misting over. "She loves being around people. On busy days, she'd greet every customer that came into the shop, and walk with me down in the bazaar. She considered it her great calling to find paths through the crowd and 'bring back the ball.'"

Charis giggled. "The ball?"

"Any ball. Well, it didn't have to be a ball. She just had to think she could fool me into thinking it was a ball, so I'd throw it for her." Haddy chuckled. "You wouldn't believe my breakage budget."

"For your balls?" Charis started laughing.

Haddy shook his head, trying to keep a straight face. "For all the things she stole in her quest for the perfect ball."

Charis squeezed his arm. "She's a sweet dog. Even Pop loved her."

"Really?"

"Mmm. And he hates dogs. But that first day when you were at work, she wore him down, and they got to be best friends. She followed him everywhere, whenever you weren't in the room."

Haddy smiled. "That's Josie."

They walked along a little more, but the crowd was getting too thick to be worth the trouble.

When Haddy asked what there was to see that *wasn't* touristy—he lived in a tourist district and had breathed the commercial air his whole life—she took him up to the tram, where they traveled downstation all the way to the massive blinding white area that Haddy had seen before.

It was, he learned, an immense wall of fiber optic pixels. A few hundred kilometers away—so as to be outside of the traffic pattern—an array of enormous mirrors orbited the station, bouncing sunlight down onto five collection ports around the hull. From there, the light was carried down thick fiber cables that split into the millions of pixels which bathed the bore with dazzle.

He also found that, up close, the light wasn't nearly so blinding—it was intense enough that he needed sunglasses (which he purchased from a vending kiosk) but no more intense than that.

"Why are we over here, other than the big bright wall?" Haddy asked after he'd got his sunglasses on.

"This way." Charis took his hand and flew with him out of the tram station and, instead of taking an elevator, took him through a hole in the floor, which quickly became a ramp leading down a few dozen meters to a gantry that stretched between two of the elevator struts.

As they descended, a guttering wind gained strength, until down on the gantry itself it had become a steady breeze.

"I don't see any fans," Haddy said.

"What?"

"The wind," Haddy raised his voice so she could hear him over the buffeting. "How do they make it without fans?"

"The station is spinning at a hundred kph. That turns the whole sky into a vortex, not everything moves at the same speed. The sunlight also warms things up, and that makes air rise, but since there isn't any gravity without acceleration, it doesn't act the same way it would on a planet, so we get all these crazy mixing winds and weather patterns."

"Weather?   Sounds nasty." Haddy had thought weather was a peculiarity of Earth, a destructive consequence of having too much air moving around in an unconfined space.

"It keeps things interesting."

"Yeah, especially when we get the wings up here. This is where you want to take off from?"

The view from this end was no less spectacular than it had been from the other end. And from this end, with his back to the light, Haddy could see much more detail in the green areas. He could also see the upstation wall, which wasn't so much a wall as it was a mass of windows all arranged in concentric circles pushing his eyes in toward the center, where the tram tracks ran.

"Expensive apartments?" Haddy pointed at the far wall.

Charis laughed. "You have *no* idea. Makes the Rim District in Luna City look like skid row."

Haddy whistled.

"You can't see them from the other side because of the light," Charis said, pointing upstation through the haze, "but look close and you can see. There are gantries like this making a full circle at each of the major stops."

"What are they for? Just view platforms?"

She shook her head. "Shortcut for foot traffic. People ride the lifts halfway up, walk across to the lift they need, take it down. It's a lot faster than walking along the outer decks. Really helps on high traffic days."

"They're all about this big?" The platform they stood on was about ten meters wide with meter-and-a-half fences running down either side.

"Yeah. The wind is better on the middle ones, but the view's better from here. But this would be the kind of place to set up a booth.

"What kind of permission would I need?"

Charis shrugged and said something, but it was garbled by the wind.

"Say that again?"

"I said I have no idea, but I know where to find out."

"Great." Haddy waved his hands at the wind. "What say we get somewhere quieter?"

"Want to go swimming?"

"Actually that paintball arena looked fun."

TWO HOURS LATER, battered, scraped, paint-splattered, and covered in defeat, Haddy stumbled into the locker room. After the first couple matches, he'd goaded Charis into joining a championship tournament—and she'd proceeded to mop the floor with him.

When he asked her how, she just shrugged and said "Guess we have different hobbies," which didn't explain either the accuracy or the brains she showed in planning an ambush, but Haddy hadn't had time to think about that. He'd been too busy trying to find cover and return fire.

He didn't stay in the arena very long after he'd been eliminated. A few minutes—enough to watch Charis's technique. Now that he wasn't fighting her, he could see how she'd seen him coming around corners. She kept a flip-out dental mirror up her sleeve that she used to clear her path and spy from hiding. He'd have to find out where to buy one, and then use it against her next time they went on the course.

But now, Charis had two more rounds to fight, and Haddy was just as happy to get out of his rented tac suit with all the paint crust he'd earned. Once he was out of it, he wouldn't be announcing to everyone just how badly he'd gotten his ass kicked.

The locker room wasn't huge, but it could accommodate fifty or sixty people at a time. The bare walls and floor made the chamber ring with the occasional thunk and ping of lockers opening and closing, the clops of shoes and the slaps of feet on the floor, and the maniacal laughter of a girl taunting her kid brother and their father trying to get her to stop causing trouble. Haddy couldn't make out the words exactly, but he recognized the father's harried tone, as he'd been on the receiving end of that same tone from both parents on more than a few occasions.

Haddy found his locker, keyed it open, and emptied his pockets into it. There wasn't a lot in there—a couple spare paintballs and a load of spent CO2 cartridges. He wanted to keep at least one of each as a souvenir. He also took his competitor patch off his breast pocket and put it in the locker as well, and pulled the complimentary towel-and-soap bundle out of the locker's side-cubby and set them on the bench.

He peeled off his mask, undid his rented booties and weapons harnesses, set them on the bench next to the toiletries, and peeled off his suit. He wadded up the rip-stop trousers and shirt in a bundle with the codpiece, then shouldered the weapons harnesses, and walked bare-skinned to the end of the row of lockers. There, he dropped the clothes in a green bin labeled "dirty suits" and hung the harnesses on a rack above labeled "used harnesses." Then, he scooped up the toiletries pack on the way past his locker to the gang showers, dodging his way between fellow patrons and around a family that was getting ready to head into the arena.

Right before the showers, he passed a full-length mirror, and caught sight of himself. From toes to crown, his olive skin was pockmarked with bruises. If he'd been a Caucasian, he'd have looked like a grape-stained snow leopard. So much for leaving the evidence of his ignominious defeat behind with his paint-smeared suit.

Haddy was suddenly *very* relieved that he'd listened to Charis when he'd decided not to rent the body armor, and at least had used the codpiece. If the paintballs had marked him up that badly, a hit to the balls would surely have sent him to the medics and left him walking funny for weeks.

He tore his attention away from his polka-dot hide and slap-footed into the shower, avoiding a relatively un-bruised group of boys and girls about his own age laughing and playing grab-ass around a center spigot tower in favor of a corner where he could nurse his wounded dignity in private.

When the hot water hit his skin, the bruises stung all over again. It actually felt better having them sting than not—he'd earned them honestly, and at least he'd been beaten fair and square. Next time, he'd give Charis what-for. He just needed to make sure he got some practice in before he called a re-match.

Haddy heard someone behind him, saw a shadow approaching a spigot to his left out of the corner of his eye. So much for privacy.

He jumped when the shadow spoke.

"Don't turn around," a woman's voice whispered from behind him.

"Sil?" Haddy dropped his soap.

"Keep it down. We don't have a lot of time. No, don't stop. Keep washing."

Haddy squatted down and scooped up the bar of soap, decided to get his legs and feet while he was down there.

"Where have you been?" he whispered.

"Shh. We can't protect you if people see you walking

everywhere with bodyguards." Sil squirted some sham-
poo into her hands and lathered up her head. "The girl
you're staying with..."

"You mean Charis?"

"Yes. You need to be careful."

"You're crazy."

"You went to the bar she's working at?"

"Phalanx, yeah."

"It's a CIA front."

Haddy felt as if all the blood had just drained out of his
body.

"Keep washing."

"Oh, yeah, right." Haddy forced himself to stand up
and get on with scrubbing all the places that made him
smell like a barbarian when he worked out. "We've got to
get her out of there."

"If you do, they'll snatch her. If she starts acting out-of-
the-ordinary, they'll disappear her. We have to be careful.
Pretend like everything's normal. We've got our eye on
them. We're listening to their chatter, we'll be able to get
you both clear if something happens."

"What do I need to do?"

"Keep your eyes peeled. If I need to talk to you, I'll
leave a chalk mark on the lintel above your neighbor's
door—the one directly across from you. When you see
that, meet me at the coffee stand in Allenston Park at 1100
the next day."

"Allenston Park, coffee stand. Right." Haddy started
repeating it to himself.

"Don't worry," she said, "we'll keep you safe."

Sil turned her shower off, and walked away. Her
fingers brushed his shoulder as she left.

Haddy finished his shower as best he could, trying to keep himself from shaking.

It was one thing to hear Sil and Malcolm talk politics and espionage while on the *Buchman*. That was a place where the world was on pause—the events blowing up across the solar system were killing his family and his friends, but there was nothing he could do about it, and there was nothing those events could do about him. He'd been sidelined, wrapped in a protective bubble, and it dulled everything. Made it somehow academic.

But now, here? Not even a day into port, and he was already starting to settle into every-day-life again, and Sil's presence crashed through that tissue-paper normalcy like a meteorite through a pressure dome.

He was being watched, and not just by people who meant to protect him, either. He was a target here, and so was Charis, and there wasn't anything he could do about it.

You know when those tourists go fishing, Haddy? Haddy said to himself. *This is what the bait feels like.*

He was still trying to get himself under control when he got to his locker. A second or two later, Charis floated in on a cloud of victory.

"You look pleased with yourself," he said, trying to keep his voice light.

"And you look like you got hickies from an octopus."

"What's an octopus?" Haddy threw his towel down on the bench and pulled his yellow slacks out of the locker.

She rolled her eyes. Even though he wasn't watching her face, he could hear it in her voice and her breathing. Maybe the spy training had done some good after all.

"Never mind." She whapped his bare butt with her gun barrel, then passed him to get to her own locker, two slots away. "I'm starving. I'm thinking Italian. What do you think?"

Haddy stepped into his pants, not quite realizing she'd been talking to him. He'd heard her speak, sure, but he was too preoccupied to actually process the words.

"Hey, cuz!" she said.

"Huh? Yeah? What?"

"Food. You. Me. Eat."

"Oh, sure, yeah, good idea." He wasn't hungry in the slightest. The adrenaline in his system had all gone straight to his stomach and turned it sour.

"What kind of food? Italian?"

"Sure, yeah, fine, whatever. Italian's great."

"Haddy." She laid her hand on his arm, ducked her head down into his field of view. "Are you okay?"

"I'm fine. Just been a long day."

She looked skeptical.

"But you—you won. Congratulations. We should definitely celebrate." He tried to sound enthusiastic, but he could tell from the way her face fell that he'd been about as successful as a groundhog trying to walk like a Loonie.

Then, suddenly, she was holding his face in her hands, looking into his eyes, her eyes brimming with tears.

"I miss them too, you know," she whispered.

"Yeah," he said. "I know."

HADDY LAID AWAKE that night.

In Lunar gravity, and even in the quarter-g acceleration on the *Buchman* once he'd gotten used to it, he weighed so little that even a stone slab would have been comfortable. Mattresses were for the kind of high impact activities he hadn't yet added to his personal entertainment repertoire, and sheets were just for making your skin feel well-cared for and cozy as you drifted off into dreamland.

Here, even on the forgiving mattress of his new bedroom, everything felt hard and uncomfortable. Every time he closed his eyes and started to drift off, he felt as if he were falling off a cliff, and jolted awake in a panic. And despite his experience on Earth, some part of his brain was afraid that if he fell asleep under this much gravity, his diaphragm would stop working and he'd suffocate in his sleep.

He didn't see how people could keep on day after day, when each day was worse than the next. First it was Mom. Then it was Ring Alpha. Then it was Uncle Amit. Now it was waiting around to be kidnapped, and not even being able to tell Charis about it, even though she was waiting around to be kidnapped too. She at least had the right to know. That seemed only fair.

But if he told her, and that made her do something that attracted attention, then it would be his fault. She, or he, or both, would wind up in an even worse position, and it would be because he couldn't keep his big mouth shut.

No, he couldn't tell her. He just had to work on trust. They had a good vibe going on, if he could keep getting close to her, he could relax some, because he'd know that if he ever shouted "RUN!" she'd run without stopping to ask why.

He wondered how Josie was doing. With him gone, and now Mom gone too, what must she think of everything? She must feel like the world was disappearing around her.

He'd give anything to have her curled up in the small of his back right now. Just thinking about her made him cry. Missing her was more real to him than his mother's death. With his mother, he simply couldn't imagine a world without her in it, even now. He hadn't seen the empty apartment, or dust collecting on her desk at work.

But Josie?

He'd left her himself. He'd said goodbye. He had a picture in his head of what the world was like with her stranded at home and him all the way out here in the cold-and-dark, tens of megameters from anywhere.

HADDY WOKE UP at 0900 to find he had the day to himself. Charis left a note telling him she'd re-arranged her work schedule so that she could work a few full days a week and have the rest of the time free, which didn't help Haddy at all.

He poked his head out the door in hopes of finding a chalk mark on the lintel across the hall, but didn't have any luck on that score. He officially had a day in which he had absolutely nothing to do and nobody to do it with.

Well, that wasn't quite true. He could get some break-fast and then sit down and figure out how much it was going to cost him to go home on a high-boost ship, and how long it would take him. Charis might not be willing to leave until...what was she waiting for, any way? She said it was a rendezvous, but her mother was dead and one of her fathers was dead and her other father and her brother were back on Luna...

Haddy, you idiot, she thinks Aunt Min is still alive.

Of course she did. In the absence of any other evidence, Haddy would think the same thing about his mother. But that didn't mean waiting around here was a productive thing to do.

No, if what she said about the zero-day exploit was true, they needed to find it.

Fine, but breakfast first.

Breakfast was coffee, two fresh tangerines, a steak he found in the freezer, and five eggs. He scrambled the eggs and made them into a topping for the steak—it was a technique he learned from his mother, a fact he didn't think of until he was two bites in and found himself thinking that mom always remembered the garlic and that made the meal into something grand, at which point he decided he didn't want to eat and left the plate on the fold-out table in the living room.

He looked up ticket prices for ships heading back to Luna in the next couple of weeks, and lost whatever was left of his appetite. He'd known fast-ships were expensive, but he didn't realize they'd take everything he'd made on the deal with Mannix Spaceways (and then some). He'd thought mass driver and nuclear pulse were the two most economical engine designs in the solar system. They were *better*, not just because they were faster, but because they were cheaper than anything else.

Well, okay, not cheaper than solar sails or ion drives, but you couldn't push humans around the system in those. They had top speeds fast enough to let probes do fly-bys of Proxima, but they took *months* just to get up to speed. So cargo, sure, but not people. People traveled by chemical rocket, ITN, mass driver, or nuclear torch.

The new engines *were* cheaper to operate than chemical rockets, but they were also comparatively rare. Anyone with a couple hundred thousand bucks to spare could get themselves a second-hand ITN ship with chemical rockets in good working order. Okay, so it wasn't exactly the price of a cup of coffee, but it was the kind of price a small businessperson could afford to pay cash for if he was patient and frugal.

But the new engines were in *high* demand. They didn't cost anything to run, but they sold new for whatever the traffic would bear—and when the traffic included every corporation and government that had any prayer of running operations outside of low-earth orbit, the traffic would bear quite a lot.

Charis had a ship, though: The *Rising*. And she *was* a torch ship. Well, Charis's family had retrofitted a torch onto it anyway. It had originally been a heavy-water ship, using a fission reactor to generate power to split water into chemical fuel on the fly, and using steam jets for fine thrust. Economical for a family yacht, all you had to do was load her up with a bunch of ice every few thousand operational hours and she'd run more-or-less forever.

But now it was a torch ship, and it could push at full g all the way across the solar system.

He just had to figure out how to convince her to take him back to Luna.

ALL KINDS OF TROUBLE

WITH CHARIS TALKING politics in the evenings, and the time he'd spent on the *Buchman* with Malcolm and Sil, Haddy felt as if he'd been thrown into a swimming pool before he really understood what water was. He was tired of feeling that way, and, finding himself at loose ends, he decided to do something about it.

He also didn't want to go back and practice paintball until his bruises healed.

As far as flying was concerned, Charis's boss was printing out parts and pieces—unassembled—during times when the bar didn't need its printer for creating unusual tableware, ingredients, or replacement parts for furniture and equipment that got broken in the occasional brawl.

Or bombing.

Haddy still couldn't believe the place had been bombed just a few weeks ago. He made a note to ask Charis about how they'd managed to get the place fixed up and open for business so fast. That kind of logistics savvy might come in handy some day.

But for whatever reason, the orn-suits that should have taken between six hours and two days each to print out (depending on what model printer they were using) were going to take a week, and then Haddy would have to assemble them by hand instead of getting them all completed straight from the finishing stage.

He wasn't about to let the time go to waste. If he was stuck in this war whether he wanted to be or not, Haddy was determined to understand what was going on, somehow. While Charis worked, he holed up and read everything he could get his hands on.

It wasn't as easy as he thought it would be. The net was filled with articles and guides-to-the-conflict and news reports and commentaries and infographics of every kind, all of them trying to convince him of something—that the Americans were monsters (which he would have readily believed if he hadn't been to Reno himself, or dealt with tourists his whole life), that the Loonies were endangering the fabric of human civilization (which he wouldn't have believed, ever, since he'd been a Loonie his entire life and he knew for a fact that Luna City was the most civilized place in the solar system), that the Persians wanted to bend the entire universe to their will (which he didn't have any way to evaluate, but was inclined to disbelieve based on the similarity in tone between those articles and the articles pushing the first two points of view), that the Sigma Five research complex near Luna City was trying to put an end to humanity (which was something only a supernova could do), and that the recent events were evidence that God was preparing the world for the final judgment and the end of the universe (which Haddy had no mental categories for even thinking about)—but none of them seemed to be interested in telling him what was really going on.

And every time a new news report came out—like the unconfirmed stories of a big fight at Gagarin—the same writers and reporters reworked their theories so that the new facts fit, which did not enhance their credibility, at least to Haddy's way of thinking.

After two days of slogging through the net, he knew less than he had when he started. He didn't even know where to begin to evaluate it all. All he really had to work from was what he'd heard in the Bazaar, and what he'd heard from his parents.

The chatter in the Bazaar had been mostly about taxes and arguments about legal this and constitutional that, and the chatter always got loudest when there had been something going on with the port or when someone's assets were seized because they got caught up on the bad end of some Terran AI's data mining agenda.

It probably wasn't a coincidence that those were the times when tourist traffic slowed to a crawl and business dried up, though Haddy hadn't noticed the correlation before.

And his parents? Well, that was where he'd learned about how wars were conducted. Cities got destroyed, people died, got raped and tortured, civilians got targeted, killer robots ran amok, and people who were in the way got sent to relocation camps and death camps. *Wars are a side-effect of politics*, they told him. *They're used to settle arguments, but in wars it doesn't matter who's right, all that matters is who wins.*

According to them, the only way to survive a war was to stay out of it. They'd taught him about Switzerland, and how that small country had managed to prosper while the world burnt down around them time and again over the centuries, because they refused to take sides.

It's smart business, his mother told him during one of his lessons, *when people are fighting, you sell them equipment and medical supplies and food. You become valuable to both sides, your family prospers, and nobody can afford to put you in the middle of the fight.*

Except that he *was* in the middle of the fight. Luna City wasn't neutral. Luna City had been attacked. His home town—his own family—had been smashed by the American war machine.

More than that, he *personally* was a target. Now that he knew about the zero-day exploit, he had some inkling of why he might make a valuable target—but by that same logic, Charis was a *much* more valuable target.

And she was working for the very people that were hunting her mother.

Or maybe, who had taken her mother.

Haddy swore to himself.

He had to tell her. He *had* to.

He'd promised not to, to keep her safe, but he could tell her anyway.

Yes. He could tell her, and convince her to just jump station with him and head back for Luna City. It wasn't like the Americans could stop her...could they?

What if they locked her ship down? What if they saw her acting strangely and kept her from coming home from work one evening?

How could he and Charis *possibly* get around that? Nineveh wasn't just a colony. It was a *space station*. On Luna, if the worst came to the worst, he could get a pressure suit and escape out an airlock—or take a welding torch, cut a hole in a wall and go outside, and hike to another building, or another colony, or a ship that was standing free on the surface. Even if one person had control of all the colony's computer systems, Haddy would still give himself (or any other native Loonie) even odds of being able to get a few kilometers head start on any search party.

But on a space station, there was nowhere to go unless

you got onto a ship. And while you couldn't prevent ships from taking off from a planetary base—on Luna City you couldn't even shoot them down—on a space station, all ships were anchored to the station with electromagnetic docking clamps. Even if you got onto a ship to make an escape, that didn't mean you could take off without ripping your hull to pieces.

Aside from research that seemed to lead nowhere, and occasional exploratory expeditions to get the feel of the station or find something to eat, Haddy looked for solace in a call home. He wanted to see Josie, and talk to his Dad, and hear more about Mom, and how everyone was coping, and what was really happening back there.

It took several tries before he found his father near enough to a screen to assent to a brief hello-how-are-you. But despite Haddy's hopes, Vin's demeanor was cagey and absent-minded. He kept the conversation to business, and how it hadn't picked up again since the Battle of Grissom, which is what the news was calling it now. Vin insisted on calling it "the riots" rather than "the attack" or "the battle" or "the war." Haddy couldn't understand why, but he didn't press. The lines of pain had already settled into his father's face like chatter-marks on a cavern wall. Vin clearly didn't want to talk about anything that might hurt.

"Dad," he said when his father was about to pass him off to Ulmar, "You said you'd have a message for me when I got here."

"Charis found you, didn't she?"

"Yes."

"Well, then, sit tight. I'll call you when it's safe to come home."

Like hell I will, Haddy thought. But he nodded like an

obedient son, then said hi to Ulmar and to Josie before signing off, swearing to himself that he was going to find some way home, even if he had to steal a ship and brave enemy fire to do it.

THE THIRD NIGHT, he prevailed up on Charis to go out for a walk after she stumbled in from work at 0300. After half a week of being cooped up in the apartment, Haddy wanted to get out and fly. But, since he didn't have any wings available yet, he needed *some* kind of exercise.

She took him walking—he suggested a park, and she told him there was one just nearby. They rode up a few levels to the greenbelt, and she led him into an area of hills and dense trees. Being the wee hours, the ambient light in the greenbelt was dimmed down to a pale wan glow as one might expect during a full moon in the Nevada desert.

Haddy noted the sign as they entered the forest:

Allenston Park

In truth, it was less a forest than it was a grove. Hazelnut and almond trees planted in a chaotic pattern gave the impression of well-kept forest. But like everything on Nineveh, whether it was obvious or not, the space did double or triple duty or more—in this case as a farm, a pleasure space, a piece of the sewage treatment system, a link in the atmosphere recycling chain, and those were just the obvious functions it served.

Charis didn't have a lot of oomph in her tonight—like it had when he'd first arrived on the station, exhaustion seemed etched deeply into her features—and she announced, after half an hour, that she was going home. Haddy decided to stay. He had a lot of thinking to do, and he thought better when he was moving than when he was sitting still.

He followed the trail through the forest and out again onto the edge of a lake, and around the lake on the running trail.

One thing kept circling in his mind didn't make sense to him: If the family had a standing protocol to regroup at Nineveh, then why had they gone to Luna City?

Charis had said: *Pop thought Mom might be on Luna.*

But that didn't seem right. If Min was on Luna, why wouldn't she call them or drop them a message? It wasn't as if it was difficult to find an open public terminal or borrow someone's PPD or pick up your own for the price of a meal.

"Excuse me," said a man's voice from a bench beside the trail. He sounded Russian. Haddy couldn't make out much more than a dim shape in the gloom. "Do you have a lighter on you?"

"Sorry," Haddy said as he walked past. "Don't smoke."

"Too bad," the man said.

Haddy heard something move behind him.

"Stop there," the man said. "Don't move."

Haddy stopped, out of reflex more than anything. He started to turn around saying:

"What do you..."

"Do not turn around." The man's voice injected ice straight into Haddy's veins. "I have gun here, is pointed at your back. I will shoot you unless you do exactly as I say. Tell me you understand."

Haddy understood, despite the almost unintelligibly thick Muscovite vowels, and he said so.

"Good. Take off your clothes. All of them."

"My...what?"

"Take them off now. I will not ask again."

Haddy wished he had some kind of weapon, or even a PPD, that he could throw at the man to distract him. If he could get just a second or two, he could close the distance and punch him in the face.

At least, he could if his hands would stop shaking. He couldn't even make his fingers work well enough to undo his shoelaces.

"Come on, come on, hurry up."

"I'm doing my best," Haddy hissed.

He managed to get one of his lace-ends caught between both palms, and he pulled it, and then was able to get his trembling fingers into the loosened knot and get his high-top sneaker loose enough to kick off. Then he set to work on the other one. With those off, he took his pants down, then peeled his shirt off, and stood scrawny and naked in the dark simulated night.

A cold night, too. The irregular breeze chilled him straight through.

"Throw it all in the lake."

Haddy complied.

"Get on your knees," the Russian voice said.

Haddy had seen scenes like this in movies. The next thing that happened was a bullet to the back of his head. He was going to die right here.

He *couldn't* die here. He had to get back home. He had to see Josie again. He had to do something to help his father.

He had to say something. A magic phrase, anything that might make this maniac decide not to kill him.

"P...p...p...please, look, sir, I'll do whatever you..."

Haddy didn't get to finish that sentence. Something cracked across the back of his skull, driving him down to his knees.

Then it cracked again, and he was face first on the dry clay path.

The blows came fast after that. Haddy's whole world exploded one impact at a time. His face, his ribs, his legs, his stomach. The beating continued until long after he passed out.

"HADDY," A SHARP whisper penetrated his consciousness like a fork stabbing through raw flesh.

He groaned.

There were hands on him. In tender places where his flesh puffed. One on his shoulder. One on his hip. They were rocking him.

It wasn't bright yet. Everything was perfectly dark behind his eyes. Nineveh hadn't yet seen fit to simulate dawn for the benefit of the plants in the green belt.

"Haddy, wake up."

Everything hurt. Even his ears hurt.

He couldn't breathe without his mouth open.

He was naked, curled into a ball, laying on the path in the same place he'd been last time he remembered anything.

And someone was still shaking him.

Haddy tried to say "stop" but it just came out in a grunty-groan.

His fingers searched for his throbbing nose, and found a mass of crusty, tacky, boogery blood.

He grunted again. This time "Stop" did come out, barely.

"Shh. Keep quiet." It was Sil's voice. "Who was that?"

"Who? What? What are you doing here?"

"Come on." Her hands closed over his forearm. She hauled at him, her fingers digging into the pulped flesh, making him cry out.

He tried to pull away, but her fingers were like iron pincers. The end result of his pulling was to haul himself against her counterweight until he was standing.

His head was swimming like koi in a fountain. He had to swallow hard against the gorge rising in his throat.

"Shh. Shh. Stay still. Wait till you get your balance. Are you okay?"

He wasn't, but he didn't want to talk. He was afraid if he opened his mouth his dinner would come out. He shook his head instead.

"Here," She slung his arm over her shoulders and half-carried him over to the bench. "The cameras went out. I got here quick as I could."

"Huh?"

"I said we were watching," she heaved as she set him down. "'What happened?'"

She started running her fingers through his hair.

Haddy told her what happened, as best he remembered it. He spoke in fits and starts, because every time she found a bump on his head he had to control his urge to scream.

As he spoke, she finished checking his head and moved on to the rest of his body, going over it in surgical detail.

"That's...that's all I know. Why..."

"It's a warning," she said.

"For me?"

She shook her head. "For me. Me and Malcolm. They know we're watching." She looked up from inspecting his wounds. "They're letting us know they can get to you."

"I don't think I want to play anymore," he groaned.

She kissed him, then looked in his eyes. "Neither do I, baby, neither do I. But the game's bigger than that, and we don't have a choice. So I'm going to find out what happened, okay? You need to get to a scanner and get patched up. I'll leave you a mark when I've got some answers. You just stay low and stay quiet, okay? Keep your door locked unless you're using it. Don't go anywhere there aren't a lot of people around. Understand?"

Having her that close to his face made his vision swim. He couldn't focus that close.

Haddy choked down another load of bile. He managed a nod.

"Yeah. Yeah, I got it."

"Okay." She smiled, patted his cheek, and then flinched when he winced. "Sorry. Here."

She put her arms around him, under his arms, and hauled him back to his feet. This time, he managed to stay standing without help, though it took some effort.

"Now, get home as quick as you can."

Haddy didn't have any clothes.

"Um..." he looked down at himself, cupped his right hand over his genitals. "I can't go home like *this*." He didn't know what the rules about nudity were here, but he was given to understand that, at some of the more backward ports in the solar system, they were positively draconian. Some places even threw people in jail just for taking off their clothes, or put them on lists that kept them from ever getting a job, at least according to some of the rumors he'd heard.

"They took your clothes..."

"No..." That didn't sound right. Haddy tried to remember what had happened before all the hurting started. "He...he...he made me throw them away. The lake. They're in the lake."

"Stay here. I'll find them." She faded away. The lake was only a few meters across the path, but by the time she got there he could barely make her out—a swimming blue shadow against the deeper blue shadows of the surroundings. The only illumination came from the lights from the upstation apartments and the vertical farms, and the merest pale glow from the light pipes. He could see scattered reflections shimmering on the water as she waded in.

"Did you see who it was?" She was still whispering. Somehow it carried to him in the still night.

"No, no. It was dark. He was Russian, though. I could tell from his voice."

He tottered across the path on ginger feet.

"Found 'em," she said. She met him at the edge of the path with the sopping bundle in her arms. "Reach your arms out."

He did. He was rewarded with a soaked, dingy, cold and heavy cloth tube getting shoved around them and then yanked down over his torso.

It smelled foul. He was going to have to shower when he got home. And use a lot of disinfectant.

Sil squatted in front of him and fumbled with more wet-sounding fabric. "Okay, right leg. Step."

Haddy put his right hand on her shoulder to steady himself, and stepped in with his right, then with his left.

The wet-and-cold slithered up his legs like an enormous slug. He shuddered when the clammy fabric touched his scrotum, and had to resist the urge to scream and wriggle away in revulsion.

"Now the shoes."

"I'll carry them." He didn't think he could cope with the extra ick of walking home on squishy feet.

"Okay." Sil handed Haddy his shoes. Then she took his face in her hands. "You be careful, okay? I don't want to lose you."

She kissed him like she was afraid she'd never see him again. By the time she was done, Haddy didn't know whether he was dizzy from the beating or the way she made his heart beat.

"Now, get home quick."

"You're not coming?"

"I can't be seen with you. Now go."

She slipped away into the dark before he could grab on to her, leaving him alone, cold, and wet, with nothing else to do but follow instructions.

And hurt. He did a lot of hurting during the long stumble home.

A longer stumble than Haddy expected, too. As he was leaving Allenston Park, his foot caught on something soft, sending him down again where the ground hit him in all the places that hurt.

When he regained his footing and investigated, his throat nearly closed up.

He'd tripped over something sticking out of a bush.

A foot.

Attached to a smooth, feminine leg.

Haddy dove into the bushes next to the path. Beneath, he found a woman's nude body sprawled on the ground, bleeding from a beating at least as bad as the one he'd taken.

Even before he turned her over, the chopstick in her hairdo left little doubt in his mind about who it was.

Charis.

THE PRICE OF A CIDER

CHARIS WAS BEAT up pretty badly. Like Haddy, her clothes had been wadded up and thrown a few yards away, and Haddy had found them while Charis was finding her feet. She looked none-too-steady when they started off walking.

But about halfway home it had become clear that, of the two of them, Haddy was having more trouble walking. He didn't put up much of a fight when she peeled off his rancid-smelling clothes and insisted that he submit to the scanner first.

Which meant he had to stand up and stand still, which he could only do with the help of a friendly wall.

After running her PPD around his head, she said:

"You've got a concussion," she said. "No fracturing though. Your pupils are even. No sign of serious brain damage. How do you feel? Nausea?"

"Yeah, don't need any more, thanks," Haddy groaned.

She continued down his body with the scanner. "No internal bleeding in the body cavity...a cracked rib...no, make that two...not serious enough to need repair work. You're going to be fine after you get some sleep."

Haddy didn't have enough bravado to come up with a clever rejoinder. He was too busy trying to keep the icepicks in his eyes from etching spirals into his brain.

The sick stone in his stomach suddenly felt lighter, and a rush of hot saliva came into his mouth. Haddy let go the wall and tore through the air with flailing arms, reaching the toilet just in time.

When he was done with the vomiting and coughing, the momentary euphoria of relief lasted just long enough to let him get back on his feet. As soon as he was at full height, his temples started pounding. It felt as if two people in cleats were kicking him in the side of the head in time with his pulse.

Charis was suddenly under his left arm, keeping him upright, leading him into the sitting room.

"Take a minute," she said through gritted teeth, sitting him down on the sofa. "Let your equilibrium settle, then do me."

Haddy didn't think he could focus on the screen well enough to do the job, but despite her brave front she wasn't doing much better than him.

She left him for a moment. Haddy didn't much pay attention. When she returned she said:

"Here, might as well get fluid samples while we're at it." She dabbed a swab at his lips, then a different one at an open wound on his chest. Haddy knew the drill. Blood and saliva—she'd swab them across the sensor, one at a time, on the back of her PPD, and it would take a spectrogram, and in a few minutes it would tell him if he had any exotic diseases or chemicals in his system. Like almost everybody else in the world, he didn't really care how it worked or what it did, as long as it told him what was wrong and how to fix it.

After a few minutes, he had enough equilibrium to make a go at scanning her. He helped her peel down and then got to work with the PPD. He started with the blood and saliva samples, since they took a while to process, then got on with the scanning. He'd done this before, just never to a whole body. Then again, nobody he'd ever had to scan had been knocked to the ground and kicked into unconsciousness before.

Ultrasound, terrahertz, ambient radiation, infra-red—if the human body emitted it or responded to it, the PPD picked it up and analyzed it and correlated the readings with the sum of current human medical knowledge to return a diagnosis, prognosis, and schedule of treatment. If the illness or injuries were severe, it would recommend treatment at a medical facility. Otherwise, it prescribed whatever medication or treatment device might be appropriate, sent that information to the household printer, and—metaphorically—sent the sick child to bed to let his or her body heal up.

It turned out she actually was in worse shape than he was. She'd gotten a hairline fracture in her left ulna, right under a hell of a cut where her skin had split open as if she'd used it to deflect a blow. That would require a matrix injection to stabilize the bone and make it knit faster. She wasn't bleeding internally, but she did have a concussion from a crack on the back of her skull. Her eyes weren't tracking right. She said it was because she was dizzy.

But she wasn't throwing up, and she wasn't acting like she had a migraine, so it must not have been as bad as his.

The cuts on her body were mostly superficial, but there were a *lot* of them. Like him, she'd been kicked repeatedly, and had bruises flowering all over her, though she didn't have any cracked ribs.

It was as if they'd been beaten by the same person, following the same script. Haddy had heard of serial killers—was there such a thing as a serial kicker? Where would the CIA find someone like that? Did they have their own affinity groups?

The PPD dinged in his hand. He handed it to Charis, on the grounds that he couldn't read the small print below the "fluids test" headline.

"Well, that's comforting," Charis said.

"What?"

"Check me for needle marks. Whoever did this didn't beat us unconscious," she said. "They drugged us."

NEITHER HADDY NOR Charis left the apartment for two full days. At first, it was mostly sleep, or at least, an attempt to sleep. Truth to tell, they were both so frightened that, even though they had to fight to stay upright, neither could quite surrender to the blackness enough to fall asleep.

Eventually, they huddled together in Charis's room, each holding knives from the kitchen. Haddy took the side of the bed nearest the door, on the grounds that he still wasn't sure whether his stomach was going to stage another full-scale revolt, and he wanted to be able to dash for the bathroom if it did.

Once they were in the same bed, however, sleep found them both quickly. A company of Marines could have stormed the front door and neither would have noticed.

The nausea passed for Haddy after a couple long naps. After that, recovery consisted mostly of curling up on the couch with Charis and watching movies.

They didn't talk much about what happened, at least, not at first. It seemed to Haddy that they had made a silent bargain with one another: if they didn't talk about what happened, it might not happen again.

It might work, Haddy told himself. *Besides, even if it doesn't, at least neither of us have to go through this alone.*

He had to admit, if he had to pick anybody to be with

while the world was falling apart back home, it would be Charis. It wasn't just that she was smart and strong and a good flyer and easy to talk to and easy to look at, she also understood...well, everything. He felt like, for the first time in his life, someone really *knew* a secret part of him that he hadn't been quite aware of himself.

And she was so, so, wonderfully comfortable to snuggle up with. Maybe even better than Josie.

CHARIS WAS EXPECTED back at work on the third day. The bruises on her face had faded from deep purple to yellow-green, making her look like something out of a horror movie, at least until she put some concealer on.

Station security hadn't been able to help. Of course they hadn't, because they didn't know the first thing about what was going on right under their own noses. The cameras in the Allenston sector had gone dead on the evening of the attack, as had several on the paths leading into the area. There was simply no way to tell who had gone in and out, and who might have perpetrated the attack. However, the officer who took the report was happy to hear that nobody had been permanently damaged, and said he would like to make up for the difficulty by offering some vouchers for printer feedstocks and meals, as they would doubtless come in handy while Haddy and Charis recovered.

Charis refused, but Haddy accepted them with bad grace. If security was going to be useless, he figured, they ought to at least pay for the privilege.

CHARIS LEFT FOR work at 1030 on Thursday morning—she was on the lunch and dinner shift today. Haddy saw her to the door, hugged her goodbye. She kissed him on the cheek—just a normal warm goodbye, but it made Haddy warm all over—and held his arm with her hand for a lingering moment.

He didn't want her to go any more than she seemed to want to leave.

But the real world lived outside their door, and it wasn't going anywhere. Haddy had the terrible feeling that hiding from it longer than they had to would just make things worse when they finally stopped hiding.

Charis's hand, at long last, slipped away.

Haddy's eyes followed her as she left. He had to go out himself, today. He needed to appear, in person, at the Chamber of Commerce in order to get a tax account for his business.

He would, after all, have to kick in for his half of the rent, and he couldn't live off his savings forever. Charis had offered to get him a job at Phalanx, but he had demurred. He wasn't used to working for other people, and didn't think he'd like it. He also didn't like dealing with entitled customers, and from what he understood, restaurant customers were about as entitled as it got outside of a brothel. And he didn't think it would be a good idea for them *both* to be working for the enemy—as it was now, if something happened to Charis, at least Haddy might be able to rescue her. If he was working there, too, that probably wouldn't be possible.

No. He needed to put together the flying franchise.

He faded back into the apartment and spent fifteen minutes trying to figure out which of his sets of clothes would be less offensive to the bureaucrats. He'd washed everything the previous night, so that wasn't a problem. It's just that, working as he did at a storefront in Luna City, he had about as many sets of formal clothes as did a deck hand on an Ensenada trawler.

It didn't occur to him to buy a new set of clothes on the way, so, in the end, he figured the loose green t-shirt and gray BDUs would be marginally less offensive than the orange lycra or the pink shorts.

Haddy found some shoes and headed out himself. Out of habit, he looked at the neighbor's lintel across the way.

There was something there. Just the slightest, lightest stroke of white chalk on the granite-gray. Haddy only spotted it because he'd gotten into the habit of checking for it every time he walked through the door, or by the door, or stuck his head out the door in order to make sure the door across the hall was still there and chalk-mark-free.

He'd memorized that lintel, every dust speck and paint fleck. The minuscule change leapt out at him like a neon sign.

Seeing it lifted Haddy's spirits. Not that he was desperate to return to Allenston Park, but knowing that Sil and Malcolm had something for him gave him hope that he might get to be more than a pawn in this damned spy game.

Haddy took his PPD off his belt and looked at it. 1045.

How long had the mark been there? Did they just put it there last night? The night before? Or just this morning? Haddy had no way to know.

Sil hadn't said anything about what would happen if he missed a rendezvous. It hadn't occurred to him to ask, because he'd never done anything secret before, not really. Private, sure, but not secret.

So was he supposed to go up to the park today?

If I were Sil, he reasoned, *if someone missed a secret meeting, and I didn't want there to be any confusion, I'd take the chalk mark down. I would only leave it up if I wanted to keep trying.*

He had just enough time to make it.

ALLENSTON PARK LOOKED different during the day. The other night it had seemed eerie, with the kind of air that made you feel like the you were standing on the precipice of a change that would ripple out and shake the whole universe.

This morning, it just looked like a little stand of trees. It would have looked quaint, almost pathetic, if Haddy had come from a place that actually had trees. Since he didn't, it still looked impressive, just not *as* impressive as it had in the dark. In the daylight, it even looked as if it wasn't the kind of place where you might get stripped and beaten half-to-death for no reason at all.

While Sil had said "the coffee stand in Allenston Park," she hadn't said *where* the coffee stand was. Haddy had assumed that it would be somewhere obvious, like by the entrance, and she would just be standing around there waiting for him.

It was only when he got there that he realized how stupid an assumption that was. Of course she wouldn't just hang around. She would look like she was there for a reason, like everyone else. Taking a walk, reading a book, having a picnic, or whatever people did near coffee stands in parks—Haddy didn't have a lot of experience with parks, so he was really just guessing.

Still, he tried to look like he was there going about his business, just like everybody else. He decided that his business was a stroll. He just had to brazen out his impulse to flinch every time there was a tree too near the path.

Where someone could be hiding.

There were security people here. He passed two of

them as he was walking. Maybe they always patrolled like this. Maybe they'd started because of the report he'd filed. He didn't know why, but the sight of them made him uneasy.

Halfway between the start of the trees and the point at which the path left them behind, there was a coffee stand, but no Sil.

As he approached, figuring to buy a drink, he saw a clearing in the forest off the path, behind the stand. There was a woman there, laying on a towel and reading a book. Her hair fell in an A-line instead of the longer style she'd worn since he met her, and she was dressed in navel-high shorts and a button-up shirt knotted beneath her breasts, but she was, unmistakably, Sil. Perhaps it was because she was the first person he'd ever kissed, but whatever the reason, the lines of her body were cut into his mind like the Ichi scar lines on a Nri Nigerian's forehead.

Haddy left the path, made his way between the trees to the grassy clearing, sat down next to Sil with a groan.

"Next time, stand nearby and light a cigarette, and don't look at me when we talk." She said it without looking at him.

So, that's the kind of meeting it's going to be?

"Sorry, I'm kind of new to this," Haddy growled. He'd been hoping for some kind of news. Some kind of answers. A kiss and a smile, or at least some kind of reassurance.

"Well, learn faster. All of our lives depend on it."

"Yeah, well, I'll try to work on that in between beatings."

"Relax, babe," she said with her voice all smiles, "relax. I got the guy who mugged you."

"You got him?" A flush of relief pushed through Haddy, but it was chased up by a sick feeling in his guts as he realized that Malcolm and Sil weren't cops, so *got him* might mean something terrible. "You didn't...um..."

She laughed. "No, we didn't kill him. We just know who he is, and we're keeping an eye on him."

"So who is he?"

"Oh, he's one of them."

"Them? Like *them* them? Phalanx them?"

"Yes."

That meant Charis was working alongside the man who beat her.

"I'm getting her out of there." Haddy kicked his legs and rolled forward to stand, but before he could get all the way up Sil grabbed his arm and yanked him down.

"Shut up and sit down. You're going to get her killed. We've got something else for you."

Haddy turned and glared straight at Sil. "Forget it."

She took off her sunglasses. Her deep browns with their pin-prick pupils looked at him as if they could squash him all on their own.

Haddy blanched.

"Good," she said. "Now, if you're done acting like a child, we have work to do."

Haddy felt as if she'd pulled the plug on him, and he'd deflated all at once. Sil knew him. She trusted him. He trusted her. *Acting like a child.* How could she even *think* something like that?

She must have seen his jaw set as resentment settled over him, because she said:

"Well, then, what would you call it? If you storm in there, and create a scene, you're just going to tip them off. If you want to win this game, you have to be subtler. Sneakier. You have to out-think them. They don't respond to righteous indignation, because they're playing a long

game, sweetheart. They're worried about *winning*, not about who's right."

A chill shot up Haddy's arms.

In wars it doesn't matter who's right, all that matters is who wins.

That's what his mother had said.

"So this really is war," he muttered.

"Yes," she said. "And we have to win our little corner of it."

Haddy took a deep breath. "What do you want me to do?"

"There is a room behind the bar in Phalanx. I need you to plant a listening device in it."

"Oh, and how am I going to do that?"

She smirked, and shrugged, as if the rest was his problem. Then she slipped a thin paperback from under her body and slid it across her towel until it was within his reach.

"This is the part where you go home now."

"Home. Right." Haddy reached for the paperback.

Sil laid her hand on his.

"We have to be bold, but cautious." She said it in a husky voice that melted the last of his resentment. She stroked the back of his hand. "I know it's hard."

She was right. It was. Haddy found himself struggling to catch his breath, and shifting his posture to maintain his modesty.

"It's not fair, but it's the game we're in."

Haddy nodded absently. Her touch had leeched all his anger away, leaving a void of need he didn't have the words to describe.

"I guess I'd better get on with it then."

DESPITE HAVING GROWN up with the expectation that public spaces could be monitored at will with cameras, microphones, and sniffers, the thought of actually *planting* a bug in someone's private space made Haddy feel dirty.

Even an enemy's private space.

He didn't like carrying the bug either. As long as he had it on him, he didn't have any private space. Sure it was only Sil and Malcolm listening at the other end, but that wasn't the point.

He left it on a table in the waiting room when he went to see the Chamber of Commerce representative. It didn't take long to get his tax certificate, but then he made the mistake about asking whether it would be possible to rent spaces on one of the high catwalks to set up his booth.

Then, suddenly, the man on the other side of the counter went from congenial and efficient to probing and cautious. It seemed that business was very welcome on Nineveh, but new-and-different ways to use the real estate...weren't. It took a good part of the afternoon to explain about the kind of business he intended to open up.

"So you're telling me that because the station has effectively zero gravity, people can fly out there." The scrawny functionary behind the counter had a sallow, pinched look, as if the entire world smelled like a particularly noxious fart. His voice sounded like he'd lost a fleet of rubber stoppers up his nose.

"Yes." Haddy walked him through the physics again, resisting the temptation to point out that the station didn't have gravity, it had spin. There was no "effective" about it—the airspace *was* gravity-free.

"And what happens if one of these flyers gets too close

to the ground?"

"Too close?"

"Crashes into it."

"Well, I suppose it would depend on the difference in speed. If they were flying spinwards, well, as long as they matched speed they could land as light as a soft hat."

"And if they were going counterspin?"

Haddy made a sour face. "I don't see how anyone could survive that. The speed that hull spins at...messy's the word, I think."

"I see. And how will you prevent that?"

Haddy shrugged. "I never let anyone fly alone first time out. I keep tandem hooks on me in case something goes wrong. All my instructors are experts, and they practice their emergency hook-ins."

"And when you can't prevent them from doing wrong?"

Haddy shrugged. Tourists who were too stupid not to crash, crashed. That was their prerogative. But he sensed that wouldn't be a good thing to say aloud.

"I'll have a release for them to sign. And I would keep them away from the parks," Haddy explained about how ceilings and hard decks worked, and how they were enforced in Luna City.

When Haddy finished, the functionary mulled the information and shook his head. "You're going to need insurance," the functionary said. "Good insurance with low deductibles and high limits."

"I wouldn't dream of doing business without it." Haddy could feel his wallet convulsing in pain as he said it.

"There are some other concerns, too..." and the functionary launched into a lecture that just about made

Haddy lose all hope that the future of the universe contained anything but rules and roadblocks.

THE BUGGED BOOK, his tax certificate, and a twelve-kilometer-long to-do list in hand, Haddy found a lift and descended from the lighter levels where the station offices were to the heavier levels where all the commerce happened.

One of the things that the functionary had said in the meeting got him thinking:

New recreational activities are difficult to evaluate. We might not be able to issue you a permit.

Well, new recreational activities might be difficult to evaluate, but *old* recreational activities weren't. After all, if orn-suit flying became an established thing on Nineveh, even as a guerrilla activity, then the station government would *have* to do something to provide space for it sooner or later. That was how things had worked in Luna City.

Maybe he shouldn't worry about the franchise just yet. Maybe he should just sell suits. The zero-g rigs he'd sold to Mannix folded up on demand. It wouldn't take a lot of work to tweak the design a little more, and make them easy to conceal under a coat.

Haddy could sell the rigs retail—which didn't require any kind of special permit—and let the public do his work for him. He could even market them for their utility function in free fall, and then occasionally fly around himself to help people get the idea that the center of the station was the biggest pressurized free fall area in the whole solar system.

By the time he reached Phalanx, he was positively humming with delight over his plan. Sil had said subtle and sneaky was the way to win the war, but the advice went double or triple for starting a business that nobody knew what to do with.

He went inside and strode up to the bar as if he belonged there. Even if he didn't, there was hardly anyone else around. A few poker players around a table in one corner, a family nibbling on onion rings and potato skins in a booth near the door, and a bored waiter walking around checking to make sure everybody was doing okay. Haddy figured it was the wrong time of day for a big crowd—too late for lunch, too early for dinner, and way too early for the hardcore drinkers.

The barkeep was big, and a bona fide Nri, complete with Ichi scarring on his coffee-black forehead. Haddy knew the look from Luna City, and he'd seen a lot of Nigerians around Nineveh, but hadn't realized there were enough Nri that had escaped the tribal genocide that they were all the way out here, too.

"You coming in here young'n, sid?" He had one of those deep, rich voices that Haddy always liked hearing in movies, even though he could barely understand the dialect. It was some new pidgin Haddy hadn't heard before, not a typical Nri accent. "Whiskey not quite so good less'n you wanting the new livers early."

Haddy shook his head. "I just want cider."

"Oh, sid sid, yes, we can go and do dat. We go get 'em for pear, peach, cherry, plum, apple."

"Plum? I guess." Haddy had only ever had apple cider. It was a family specialty. He'd never tasted a plum before, but he'd heard good things. "How much?"

The barkeep reached under the bar and produced an icy pint glass in his left hand, a tap-hose in his right, and filled the to the top glass with a sparkling light amber-green liquid. He set it on the bar and said, "Twelve and thirty."

"*Dollars?*" Twelve dollars and thirty cents for a glass of cider was the kind of price even the most audacious Luna City merchant wouldn't dream of asking for.

"Sid sid. We make 'em right on site. Not cheap with the orchard spaces." The barkeep pointed up in the general direction of the greenbelt.

Haddy swore, then pulled his credit jack out and handed it over. "Well, I hope it's good."

It was. It tasted like someone had bottled that feeling Haddy got from pulling a swoop out of a hard dive straight down to the bottom of the Gallery, with only a few centimeters to spare. Light and giddy and sour and sweet and sparkly all at once.

"Excuse me?" Haddy said to the bartender.

"Sid sid?" The Nigerian looked up from the till where he was poised to dock payment from Haddy's jack.

"I was wondering, is Charis in? The waitress?"

The Nigerian looked puzzled for a moment, then his face opened up as if he had just figured something out. "You the boy she be talking on all these days. Hadrian, yes?"

"Uh, yeah, that's me." He wasn't sure he liked that Charis was talking about him to her co-workers. But then, she didn't know her coworkers were working for the Americans and might know what happened to her mother.

"Mondu," the Nigerian extended his hand. "This is the place I run, here. Charis is a good girl, top skill smart-and-sharp. You be sure you treat her good, you okay?"

"Yeah, yeah, I know. She's great."

"Okay, good." Mondu handed Hadrian the credit jack back without swiping it. "Drinks are for free on family, okay, sid sid."

Haddy wasn't about to pass up a chance to not-spend twelve bucks and three cents. He took another drink, then asked again:

"Is Charis here?"

"Out on the errand, but not for soon she will be back in now."

"Okay, thanks." Haddy couldn't quite tell whether that meant she'd be back soon, or she wouldn't be back for a while.

It turned out to be the former. About four minutes later, Charis ran into the bar, spotted Haddy, made a beeline for him, and yanked him off his barstool. If he hadn't just finished draining his cider, he'd have wound up wearing it.

"Hey, hey, what's up?"

"Shut up," she said, "quick."

They cleared the entrance to Phalanx. She turned left and marched him toward the heart of the adult entertainment district. She kept mumbling to herself, but Haddy couldn't make it out.

"Charis," Haddy yanked his arm loose but kept pace with her. "What's the problem?"

"I saw him I saw him I knew it I *knew* it."

"What? Who?"

"You know how I told you that right before Mom disappeared, we were in the greenbelt on Sidon?"

"Yeah."

"Well, there was someone else there. Just a guy, walking around. Another tourist. It's the kind of thing we're supposed to watch for, but he just blended in. I only remember him because Mom and Pop drilled me all the time on noticing people."

"And?"

"He's here. I just saw him."

"And you just came back to work?"

"Well, yeah, where else was I going to get a tracker to plant on him?"

"What?" The number of levels on which she was making sense seemed to Haddy to be shrinking rapidly.

"Now that you're here, you can help me follow him. We'll find out where he's staying, and then we'll figure out how to get him."

"Get him?"

"He knows what happened to Mom. He probably took her. He maybe killed her. We have to find out what he knows."

Charis slowed the quick-march down to a slower stroll, then steered them both toward the wall.

"He was at the strip club around the corner up here, he just ordered a cappuccino from the coffee stand in front..." She slowed to a stop just shy of the corner, bringing Haddy to a stop behind her with a wave of her hand. Then she squatted down to little-brother height and very, very slowly rolled her left eye till it was just poking around and she could side-eye whatever was out there. "Thank God."

"What?"

Charis backed off the corner and stood up. "He's still there. You'll help me track him? He won't recognize you, so you can help me tail him."

"Sure. Yes. Of course."

"Okay, do what I did. Stay low. People don't look for faces below head-height, so even if he sees you he won't notice at first. Good. Now roll out just enough that you can barely see that place called Meow Mix out of the corner of your eye."

Haddy strained to figure out what was happening around the corner. After a half-second, he figured out that if he closed his right eye, his left would focus properly, so he did.

There was blue store-front with pink neon signage blinking with two figures of naked women with cat-ears and wagging cat-tails about four stores in from the corner, across the way.

"Okay, I got the club."

"Now look around the front, see the coffee stand?"

"Yeah, I see it." It was on a cart with a green awning.

"Now, look for the man in the brown leather jacket, pale green corduroy pants, and the high boots. He's right on the near side of the stand, looking at the club's show schedule."

Haddy scanned right.

He found the man.

"Oh, s'crats." His stomach dropped through the floor.

It was Malcolm.

SECRETS MOST LOFTY

"S'CRATS S'CRATS *S'CRATS!*" Haddy said as he pulled back behind the corner.

Charis was looking at him as if he'd just grown an extra nose.

"This won't work. He knows me." Haddy was scrambling inside, trying to keep some kind of bearings as his entire understanding of the world re-oriented itself around him. Malcolm *took* Aunt Min?

That couldn't be right. Malcolm and Sil worked *with* Aunt Min. They'd been on Sidon to meet her, they'd said. If Haddy ran a spy network, that's the way he'd do it. Come in to port, meet everyone there that might need a meeting, then leave again.

"He knows you? How?" Her bafflement was quickly turning to suspicion.

"He was on the *Buchman*. We were in the same centrifuge therapy slot. Had lunch a few times." Haddy decided, as he spoke, that he couldn't tell her everything. Not yet. Not until he was sure what was going on. If he spilled the beans and Sil and Malcolm *were* on the up-and-up, he'd have just put Charis's life in danger.

"Perfect!" Charis grinned slyly.

"How?"

"Look, you wait here. Stay out of sight. Stay on him. I've got an idea."

"What?"

She rolled her eyes. "Look, I know how to do this. Just stay on him and *stay out of sight* okay?"

"Okay, okay, fine."

"And call me if he starts moving," Charis tapped the PPD at her belt.

Haddy blinked. It was her own personal PPD, with the hand-painted wings all over it. He'd never heard of any restaurant that let their wait staff carry personal PPDs while on the job—it distracted you from the customers and made for bad reviews.

"Sure, sure, yeah, I will."

Charis squeezed his hand. "Back in five minutes."

Then she turned and ran back the way they'd come.

Haddy squatted down and rolled his head around the corner again.

Malcolm was still there, though he'd lost interest in the program and was milling around as if he were waiting for someone.

And squatting in this position was giving Haddy a crick in his neck. He needed a better way to keep an eye on Malcolm. A periscope would have done the trick, except that Haddy lived in a world without periscopes and, having never watched a film about submarines or tanks, didn't even know the word.

He took out his PPD, thinking he could use the camera on it to look around corners. He turned it on, snaked it around the corner, and watched the viewfinder.

It worked, but he was getting dirty looks from a shopkeeper across the way. Walking around with a live camera and surreptitiously filming people was the definition of bad taste in Luna City—there were booths in the Bazaar that actually rented antique-looking camcorder cases for PPDs, so that people who were being filmed would at least have fair warning that it was going on. It didn't really stop people recording—blink-lenses could do that if you set them up right—but it was one of those things that just *wasn't* done, and if blink-lens footage went public, the person who posted it was in for a good thrashing. It was a matter of manners, not law, but in Luna City, manners were more important. Evidently that was the case here, too.

Haddy put the PPD away and cast about for a different solution. He was hoping for a handicrafts booth, maybe someone selling mobiles or hanging art that had mirrors on it. If he could find a mirror small enough to palm, that would solve his problem. He could look around corners without looking like he was looking around corners.

But since this was the adult entertainment district—the locals called it "The Zoo"—there weren't any handicrafts stands knocking about. Those businesses tended to cluster in the family-friendly district where they got more foot traffic. All he could see from where he was standing was a head shop, a brothel, a VR arena, a shooting range and a laser tag arena with a "combat supply center" sandwiched between them, and something called "Zoe's Platter Paradise" which looked like a very classy restaurant, and a body mod shop.

Maybe he could use his PPD screen...

Nope. Matte finish. No reflectivity.

The combat supply center.

When they'd been paintballing, Charis had used a dental mirror...he bet that's where they sold them.

Haddy chanced one more look around the corner. Malcolm was sitting down now, drinking coffee at a table near the coffee stand with four other people, none of whom Haddy recognized at a quick glance. So he ought to be tied up for a few minutes, at least.

It was worth taking the risk. Haddy jogged a few yards along the wall so that he'd be well-sheltered from Malcolm's eyeline, then he sprinted across the thoroughfare and slipped into the thick foot traffic in front of the shooting sports shops. Standing a head taller than most of the people in the crowd—his height was a side effect of growing up in Lunar gravity—Haddy stood a good chance of getting spotted. He tried to mitigate it by walking hunched over and sticking as close as he could to the few tall people he could find.

Inside the shop, he found a wide array of arena weapons, harnesses, body armor, scopes, blink-lenses, goggles, holsters, magazines, gas bottles...

And mirrors.

Haddy grabbed one of the mirrors, waved his credit jack through the counter top payment alley checked himself out, but stopped before he left again.

He didn't want to be spotted. Maybe he ought to change clothes.

There were urban camo combat jackets here, soft high-grip boots, utility pants, black lycra shirts, shielded caps...

He grabbed one of each in his own size, checked out, then changed in the store—which didn't endear him to his fellow patrons—before heading back out into the street. He risked a quick eye-check at Malcolm's position as he came out the door, and found his friend still holding court at the coffee bar.

Haddy hurried out of sight before Malcolm could spot him. He threw the bundle of his old clothes into a trash bin, and returned to his post. He extended the dental mirror and snaked it out around the corner.

Now he could see Malcolm, and he wasn't attracting

attention to himself, and his neck wasn't hurting. He felt a little thrill surge through him—not just from his triumph, either. He was watching someone who did not particularly want to be watched, who didn't know he was watching, and who he was deliberately hiding from.

It was...perverted. Deeply, unsettlingly perverted. The kind of offensive behavior that would earn a beat-down from any self-respecting fellow citizen, at least back in Luna City. The most basic rule of modesty was *don't stare when you're not invited*. He was staring where he surely wasn't wanted. It made him feel powerful, giddy, and it frightened him.

Someone was approaching from his right. Haddy turned to see Charis bounding up to him.

"Got it," she said. "What happened to you?"

He filled her in on his brainstorm.

"Hmph. Now I wish I'd thought of that. Good going, cuz."

"Thanks. What did you get?"

"Tracker." She opened her palm to reveal what looked like a crumb from a burnt piece of toast.

"You got that at work?"

She looked up, bobbed her head from side to side, and said, "There's a lot about my boss you don't know."

Yeah, I'll bet. Like he works for the CIA. "Like what?"

"Later. Here." She took his hand and dumped the bug into it. "All you have to to is touch him. It'll stick to fabric. He won't even notice it."

Haddy examined it. It wasn't *quite* black, but it was definitely dark. It would need to go somewhere dark. Malcolm was wearing a dark brown jacket, so that should do the trick.

"Okay," Haddy said. "You take this." He handed her the mirror.

"Don't move. He's behind you."

Haddy's heart tightened. "What?"

"He's on the move. He's walking toward the bar up there," she looked over Haddy's left shoulder, past the intersection. "Just don't move and as long as he doesn't turn this...uh-oh."

A flash of panic crossed her face, and Haddy did the only thing he could think of to keep her from giving them both away.

He seized her arm, pulled her to him, and kissed her.

She didn't struggle. She did pull back enough to whisper "What the hell are you doing?"

"He can't see our faces, he won't see who we are," he spoke against her cheek.

She chuckled. Her arms went around him.

"What? That's funny?"

"No, no," she said. "It's the dumbest excuse anyone's ever had for kissing me."

"Oh, what's the best?" Haddy suddenly forgot where he was entirely.

"That they wanted to." Her voice was warm, like all the smiles in the world packed into one sound.

"Well, now that you mention it..."

He kissed her again. She kissed him back. For a long, glorious moment, the entire Zoo faded into silence around them. He could feel her heartbeat through her lips. She still smelled like lemons. He hadn't noticed it until now. He'd gotten used to it, but now the lemons were wrapping up his entire world.

This was nothing like kissing Sil. This was like some deep part of him had been crippled his whole life, and now, suddenly, it knew what it meant to run and jump and be truly free. It shook him with a kind of terror that he would happily die just to avoid recovering from.

"Mmm..." she said.

"Mmm hmm." he said.

"Mmm mm!" she pulled away. "No, I mean he's moving again. Look."

She nodded past him. Haddy looked left over his shoulder.

Malcolm was walking away from them, heading spinwards toward the other end of the Zoo.

Reluctantly, Haddy let go of Charis. He wasn't sure whether he was more afraid that she would pull away fast, or want to stay close, but it did give him some small measure of comfort that she, also, lingered longer than was strictly necessary.

They followed. All they needed was a chance to get close.

The flow of the crowd meant they had a tough enough time just maintaining a constant distance, to say nothing of gaining on him. Traffic was heavy, but didn't grow heavier until Malcolm had made significant progress around the station. As he approached the spinwards edge of the Zoo, however, traffic picked up again, and Haddy and Charis went from struggling-to-keep-up to definitely-falling-behind.

Haddy suggested heading a block upstation and taking the service alley—a wider space where deliveries were made to the rears of the shops, but where commerce was disallowed and pedestrians were not supposed to tread for fear of their own safety—reasoning that they could catch up quickly and then pace him one block to the next.

Charis nixed it as soon as he mentioned it. "There are too many places where he could slip away. This place is honeycombed with ventilation, access ports, back doors. It's not like Luna City where everything is public—here, all the operational traffic happens backstage."

"Backstage?"

"This is a theme park," she said with a mischievous sparkle. "Didn't you know?"

Haddy hadn't realized that, but since he also didn't know what a theme park was, he thought it best to leave the subject alone.

The edges of the Zoo were the primo real estate—close enough to the family centers that groups could split up and take their leisure in whichever flavor they saw fit. The Zoo and the family-friendly districts each took up half the station—Phalanx was poised on the counterspin border of the Zoo. They were now approaching the spinwards border, halfway around the station from where they'd started.

"If he keeps this up much longer," Haddy said as he broke a trail through a knot of people, "We're going to lose him."

"Where the hell is he going anyway?"

Haddy shrugged. "Maybe he's trying to get his steps in for the day or something. He was kind of a fitness nut on the *Buchman*."

"Hold a mo, I got a notion." In spite of her words, she kept on pushing from behind.

"What?"

"Keep your eyes peeled for pickpockets."

"What, do they wear uniforms around here?"

"Don't tell me you never had your pocket picked."

"Too many times, and I never caught them."

"How good's your visibility up there, Mister Skyscraper?"

"That's pretty rich coming from a woman who busted one-eighty like an old coffee mug."

"Shut up. Really, how much can you see?"

"More or less everything."

"Do you see anyone stumbling into other people a lot, making brushing past each other closer than they need to?"

Haddy looked around. People in crowds had particular rhythms and currents they followed. He'd seen it often enough from a flying position in Luna City. So, if he got a feel for the current of the crowd, and looked for people bucking the current in unnecessary ways...

"There's a guy that needs a shave over there," Haddy nodded spinwards on the upstation side of the street. "He's stumbling around the ends of the line for some food stands. It looks like he's indecisive, but he's bumping into a lot of people."

"Let's try him. Head that way."

Haddy changed course, veering upstation to intercept the could-be-pickpocket.

"Plaid jacket?" Charis asked.

"That's the one."

"I see him."

When they got inside shouting distance, Charis peeled off, heading at the guy head-on. Haddy decided to cut off his escape in case she spooked him, and hooked wide to come in on him from the spinwards side.

As Haddy drew up behind their target, he could actually see the man working the crowd. Quick, very smooth movements—a hand darting into a pocket, coming out, never making so much as a ripple in the fabric, not so much impact as to leave a hair out of place. Nobody in line would even know they'd been had until they reached the front.

When they had him sandwiched, Charis said, "Excuse me, I was wondering if I could hire you for a job..."

At which point the man bolted.

So much for inconspicuous, Haddy thought.

But Charis had the jump on him. She sprang up on a trash can, leapt over the heads of several other people in the crowd, and landed in a head-first dive-and-roll in a clear space behind the bolting pickpocket.

Haddy did his best to keep pace with them, while keeping his back to Malcolm to stay one more body in the sea of bodies.

It was a losing game. They were well counterspin—to the next block, at least—before he found a significant break in the crowd and was able to pick up speed.

Charis had thrown caution to the wind. She was keeping up with the pickpocket by using the local geography—walls, trash bins, booth counters. Haddy'd seen parkour before, mostly in Lunar gravity and some on the *Buchman*. It didn't occur to him to think anyone could move like *that* under a full g, and yet there she was, scampering across the landscape as if it she'd evolved in it.

Just as Haddy closed the distance, Charis ran up the downstation wall, sprang off a protruding chevron at about head height, and dove for her quarry.

She came down on his shoulders, knocking him forward into a sprawl on the deck.

The pickpocket made a noise that sounded halfway between a whine and a stream of profanity.

"Now," she huffed. "Like I said, I want to hire you for your professional skills..."

"Hey hey hey!" A security guard skittered up with her deputy in tow. She looked at the pile of bodies on the street and said: "We got a call for a running chase and we find a wrestling match. You better have a tax certificate for public entertainment."

"Not a publicity stunt, officer" Charis said.   "Just crossed wires." She stood up, offered a hand to the pickpocket.

He took it warily, and pulled himself to his feet.

"I heard that Tim here was a good man in a pinch and needed a job, and we're understaffed for this evening down at Phalanx. I saw him in the crowd and shouted out to him, and he mistook me for his ex-wife. I had to chase him because my boss said if I don't bring him in it's my ass."

"That right?" The guard looked back and forth between them, suspicion written on her face. She was shorter than either of them—maybe Ethiopian, probably raised on Earth—but what she lacked in stature she made up for in presence. She glanced at the pickpocket. "I asked you a question."

"Yeah," he said, clearly not sure he believed he was lining up with such a ridiculous story, "Yeah, yeah, that's right. She's a dead ringer for Alice, man. It's spooky, I'm tellin' you."

"You," the guard looked straight at Haddy. "What's your business here?"

"Me?" he said. "I was just, uh, heading...she offered me a job too. At Phalanx. I was heading back with her."

"You don't say." The cop clearly didn't believe him. She did another round of the suspicious looks, then said,

"Phalanx, eh? I guess that's okay. You better get on with your business then, stop disturbing all these good people."

They all agreed. As soon as the cops turned their back, the pickpocket said:

"Okay, you didn't bust me. What do you want?"

Charis ran him through the job.

"Easy. What are you offering?"

"Charis," Charis extended her hand.

"Just keep calling me Tim." He shook her hand with a cagey look on his face.

"Okay, well, like I said, I work at Phalanx. I'll get you free drinks for the evening."

"At *Phalanx?* Consider it done. Who's the target?"

"Um..." Haddy said looking around. "There we might have a problem."

The two minutes the chase had lasted plus the three the cop had detained them added up to a hell of a head start for Malcolm. Haddy had pretty much given up on the possibility of finding him again, but Charis wasn't so easily deterred. She backtracked their steps and got up on a convenient wall to try to get a vantage all the way to the end of the station. It must have worked, because she pulled her PPD off of her belt and held it up as if she was taking a picture.

She hopped down and showed the screen to the putative Tim.

"He's in line for the burrito stand," Charis said, pointing at the screen.

"Hmph," Haddy said, "Sounds like him."

"Haddy, give him the bug."

Haddy complied.

"Then come to Phalanx at 1900," Charis said. "You'll have an open tab—but just for you. Don't go bringing half the station in."

The putative Tim smiled. "You got a deal."

THE MISSION WAS a success. From her high vantage, which she crawled back to, Charis reported watching Tim brush past Malcolm as he was leaving the burrito stand and wading through the crowd. Malcolm didn't appear to notice at all.

Charis then begged off, saying she had to return to work. It was only after she left that Haddy remembered the book with the listening device that Sil had given him, and wondered where he'd dropped it.

On the walk home, he mentally retraced his steps, and concluded that he must have left it on the bar, so it would be in whatever Phalanx used for a lost-and-found, if anything. He would have to go in and claim it at some point...

But not before he knew what was going on.

Malcolm and Sil's story still sounded plausible to him. They were good people. They cared about him, and about Luna City. He didn't think he would have made it through the journey aboard the *Buchman* without their help.

They'd never said anything incompatible with Charis's story about seeing Malcolm on Sidon. And it did make sense that they'd have headed to Nineveh after Min disappeared.

The problem was Charis. Watching her on her game this afternoon made a whole bunch of other things not add up.

Like that tracker. She took a tracker from work. What kind of bar kept trackers just laying around like that? She *had* to know she was working for some kind of shady operation. Did she know it was CIA? If she didn't, what did she think it was?

The tracker would solve it. And when it did, he'd tell Charis everything.

Until then, he settled in to more of his reading up on the war. He still didn't know what to make of it at all, but he was beginning to think that maybe that was the point.

But if that *was* the point, if *nobody* knew what to make of it, then why the fight in the first place? Sure, nobody liked the American government—at least nobody in Luna City—but Luna City would be a boring place without the Americans coming up to do the touristy things. The entire city was built on Americans, and people from all over the place who came up out of the gravity well *because* of the Americans' space elevator. If the Americans left...what would happen?

They wouldn't kill all your friends, that's what would happen.

Haddy felt like he'd gotten caught between the gears of history. He had to do something about it. And if he was going to go against everything he'd ever been taught, and actually pick up a gun and shoot it *at* somebody? He wanted to know why.

He just wondered if he'd still feel that way when he got home. When he walked into the apartment and his mother wasn't there. When he felt her absence all around him in the way that he couldn't in this strange place.

No, he decided, *that* can't *matter. I can't let it.* Not if he wanted to respect himself. What kind of a man was he if right and wrong changed with his mood?

No. He needed to decide what side he was on—if he was going to be on any side—before he got home, not after.

Deep in his mental meanderings, he didn't even notice the sound of Charis unlatching the door. It was only when she banged on it that he jumped.

He'd thrown the hook-lock when he got home. He hadn't even noticed—the practice had become automatic.

Haddy rushed to the door, checked the monitor, unhooked it and let it slide open.

Seeing Charis put him right back in the Zoo. Her smell, her taste, the texture of her lips, it all came flooding back to him at once, and he couldn't look her in the eye.

"Sorry about the door..."

"Don't worry about it," she pushed past him, shrugging a satchel strap off her shoulder as she moved. "I've been waiting for this all day."

She sat down on the sofa, looked back at him standing uselessly near the door as it slid shut again. She patted the cushion next to her as if he was keeping her waiting.

"I, uh...have to throw the lock...just a second." *What is wrong with you? It's the same Charis, just talk to her like normal.*

Except that wasn't true. Now she knew how he felt about her—she had to, after that kiss. Worse than that, now *he* knew how he felt about her, and he wasn't sure he was prepared to deal with that.

"Haddy, come on."

Haddy joined her on the couch. She produced a tablet from the satchel and slid next to him.

"Want to see where he went?"

"Yeah, I guess. What'll it get us?"

"It'll tell us what he's looking for."

"How's that?"

"Well, there's a microphone on it too."

Haddy felt uneasy. He didn't know what he wanted to find out, but he suspected that no matter what the tracker showed—whether it confirmed Malcolm and Sil's story, or told a different story entirely—it would wreck some part of the life he'd been able to somehow knit together in the week since arriving here.

It was a life that he really liked—though he was surprised to realize it.

Charis didn't wait for his go-ahead. Why should she? This whole thing was her idea. She activated the tablet.

The opening screen showed a three dimensional plot of movement, color-weighted for time, and overlaid on a three-dimensional map of the station.

The line of Malcolm's track wound around the Zoo, then headed up to the tram at the center of the station. Then it did something...impossible.

"Is that doing what I think it's doing?" Haddy said.

"What, you mean stopping between stations in Sections B and C?"

"Yeah. And what's this?" The tracker's line just didn't fail to make the full trip between stations. When they zoomed in, it moved off at a tangent, away from the tracks. "There isn't anything up there, is there?"

"I don't know," Charis said. "I've never been close enough to be able to see it. But..."

"Backstage?"

"Huh?"

"You said that there's as much 'backstage' about Nineveh as there is in public view. What kind of stuff happens backstage?"

Charis shrugged. "Deliveries. Maintenance. Almost everything else is a subset of one of those."

"The very end of this line is blue."

"He spent a long time there. An hour."

"That's not a lot of movement..."

"Way ahead of you." Charis manipulated the screen, flipping through options the way only a seasoned expert could.

"Where did you learn all this stuff?"

"Here we go," she said, ignoring the question.

She played the audio. There was a lot of background noise. Some shuffling. Then voices.

Malcolm's first. "Lunch call! Gotcha some Mexican dontchaknow."

"Did you get my message?" That was Sil's voice.

"Yeah. We missed each other no problem."

"Just barely. He was within fifteen meters of you for almost three minutes, then he went into this store over here, came out, and poof."

"Poof?"

"According to this, he's been standing in a trash can for the last seven hours."

Charis paused playback and looked at Haddy. "They're talking about you."

Haddy nodded. "The woman is his wife. Or was traveling as his wife."

"What happened with the trash can?"

"That's where I dumped my clothes." Well, they did say they'd be watching. Now he knew how.

"Shit," Charis said. She pressed play again.

"They were trying to follow you," Sil said. "The girl spotted you on Sidon. She thinks you took her mother."

She stopped it again. She looked at Haddy.

"Where are your other clothes?"

"In my room."

"Shoes, underwear, everything?"

"Everything." Haddy didn't wear underwear when he could help it. It always bound up around his balls and made him itch.

Charis looked up at his bedroom door. Haddy followed her gaze. The door was closed—a necessary habit when you have younger brothers who were prone to invading your privacy without the slightest provocation—and breathed a little sigh of relief.

"They've bugged your clothes."

"I'll toss them."

"Don't. They might be useful."

Haddy looked at her with new eyes. It was slowly dawning on him that the world she lived in was a far darker place than he'd imagined. He wondered if he should be afraid of her, of what kind of secrets she might be keeping.

"What about this?" Haddy held up his PPD.

She shook her head. "They lost you when you dumped your clothes. I'm guessing you never had your PPD out of your possession on the *Buchman*, right? You never left it in your quarters when you went out, nothing like that."

Haddy thought back. "Yeah, I think that's right. Not after I met them, anyway."

Charis sighed. "Well, there's that at least."

She un-paused the recording.

"And the boy?"

"Still behaving. He's a good little soldier." Haddy didn't like the tone in Sil's voice. Something about it seemed almost to be mocking him.

Malcolm and Sil talked about the food while they ate. It occurred to Haddy that this place was their surveillance nest. It was a good location—high up in the sky with nobody around to see them come and go. Well, except for the people on the tram.

After a few minutes, Malcolm said:

"Anything new today from in there?"

"Not a peep," Sil said. "Tough bitch."

Malcolm swore. "Where's Andy?"

"Sent him out for some sack time."

"I guess that's right enough. We can't keep churning like this, for sure." He was quiet for a few moments. "I'm gonna take a run. It's time we start pushing on the soft spot I think."

"Well, it is feeding time. Maybe her appetites can do with some adjusting, you think?"

"You are positively evil, you know that?"

"That's why you love me."

"All righty," Malcolm said, "let's do this."

There was some rumpling noise, and a door. Then Malcolm said:

"Lunch call. Brought you a burrito today. Chicken, this time."

There was some more rustling, then the sound of foil tearing.

"The proper response," Malcolm said, "Is 'thank you.'"

"Fuck you very much." It was a woman's voice.

Charis stiffened, and Haddy knew who it had to be. "Min?"

Charis nodded. "Min."

CONFESSIONS AND REVELATIONS

ON THE RECORDING, Malcolm clucked his tongue. "Aren't you being a tad ungracious there, lady? I did spare your girl and your nephew, dontchaknow."

Min snorted. "So you said."

"You should thank Andy there, when he gets back. He's the one kept me from hurting them too bad. I don't think he showed you the photos, did he now?"

Min didn't answer. The sounds of her eating stopped, though.

"Oh. Well, maybe that's for the best, after all. It would ruin your appetite. I mean, just look at that face..."

Min still didn't answer, but Haddy heard what sounded like a gasp.

"Yeah, that's what I thought. Now, don't get me wrong. I like the boy. He's a good lad, really stand-up. You'll be proud when you get to see him again, for sure."

"Oh my god..." Min whispered.

"And that girl of yours, well, I've got a bit of a heavy boot, so they brought in someone with a lighter touch. Delicate bones, a girl that willowy. Don't want to do more damage than you intend to..."

A choked-back sob answered him.

"Now look here," Malcolm's voice was soft and sympathetic, "We've had some good times, unfortunate circumstances aside, am I right? I mean, you're up, what, seven hundred on me?"

"Seven thirty-five," Min gritted.

"Right. And we're treating you decent up here. There's no reason to get nasty. But the world moves out there. I don't know what Andy's been telling you, but there's a real goddamn war on out there, ma'am. Incandescent. And your people are dying."

"Hmph."

Malcolm spun a yarn about Gagarin Station and the Persians that Haddy didn't quite catch, but he figured that it must have something to do with the rumors he'd read. Malcolm *didn't* say anything about Grissom, or Ring Alpha, which Haddy found odd. If he was trying to pressure her, why would he hold back? Did she already know? Or was he saving it for a second round of shock?

"Now here's the thing, Min. I don't want to spoil our relationship, I really don't. When we let you go, I want to keep up with the cards, cause you're damn good, for sure. I'd love to have a game in Phalanx one day when this is all over. But I've got pressure on me, youbetcha. You've got to give me something. If you don't, I'm going to have to squeeze. Oh, I know you're not going to break, I'm not talking about torturing you. But your girl, Min. And that boy. They're all out in the open. I've got the lock code to their front door..."

"That lying sack of..." Charis said as she paused the audio again. She looked up at Haddy. "You didn't give him your code, did you?"

"Of course not, what do you think I am?"

Her expression darkened.

"I wonder." She said it coldly, then un-paused before Haddy could protest.

Malcolm's voice continued: "...we've got trackers in their clothes. I can find either one of them within a meter, and deliver the same or worse."

The words hung in the air for a moment, then Malcolm said:

"I don't want to do that, Min. You bet I don't. They're good kids. They don't deserve to be in the middle like this, and that's for sure. But we're playing for bigger stakes now, and you know as well as I that the lives of two horny teenagers don't make for a good goddamn, and neither does how hard they die." He lowered his voice to a whisper. "You know they laid like that, out in the park, for an hour before we woke 'em up?"

Min mumbled something.

"Sorry, ma'am, I didn't hear what you said."

"I said get out of here you son of a bitch."

Charis hissed "Yes!"

Haddy realized he wasn't breathing, and took a big gulp of air.

"I'm sorry you feel that way, ma'am. Really I am. Next time we talk it ain't gonna be so cordial I don't think. Hope you sleep well. We're in for a long one tomorrow, yessirree."

Charis stopped the recording. She turned her intense eyes on Haddy, and he couldn't tell if she was angry, or relieved, or wanting to kill him, or kiss him.

"'A good little soldier,'" she said. "'A friend of mine.'"

Haddy gulped. He started shaking all over. He was sure his face had gone from its native olive-tone to ghost-white.

"I...it...Charis I...I...I can..."

"Yes," she said in a dangerously quiet, measured voice. "And you better start. How do you know these people? Tell me *everything*, from the moment we got separated till the moment you showed up here."

Haddy shifted to the far end of the couch and stared at the cushions between them. It took him a long time to find his tongue, but Charis didn't goad him. He almost wished she had—it would have been less humiliating to get in a fight and shout the truth than it was to have to recount every detail.

But he did recount every detail that he could remember. She seemed to be able to tell when he left something out. He wanted to skip over the stuff about Sil trying to seduce him, but she spotted immediately when he did, so he had to go into *everything*. What had seemed fun and world-changing and mind-blowing at the time now seemed petty and stupid, like he'd been led around by his penis, like he was too horny and lonely and pathetic to think straight.

Charis let him squirm until he was done.

Then she asked: "Why didn't you tell me?"

Haddy shrugged. "Because if you knew, and your behavior changed, your boss might kill you."

"What?"

"Oh." It dawned on Haddy that the entire story about Phalanx being a CIA front was part of the story they fed him, and he'd better tell her. "Well, it's part of what they said. They said Phalanx was a CIA front, and that the CIA were the ones that had disappeared your mother. This morning they gave me this bug..."

"This *morning?*"

Haddy realized that there was more to tell, so he told her about how Sil had contacted him in the showers at the paintball arena, and about the chalk signal, and about the conversation this morning.

Charis whistled.

Haddy gave her a questioning look.

"They really screwed up. They also did a hell of a number on you."

"How? I mean...to both. How to both?"

"They screwed up by underestimating you, and me. They figured they could lead you around by your prick and your heart. It's tradecraft 101. You build trust by inducing a bond with your target. Make him want sex. Make him depend on your friendship. They figured if they could make you trust them, you'd fall for it all hook, line, and sinker."

"But I *did* trust them." He was building up a powerful rage at just how badly he'd been taken.

"Trust me, Haddy, they were sweating bullets after you didn't have sex with Sil that first night she offered. I guarantee you they were going *crazy* once you made that deal with Mannix without talking it over with them first."

"Why? And why would they have a problem with that deal, anyway?"

She sighed. "It...it'll take a long time to explain. Look, what you have there, with Malcolm and Sil, they're company handlers. Have to be."

"Company?"

"CIA. And trust me, they're good. Very slick, with this whole thing. But based on what you're telling me, they needed you on-side. They want ears in that bar, and you're the way in. And they want you close by to put pressure on Min, which is a bonus and...god, it's brilliant. And then they get lucky..." She shifted her posture. "Look, here's how I figure it went down. They're after the exploit. They have to be..."

"Why?"

Charis rolled her eyes. "Because if they were just trying to bust the network, they wouldn't have started hunting us almost right away. So they grab Mom, and she doesn't have the exploit on her. So they flag Pop and Dad and probably me and Arn at ports, and when we buy tickets for the *Buchman*, they've got us. They put people at customs to try to get the exploit the easy way, and then they're on board the ship personally, just in case..."

She stopped for a moment, looked up, and her head bobbed a few times, like she was ticking off items on a checklist, then she continued.

"Yeah. They're expecting Pop and Dad and me and Arn, but we never made it aboard, so they find out you're there and they adjust on-the-fly. They figure if they can get you on-side, they can use you for bait, or leverage, or both. They can even use you as a mole. It's perfect. Except for your goddamn stubborn independent streak. 'Typical Loonie,' they think, but they adjust and get as close to you as you'll let them anyway. The honey trap doesn't work...'"

"Honey trap?"

"Uh..." Charis blushed. Haddy had never seen Charis blush. "The honey is the...uh...when a girl gets excited...dammit why do you have to be a virgin? Okay, forget all that. It's an industry term. For when you use sex to lure someone into working with you, okay?"

"Okay." Haddy wondered what it could be about that term that was making *Charis* blush.

"So the honey trap doesn't work, at least not all the way, and then you make the deal with Mannix, so they can't get you on the money angle—if you were broke, they could get to you a lot easier—but they get the lucky break when the news comes in, and they use your grief to get you to depend on them. And so they play like they're on my team, and they start training you to be a mole, so they can get you to infiltrate Phalanx for them. The would have told you it was a Company front pretending to be a node in the resistance network, and then they'd have had you inside. They'd have had you beaten just like they did, to put the squeeze on Min. But then you get here and, ta-da! There I am. And they think they've scored big, because I'm better leverage and I'm already inside Phalanx. But they don't realize that I've been in on the game since I was fourteen, and that Mom was priming me for it before that. Gods, they must have dropped a galactic load when they heard that I was part of the team, and not just a kid along for the ride."

She was looking at Haddy's bedroom door, her tongue poking around in her cheek, like she was scheming, and half her mouth turned up into a smile. A real *oh, boy did they screw up and are we gonna get 'em for it* smile.

Charis made eye contact, and Haddy looked away. He had never felt so used, so humiliated, so blindingly stupid in his entire life. He wished he had an airlock to step out of.

He felt her hand under his chin. She raised his face until he couldn't *not* look at her without closing his eyelids or looking way away with just his eyeballs.

"Hadrian," she said, "You should be proud of yourself. This scam would have taken *anybody* else. You stayed skeptical the whole way. You stayed *Loonie* the whole way. If you hadn't, you'd have trusted them the whole way and played me like a fiddle. You could have, too." A look came over her face that he didn't know how to interpret, but it made him want to kiss her again.

Instead, he said, "So, uh...what do we do? We've got to get her out of there..."

"Well, that's where we've got a problem. They've gotta

have someone at station ops in their pocket to be able to make those unscheduled tram stops for their base up there. And we don't, so we can't actually get to her. Even if we could, that can't be a big place. If we went in they might trap us in there, and we're worse off than before."

She held up her fingers and started ticking off more problems:

"And if we somehow get Mom out, we have to get her off station, and if they've got ops in their pocket, they might be able to lock the ship down, or lock us in, or get us arrested."

"Yeah," Haddy said, the shadow of an idea growing in his mind, "But we do have something they haven't got."

"What's that?"

He smirked. "Twenty-five years of combined flying experience."

Her eyes opened wider than he'd ever seen them. "Brilliant." Then her eyes darted over to his bedroom door. "Hold on, right there, I've got an idea."

THE BRIGHT AMBER sign by the gantry door said "Danger: High Winds. Hold railing at all times when lit." It blinked, too, just to make sure that nobody missed it. Accidents up here were messy, dangerous things.

The sign blazed and blinked whenever the auxiliary railings deployed, which turned the wide open gantry into a series of five parallel narrow walkways bordered by rails. It was an automatic safety system, which activated whenever gusts topped eighty kph, as they frequently did at night as the greenbelt cooled down.

On decks this high, with gravity less than Lunar, a wind that fast would blow a large man away like he was made of kite tissue, if he didn't hold on.

Tonight, the wind whistled violently in the midnight dark as two hatted, long-coated figures crept out of the shelter of the lift bay. Nothing unusual in their appearance, so far as longtime Ninevites were concerned. Nothing to attract attention. That was Haddy's part of the plan.

Charis had come up with the other part. A performance, the kind that would drive Sil and Malcolm around the bend, along with whoever else was listening. According to Haddy's blink-lenses, they should be getting to the good part just about now.

It had taken a day to get everything ready, which was longer than they each were comfortable with.

First, Charis had gone to the door and monkeyed with the entry controls, then she'd gone around the house scrutinizing cupboard doors, surfaces, and seemingly random pieces of the floor in minute detail. When Haddy had asked her what she was doing, she'd only held up a finger, so he'd shut up and waited.

Once she was done, she's told him that Malcolm not only couldn't plausibly have the door code, but she was certain nobody else had been in the flat except for Haddy and Charis themselves. There was no record of other access on the door's log, and she had a secondary, detached system that recorded the face of everyone who walked through, and neither system had recorded any access. She also had what she called "tell tales" set up around the apartment—which she'd go into later—and none of them indicated the presence of anybody but herself and Haddy.

That out of the way, Charis sat back down and explained to Haddy that Phalanx was a nest of spies—and a vital part of the private intelligence network the Resistance depended on, and that Min had helped build. Min hadn't helped set Phalanx up, but she used it regularly. It was why Nineveh was home base. If the family got separated, all parties were supposed to rendezvous back here, on the assumption that if someone didn't make it, Phalanx's network of human assets might have heard something.

That's why the CIA wanted an ear inside. That was probably why they brought Min back here instead of taking her down to Earth and disappearing her inside some hole in the ground: up here, anything they found out, they could use immediately. And here, they might be able to trade her for something else they needed.

That was Charis's guess, anyway.

Then Haddy had explained his plan. *There isn't any way in there without letting them know we're coming,* he'd said, *so we don't go in there. We go* out *there. We fly.*

Charis liked the idea. Kind of. *How do we get Mom out? Assuming we can find a way in from the outside, we don't have three suits.*

We also don't have gravity, Haddy had said, *We bring a harness and tandem hook her. If we land up high, near the hub, we don't have to worry about an unsafe landing.*

We're going to have to be off-station before they raise the alarm, Charis had said with a sparkle in her eye.

And we've got to make them believe we're in our quarters, or somewhere else like that, Haddy had pointed out.

I know just the thing.

After that she had gotten on the link to Phalanx, talking to Mondu. The orn-suits were a matter of "vital strategic interest" now. There wasn't a better term for it. "National security" didn't apply because the loose alliance of colonies fighting against the Americans and the Persians weren't anything approximating a "nation" and might never be.

When she had hung up, she'd said that they'd have the suits in twelve hours. They had until then to get ready.

First step: Haddy went to Phalanx and pretended to claim the book from lost-and-found. He had pretended to riffle through the book and find the listening device, then had pretended to accept the offer of a job interview, and had gone through all the motions of answering questions about previous employment, skills, and the like. Then he had pretended to ask for a tour, and then pretended to plant the bug in a location that he pretended was the secret back room that Malcolm and Sil wanted access to.

Which was to say, he'd done all those things with Mondu's active knowledge and participation, except for planting the bug in the back room. For that, Mondu had instructed Haddy, by gesture, to put it in a closet containing speakers that ran chatter to the room. With any luck, it would sound to the spies as if the bug were in the proper room after all.

Second step: Haddy returned to the apartment, where he and Charis put his bugged clothing—and everything else he'd brought from Luna City—under the mattress in his room, and then retired to Charis's room, where they spent several hours recording innocuous and utterly inconsequential conversations, culminating in the two of them pretending to have sex, and then go to sleep.

Haddy only had vids to go on as far as knowing anything about how sex sounded—and those of wildly varying levels of artistic quality—so he'd followed Charis's lead and generally pretended to be as shy as he felt.

Third step: Packing. In Haddy's case, this meant "PPD and credit jack." In Charis's case, that meant grabbing something she called a "go-bag" from under her bed.

Fourth step: Haddy sat down to read for a few hours while Charis worked some magic with the drivel they'd recorded, plus a couple of films for good measure.

Fifth step: Haddy piled his bugged belongings on the vacuum robot along with a small tablet. Charis set the vacuum to move randomly throughout the house every-so-often, with movement starting about the time Haddy would normally wake up, and the tablet to start playback at about the time when she would normally get home from work.

Sixth step: Leave the apartment.

On the way out Haddy had looked for a new chalk mark on the neighbor's door lintel, and breathed a sigh of relief that there wasn't one.

They had beat a hasty path to a hotel a few levels up from Phalanx, one that they hoped wouldn't be under any kind of special scrutiny from the Americans, where they found four large totes waiting for them at the registration desk.

"Supplies," Charis had called them.

She wasn't kidding. Mondu, or one of his people, had done some shopping on their behalf. One of the totes contained tools, another contained food, a third contained two custom-fitted, freshly printed orn-suits, completely assembled.

After that, they grabbed all the rest and food they could get—in between testing the new rigs for fit and finish, and walking verbally through the plan so many times that Haddy was dreaming about it whenever he closed his eyes, even to blink.

But now that they were all the way up here, in the dead of night in what felt like a junction duct in a badly plumbed HVAC system—and Haddy knew, since he'd crawled around in a few when he was younger, just for fun. Haddy was tempted to call it off when he stepped out of the lift bay and felt the strength of the wind. A daring plan was all well and good, but if it got them killed, it wasn't daring. It was just stupid.

"You think you can handle the wind?" Haddy said. He had to almost-shout it over the howl of the air whipping its way over and under the gantry.

"What I'm worried about is these suits," she shouted back.

"Relax," Haddy said, "I built 'em to take four g's in the turns. Your arms'll give out before these babies do."

"That's comforting." Charis scanned the center bore above them.

"Do you see it?"

"Yeah, I think so. Give me a minute, I'll paint it." Charis took her overcoat off, fishing out a suction cup with a ball joint, a little arm, and a near-IR laser in the process. She stuck the suction cup to the wall, fitted the little arm into it creating a ball-and-socket wall mount, and fixed the laser to the end of the arm.

Then she aimed it.

"Okay, I think we're painted. Can you see it?"

Haddy scanned. The night looked less night-ish in near-IR. The ground was bright with radiating heat. Plumes of warmth billowed up from it and blurred in the swirling air like ink being poured into a whirlpool. The gantry in front of him was nearly black, and the tram tracks around the spindle showed up as black silhouettes against the ground above, dotted by lights and radiators which glowed white.

Above him and forty-degrees upstation, a little

complex of tubes and spokes jutted out from the superstructure—in this waveband, he could see that there were
such structures between every station stop on the tram,
they were just difficult to spot during the day due to
the lighting conditions—and on this complex there was
a broad, defocused, soft green glow as Charis's laser
bounced off of it.

"Yeah, I got it."

"Okay, good.   Now remember, that," she pointed
forward along the gantry, "is counterspin."

"Got it." Haddy shucked his own coat, and hat, took
Charis's from her, and tossed them all back into the lift
bay so they wouldn't blow around in the wind and create
more problems than he and Charis were about to manage
on their own. "Check my rig?"

Charis knelt in front of him, checking his tool bag
and tugging on the spare harness—both of which he had
strapped to his front—doing her best make sure they were
each well-secured and out of his way, and also that the
tandem harness he was wearing was on properly. They'd
done this whole routine at the hotel, but Haddy wasn't
about to take a chance on not checking twice.

Once she'd done with his front—including checking
the fastenings on his gecko booties and gloves, and the
connections for all his control surfaces—she circled round
to the back and rooted around under his feathers, checking his connection points, the harness fit, and the whole
shebang.

"You're good. Do me?"

He returned the favor. If he'd gotten his way, she'd just
have worn the tool bag, and not the tandem harness or the
spare. The more parts involved, the more could go wrong.
Besides, he had stronger arms and a sturdier build; he was

going to have a much easier time carrying the extra mass when it came time to maneuver than she was.

Even though there wouldn't be any weight to deal with, the extra mass would make acceleration and deceleration much harder, and it would be hell on the arms in any high-bank turns—enough so that Haddy honestly worried about whether or not it might re-break Charis's forearm, or literally tear both her arms off at the sockets if worst came to worst.

I'm taking one, she'd said. *We don't know what will happen up there. If one of us has trouble, or gets injured, what would we do then? No, we're both wearing them, and that's final.*

Now that they were up here and feeling the wind, Haddy was glad she'd won the argument.

"You're good," Haddy said when he finished his inspection. "Guess we'd better go."

A thrill ran through him as he said it. The same kind of thrill he got anytime he stepped off a perch, or hung upside down before a dive down the Gallery, or slipped when mountain climbing on the Lunar surface. Butterflies in the stomach, chills on the spine, a fluttering of electricity in the testicles, and a giddiness that made him feel like he might throw up and die of delight all at the same time.

"All right," she said. "On three. I'll go first. One, two, three." She sprinted counterspin along one side of the gantry, hopped up to the railing, jumped over the edge, and was lost to Haddy's view.

Haddy counted three and followed her over the edge into the howling night.

IT'S WHAT WE SIGNED UP FOR

THE WIND HIT HARD as Haddy jumped. He'd thought to jump into the wind and deploy his wings, but that plan went moot the moment his body hit open air.

It knocked him backwards, tossing him under the gantry with centimeters to spare, the trusses barely missing his head, and that only because the under-surface was, like the rest of the station, curved, and his counterspin momentum had hurled him far enough forward that the gantry deck rose as Haddy fell.

The brutal wind whipped him downstation like so much litter, sending him into an unstoppable head-over-heels tumble toward the distant lightpipes, while the momentum he'd jumped with carried him inexorably toward the patch of ground in front of him.

The ground was all around him. He might have hundreds of meters of wiggle room in every direction when it came to correcting for mistakes, but by the same token, every direction posed a limitation more tangible than any hard deck that any air traffic controller ever dreamed up.

Haddy flailed about, trying to get purchase on the air, but his movements seemed useless. He was like a man blown out an airlock, clawing and scratching and trying to get a grip on nothing.

His wings weren't working.

Then a voice in his head said *This is the new suit, stupid.*

Bat-wings, remember? Deploy your wings before you're a smear on the greenbelt.

Heeding the thought, Haddy somersaulted into a side roll, used his body like a skydiver, splaying all his limbs facing the gale, catching the wind to stabilize his angular momentum, and hoping like hell that he didn't hit a cross-wind in the next six seconds.

It worked. He stopped tumbling.

Haddy jerked all four limbs, and deployed his wings and tail.

They caught the wind harder, and he started seriously gaining speed.

In the wrong direction.

He'd never flown into wind this strong before—he'd used gentle breezes to soar, and tail winds to give him a speed boost, but headwinds were not something that really occurred in Luna City, at least not with enough ferocity to notice.

Haddy experimented with pushing and pumping into the wind, and gave it up as useless after only a few seconds.

So he re-oriented himself into a dive, nose toward the ground, and found that he was able to tack upwind as he pumped groundwards. He figured he could ride the winds like a sine wave—outwards, then inwards, and make it to the target eventually.

But as he was looking at the ground through his blink-lenses, seeing everything in near-IR, he saw the wispy updrafts of heat, and their scattering patterns, and realized that he was seeing a *map of currents*. All he had to do was find the current going in the right direction...

There. The currents were stratified. He could see vortexes and perturbations in the laminar flow every time the currents hit a thermocline. The entire mass of air circulated gradually counterspin—which Haddy supposed must be because the air didn't keep speed with the ground once it left the layer right near the surface—but they also traveled in layers as they moved inward. The radiating heat rose a few dozen meters, where it was smeared counterspin and then carried upstation toward the magnificent heat bloom that was the high-rent district, then it curled toward the center and reversed itself and blasted back downstation toward the lightpipe panel.

Haddy realized that the currents would have to move a lot differently during the day with the lightpipes pouring energy into the place and the air conditioners taking it out, but he didn't really care about how it worked during the day.

He arrested his dive at the upstation current and leveled, then flapped as hard as he could, pushing air behind him, taking advantage of the tailwind to build up terrific speed. The ground below him slid out from under him—he wasn't keeping pace with rotation, and he could feel it in his arms. There was less and less pressure pushing him outwards toward the hull.

It took him a full two minutes to make up lost ground. He built up enough speed that he started braking long before he reached the updraft—or indraft, as he supposed it had to be called—to the downstation current layer at the core of the station.

Even with the braking, he had to pull a three-g turn on the in-swing, and then reoriented himself to push back away from the upstation wall and toward the little tower.

He fleetingly hoped that nobody was looking out their high-rent apartment window as he soared past. That might invite unwanted attention.

Haddy leveled out and found his current. It started gentle, but the tail wind kicked up fast. He found himself whirling and circling back to keep his speed low, all the while scanning for Charis's laser painting on the target perch.

The structure they were looking for was between Sections B and Station C. As he approached the hub for Section B, Haddy's gaze followed the tracks to find the little superstructure halfway to Station C.

There.

But he couldn't see the laser paint on it. He might have fallen part or all of the way around the station—he had no way to know. Charis had bounced it off a surface that *should* have been visible from this angle, but he couldn't see it.

The currents are flowing in columns—concentric circles—not vertical strata, Haddy reminded himself. *This tailwind goes all the way around the station.*

He banked into a corkscrew, and found that doing so allowed him to control his speed a lot better.

One turn around the circumference of the station brought no joy.

Two turns, same thing.

On the third turn, he swung out wider.

There you are. Dim and broad and green, lighting up the shadowy cylinder jutting out from the dark tracks against the bright ground.

Haddy circled inwards in the ghost-light, aiming for the shadow, adjusting and readjusting his speed every second or less, trying to match both downstation momentum and spin, until he found himself chasing the structure, working to stay even with it and not slip sideways before he could collapse his wings and get his hands on it...

Bam.

In one swift motion, Haddy retracted his wings and grabbed the structure, splay-fashion, slamming into it so hard it knocked the wind out of him.

He dared not move. No matter how much he wanted to beat at his chest, try to make himself breathe again, he knew that if he let go he'd get blown off into the bore and waste precious minutes and energy doing the whole damned operation over again—and, and maybe get hurt worse on the next landing, due to fatigue, and maybe botch the whole job and maybe cost Charis her arms, or Min her life, in the process. He just hung there while the panic built, and built, and built, until all he could think about was air, and how he wasn't breathing, and how his throat was collapsing, and how he was going to die up here, and no one would find his body until pieces of it started rotting off and floating lazily out to ground level.

He wasn't going to last another second.

He had to let go and move to try to make his diaphragm work again somehow or he was going to black out.

His chest shuddered like a stubborn diesel engine.

Something caught.

Glorious air rushed into his body, air sweeter than any other taste or smell he'd ever known.

And suddenly, he was breathing again, like everything was normal. His heart pounded as if he'd just taken a straight dive two hundred meters down and not used his wings until the last possible second. Like he was kissing Charis for the first time all over again.

He gulped the air in, then whooped into the wind.

"Woo hoo! Oh my god *damn* what a ride! Charis, you here?"

He climbed hand-over-hand, being careful to maintain contact with three of his four points at all times. The booties and the gloves had surfaces textured like gecko's feet—under Earth-normal gravity, the friction they generated when put under load would make even the world's fattest man stick to a glass panel with no other support. His arms would give out before the grip did.

Up here, though, with no gravity to speak of, Haddy had to keep each point pulling inwards toward each other to maintain the friction load, which was both counterintuitive and devilishly difficult.

He managed it though. He just had to hug the curve of the structure as if he were a baby chimpanzee clinging to its mother's back.

"Over here!" Charis shouted. She sounded like she was around the lip of the cylindrical structure to his left.

He scampered to her and found her tied in to a pad-eye with one of the carabiners on her tandem harness. She was leaning out against the tether, using a microwave camera on the end of a collapsible stick to scan through the fullerine walls.

"Did you find her?"

"No. Not over here."

"You work left, I'll work right."

"What?"

Haddy scampered closer and shouted again, practically in her ear.

"Got it," she said, and went back to work.

The entire cylinder was only about twenty meters in diameter, and they knew from the tracking information that Min's room was somewhere on the outermost level. All they had to do was find it.

Haddy scampered around until he was over the horizon from Charis, found a pad-eye, and hooked in. He should have expected pad-eyes up here—maintenance people would need to be able to get out and do work on the external walls, to repair UV damage from the lightpipes if nothing else.

With his hands free, he opened his tool bag and produced a camera and stick, being careful not to disturb the other contents so much that they bounced out in the microgravity.

He was light up here. He had weight, but he'd have laid good money that this close to the hub he'd tip the scales at under a kilogram.

The camera didn't look like a camera—there was nothing on it that looked like a normal lens—instead, it was a small plastic do-dad, about the size and shape of a deck of cards. One side was covered in gold mesh, which was actually the lens overlaying the sensor, appropriate to the scanning wavelength. It worked like a polarizing filter to help the sensor produce a clean image. He attached it to one end of the stick, then flicked the stick out to its full two meters extension.

The controls on the stick's handle allowed him to transmit to his blink-lenses, and the net effect was that he could look right through the fullerine hull into whatever room was beyond. At this wavelength, only water and metal and other high-conductivity materials scattered the waves back.

He found a room with a desk and some screens in it, along with a ghostly squeeze-bottle of water floating on what appeared to be thin air, though logically Haddy knew it had to be resting on some surface made of fiberglass or fullerine or some other carbon composite.

But no Min.

He shuffled along another four meters and repeated the process. This was some kind of closet, there were racks full of metal tools etching their ghostly images across his vision, but still no Aunt Min.

One more shimmy round brought him within sight of Charis again.

"Anything?" he shouted.

She held up a hand, continued her sweep. Haddy secured himself into a pad-eye near at hand and leaned back against his harness, then started his.

An empty room again—some furniture, but not much.   Ghosts of something gossamer—wet cloth, maybe—scattered on the floor, and a lump of something...

Min.

Her head was pointed towards his position. About a meter or so inside.

"I've got her!" Haddy shouted.

He didn't hear anything back from Charis, so he collapsed his stick and worked around.

Haddy found her right where he left her, but she wasn't actively scanning now, she had a worried look on her face. When she saw him moving her hand went up again, gesturing for him to stay still and stay quiet.

Then, her hand went down, she unhooked, and she moved over towards him with an immense amount of care, as if she were trying not to disturb a sleeping person.

When she got to where he was, she pointed further along the hull, so he unhooked and lead her over the horizon from the cylinder, counting the arm-spans so he'd know where he was in relation to Min.

They stopped on the border of Min's room and the closet, when Charis hooked in.

"We have a problem," she shouted. "There's someone in there, they're awake and moving around. I should have expected it, I'm sorry."

"How many? Just the one?"

"Just the one," Charis said. "I figure there's the three of them, one for each shift."

"Malcolm, Sil, Andy. It makes sense. I found her."

Her eyes opened wider. It looked odd in the ghostly near-IR. Instead of getting lost in her sparkling, electric blue eyes he was looking into two glazed, dullish gray-green pits where her eyes should be, so he imagined her eyes there instead. Less creepy that way.

Haddy pointed to the hull just to their right. "She's right in there. Just gotta decide where to cut through."

"We can't cut through," she said. "He'll hear."

"Plasma cutters don't make noise..."

"They make *heat*. I planned for that but..."

"Why wouldn't he just run?" The fire suppressors and alarm had been part of Charis's plan. The moment they lit up the plasma cutters they were operating on borrowed time because it would let Malcolm and Sil know that there was something going on up here. They'd accounted for all that. In fact, they had been depending on it as a diversion to help the rest of their escape.

"After all they've gone through?"

"Right, right." Haddy swore. He wanted to smack himself for being stupid, and then do it again, and again and again until at last the smallest part of the world started cooperating. "What the hell are we going to do now?"

Charis set her jaw. She pursed her lips. She started grinding her teeth. Haddy wished he could see her in real color—the ghostly IR added one more string of disquiet to Haddy's mind in the midst of a blaring cacophony of it.

Then she closed her eyes.

"Charis?"

She swore.

"Charis, what?"

"We can't make it in."

"We can't give up now!"

"Have you got any idea for how to get in, genius?" she snapped. "Cause that's *my* mother in there less than *eight* centimeters through that wall and there's double-aught we can do to get her out!"

The end of her words was nearly choked off by a sob.

Haddy felt like this was all his fault, somehow.

It *was* his fault. If he hadn't let Malcolm and Sil bamboozle him, if he...

He didn't even know how to begin to catalog his mistakes.

Haddy closed his eyes, shook himself loose. That kind of thinking wasn't going to do any good. They were here, now, and they had to do *something*. They couldn't just go home. They *had* to get in there somehow...

"What about Mondu?" Haddy shouted. "Can he send anyone up here knock on the door or something?"

Charis shook her head. She opened her mouth as if she was going to say something, then closed it again. Then, more deliberately this time, she opened it up and shouted:

"Take my torch."

"What?"

She reached into her tool bag and produced her plasma torch and a tank the size of a football. The thrust it towards him.

"Take it!"

Haddy took it, dubiously. He didn't like where this was going.

"Wait three minutes. *Three minutes*, you got me?"

"Charis, this isn't..."

"Yes it is! Now get through that wall and get my mother out, and if you don't start cutting in three minutes we're all three wrecked."

Haddy couldn't refuse. Event through the IR haze the look on her face didn't leave any room for argument.

"Okay," he noted the time in his blink lenses. "Three minutes. Starting now."

Charis unclipped, gripped the wall, and pushed with all four limbs, throwing herself toward the spindle and tracks at the center of the station.

After ten meters, when the structure necked down to a narrow passage, she snap-deployed her wings, canted inward, and disappeared from Haddy's view.

Now he waited. He spent the time positioning himself at Min's room and scanning the wall as close to the floor as he could get. There was still spin on up here, and gravity, if ever so gentle. If he opened the wall as close to the floor as possible, she could just crawl straight out.

He found a spot, not too far off from where he was hoping to, where he could cut through without hitting any wires or other metal brick-a-brac that was inside the wall.

Haddy stowed the camera and stick, took out the plasma cutter, leaving the tank in his tool pouch. There was enough hose length to feed the fuel without bringing it out, and he needed his hands free.

Thirty seconds left.

Haddy positioned the cutter against the bulkhead, flipped the power switch, and counted down.

Five.

Four.

Three.

Two.

One.

Haddy squeezed the trigger.   The plasma cutter erupted in blinding blue. He closed his eyes against the glare—but it didn't stop the blink-lenses. They picked up the IR bleed through his lids and gave him a fuzzy picture of the wall, with pinpoint sharpness where the plasma flame was.

The wall around the torch flickered and flared as the carbon in the fullerine caught fire, then guttered out as the other chemicals in the matrix—chlorine and fluorine—vaporized and smothered it out.

He had to force his hand to stay slow and steady, and not to rush. He repeated Charis's instructions to himself.

Move slowly. No more than a centimeter per second.

At that rate, it would take almost three more minutes to make the hole big enough for Min to fit through. If the wall was more than eight centimeters thick, he'd have to cut twice, maybe more, in order to get all the way in. How in the hell was Charis going to keep whoever-was-in-there busy for all that time? The only thing Haddy could think of that might give him enough time to escape with Min was...

Oh no, she isn't...

She can't!

Haddy ground his teeth together as the seconds melted away with the wall, the panic growing in dry, itching his throat with every passing second.

Halfway done now. Charis, come on, don't do anything stupid please please please.

He couldn't lose her. Not her. Not after everything else. He *couldn't.*

Overhead, a red light blinked. A siren blared through the wall. Haddy could hear it.

The fire alarm.

Charis I hope you got them out of there somehow.

Almost there. Almost...

The cutter completed its circuit. Haddy threw it away and kicked the panel with all his might.

It buckled inward.

Haddy looked inside. Through the heat haze bleeding off the edges of the cut, he could see Min looking around in confusion.

"Min!" he shouted. "Aunt Min! It's Haddy. Come on, quick!"

"Haddy?" She sounded confused. Then, after a half-second. "Hadrian Jin?"

"Come on, we don't have any time."

She didn't waste any. Min faded back to the opposite wall, kicked off, and shot toward Haddy.

Haddy shifted up to block the hole with his body, and took the full force of her mass straight in his solar plexus, letting it snap him back against his harness.

Min grunted.

"You okay?"

"Yeah. Yeah."

"Okay. Good. Grab on. That's it. Arms around me. All the way out. Quick, now, quick! Don't let go!"

Min cleared the little hole. Haddy swung her out into the emptiness.

"There's almost no gravity up here. Grab the harness, here, on my legs. These straps." He guided her hands to the loops around his legs. "Got a good hold?"

"Yeah. I got it."

Haddy could barely hear her over the howl of the wind.

"All right, I've got a tandem harness here. You remember how those work, right?"

"Of course I do! How are we going to get down from here?"

"Just put the harness on when I pass it to you, but don't let go. I don't know if I can catch you in this wind. All right?"

"I read you."

Haddy unclipped the tool bag covering the tandem harness and threw it away, trusting to luck that there wouldn't be anyone down in the greenbelt that would get hit by it at this time of night.

He handed it to Min. She took it with her left hand and started struggling into it, a devilishly difficult thing to do one-handed with no ground to balance against.

Min switched hands and contorted around beneath him.

A white-hot blur streaked past Haddy's vision, and he jumped reflexively.

"Okay, I got...whoa!" Min's grip failed, and she fell. Another white-hot blur—a plasma burst from a thermal weapon, streaked out the hole.

Then a body.

It was Sil. He could tell from the silhouette. He'd know the shape anywhere. Those hips were still burned into his memory, probably always would be.

Haddy swore.

Charis rocketed through the hole right after Sil, arms in front of her in a full dive, and deployed her wings.

"I lost her!" Haddy screamed. "I lost Min!" He fumbled with his carabiner, trying to get loose and go after his aunt.

Charis wheeled around and flapped hard, rocketing past Haddy toward where Min was blowing away downstation. Haddy barely had time to notice it. The hull in front of him bloomed with heat as the helium plasma fire from Sil's thermal pistol struck it. He jumped back, against his tether, and Sil's body caught the wind, whipping her downstation past him, her flailing fingers missing him by only a few centimeters.

Haddy wrestled the carabiner loose and found himself floating into the high wind.

He cupped his body, getting maximum friction, turning in mid-air, trying to figure out where everyone had gone.

There. In front of him a couple dozen meters, Sil was twisting wildly trying to get control of herself. She fired off a couple more thermal shots downstation, toward another body, this one with wings.

The shot missed Charis, just barely. Charis herself was closing on Min fast.

Too fast too fast too fast.

Haddy held his breath.

Charis spread her wings, flapped to brake, then retracted them and hit Min hard, catching her in a bear hug, sending the two of them into a high-speed tumble.

A controlled tumble.

Haddy let his breath go as he recognized the textbook rescue maneuver. It looked different without the wings deployed, but Charis was jostling around to Min's back and hooking her in.

That just left Sil to deal with. She was lining up, trying to get a bead on the retreating twosome.

From Haddy's position, it looked like she had a pretty good shot.

Haddy deployed his wings and spread wide, letting the wind kick him forward, then he flapped, pouring on more speed, heading straight at Sil's back.

With two meters left, he collapsed his wings and kicked his feet forward, aimed straight at Sil's shoulders.

He hit her with a sickening crunch.

Sil shrieked in pain.

The gun tumbled away into the wind.

Haddy doubled forward and grabbed Sil around the waist with his legs. He fumbled with her clothing, found her belt, and clipped it to his tandem harness.

"You try to get loose, Sil," Haddy yelled, "You'll fall and die a smear on that deck. Stay still, I got you." Haddy let her go, trusting her belt to hold her, and deployed his wings again. He aimed for the deck, flapped outwards, pushing down through the thermoclines, losing and regaining his balance as the winds shifted and tossed them backwards into a tumble.

Twice he lost his bite on the air. Each time he retracted his wings, muscled Sil with his legs to reorient them both, and deployed his wings again.

Now he had to match spin, and match it without grounding himself. He scanned the ground for somewhere to drop her.

He spotted a yawning maw of black below him. That had to be a lake. The cold water would suck heat in in weather like this.

He resisted the urge to swoop down. He was going to have to gamble. She'd be hurt, maybe paralyzed for a while, but as long as she hit the water...

Haddy retracted his wings. He reached around Sil, who started struggling like crazy. Somehow, through the writhing battle of muscles, he found her belt buckle. It had a pushbutton release.

He pushed. Then he kicked her away and spread his wings once again, flapping hard against her, nearly tearing his arms out of his sockets trying to pull back from the ground rushing up to meet him.

Sil tumbled away, almost lazily, toward the ground below, which spun at roughly the same speed she was moving spinwards.

Haddy kept flapping, braking his momentum and whirling back over the land to catch the rising thermal. His wings shimmered and shook as they bit into the thermal, and suddenly he was riding the rising current in an accustomed corkscrew.

He chanced a look down in time to catch Sil colliding with the water with a splash that looked almost gentle.

Thank God for that.

But it wasn't over yet. He looked inward to see Charis and Min trying to negotiate the transition down the thermocline. He blink-zoomed in on them to gauge the distance, then swept his eyeline to take in the surrounding weather. He was going to have to climb straight inward, past the upstation current to the downstation current, then circle back in on them from behind.

Charis don't be stupid. Don't take any high-g turns, please please please.

Haddy climbed fast, working his arms harder than he'd ever worked them before, even in competition races. He broke through the upstation current, then to the downstation current, and rode the winds downstation, then swung outwards and caught the next draft coming back upstation, speeding up on them from behind and matching speed.

He fell into formation off Charis's starboard wing.

"Woo hoo!" he whooped. "We made it!"

Charis didn't answer.

"Charis! You okay?" he shouted, then realized he didn't have to shout loudly with them both keeping pace with the tail-wind.

"Yeah." Her voice sounded strained.

"What's wrong?"

"My leg," Charis grunted. "I think she hit me."

"Cut Min loose! I'll take her."

"Hell no!"

"You can't land with all that mass on you with a busted leg."

"I've got it! Don't jiggle my arm!"

"Charis," Min said, "Cut me loose."

"No." Charis flapped to get a little ahead. Then she wobbled. "Mom, what are you... Mom, no!"

Min separated, drifting slowly away from Charis, sliding sideways to starboard. The push sent Charis into a portways tumble, while Min shimmied, spread her arms in the wind, and stabilized herself like an old hand at the wings.

Haddy swooped down, matched pace with Min.

"I'm right above you Min. Ready to hook in. You good?"

"I'm good."

Haddy descended, centimeter by centimeter, until they were almost touching. Having matched speed with the tail wind, they were both effectively floating, so there was no turbulence to deal with. Haddy did the rest from memory.

In one motion, he brought both his arms across his body evenly, so as not to create uneven drag with the wings. He seized the tandem straps and brought them down to the D-rings on Min's hips and clipped himself in, then extended his arms again.

They were locked.

"Hell of a family reunion, eh Aunt Min?"

"I don't think I've ever been so happy to see anyone in my life."

"Well, hold that thought, we're not out of this yet." Haddy looked up to see Charis had fallen back into formation just above him and to his port. "Ready Charis?"

"Ready." She sounded pissed. "Let's go."

The two of them laid on the speed, flapping upstation and aiming towards the center, riding just below the thermocline until they got past the lift spokes for Sector B.

"Do you see it?" she shouted.

Haddy looked toward the center, just on the inside of the hub. He spotted the gallery at the customs area—or one like it. The way Nineveh was designed, there must be one on each quarter of the station's hub.

"I see it," he shouted. "How can we be sure it's the right one?"

"It is."

That was good enough for Haddy. As they approached the upstation thermal, he cut his speed, then swooped in a gentle turn and rode the thermal up the face, flapping to brake as he approached the reverse current.

"Okay, Min, hold on, this is gonna be a little bumpy."

"I'm ready."

He settled in to within a meter of the wall, flapping hard as they hit the reverse current. At this distance from the wall, the resistance was slight enough he could over-come it, even with the extra mass he was carrying.

He came in for a hover next to a railing very similar to the one he'd looked over when he came on station. A blast of air coming in from the balcony hit him in the face, and Haddy had to flap again, so hard that he was sure his shoulders were going to dislocate. He curled his elbows to reduce the resistance from the air, aimed their bodies straight into the wind, and pushed pushed pushed.

Then, all of a sudden, he was through, flying into a wide lounge that looked, at first blush, like the customs area.

But it wasn't the customs area. That was on the other side of the hub. This was the embarkation lounge. Same floor plan, same design, but with the traffic directed toward the outbound ships instead of bringing people in.

Haddy retracted his wings, stuck his feet out, and touched the ground.

Charis was already there, working her PPD. Haddy looked over at her. Her left calf was bleeding, a nasty burn streaked across it. Haddy caught the sickly whiff of frying skin.

"Are you okay?" He asked her.

"I can make it," she grunted, then said into her PPD. "Mondu, we're all set."

"Transport is ready for you," Mondu's voice came through the PPD's speaker.

Haddy reached his left hand up to his eyes and pressed his fingers against them and pinched, sliding the blink lenses out. He shook them off his fingertips as Min launched herself at Charis. The older woman caught her daughter up in a bear hug, raining kisses and tears down on her face.

"Mom Mom MOM! Save it, we gotta run."

Min withdrew from Charis, with visible effort, and nodded.

"Okay," Min said. "Let's go."

Still in their harnesses and rigs, the three of them ran in long loping strides up the ramp to the docking area. Min was unsteady in the low gravity, having only regular shoes to rely upon, so Charis and Haddy each grabbed a strap of her harness and lifted her, using her mass to give extra grip to their gecko booties.

Haddy and Charis ran as fast as they could manage and still maintain control. They had a few minutes, maybe, to get clear of the station before they were locked in.

"This way!" Charis pointed at a side chute, away from the commercial traffic area. They took the spur through a narrow hall to a small terminal room with a large bay window looking out at the stars and a small shuttlecraft clamped to the side of the station.

The airlock door was open.

As a unit, the three of them leapt the final distance to the door, barreled through and skittered to a stop.

Haddy punched the lock-cycle button as they sailed through, and the door snapped shut behind them. He found himself in a small shuttle, six meters from end to end and three meters across, remotely piloted, with only about twenty seats in it.

"Hell yeah!" Haddy whooped.

Charis slapped him.

"What was that for?"

She answered by kissing him, hard, then pushing him back away.

"Okay..." Haddy said, "What was *that* for?"

"If you don't know," Charis said, "I'm not going to tell you." But she said it with a hint of a smile.

"Fine. Whatever. That's stage two," Haddy said. "So far so good."

There was a powerful *thunk*, and the ship shifted around them.   All three of them reflexively grabbed hand-holds.

"Stage two?" Min said. "What's stage three?"

"Well," Charis said, "That's the tricky part."

"Why?"

"Do you have the exploit here on Nineveh?"

Min shook her head. "I destroyed it when they grabbed me."

"Well, that's one thing at least," Charis said. "Now we just have to get underway before they lock the ship down."

"Did Sil have a chance to raise the alarm?" Haddy asked.

Charis shook her head.

Haddy breathed a sigh of relief. "We might get away with this, then."

"With what?"

Charis filled Min in on her suspicions that the CIA had someone in station control, and how she was gambling that Mondu could use Phalanx's back door access to prevent a lockdown, and how not even Mondu was sure it would work.

Min nodded.

Seeing the two of them together, Haddy was struck by how much Min's daughter Charis looked. They shared the same willowy, wiry build, the same shape, the same powerful shoulders. Min had longer bones in her face and dark hair—Charis's squarer skull definitely let on that Amit was one of her fathers, and her hair testified to Mike's parentage as well.

But those wasn't the only differences. Min looked older. Older than Haddy remembered. Older than most people preferred to look. There was gray in her hair. Paler, too, despite her olivine skin. Crinkles around her eyes. Her cheeks were thin and drawn. Severe. Her eyes looked almost hollow, and her hair was matted and tangled as if she hadn't washed it in weeks. He wondered what they'd put her through trying to extract information from her—and then he wondered whether he really wanted to know.

"Thank you," Min whispered through tears of relief. "Whether we get out or not. Thank you."

Charis, soaked in sweat and looking as exhausted as Haddy felt, regarded her mother for a long moment, then said:

"It's what we signed up for, Mom."

"Yes," Min said. "Yes, I suppose it is."

Everyone fell silent after that. And for the next ten minutes, until the shuttle docked at the *Rising's* airlock, nobody said a word.

TRUTH IS EXPENSIVE—LIES ARE MORESO

AT 0123 HOURS, the robot ship made hard dock with the *Rising's* airlock.

Charis flew through the airlock ahead of them, shouting behind her:

"I've got controls. You guys strap in."

Min followed next. Haddy brought up the rear, following Min up from a hub-style annex with four doors, then up through another with six doors, then up one more level where they stopped in a four-by-five meter chamber just aft of, but open to, the bridge where Charis had already shucked her orn-suit and strapped herself in.

Min strapped in on an acceleration chair. Haddy unclipped his suit, gathered it into his right hand, and strapped himself into the chair next to her.

"There's an eluth injector in the left arm-rest, if you need it," Min said, doubtless noticing that Haddy looked a little green around the gills.

Haddy availed himself of it gratefully. Full-on free fall without a pressing mission had left him feeling woozy. Or maybe it was just the come-down from the evening's excitement.

Rising shuddered and jolted as she blew moorings. Not the most auspicious take-off. In almost the same instant, a bland feminine voice blared over the radio from the bridge:

"This is Nineveh docking control, all clearances are canceled due to a fugitive alert. Your cooperation is appreciated." Then, a second later: "*PRS Rising*, this is Nineveh docking control. You are not authorized to depart at this time. You are directed to return to your dock and submit to customs inspection."

"Negative, Nineveh, we are clear and proceeding under our own power." Charis emphasized the point by firing the thrusters, pushing Haddy down into his chair and *Rising* up into open space.

"*PRS Rising*, you are now in violation of your docking license. You are ordered to heave-to and surrender."

"Fine me."

Haddy turned to Min. "Won't they come after us?"

Min shook her head. "This is a commercial station. Their only armaments are for asteroid defense. If they shot ships out of the sky, the debris would damage the station."

"Not very good for business?"

"You got it."

"Don't worry about it," Charis said. "We know a guy who can fix our docking license for us."

"Mondu," Haddy muttered to himself. He decided, then and there, that he needed to come back here some day and thank the man personally—and maybe learn a little more about how he got involved in all this mess. Haddy's head was swimming with a couple thousand questions, but they wouldn't coalesce. Between the anti-nausea shot and the sudden feeling of victory, he found himself slipping into a comfortable, long sleep. And, try as he might, he couldn't fight it.

HADDY AWOKE SOME time later to find himself sleeping supine on a flat couch, with arm rests buttressing either side of him. The bridge was still forward, though now that meant "up" rather than "in front" with relation to where Haddy was. He definitely hadn't been moved—someone must have folded down his chair while he slept. A full gravity was pressing down on his chest, which meant they were clear of the Nineveh docking pattern and under boost, presumably heading back for Luna City. His orn-suit was gone, his safety belt was missing. The other chairs were missing, too, as was Min.

Looking around, he decided that he must be in the galley. When he'd fallen asleep, it had been a featureless room with four acceleration chairs. Now there was a table deployed to his right, and beyond that a wall had opened up to reveal a microwave oven, a sink with tap, and a pressure brewer polluting the air with the glorious scent of coffee.

Haddy's stomach rumbled in response.

He rolled off the seat—or cot, he guessed it was now—and went to inspect the cupboards. He found them well stocked, and in short order he had a microwaved ostrich-and-mushroom pirozhki in his left hand and a cup of coffee in his right.

He couldn't hear anyone else up and about, and considered exploring to find his aunt and cousin, but decided to table that until he'd finished his breakfast (or whatever it was). He sat down at the table and pretended to be civilized.

It was good food. It tasted of success—but he found he would rather have shared the celebratory meal with Charis than eat it alone.

When he was done, and had cleaned up, he found Min and Charis in a small room—almost a closet—with medical equipment. Charis's blonde hair was pulled back, a ribbed black tank top hugged her body and loose shorts fell about her hips. Her right calf was wrapped in the kind of soft resin bandages that held cellular matrix in place. When it fell off, it would look as if she'd never been burned.

This was normal to Haddy. Except for people that decorated their bodies with ritual scars, like Mondu had, he'd only ever seen scars on criminals—the kinds of people who liked to display their injuries to demonstrate their willingness to violence. Everyone else got their repairs done the proper way instead of letting the body's bumbling natural processes mark them up like dust in a crater.

Haddy shook his head when he realized he'd been staring at Charis. He wondered if there would ever be a time when it was okay to stare at someone. Seeing her made him feel giddy—no, not giddy. At least, not *just* giddy. Happy, too. Like a good healthy race round Reservoir Cave.

Charis looked like she was just finishing up a going-over on Min like she'd given to Haddy after the beating the other night, which Min was accepting in bad grace.

"Hello, Haddy," Min said, trying to push Charis away.

"Hi," Haddy felt himself blushing, having been caught looking.

But Min didn't seem to notice, and Charis was still trying to get her mother to sit still and submit to the scanner.

"Honey, really, I'm fine." Min batted Charis's hand away again.

"That's not what this says." Charis pushed Min's hand back down and kept her focus on the PPD's screen. "You're undernourished and dehydrated, you've lost sixty percent of your bone mass and forty percent of your muscle mass, and you've got a badly-set broken arm. We're going to have to re-break it and re-set it."

Min shook her head. "I'll get it done when we dock."

"That's going to be a problem," Haddy said—then realized that he'd spoken when he hadn't intended to.

Charis shot warning eyes at him, then closed them in consternation when Min said:

"What do you mean?"

"Fine," Charis said, turning off the PPD. "You might as well tell her. I was going to let her heal up first, but you go right ahead." Charis threw her arms up in apparent exasperation, but the tears welling up in her eyes betrayed her; it wasn't Min that Charis wanted to protect. It was herself.

Charis walked to the wall behind the bench where Min was sitting and attempted to look too busy to make eye contact.

Haddy decided to steer clear of the subject of Amit for the time being.

"Ring Alpha's been destroyed," he said. "There's nowhere to dock."

"It's been *what*?"

"Nuked," Haddy said. "Vaporized. The news says it was the Americans. The Marines came through after the big battle back home..."

Charis winced, and Haddy realized he'd just opened the subject of Amit's death whether he intended to or not, so he girded his resolve and plowed on.

"...they evacuated the station, then they blew it up. It's gone. We don't have anywhere to dock. We'll have to go to Gagarin and take a shuttle or..."

"Haddy," Charis said with a dangerous edge in her voice, but still looking at the wall "We're boosting at one gravity."

"So?"

"So don't you think she'll be fine sitting on the ground in a Lunar field? We have landing struts, you know."

Haddy hadn't thought about that. There wasn't any atmosphere on Luna, so any ship with landing gear could land, no matter whether it was streamlined or not, so long as said ship could take the structural stress of one-sixth g pushing on it constantly for as long as it sat on the ground.

Rising was a boost ship. It was designed for high acceleration. Luna's pitiful gravity well wouldn't bother it.

Min's face, meanwhile, took on a very worried look. "Why are we going back to Luna City? Nineveh has the network. We'd have been safe, even if they locked us in."

"Not with those people running around!" Haddy objected.

"Charis?" Min turned around to look at Charis, who was hiding behind her. "Is that what you told him?"

Charis turned to face her mother. Her cheeks were red, her eyes boring a hole in the floor in front of her.

"Wait," Haddy said, "we *would* have been safe staying there?"

"No. Well, okay, not really. Not with..." She looked up at Haddy, "...everything else."

"I think you had better tell me everything." Min was still looking at Charis. Her tone made it clear that it wasn't a request. "You start. What happened since Sidon?"

Charis told her. It was the same story she'd given Haddy, but with more detail, and more jargon.

She ran through the family's evacuation from Sidon, their stopover at Gagarin on the way to Nineveh, and then

Amit's last-minute decision to go to Luna City to follow up a rumor that Min had surfaced on Luna.

"I was there," Min said. "Well, almost. And only for about five minutes."

"What did happen to you?" Haddy asked.

Min sighed. "They—the team that was holding me, I mean—had picked up info about the exploit somehow. They were there waiting for the exchange. When they picked up the man who gave it to me and he didn't have it, they zeroed in on me. They hit me with a taser in the greenbelt on Sidon and dragged me a few feet off the path when nobody else was looking. They drugged me, and the next thing I remember they're pushing me through a transfer point on Ring Alpha. I got loose...well, I didn't get loose for long. Then I was packed up on a ship again for Nineveh, and I woke up in a cargo tub in that little room you found me in. The rest...the rest I'd rather not talk about."

Min's face said a lot more than her words did. She shook it of after a moment, looked at Charis again. "So what happened in Luna City?"

Charis shrugged. "We didn't find anything. Pop thought it was a rumor, but by then the *Rising* was attracting attention. There were Marines there in the city, and they were looking her over. Then we stopped in to check with Vin and Nita, figuring maybe they'd heard form you. And Vin asked us if we could take Haddy to keep him from trying to join the fight when it broke out..."

Haddy fumed. This was *not* the version of the story his father had given him. Vin had said Haddy might be drafted, and that it was Mike's idea to take him off into that stupid exile. Okay, sure he'd been able to help save Min, and that was good. He was glad Charis had her mother back. But if he'd been there, at the shop, when that riot broke out, he knew *he KNEW* that his own mother would still be alive right now. He'd have thrown her over the side of the Gallery himself and then flown down to save her.

Mom was dead because Dad was a goddamn coward.

But Charis was still talking, relaying her end of the incident in customs while trying to board the *Buchman*, and then the story about coming to Nineveh on her own to make the family rendezvous, but how when she showed up at Phalanx there wasn't any word, so she took a job from Mondu so she could be near at hand in case any chatter about Min floated by.

"Why did you go on your own?"

"Oh." Charis said unenthusiastically. "That was Pop's idea. He said we'd have a better chance if we all split up, so I hired a crew and came along ahead without him or Dad."

"A crew?" Min said reprovingly.

"Jack's boys vetted them, Mom," Charis rolled her eyes. "They were safe."

"All right, if you say so," Min sounded like she didn't believe...well, no, not like she didn't believe. She sounded like Haddy's mother did when Haddy had done something that she found worrying, or thought was ball-breakingly stupid.

Haddy chuckled silently to himself. No matter the training, or the trust, or the partnership in espionage, before and after everything else, Min really *was* Charis's mother. Seeing them not-quite-bicker made Haddy feel like he belonged again. Like he was home, maybe. At least a little bit.

He just wished he could've gotten the chance to fight

with his mother like that again.

"Anyway, Mom..." Charis resumed her story. She relayed how she'd fought with Mondu about putting a bounty out on the Persian destroyer exploit—she wanted the whole network looking for it, but Mondu had pointed out that people in the network might kill to get the information just to pass on, and that wouldn't do Min any good if she was still in possession of it. In the end he had put out a bounty on information about Min, worded so it was made clear that she was wanted alive and unharmed.

"Wait wait wait, bounty?" Min said. "Didn't you deliver it to Phalanx yourself?"

Charis waved Min's concern away, saying "Mom, if someone got it from you, they'd try to sell it, wouldn't they? Unless they already worked for the Americans, I mean, but then we'd hear something through the leakers, right?"

"Yes, I suppose that's true."

"Well, then I just waited for Haddy to show up. And he did."

It filled in a lot of pieces in Haddy's understanding of the narrative, but he couldn't help but notice that Charis had left out the most important part.

And when Min turned around to ask Haddy for his story, Charis's eyes pleaded with him not to mention Amit's death.

But Haddy didn't know how to tell his story without the loss. His whole story was *about* loss, and stupidity, and dumb luck. Luck that he got that Mannix contract. Luck that he'd met up with Charis. He felt like one of those castaway characters in the movies, thrown out into a storm on a nothing-raft, trying like hell to steer when they were just lucky to hold on tightly enough that they didn't get drown.

So he told it, best as he remembered it, one end to another. Min was very interested in the Mormon family, and frustrated that he hadn't spent more time with them. When he asked why, she just shook her head and said "It's another matter entirely. Not important right now." So Haddy shrugged and carried on.

He told her, in as much detail as he could, about meeting Malcolm and Sil, and his conversation with his father, and then about the information blackout to control rumors.

"Hold on there, what rumors?"

"About the big fight in LC. Well, fights. Marines in the spaceport, war against the civilians."

"Oh my god, they went and done it," Min gasped. "Those two-bit bastards went and done it. It's started."

Haddy shrugged. "I don't know who did it, but yes. It's done. There's a war on...but I didn't find that out until later."

He continued with his story, sparing details in the more embarrassing parts—he just talked about Sil trying to seduce him, rather than going into the kind of gory details he had when he'd told Charis—but then he got to the Mannix deal, and the news he learned when he got net access.

"Dead? Nita?"

Haddy nodded. Telling the story had smeared his cheeks with tears again as he relived the shock, but the question itself pushed him back to one remove, as if the facts of the case didn't have anything to do with his feelings.

"In the attack. Charis was there, she saw what happened." He almost didn't say this last—Charis was clearly desperate that he not mention it—but something about the way Min asked questions made him feel obligated, somehow, to complete answers.

Or maybe he'd just finally decided that he'd had enough of being buried under lies, and wasn't willing to add any more of his own to the pile.

Now Charis was fuming.

"Charis?" Min turned to Charis, so Haddy couldn't see Min's expression. But her tone shook him to his center. Disapproval and terror wrapped tight under a calm, collected veneer.

"It's not important. Not right now..."

"What happened?" Min said. "Tell me."

So Charis told her. Everything.

Haddy could barely stand to listen to it.

Min nodded grimly as Charis finished.

"How long until we make planetfall?" Min asked quietly.

"Three days. Well, a little less than that now."

Haddy started out of his misery at the figure. Like anyone who knew anything, he was aware of how fast a ship moved under constant boost, but living the difference between an ITN liner and a torch ship in the space of a week knocked him back on his heels.

A hard look came over Min's face.

"Very well," Min continued with an eerie false-calm. "I think I need some time. I'll see the two of you at breakfast tomorrow and we'll pick this up then. And no more evasions, either of you." She looked at Haddy. "You don't know how serious this is," she turned to Charis, "and you only think you do. If you hold something back, we will count the cost in blood. Maybe a person's. Maybe a city's. Do not test me, children."

Haddy found himself nodding and promising to cooperate. Charis merely grunted.

"I mean it, Charis," Min said.

"Okay, okay, fine, okay? I got it. Jesus, Mom."

"That'll do for now." Min pushed herself up to standing. "I'll be in my room."

She walked toward the door with great difficulty. The weeks spent in micrograv had weakened her to the point of frailty. Haddy offered to help, but Min waved him off.

When she reached the door, she stopped, looked back at the two of them, and said:

"When I was in there, I didn't dare hope someone would find me. I never dreamed it would be the two of you. Thank you. It was an incredible plan. And you," she pointed a shaky finger at Haddy, "You're going to have to show me the way around those new suits of yours."

"Yes, ma'am," Haddy said.

Min hobbled out.

Haddy sighed, not knowing how to feel anything in particular when he had so many different, contradictory emotions knocking around inside of him.

Not that he had time to think much on it. As soon as Min was out of earshot, Charis was out around the examination bed.

"Thanks, genius. I wanted to save that little gem until she'd had something to eat and some sleep. Is that too damn much to ask?"

Haddy shrugged. "Waiting would have just made it worse."

Charis's right arm flew up to slap him. Haddy caught it this time, and held it.

After a moment, Charis closed her eyes and took a deep breath.

"That just shows how much you know," she snarled, and ripped her arm free of his grip, and stalked out.

WITH MIN IN her quarters, and Charis resolutely refusing to speak to him, Haddy had to figure out where he was going to bunk without any help from the people that actually owned the ship.

Not that he was at a loss for options. Haddy found that he could take his pick from four of six small staterooms—the other two were occupied by Charis and Min—each barely big enough to fit a queen-sized bed and a smaller shelf-bed above it, both of which folded out from the walls. They had vacuum-driven toilet facilities in-room, and they were arrayed like slices of an angel food cake around a central area where the shower cubicle lived—the ladder leading up-and-down between decks ran along the outside of one of the cubicle's wet walls.

Thusly arranged, the entire crew quarters area occupied the whole of the second deck aft from the bridge, one deck back from the area with the large galley, the tiny infirmary, and a presumably large auxiliary room (Haddy found the door locked and didn't have the code) where Haddy had spent his time aboard thus far. He figured it must have exercise equipment in it, or something else to fight the boredom in stretches between planets.

Haddy mentally claimed one of the four identical empty rooms, then strayed down one more level to find himself in another hexagonal annex with one of the cake-slices removed, creating an open space leading to the airlock and a series of cabinets filled with pressure suits and other vacuum gear. The rest of the cake slices were fronted by locked doors marked "Service Personnel Only," and a room number.

So much for exploring.

In Haddy's limited experience, it seemed like a good logical layout for a ship. A damn-sight more logical than Charis's weird attempts to spare her mother the bad news...

No. That wasn't fair. She'd *panicked* any time the truth got anywhere close to Min. No matter what she said, she wasn't trying to protect Min from the hurt. Or at least not *just* that. It was something different. Almost like she wanted to protect Min from knowing at all.

Yes. Of course. Everybody else knew. Everybody in the family, everybody in the universe. But as long as Min was ignorant, than there was some part of the universe where Amit was still alive. If only for a little bit longer.

Haddy climbed the ladder and went into his room. He pulled out the bed and sat on it, and sulked. He really had done it now. He had officially graduated from "clueless with girls" to "insensitive bastard," and without even trying. Any more not-trying would probably get him promoted to "world's biggest asshole" by the end of the week.

After an hour of mulling things over, and not coming up with any better conclusions, he activated the terminal in his room and tried to connect to the net. It took a few minutes for the ping to turn around, but that would be enough. Haddy used the time to write a note to Charis explaining how he'd realized he was a jerk, and then sent it off, mainly because he couldn't stand the thought of her sitting up on the bridge all alone and hurting like she was.

Then, lacking anything better to do and being exhausted from the roller-coaster, Haddy pulled up a slide show of Josie on his PPD, and propped it next to his pillow where he could watch it, and he drifted into a fitful sleep.

TAP TAP TAP tap tap tap tap

Haddy buried his head under his pillow and went back to snoring.

Tappity tappity tap tap tap

"Oomrefffrrgglle go away!"

But the tapping continued. Persistently. Mercilessly. Long enough that it actually woke Haddy up, if you could call feeling like you'd been run over by a tram car "awake."

Haddy sighed heavily. "Come in."

The door slid aside, and Min tottered in. She'd showered, and dressed in a fresh orange shipsuit, but she didn't look as if she'd rested. Her eyes were puffy, red, and swollen, and she still moved like her body couldn't bear her weight.

"Aunt Min. What's wrong?"

She sighed. "I don't like to wake you, but I need to speak with you alone. Do you mind if I..." She looked enviously at the foot of his bed.

"Yeah, sure, sure, sit down. God, I'm sorry. You could have paged me, I'd have come to you so you didn't have to..."

She shook her head. "I have to walk as much as I can bear if I want to recover."

Haddy couldn't think of anything to say that wouldn't make him look stupid or useless, so he kept his yap shut.

She reclined across the foot of his bed, laying on her side facing him, propping her head-end up on her elbow. There were little beads of sweat on her olive forehead, and lines of pain down her neck and around her eyes. Haddy handed her a spare pillow to use as a prop instead. She accepted it graciously, but didn't use it.

"I need you to tell me the rest of the story. Every detail. Don't worry about upsetting me."

Haddy took a deep breath. "Well, after I read the news in that conference room..." And he told her the whole thing. This time he left in everything—all the embarrassing details, all the stupid mis-steps. Any time he felt like covering something up in order to make himself look less stupid, he forced himself to leave it in.

"...and, well, that's when I kicked the wall in, and you know what happened after that." Haddy's heart was thumping like a caged animal. He felt like he was waiting for a judge to pass sentence on him. He didn't know why, but all he wanted to hear now was that he'd done *something* right.

Min watched him for a long time, as if she was looking for something deep inside him. He wanted to squirm, turn around, look away, but something about her gaze held him for a long time.

Finally she said:

"You love her, don't you?"

Haddy crinkled his brow. "Who?" The question was so far out of what he'd expected that he wasn't sure he even understood what she was asking. "You mean Mom? Of course I do."

Min smiled, just a little.

"Charis."

"Charis?" Haddy scrambled. He felt as if he'd just run off the edge of a cliff. He was sure that he'd never thought about Charis exactly that way—well, not *exactly* that way, at any rate—and yet he was equally sure, at the same time, that Min had spotted something that he'd been struggling to keep secret even from himself.

And it scared him to death.

"Yes," she said. "Charis."

Haddy looked at the bedspread, too embarrassed to look Min in the eye.

"I...I...I guess, maybe..." he stumbled, and stopped. Did he love her? Really? Or was she just exciting?

Sil was exciting, or had been. But that had been different. He'd known, right away, that there was nothing more there. That's why he'd put her off as much as he did. He didn't want *just* exciting. He wanted a girl who he felt about...he felt stupid even *thinking* it, but he wanted a girl who he felt about like he felt about Josie. Someone who he could matter to. Someone who he could just be near, who made him feel like some part of the world was good, even when everything else was crazy and dark and terrible.

But he wanted more than that. He wanted someone who would play goofy games with him, and who would go flying with him, and who he could work with.

Someone like that, who was exciting too.

Someone like...well, like Charis, now that he thought it through.

He took a big breath. It wouldn't make any difference now, anyway, after everything else he'd just told Min about himself. She saw straight through him. It wouldn't do any good to lie. "Yes. Yes, I think I do."

"You should tell her, you know."

"But...why?" The last thing he wanted was another slap, especially today. He just wanted to get home and see Josie. He wanted to see the shop. He wanted to talk to his father, even though his father had set the whole miserable thing in motion and he wanted to punch him in the face...he was still Dad. Why complicate things even more than they already were?

"Because if you don't, you will always wonder. We're in a war, Haddy. We might all survive. Or any of us could die in a bombing, or an invasion, or by pirate attack. We could get knifed by someone trying to contain a secret that they think we know, even if we don't. How would you feel if she died, and you never told her?"

Haddy felt icy fingers grip his heart. As if Min had just turned on the tap deep in his soul, his eyes welled up and he couldn't get control of himself.

"The truth is expensive," Min said. "It's risky. But I can promise you, as someone whose business is deception, that lies are moreso."

"And you...you wouldn't mind? I mean, if she felt the same way?"

"You have a lot to learn, Hadrian. One of those things is that no matter how good humans get at fixing injuries, or bringing people back from the brink, or rejuvenation, or curing diseases, none of us knows how long we have. Life is change. Life ends. But whether it's for a week, or a month, or for life, she could do worse." Min reached out, took Haddy's hand. "You're a good man, Hadrian. I think Charis would be a lucky woman to have a man like you in her life. Don't miss your chance to find out if she feels the same."

Haddy nodded. He didn't know what to say.

"Hey," Min said nodding at his PPD, "Who's that on the screen?"

"That? That's Josie. Here." Haddy seized the device and started showing pictures, telling Min all about how he'd saved up for her, and the crazy energy she had, and how much work it was to train her, and how he'd loved every minute of it...and then he suddenly realized he was exhausted again. "I think I need to sleep some more. What time is it anyway?"

"About 0600. You only slept a couple hours." She squeezed his hand and then heaved herself to a sitting position. When she spoke again, her voice was all business. "I'll need to talk to you both tomorrow. Set your alarm for 1400, meet me in the mess. There's one more problem in all of this, and I will need all the help I can get."

A Fast-Approaching Problem

HADDY'S ALARM BEEPED briefly. He waved his arm around, searching for his PPD.

Instead, he found something soft and warm.

For a moment, he thought he was back in his bed at home, with Josie stretched out against his back, and the whole adventure had been a terrible dream.

But his weight was wrong. His arm was too heavy for Luna. This was a full-g field.

And Josie never slept *under* the covers.

Haddy turned over, and found himself face-to-face with Charis.

"Good morning," she said.

"Um...hi." And then, because he felt stupid just saying hi: "How did...I mean...why did...I mean...when did you get here?"

"A while ago. I found your message after I woke up."

"Oh."

"I didn't want you to start the day thinking I didn't."

"Uh...thanks, I guess."

Charis reached for him, ran the backs of her fingers down the side of his face.

"I'm sorry," she said. "I shouldn't have...well, I shouldn't have blamed you for that. I just...you were right. I didn't want him to be dead."

Her chin was trembling.

"I understand," he whispered.

"Haddy?" She was so close now that her face was a soft, jumbled, wonderful blur. "I...I...I couldn't have done it without you."

Haddy smiled. He wanted to tell her he loved her, that waking up to her face was the finest thing that ever happened to him, that he wanted it to happen again sometime. Maybe all the time. But all that came out was:

"We make a good team, don't we?"

"Yeah," she breathed.

He felt her breath on his cheeks.

And her forehead against his.

And then he was tasting her. Kissing her like he meant it, because he did. And she did too, or at least she seemed to. He lost track of where his face ended and hers began. Of where her breath ended and his began. Of where her hands ended and his body began.

Haddy came up for air only reluctantly, when he was afraid his heart would explode in his chest.

Charis's lips on his ear sent electricity all down his body. "I hate to say it," she said, "But Mom needs us in the mess."

Haddy shuddered. "She's a smart lady. She can manage without us."

Charis chuckled. "Oh, god, you have no *idea* how much I wish that were true."

"Really?"

She pulled back and held his gaze.

"Really."

"Wow."

She slipped back out of his bed, standing in her half-unzipped white denim shipsuit. She looked down, laughed, and zipped it up.

"You're sneaky," she said.

"Hey, it's not my fault, I didn't even know I was..."

But she was laughing again.

"Come on," she said through her laughter, "We have work to do."

BREAKFAST WAS BAGELS and bacon and dried mango. Not exactly steak and eggs, but there was enough for Haddy to get four servings, which was just about enough to quiet his ravenous appetite. Every time he got up to get another helping, Min looked like she was about to collapse from trying to contain her laughter.

"What?" Haddy said. "Do I look *that* funny when I eat?"

"No, no, no, you just look *exactly* like your Dad did when he was your age."

"Gee, thanks." If there was one person he didn't want to be like right now, it was his father.

"It's a good thing," Min said.

"I'll have to take your word for it."

"Okay, Mom, enough. What did we have to get out of bed for?"

Min raised an eyebrow. "We?"

Haddy felt his ears catch fire, and he concentrated firmly on his food.

"Oh shut up," Charis said.

Min shrugged, then leaned forward with her elbows on the table.

"How many hours until turnover?"

"About six hours to the halfway mark," Charis said. "It's all downhill from there. I've got us plotted into the main Grissom approach orbit. We should be on the ground in about forty hours."

"Very well," Min said. "We have forty hours. Thirty nine, since you'll have to be at the controls for the final hour."

"Thirty nine hours to do what?" Haddy asked.

"To figure out where that exploit went."

"Mom, it's gone. It wasn't on Pop when he died."

"He wouldn't just let it go, would he?" Haddy said.

"No," Charis said. "He wouldn't have even told me about it, normally."

"But he did," Haddy said. "Why?"

Charis shrugged. "I have no idea. Unless...I don't know, maybe he wanted me to tell Mondu if something happened to him? So Mondu could watch the Persian darknet to see if it popped up somewhere else?"

"I don't think so," Min said. "The man who leaked it claimed he discovered it. He said he was giving me the only copy."

"So why don't we find him again?" Haddy said. "Ask him to, I don't know, re-create it?"

Min shook her head. "He was killed in an accident shortly after he talked to me."

Haddy cocked his head. "Even if that's true, how could you possibly know that?"

Min took a PPD from her left breast pocket, set her fingers dancing across it, then placed it on the table between Haddy and Charis.

The screen showed a headline:

Six Dead in Airlock Failure

Scrolling down, Haddy saw there were pictures of the deceased in the article.

"How did you find this?" Haddy asked.

"I haven't slept yet."

"Mom!"

"Don't 'Mom' me, young lady. Listen: We have to find that exploit. Or, at the very least, we have to make sure it was destroyed. The only thing worse than not finding it is letting the Americans get to it."

"Okay, I get that it is. I believe that," Haddy said, "You can steal a warship with it, and that's a big deal. But why is it *this* important?"

Just as Min opened her mouth to answer, Haddy found himself continuing at an almost frantic pace:

"Come to think of it, why is *any* of this going on? I spent a lot of time on Nineveh trying to read up on all this crap, but I couldn't find anything *anywhere* that would actually explain why this war is even *happening*. Everyone seemed to, I don't know, *assume* that I understood it already. But I don't. I don't and it's making me insane. Why would the Americans send the Marines to blow up Ring Alpha? Why would they invade Luna City? Why would we declare independence instead of, I don't know, filing a lawsuit or something, or bringing the assholes who ordered the raid up on charges?"

"That's a long story, Haddy."

Haddy shrugged. He didn't care how long the story was. "Look, you two live and breathe this stuff. I *don't*." He looked from Min to Charis, then back to Min again. "Aunt Min, Charis told me why you left the business, so you know how Dad and Mom are. Politics makes about as much sense to me as Greek Mythology. Actually," Haddy took a deep breath, and let itself out, trying to slow himself down so that he could actually speak sensibly, "it makes less sense, now that I think of it. But what I *do* know is business. Vested interests. Competition. Customer service and everything. If you want me to be any use here, I need to know *why* everyone cares enough about this whole situation to...well, shoot people over it, and blow up ships, and invade cities, because this has all seemed completely bug-nut crazy to me ever since Dad told me I had to run away to Nineveh so I didn't get drafted."

Min snorted into her coffee. "He would put it that way."

She took a drink, set the coffee down on the table, and folded her hands in front of herself again.

"Okay," Min said, "quick version.   There hasn't been a major war on Earth for almost a hundred years. Minor wars, sure. Regional conflicts, especially as the Persians expanded fifty years ago, but nothing like used to happen."

"What used to happen?"

"For a thousand years before that, there was a major war every twenty-to-fifty years, with a couple exceptions."

"Why?"

"There are a lot of reasons," Min said. She pursed her thin lips together, as if she was trying to choose her words carefully. "And, keep in mind that this is a gross over-simplification. Not *all* wars start this way, but...most wars, almost all of them, come down to the fact that a government's power depends on its ability to protect its people from famine, drought, disease, and invasion. A government that doesn't do that loses its power pretty quickly. People revolt..."

"...like we're doing now?"

"Yes. Like we're doing now. A lot of Loonies think the government hasn't been doing its job keeping the shipping lanes safe, or keeping the colony safe, and they're angry at having to pay for services they don't feel like they're getting."

Haddy nodded. That made good sense to him. He'd

seen what kind of lengths irate customers were willing to go to.

"Anyway," Min took another sip of her coffee, "Earth has a problem. It's always had this problem: there aren't a lot of places on Earth that are safe from all of those things. Crops grow most easily on open plains which you can't defend—remember, vertical farming only came in in the last eighty years—metals only show up in certain kinds of geology, and it's rarely the same geology where farming happens. So, every generation, neighbors fought over farmland to grow crops, and river access to run the mines and move their harvests, and because the country next door had better mines and was building bigger weapons and that meant they could steal your country if they decided it was in their interest."

"That's...awful."

"Yes."

"What do you mean by a 'major war?'"

"Big enough to wipe entire countries off the face of the Earth. Battles where tens of thousands of people would die in a single day. Whole cities would get bombed or burned out of existence, or, before that, starved to death, or have plagues sent against them—you've heard of biological warfare?"

"Yeah, of course. Using diseases as weapons. But nobody does that, because the diseases are just as dangerous to the people who cook them up."

"Yes," Min said. "Now."

The way she said it sent a chill through Haddy.

"Until two hundred years ago, people used them all the time. Back before there were guns, people would dip arrows in raw sewage to infect the enemy. Even a slight wound would kill someone, and if it was the right disease that took hold, it would kill a lot of someones."

Haddy decided that he'd had enough to eat, and pushed his plate away so he didn't have to smell the food.

"Okay," he said, "So what changed two hundred years ago?"

"Cameras and fast travel," Min said, "And nuclear weapons."

"Why would that make a difference?"

Min sighed. "The short version? For most people, most of the time, it takes a lot of...conditioning...for a human to want another human to suffer. Cameras made it harder for governments to justify the destruction to their people. As for airplanes and railroads and ships...when people can travel quickly, they interbreed. Cultures mix. Countries trade with each other, and it stops being in anyone's interest to start a war. Or, at least, a major war. You'll always have little wars—people who are cut out by the system, who want a better deal, and don't think they can get results any other way. But nukes were the big one. Nukes made war too destructive. When one country can destroy the rest of the world in the course of winning a war, and another country can finish off the 'winners' with automatic retaliation, war stops being something you can win."

Haddy scowled. Outside of Earth, nukes were cheaper to build than chemical bombs, and they were safer to use in open space. The entire solar system was built on trade and travel, and cameras were everywhere. "If all that's true...how can we *possibly* be in a war now?"

"Because it's inevitable."

"What? How can a war be inevitable?"

Min looked tired, as if she didn't know which way to turn on a long, long walk.

"What happens when a meteor hits a planet?" Charis asked Haddy.

"If the meteor is big enough?" Haddy asked.

Min and Charis nodded in unison, as if they'd rehearsed.

"It might wipe out an entire planet. All that kinetic energy..."

"Exactly," Charis said.

"But we defend against asteroids. We have telescopes, and probes, and solar sails, and missiles. Asteroids heading for the Earth/Luna system, we spot them and tow them into orbit and mine them. No big deal."

"Would you be able to defend against, say, a gigaton's worth of asteroids that the spotters failed to notice until after they'd passed Luna on the way to Earth?"

"No, of course not." This was all grade school physics, as far as he was concerned. Asteroid impacts were a fact of life on Luna. Asteroid defense was one of the biggest jobs the Colonial government did. Haddy felt as if there were something big and blurry floating right in front of him, but he couldn't bring it into focus.

"Correct," Min said. "Now, forget what you think you know about people. Imagine instead that people are truly, properly crazy. The biggest fear everyone had during the early nuclear years was that some megalomaniac nutcase would get into power and launch all the missiles even though they *knew* it would be the end of the world. Or, worse, that a plane would malfunction and drop a hydrogen bomb by accident, or a missile control system would malfunction and launch on its own. It was a real danger—it almost happened a few times. No, I'm serious. There were at least four occasions when exactly those thing did happen, and it was only luck that the bombs didn't go off."

Haddy gulped down the knot rising in his throat.

"Imagine you're living on Earth, at the bottom of a gravity well so deep you don't even realize it's there. You have a whole universe above you—not around you, but *above* you. And it's filled with asteroids. You have people living on the moon, people with mass drivers that are supposed to be used for cargo. People that wrangle asteroids to mine them, that keep a stock of asteroids in orbit with rockets attached to them. You don't know these people. You don't know what might happen. What do you think you might do if you got nervous and about whether someone *up there*—who's culture you don't know, whose concerns you don't understand—is going to start dropping rocks on your cities? What if you're Persian, and you look up and you don't see Luna; you see a gigantic missile base owned by the Americans that you can't possibly defend against. What would you do?"

Haddy gulped again. "Build a fleet of warships to make sure I controlled that base."

"And if you're American," Charis said, "and you see massive Persian warships showing up in the sky around your space stations and planetary bases?"

"I'd...oh no."

"Go on," Min said.

"I'd do anything in my power to make sure they didn't get a foothold. I...I don't think I'd care how many people had to die out here, because there are billions more down there that I'm supposed to protect."

"And," Min said, "If you were a colonial? One with power, and money, and an entire civilization out here that you felt invested in?"

"I'd do anything to keep both of them out."

Min nodded gravely. "The moment that Armstrong and Aldrin set foot in Tranquility Basin, this war became inevitable. There are only three outcomes: Either the Persians control the moon and relegate the Americans to a second-rate power, or the Americans control the moon and relegate the Persians to a second-rate power, or the Loonies hold the sky on their own, and Earth learns to live with it."

"Oh my god."

Min finished her coffee. "I believe that if we Loonies don't win this war, we're going to spend the next several centuries dealing with Terran governments trying to control the solar system. It will be the kind of world we had back in the bad old days, where war was a constant fact of life. I don't want to live in that world. I don't want my children to live in that world, and I certainly don't want *their* children to live in that world. We have a chance, right now, in the next few years, to make sure the Terran governments stay on the ground where they belong."

Haddy let out a long sigh. He had wanted to know why in the world he might ever even *consider* killing another person, let along get involved in an interplanetary war. Now he knew.

And he really, *really* wished he didn't.

"So if the Americans get their hands on this," he said, "they can steal all the Persian ships, and we're not going to be able to beat them."

"Very likely," Min said.

"And if we don't get it...the Persians can use those ships to beat the Americans and take us over?"

"Probably, yes."

"And Amit wouldn't have sent it over the net because

someone might break the encryption?"

"See, Mom," Charis said, "I told you he was quick."

"Okay, so how do we find it?"

"We need to reconstruct the chain of custody. Where was Amit, and when? Who did he have contact with? Is there anywhere he could have hidden the exploit that he might have thought was safe?"

"That's a lot of ground to cover," said Charis.

"Well, we'd better get started."

OVER THE NEXT thirty-eight hours, Charis and Haddy huddled around the galley table, reconstructing Amit's final days. They started with Charis's memory, then—after being warned not to mention that they were on the way back to Luna, for fear the call might be intercepted—Haddy called home to ask his parents about everything they could remember, only to discover, again, that his Mother wasn't there anymore.

It hit him hard enough that he had to turn the call over to Charis, who spoke with Mike for over an hour—then she had to turn Mike over to Min. Haddy took notes, and then they reviewed the call together, checking the notes and filling out their timeline.

Then they repeated that process with the other members of the ad-hoc Jin household: Vin, Ulmar, and Arn. Then they moved outward to the people that showed up regularly in each account.

By the end of it, Haddy got up to stumble to bed, too tired even to want Charis to come with him.

Charis yanked him back down into his chair at the galley table and said "stay," like he was Josie or something.

He was too tired to do anything but obey while she

left the room. She returned a few moments later with a pressure injector.

"Give me your arm," she said.

Haddy complied, and was rewarded with a sharp pain as the gun sent a pressurized thump of some kind of drug into his system.

"Benzedrine. It'll keep you up for a while."

Charis then turned the pressure injector on her own arm and repeated the operation.

"And me too."

Five minutes later, Haddy was concentrating better than he had in hours. The swimming emotions about his family and his mother's death faded into the background, and he focused down on the mystery at hand.

Amit, it turned out, had regular habits, even in Luna City. He had certain shops he frequented, certain people he socialized with several times in the day he'd been there. Charis couldn't be sure whether they were old friends or whether they were network members, but she took a run at calling them. When they acted cagey, or she felt they were guarded in their speech somehow—and also in the one case where a woman hung up on Charis at the mention of Amit's name—she put them on the "network members" list. She figured those were the people that Min would need to talk to personally when she woke up.

Not that Charis gave her a chance. Any time Min tried to get out of bed, Charis badgered her to go lay down and get on with recuperating. On two occasions, the conflict escalated into a shouting match which carried straight up through the floor.

Haddy didn't care for the shouting—shouting was always an extreme event in his household, since his parents were both very even-tempered—but he had to admit his admiration for the variety and facility of profanity and rhetoric on display. He wondered what kind of business he'd go into if he had that kind of verbal imagination.

About thirty hours in, Min emerged from her hospice to review their work.

"It smells like a musk ox died in here. You," she pointed at Haddy, "Shower, now. Charis, for gods' sake, get him a shipsuit and burn that body stocking he's wearing."

Haddy looked down and realized that he was still wearing his orn-suit unitard from the rescue mission, and beat a hasty retreat to the shower cubicle in order to try to resuscitate his dignity, assuming it hadn't suffocated after being trapped in the suit with his smelly hide.

He emerged five minutes later to find Charis waiting for him with a kiss, a fresh dose of Benzedrine, and a shipsuit.

Haddy wasn't sure that he could decide which of the three was more wonderful, and contented himself with the fact that nobody was quizzing him on the subject. The shipsuit's light, loose blue denim felt like a dream of relaxation after the last who-knew-how-many hours in the unitard.

While Haddy was dressing, Charis was stripping down for the shower herself. He tried to put off dressing, on the grounds that his character would benefit immensely from a second scrubdown, but Charis just swatted him and said:

"Oooh no. You come in here with me and we're never getting out, and we've got work to do."

Up until that moment, Haddy hadn't ever expected

that he'd resent having to work.

MIN, IT TURNED out, had used her "sleep" time to pursue her own research agenda. She had been on the link, pouring through news reports and local chatter and public camera feeds, trying to find information that might fill in the cracks. While the teenagers had been getting cleaned up, Min had been integrating what she'd learned into the timeline that Charis and Haddy had been piecing together.

When Charis and Haddy returned to the galley and all parties were freshly caffeinated, Min presented the finished timeline and movement map to Haddy and Charis on the table's active surface.

Haddy was shocked. All this time he'd been looking at the text version, he'd resigned himself to the notion that, at best, he and Charis might be able to piece together a rough itinerary of Amit's hours on Luna—a list of people he talked to and in what order, maybe, or an hourly status board of where he had been at a given time.

Instead, between the three of them, they'd worked out a map of Amit's movements from the time the *Rising* landed until the moment of his death—excepting a big black hole of ignorance surrounding the week he'd been detained at Ring Alpha—without any gaps in it longer than about six minutes.

"That assumes that nobody is lying to us, and everybody is remembering accurately," Min said, "but the testimony you two procured mostly accords with what I found in the public record."

"That's amazing," Haddy said.

"No," Charis sat with one knee pulled up to her chest and her chin resting on her knee. "That's not amazing. That's us done for."

"Why?"

"Because he didn't see Jack," Charis said.

"Jack? You said something about a 'Jack' yesterday."

Min shook her head. "The less you know..."

"Oh come *on*. Aren't we past that?"

"For a great many things, yes," Min said, "But not for this. For now, let's just say that Jack is a code name for one of the key members of our network, and he has a reliable contact point in Luna City."

Haddy nodded. He disliked being kept in the dark, but she had answered the relevant part of his question, so he let it go.

Min pointed to the travel track on the map. "Amit stopped to make contact with six sources and two neighboring cell members, but no dead drops and nobody with an avenue to the right part of the network—including Jack. And Jack's the one we'd expect him to go to."

"Maybe he ran into him in the Bazaar?" Haddy said.

"Mmm," Charis said, "A brush pass would have done the job. Or a delivery. Did he place any orders?"

"That's possible," Min pressed a crooked forefinger to her lips as she mulled it over. "I didn't see anything on the video, but we are talking about Amit. The hell of it is, we only have twenty-seven hours to account for..."

"Twenty nine," Charis said. "You're forgetting the two hours after he returned from Ring Alpha." That was where Charis had been spending most of her scrutiny—that narrow window between when Amit's shuttle landed and when he died in the crush. "I think he stashed it in Vin's shop. We can take it apart when land—there are a lot of places to hide something like that."

"Did he say anything to you when he came back from Ring Alpha?"

"Um, he said hi, he hugged me," Charis looked at the ceiling as if she was scanning her memory banks. "I asked what happened. He said they searched him and questioned him, and eventually had to let him go."

"How was his mood?"

"Relieved, I think. Yeah. Very relieved. I don't think he thought he was going to make it out of there alive."

"Or," Haddy said, "Maybe he wasn't sure *you* made it out of there alive."

"That would make sense too," Charis said. "But he was also very operational..."

"Operational?" Haddy asked.

"Mmm. Like he was working. He said we needed to get to Nineveh like yesterday. At the time I assumed that he meant that we needed to catch up with you, but now...I don't know. It could have been something else. So I told him that I could go now, and he told me to wait out the shift and meet me back at Vin and Nita's place."

"It's not in the shop." Min said.

"Why not?"

"Because he was gone too long." This time Min didn't wait for the confused look that Haddy was about to give her. "The only way he could have ditched that thumbnail was to swallow it. They had him for seven days, I guarantee you they thought of that and sifted through everything that came out of him. He wasn't devastated when he came back, and his first concern was seeing that the rest of you had made it out okay, so he wasn't rushing to warn our contacts that the Americans had the exploit. QED: He never took it with him to Ring Alpha."

HADDY WAS NEVER much for mysteries. Especially locked-room mysteries. Puzzles were fun, as far as they went, but deliberately impossible puzzles dreamed up by sadistic writers who thought they were oh-so-clever just to confound people and then spring a solution on them that had been staring them in the face the whole time?

Nope. Not his thing. And he'd had plenty opportunity to find out, since that exact kind of mystery was the preferred entertainment of both his parents. Whether it was at a community theater, or a vid, or books, they loved their locked-room mysteries.

It was, Haddy reflected, just his luck that he now found himself living in the middle of a locked-room mystery, or its nearest celestial equivalent.

They went round and round it for several more hours, trying everything they could think of to come up with a list of places to search.

There was Haddy's family's apartment. That was obvious. And the shop—Amit had visited it in both time windows, so they had to check there, too.

Then there were the contacts he'd, well, contacted. Min was going to have to speak to them. She knew the secret handshake. Haddy just hoped she could get something out of them. They were, as far as he could tell, the last hope.

PRS RISING GROUNDED at Grissom Spaceport, directed by Luna City Docking Control to the far end of the concrete from the terminals. Normally, only heavy cargo landed this far out, and only for staging before being towed into the cargo bays at Termial D.

But things were not normal. And even from Haddy's vantage point on final approach, the reason was obvious.

Watching through the external cameras on his PPD from his acceleration seat in the galley, the once-pristine, perfectly level concrete slab that stretched out into Tranquility basin from the cliff wall was pockmarked with craters, as if the place had been bombed.

Well, it had been bombed. And mined. And had an army marched across it to breach the airlocks. Haddy had picked up that much from the news reports. But hearing that your hometown was bombed was a different thing entirely from actually *seeing* it.

Grissom was badly beaten, but not mortally wounded. Construction vehicles worked to repair the damage, but although they'd had four weeks since the big fight, they seemed only to be getting started on the damage.

With all that mayhem, he was astounded that the *Rising* had been able to land at the spaceport at all.

Haddy cooled his heels in the airlock with Charis, waiting for the mobile lounge to arrive and ferry them into the spaceport proper. He found himself pacing, drumming his fingers, tapping his feet. Afraid of what he would find on the other side of the ride, but unable to sit still.

"Haddy, relax."

"You relax," he snapped.

"That's not what I meant," Charis said soothingly. "This is the Benzedrine. It's washing out of your system. In about an hour you'll crash and sleep for twelve."

"Well, give me some more. We've got to find this exploit..."

"Oh no you don't." Min said it as she slid down the ladder. She hit the ground with some spring in her step, and walked upright without apparent difficulty. The Lunar gravity, being one-sixth that of what they'd been boosting at, was much easier for her to bear up under.

"Therapeutic doses only, and you two are at your limit."

The light over the airlock changed from red to green, indicating that a seal had been made with the mobile lounge's gangway.

"Let's go," Min said. She looked at Haddy. "Next stop, your place. When we get there, *I* will get started while the two of you bunk down."

A SORT OF HOMECOMING

WHEN HADDY HAD last seen it, Grissom and the Bazaar had been so choked with humanity that it was almost impossible to move.

Now, it was a ghost town. The vast half-pipes that made up the spaceport were empty, except for the occasional bystander watching the repair work, or sitting in a seat awaiting a call for a departing flight. Normally one of the arteries of the colony, it felt utterly exsanguinated.

Burns marked the walls here and there. Blood stained the carpet and the stone. It had been a hell of a fight. Haddy found himself resenting that he hadn't been here. If he had been, he could have saved Mom's life. Or, at least, he could have died fighting for her chance to escape.

Only Charis's hand in his gave him any comfort, and it was a thin comfort at that.

The scars continued halfway up the Bazaar to the Gallery. Booths still half-shambled from the crush of people. Vendors sitting behind counters empty of customers, looking listless. The whole place felt as if it was waiting for the other shoe to drop.

Haddy resisted the urge to go all the way up to the Gallery to check on the shop. There would be time for that later. Min was steering them toward the side passage that led into Haddy's housing block.

Directly, they found a door marked by a sign that read simply: *& Tonic*

Haddy punched in his door code from memory. The door slid aside revealing a living room that looked smaller than he remembered it.

"Hello? Anybody home?"

"Doesn't look like it." Charis pushed past him into the apartment and flopped down on the leftmost sofa.

Haddy didn't move.

"There's nobody here, Hadrian," Min said behind him. "They're all at the shop."

"Oh." Haddy's spirits sank. He'd wanted to see Josie. He'd wanted to see Ulmar. Maybe even Dad.

"Get to bed," Min said. "I'll make sure you aren't disturbed."

"Except for Josie," Haddy said. "Be sure to let her in."

"I'll do what I can," Min said. "You too, Charis. Bed. Sleep. Plenty of work tonight."

Charis hauled herself to her feet, grumbling under her breath. Haddy walked in on feet far too heavy for the low gravity, sliding across the floor to his bedroom door, and opened it. He stumbled inside, flopped on his bed without bothering to undress or remove his booties or even lift the covers. Charis followed him in, flopped beside him, and both were asleep inside three minutes.

IT WAS THE shouting that woke him up. Someone was in a hell of a lather on the other side of the thick bedroom door. Haddy couldn't make out the words, but he recognized his father's voice, and Min's voice.

He tried to get up, but found his left arm pinned under Charis. He was curled around her spoon-fashion, his back to the wall of his bunk-cubby, his face toward the door.

As delicately as he could manage, he slipped his arm out from under her and then climbed over her body. She curled up tighter when he disengaged, and mumbled a bit in her sleep. She wiped clumsily at her face with a sleepy hand, and then her breathing settled back in to an easy, even rhythm.

Haddy soft-footed to the door and waited for a break in the shouting, which came momentarily.

He cracked open the door, slipped out, and shut it softly behind himself again.

Vin was standing in the kitchen holding a mug, his face flushed red with anger, staring daggers at his sister who was sitting on the chair at the end of the coffee table, staring daggers back at him.

"Hello, Dad," Haddy said.

Vin dropped his mug. It tumbled lazily and clattered on the ground. "Haddy?"

"I'm home." Haddy crossed half the distance between them. He didn't know whether to offer a hug, or a handshake. Instead, he just trembled as all the rage and loss and loneliness from the whole ordeal washed over him afresh.

His fathers face went slack. "Welcome home, son."

"We found Min," he said uselessly.

"I see that. Are you okay?"

"Yeah, I'm fine..." He wasn't fine. He was barely keeping his eyes from bursting into tears. "Is...is everybody okay?"

Vin bit at his lip. "Yes. Ulmar's fine. He's at the shop."

"And Josie? She didn't get hurt, did she?"

Vin shook his head. "No, she's fine."

"Where is she? Why isn't she here?"

"She'll be back with Mike. She...we can't leave her here alone. She was sitting by the door waiting for you to get back...and Nita." Tears ran down Vin's cheeks.

"It's okay. I'm back. I'll take care of her."

Vin shook his head again. "You can't stay..."

"What?"

"You'll be leaving with Min and Mike when..."

"Oh no," Haddy snapped. "You are *not* sending me away. Not again, I have to see to the shop. I'm part owner now, and..."

"Son," Vin said, as if struggling to keep his voice under control, "There's been enough...unpleasantness around here. I'm not going to lose you too."

Haddy took a deep breath. He was spoiling for a fight now, but before he could let loose, Min cut him off.

"Perhaps we should discuss this later, when we've all had a chance to settle in?"

"You stay out of this!" Vin shouted. "Haven't you done enough to..."

"Hey, hey," Charis said blearily from the direction of the bedroom, "It's hard to sleep with all this racket out here."

Vin looked past Haddy at Charis, his eyes wide. Then he looked at Haddy, then back at Charis, as if he was trying to decide what exactly he was seeing.

Charis walked up behind Haddy and took his hand, as if to remove any doubt. Haddy looked at her. Her eyes were steel, her head was proud. He found he was proud to be standing next to her.

Vin set his jaw and turned toward Min.

"You permitted this?" he growled.

Haddy bristled.

"Yes," she said calmly. "They're of age to consent, and they do. It's not my business, and it's none of yours."

"Like hell it isn't. They're cousins."

Haddy felt his jaw clenching.

"Which Nita's parents were, too."

"This is *incest*."

Haddy felt his chest go hollow and hot. The lies and the cowardice he could understand—Vin had been trying to protect him. That made sense. But this was different. This was hypocrisy. Haddy felt as if the man standing in front of him wasn't his father at all, but some kind of fake copy without any integrity at all.

"Not in this jurisdiction, brother, and not by any psychometric theory I've ever heard. They weren't raised together, there's no bonding-confusion issue. And if they stayed together and decided to have children some day in the *distant* future they're both smart enough to use genetic screening."

"This is *my* house!"

"No," Haddy said, "this apartment is on lease to the corporation, which I now own one quarter of from my inheritance from Mom."

"I'm voting Ulmar's stock..."

"And you taught me all about shareholder oppression," Haddy lowered his voice dangerously. "Don't test me on this, Dad. I learned from the *best*."

"Get *OUT! Now!*"

Haddy stepped right up to his father, standing toe to toe in his face, and growled "I can't believe that the father who taught me how to be a man would turn out to be such a petty, sniveling child. I'm glad Mom isn't here to see what you've turned into."

Haddy whirled on his heels and stalked to the front door. It slid aside in front of him.

"Haddy!" Vin shouted.

"Go to hell, Dad," Haddy tossed it over his shoulder just before the door slid shut behind him.

HADDY STALKED BACK down to the spaceport and stood in front of the floor-to-ceiling windows that looked out over the broken landing pad. This wasn't the way he'd wanted things to go. He'd wanted a happy reunion, and to find the exploit, and then get back to his life.

But his life wasn't here anymore. Not like it used to be. He'd known that would be the case as soon as he got the news on the *Buchman*. Mom's death changed everything. He just didn't want it to. He and Vin had always been a great team. All his best memories—at least, the ones that didn't involve just Mom or just Josie—were of working in the shop with his father.

Vin was a man who'd spent every day doing what he loved. He was patient, he was even fun in his own under- stated way. He'd taught Haddy everything he knew about being a businessman, about being an adult, about sticking to your principles. Without Vin, Haddy didn't think he'd know which way was up, or why it mattered.

Face it, Haddy. You screwed it up. Bona fide, Grade A screw up. Completely plonked it in every way.

Maybe so. But none of that meant that Haddy should let Vin walk all over him.

No, but there are better ways to stand up for yourself than throwing a tantrum. So what are you going to do about it?

Haddy stood by the window for a long time. He didn't know how to feel anymore. He didn't even know if he *could* feel anymore. His insides felt as empty and broken as the spaceport itself.

After a while, his heart beat slowed. His rage quieted to a dull ache. He wondered if he'd really been angry at all, or if Vin had just poked him where he hurt the most...because Vin was hurting just as much, in just the same spot.

How are you going to fix this? he asked himself. *You have to fix this. It's your ball.*

At length, Haddy reached for his PPD, only to find he wasn't carrying it.

He looked around for a public terminal, and spotted a kiosk a little ways down the concourse. Its signs were lit. Maybe it hadn't gotten smashed in the battle. He trudged over to it and called up the public net. They needed to talk again, but there was no way they could do it at home.

Once, years ago, when Vin had gotten into a feud with a competitor who was knocking off their suit designs, Vin had invited the other man to coffee and worked things out.

Neutral ground, son, Vin had said. *You have to negotiate on neutral ground. It clears the air.*

Haddy wrote his father a note, telling him he was sorry, asking him if they could talk. He promised to be waiting at the Fly Free coffee bar in the Bazaar. It was where Vin and he always used to go to find new beans to try.

He hit send, then collected himself and trudged his weary way back up the ramp into the Bazaar and found a seat at an empty table. The barista's bench had a sign on it that said "Closed Until Further Notice," so Haddy wouldn't be able to buy a peace offering.

Come to think of it, his credit jack was back in his bedroom with his PPD, so he couldn't have been able to buy anything anyway.

Then he waited an impossibly long time. He didn't have a watch, and couldn't see a clock, so he didn't know how long. A minute might just as well have been two years.

Just as he was about to give up in disgust, Vin hewed into view between a set of booths just up the way. Haddy waved, Vin nodded, and walked toward the table.

"Dad."

"Son."

"Look, I'm sorry. I was completely out of line, I had no business saying that, I just...look. A lot happened while I was out there, and before you get mad at me again, I wanted a chance to explain..."

"Haddy, I..."

"And before that...I just wanted to say that I hope, someday, you can forgive me. I'm really, really sorry. I never wanted to hurt you. Well, I did, but not because of you, not really."

"Hold on, hold on," Vin raised his hands. "Just shut up for a second.

Haddy shut up.

"Son, I'm the one who owes you an apology. My problems with Min don't have anything to do with you. And your mom..." Vin choked up.

"I know," Haddy said quietly. "I miss her too."

Vin nodded vigorously. "I know," he whispered. "Look, why don't you go ahead. Tell me your story."

"Okay," Haddy nodded, feeling a tremendous weight lift from his heart. "So, when I got separated from everybody on Ring Alpha..."

And Haddy told him the story. Vin didn't interrupt, except to ask for clarification from time to time.

When he was done, there was a long silence. Then Vin said, "I didn't know you had it in you."

"Neither did I. I don't even know what 'it' is."

"That kind of courage."

"Courage? Dad I was scared to death the whole time..."

"And you still did everything you had to do." Vin seemed to study Haddy's face for a long moment, then said: "You did a hell of a job, Hadrian. I'm proud of you."

Haddy gulped.

Then, not wanting to sit waiting for one of them to come up with something to fill the uncomfortable silence, he said:

"What happened here? I mean, aside from the obvious."

Vin shook his head. "We'll have plenty of time to talk about that later."

Haddy nodded. "You know I can't stay out of this war."

Vin nodded gravely. "I know."

Another long silence. Then Vin said:

"I guess...I'm going to have to trust you to stick by your principles, wherever they take you. I wouldn't be much of a father if I couldn't do that."

"And this thing with Charis..."

"I can't say I'm happy about it, but...well, we can talk about that later, too. For what it's worth...I think Nita would have approved."

"You do?"

"Yes. I do."

"God I wish she was here."

"Me too, son. Me too."

THE APARTMENT DOOR slid open on a room filled to bursting with people. Min and Arn and Mike and Charis and Ulmar were clustered around the coffee table playing a raucous game of rummy. The air was thick with the smell of freshly-delivered pizza.

But Haddy barely noticed.

Haddy only saw Josie, the tips of her ears just poking up over the back of the chair nearest the door..

He clicked his tongue.

Josie's narrow, wolf-like head raised lazily. She craned her neck and met Haddy's eyes.

Then she was up, and bounding, jumping high in the Lunar Gravity and hitting Haddy full in the chest with twenty-seven mass-kilos of fur and muscle and tongue and happy, helpless whining.

Haddy caught her in both arms as she knocked him off his feet and onto his back.

"That's it, that's it, yes, oh, yes, girl, it's me. I'm home."

She wrestled around on the ground with him until she couldn't contain herself, then she leapt up and bounded all the way to the kitchen, turned around, and bolted to him, running rings around him, sniffing at his feet, whining, her ears pinned back in apoplectic delight.

Haddy snapped his fingers. She sat down smartly and thrashed her tail back and forth across the polished granite.

Haddy knelt down, reached to his left bicep where he still kept her collar, and undid it. He looped it around her neck, replacing the new collar someone had put on her, and buckled it in place.

"Here, baby, this is yours. Yes, I know. I promised I'd come back, didn't I?"

Then he took her face in his hands, and kissed her. She licked the tears of joy off his face and he found himself making promises he didn't know if he'd ever be able to keep.

"Yes, sweetie, yes, I'm back. I'm home. I'm not going to leave again like that, not ever. I promise. I promise."

JOYOUS REUNIONS AND mended fences to one side, there was still work to be done, and urgently. After Charis and Haddy took the night in Haddy's room with Josie splayed between them, and Min and Mike had the night to themselves in Ulmar's room—leaving the boys to camp in the living room under protest—Min set the agenda.

Since Mike was not allowed to know details about what they were looking for, given his inability to keep secrets under the best of circumstances, he continued serving time in the flying shop while Min, Charis, and Haddy set about trying to run down the thumbnail that Amit must have ditched somewhere in the twenty-seven hours he'd been in the city.

The three of them searched for three days, going over every booth Amit had stopped at, every nook and cranny and crevice they could find, but it was no use. Between sorties, Haddy tried to think of new questions to ask Charis, to see if together they could find any scrap of hope. But it was fruitless.

Eventually, even Min was forced to admit defeat.

"The good news is," she said as they sat in the living room having spaghetti with the rest of the adults in the family, "The Americans don't have it. None of our sources inside the American intelligence complex have found any indications that it's shown up on their radar. They're actually offering a bounty for it on the darknet."

Haddy sat in his favorite chair, back to the kitchen, scritching Josie and dangling the occasional noodle in front of her, which she took delicately. She might have been a dog, but she had good table manners. And having her there under his fingers again made the world feel less tumultuous.

"That's a relief," Vin said. "What about you? How long are you going to stick around?"

"We've got to leave tomorrow. Mannix is hosting a piracy conference on Gagarin that we need to get to. With the Americans and Persians distracted with each other for the moment, it falls to us to think up new countermeasures to protect the shipping lanes."

"Which means new designs, and more business for you," Haddy said.

"Exactly."

Charis didn't speak. She was sitting to Haddy's left, looking lost.

She has to leave too, Haddy realized with a pang.

"Um...Charis?" Haddy said. "I'm about done, and this girl needs a walk. You fancy..."

"Oh hell yes." She stood up fast enough that she lifted off the ground, then fumbled trying to get her footing.

"Then if you good people will excuse us," Haddy said, taking some small pleasure in the unaccustomed formality.

THEY WALKED HAND-in-hand, Josie trailing along next to them, just wandering, not saying much, neither of them wanting to spoil the moment with words that wouldn't matter.

But after a while, the silence slid from companionable to oppressive. Haddy realized that he was trying to find excuses not to talk, and he didn't know when they'd get another chance.

If you're going to say anything, you have to say it now.

He spotted a conversation pit a little ways up at a widening in the passage and veered their course towards it.

Haddy sat down sideways on the sea-foam velour, opening a space for Charis to sit facing him, which she did. Josie dutifully lay down at their feet.

"Charis?" Haddy said.

"Yes?"

"I just...I...I don't want you to go. I know you have to..."

"I don't want to go either." The silence hung between them for a moment. Then she said, "Look, I'll call you, every chance I get. Even when I'm out a ways, we can still see each other..." She reached out and touched his face.

"I'd like that. I...I just wish we had more time to..." *Goddammit, Haddy, out with it.* "Charis?"

"Yes, Haddy?"

Oh, to hell with it. He leaned forward and kissed her softly—then, before he could lose himself in it, he pulled back. "I love you."

She smiled, and pressed her forehead to his. "Haddy?"

"Yes?" Haddy trembled.

Then she whispered. "I love you, too."

Haddy did his best not to jump up and whoop, but inside, he was running around and bouncing just like Josie had done the other day.

"You'll come back, right?" He said. "Go flying with me again?"

"You bet your ass." She kissed him. "Every chance I get. Just promise me something..."

"Okay. Name it."

"When I get back here, after the conference..."

"Yes?"

"You'll have your own apartment where we can stay."

"Wow."

"Yeah," she said. She was trembling too. He could feel her shaking through the cushion.

He kissed her again. Really kissed her this time. He felt her whimper against his lips—or maybe it was him, he couldn't tell anymore.

And he'd never have let her go, either, if Josie hadn't jumped up and decided to join in with a flurry of licks.

Charis spat and giggled and scritched Josie. "Looks like *someone* doesn't want to be left out, do you girl? That could get to be a problem."

"We'll work it out."

"Oh, we'll *definitely* work it out," Charis said, still looking at Josie and tossing the pup's head around between her hands. "Because if we don't there's...hey."

"What?"

"How long's it been since you took her to the vet?"

Haddy shrugged. "I guess...eight months ago for her vaccinations."

"Might want to take her tomorrow. Feel this." She moved Haddy's hand to just beneath Josie's left hear. "Feel this bump. She doesn't have one on the other side."

Haddy palpated. There was a bump there. Come to think of it, it was right where she'd had that scratch when...

No. It couldn't be that easy.

But what if...

"Charis," Haddy hissed excitedly. "You told me once Amit didn't like dogs, remember?"

"Yeah, but this sweetie won him over. I was hoping that..."

"No, no, listen. He *didn't like dogs*, but he was attached to the hip with her any time I wasn't in the room, right?"

"Yes. Yes he...no. He couldn't have."

"You've got those medical apps on your PPD. Let's scan her."

Quicker than he could see, she whipped her PPD off her belt and started fiddling with it, then she brought it to Josie's head.

Josie thought she wanted to play, and started licking and mouthing her hand.

"Shh," Haddy stroked her whithers softly. "No, Josie. Stay still. Lie down." Josie climbed the rest of the way onto the cushion and curled up in a ball between them. "That's it. That's it. Good girl. What are you seeing?"

"Haddy...oh my god. Haddy, there's something here."

"Like a thumbnail?"

"Exactly like a thumbnail."

A VERY LONG ROAD

FROM HIS VANTAGE atop the long thermal column at the bottom edge of the ag dome, Hadrian Jin scoped the hundreds-meter depth below him through his blink-lenses. Flicks of his fingers tweaked the primaries on his wings, holding him in a grand circle in his designated airspace, sandwiched between a hard ceiling at the entrance to the ag dome and the top level commercial space of the Gallery.

It was his last shift as skyguard, at least for this month. In five minutes, he was due back in the shop for two more hours of work, and then he had to be down in Grissom to meet an arriving ship.

The war was heating up again. He received nightly updates from Charis over the past six weeks, sandwiched in between their more intimate moments on the long calls that lasted well into the wee hours every morning. In the time she'd been away, the shop had become the new go-to hub for the intelligence network, or at least Aunt Min's section of it.

In between times, he had abandoned his university prep studies for a curriculum in the arts of intelligence and war—a course of study set and overseen by Aunt Min. It kept him so busy he hadn't been able to get back to his writing. But he would, someday, as soon as he could make the time. Which he would, somehow.

Right now, though, his calender was crammed. He

was coming to understand that the business of intelligence wasn't just to find out the enemy's secrets so you could win the war, it was to prevent wars from escalating. He'd been shocked to learn how many times, just in the past two centuries, that world-ending wars had been prevented or curtailed because people in the intelligence communities were willing to go outside the rules and talk to the other side off the books.

Almost as shocked as he'd been to learn how many times bad intelligence and personal agendas had created wars where there needn't have been any in the first place.

This is a dangerous game we're playing, Aunt Min said. *Lose track of that, and people will die.*

People had died. More people were dying every day, out there. It was a fact that did not rest easy on his conscience, and he was determined to do his part to make sure that it stopped as soon as possible.

And it was, perhaps, only a matter of time before the war came home again.

It would be a long road before the end of the war. Haddy just hoped it wouldn't be too long.

And at the end of it, he intended to go back to Nineveh and open up that franchise. That's where the real action would be, as the rest of the solar system opened up. After the fighting was done.

Maybe Charis would go in on it with him, when all the rest was over.

A man could dream, couldn't he?

If he couldn't, what was the point?

But Luna City was on the mend. There had been no more attacks, at least not yet, and business was picking back up.

So far as anyone knew, the Loonies hadn't moved on

the exploit yet. Charis said that the people at the top were waiting for the opportune moment to play their trump card. Such weapons had to be used decisively, in circumstances where they would turn the war completely, or not at all.

But they would move on it. Of that he had no doubt.

Until then, his job was to keep his eyes open, and to pass information up and down the chain to people he'd never seen, and whose names he did not know.

His father still did not approve. But he did, at least, understand, and that was good enough for now.

As Hadrian finished up his shift that evening and went to his new apartment to clean up and fetch Josie to go to the spaceport, though, his mind wasn't on his work. It was on his other job.

Yes, he had another job too, besides studying and espionage and keeping tourists from crashing into walls. And that, too, had been given him by Aunt Min.

It was that responsibility that filled his awareness as he watched the airlock for a blonde head of hair, and a face he was aching to touch, belonging to the woman he spent his nights longing for.

"Here!" He shouted and waved his hand when he caught sight of her.

Charis waved back, and quickened her pace toward him, all smiles, only to be arrested halfway by Josie, charging forward to welcome her back into the pack.

Hadrian swept Charis up in his arms. Josie whined and ran circles around them as they kissed.

Whatever you do, Aunt Min had told him, *Do not forget to live your life. You only get one, and none of us is guaranteed a time beyond this moment.*

It seemed like good advice.

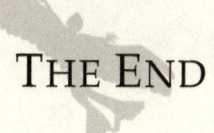

THE END

Turn the page to read a sneak preview of
The Briggs Defection
The first book of The Kabrakan Ascendency
The full story of the Lunar Revolution

I

Washington D.C.
20 December, 2124

ON THE STREET below, thousands of winking blue lamps blazed out through the mid-day gray of the urban core—the headlights of autonomous pods on spiked wheels. They were the only thing on the road. No human would dare drive on a day like this, even in a self-driver, not on rubber tires.

It was deep winter out there. The ice sat nearly half a yard thick over the pavement, the wages of the small ice age that choked the Eastern seaboard every December-through-April.

But the cold beyond the double-glazing of bullet proof transparent fullerine that made up the bay window in Rueben Briggs's office did not seep inside—not in any way that mattered.

It was a cold wind from Plymouth that he was contemplating now. His ex-wife was pestering him to come home again. Home to see his children. Home to the noise of the cat and dog fighting. Home to the din of school-agers arguing over who-took-whose-whatever. Home to an empty bed in a soulless guest room, and a woman who had no patience for his work or anything related to it.

Or anything to do with him, for that matter.

At least the ice outside was honest about its intentions.

But he supposed he needed to go, for the kids if nothing else. Joanne was right; it wasn't fair to them, him living down here since his appointment. But what was he supposed to do? The National Security Advisor needed to be within spitting distance of the President, and the DNI, and the DDO, and everyone else in town with two or more capital letters after their name, and it wasn't as if he'd come into office at the height of peacetime.

After what he'd learned in the last eighteen months, he figured he had only about a one in three chance of stopping a major war from breaking out.

The failure of his marriage had, he supposed, been a question of mutual dislike: Joanne didn't like life inside the beltway. Briggs didn't much care for life lived under threat of a Persian military presence in space.

She'd acted on her preferences. He was acting on his, as best he could. The divorce had been finalized on Thanksgiving.

If he was honest with himself, he'd rather it had been different. He'd have given up almost anything to recapture the kind of life he and Joanne had shared before Washington.

Anything, really, but Washington itself.

Mister Briggs?" Tabitha—Briggs's pasty ginger lieutenant—stuck her overly coiffed head through the half-open door, elaborate feather fanciers and all.

Yes?" Briggs turned from the window and scooped up the deck of red Bicycles on the edge of his desk and started handling them absent-mindedly. Practice for the poker tournament in Grenada late next month. He didn't get to play as often as he used to, but he'd long ago made it a matter of personal discipline to keep his fingers nimble.

The last of the local intercepts."

Local intercepts. This was the term he'd trained his staff to use for the reports that he had a special interest in, and for which he'd built his own sorting algorithm. It was a toy from his early days teaching at Stanford, one he'd tinkered with over the years as he'd advanced from academia to government. It caught mostly junk—it was designed, specifically, to catch things that the rest of the intelligence community would classify as junk—but sometimes, in his private little junk pile, there were gems.

Thank you, Tabitha," Briggs crossed to her, accepted the PPD, gave it a cursory glance. Analyst work was below his pay grade these days, but he insisted on keeping a hand in anyway. It had taken him eighteen months to get his staff to accept his hands-on way of doing things, but they were finally falling well into line.

The gems he kept finding helped.

He looked up from the device. "Why don't you knock off for the day? Beat the traffic. Give that wife of yours a surprise, eh?"

Tabitha's normally flat demeanor opened up. Briggs wasn't known for being generous with time, but facing down his own dreaded homecoming at the end of the day he thought it only proper to give someone else the chance to sample the joy he couldn't.

You're sure?"

Most assuredly. Go on, get moving. You don't want to get caught in the rush with the storm moving in."

She peaked her eyebrows and vanished silently through the heavy oak door, closing it behind her, leaving only a trace of rosemary perfume in her wake.

Briggs returned to his desk, scrolling through the PPD with his right thumb, idly cutting and re-cutting the card deck in his other hand.

He sat down in his leather wingback office chair and scooted back, propping his feet on the desk, swinging one over the other. It wasn't as relaxing a position as it used to be. Life at a beltway desk had given him the body of a bureaucrat.

Now, let's see here. Any gems in the pile today?"

The most recent significant gem he'd found two months ago, and it had brought him to loggerheads with Bill Shelley, the head of the Space Affairs Committee, a man of unimpeachable reputation. Shelley was also a man-of-the-people (at least when you placed that term in the strongest possible scare quotes). A Massachusetts blue-blood from the Adams clan, old money and power going back to the foundation of the republic, and about as connected to the concerns of his "fellow Americans" as Joanne was to her sex drive.

Briggs's own working-class upbringing in Yucatan had forever poisoned him against the pretensions of blue-bloods who fancied themselves men-of-the-people, and that was the beginning of his loathing for Shelley.

But loathing was something he could work around. At bottom, Shelley had the same policy goals as Briggs. Both recognized that the Lunar Colonies couldn't continue as American outposts forever, not if the solar system was to have a stable future. They'd made a good team, with Shelley working the Senate and Briggs working the White House, co-ordinating their efforts to push the right buttons and migrate American policy—by inches—toward something sustainable over the long term.

A return to the old Bretton Woods system, that was the aim. Just as America had once used its muscle to ensure freedom of the seas for the rest of the world, now it would ensure freedom-of-the-skies.

At least, that was the dream. If they could pull it off, they might avoid an all-out war for control of the solar system—a war that they both knew that no Terran power could possibly win.

Then, six months ago, things had started to turn. Shelley went limp just as the policy push entered its most delicate phase.

And then, one of those little gems in the junk. An intercept from a server Briggs had been watching for a while—a darknet router that got chatty anytime the world took one of its periodic lurches toward the metaphorical toilet. The messages weren't encrypted—that would have singled them out for special attention, and the encryption would eventually be broken. Instead, they were in code. Innocent-sounding correspondence, each word with a private meaning known only to the sender and recipient.

Briggs had gotten to know the writing style of this particular sender. He hadn't been able to identify who it was, yet, or who the sender was working for, but he was pretty confident that it wasn't someone working for the American establishment. This note talked about a tree trimming service and a Greek restaurant named "Chlentzos's"—meaningless drivel, on the surface. Except that Briggs had seen this combination of gardening and Greek food before in his intercepts, just often enough that it had stuck in his memory. And that day, he'd happened to have had lunch at the Greek restaurant mentioned in the email.

It was enough for him to dig into it, more-or-less on his own time. He couldn't really justify spending official resources on the longest of hunches. And he was glad he hadn't when it turned out that Chlentzos's was a real establishment with which Bill Shelley had an ongoing gastronomic love affair.

The problem that niggled him, though:

Bill Shelley was allergic to garlic—or had claimed to be at least twice at state functions where Briggs could over-hear him.

Shelley. Could he be running his own private intel service through the restaurant? Using it to communicate with assets that a senator wasn't allowed to have direct access to?

Or maybe...

If he was being pressured by someone using the restau-rant as a drop, or a clearing house, it would explain his sudden lack of efficacy on their mutual campaign.

It was a conjecture—the kind of leap of intuition that wouldn't stand up to scrutiny for a moment. But Briggs had built his career on those leaps of intuition, and he had learned not to ignore them.

Still, he couldn't afford to open an investigation. Not officially. Instead, he'd enlisted outside assistance in the form of a Russian mercenary with whom he sometimes did off-the-books business.

In the meantime, he'd taken steps to get Shelley shut out of the inner circle at the White House. Not an easy task, considering that Shelley was one of President Johan-son's old fraternity buddies.

But Briggs had not gotten to his current position by playing softball. Since there was no way to prove his suspicions—and since Shelley was an obstacle for other reasons in any case—he'd played a palmed card.

When Shelley had been widowed twelve years ago, he had turned to a friend for...comfort. That friend had been Allegra Johanson—the current President's wife, though long before Johanson had been elected—and Shelley had used that relationship to further his political game.

It was a relationship the President hadn't known about, and a relationship that had continued after Johanson had taken the White House. A scandal would have been disastrous, so Briggs, ever the loyal lapdog, had informed the President of the affair "Out of concern for your reputation, Mr. President."

And, like that, Shelley had gotten the cold shoulder, without anyone ever being the wiser.

My my, you have all been busy, haven't you?" Briggs muttered as he leafed through the discarded traffic. He recognized quite a bit of it—coded messages zipping between various criminal organizations both on-world and off. Orders for weapons shipments, counterfeit goods, money laundering, the usual background noise that the Justice Department pretended to be concerned about when they weren't trading in it themselves.

Nothing of distinctive interest...

Briggs stopped at a bounty listing. He did love a good bounty listing. They comprised an entire rhetorical art form all their own. Light on specificity, nothing that might stand up in court. A good bounty listing read like any other want ad, but there was a certain cadence in the pitch that left little doubt as to the nature of the services being sought. He kept a file on administration officials with prices on their heads, fed it regularly to the Secret Service on the QT. Since his intercept wasn't official, he couldn't put it through official channels, but someone was always trying to assassinate someone. Geopolitics was a game, and Briggs considered it a collegiate obligation to keep people on his team from falling victim to the machinations of any of the opposing teams.

Must have appropriate and current credentials for 3204-230-33456 locale.

Briggs's breath caught in his throat. That put the target in the intelligence community, and the solicitor was looking for someone with active clearance. Hiring a hit behind the gray wall.

That would make the Secret Service's job interesting. It had been a few decades since they'd had to find a mole inside the establishment.

Briggs opened the metadata on the posting. It had been listed on one of the popular industry dark sites in the South American zone...

...via a last-mile node in Vermont.

Shelley was in Vermont right now, for the Christmas holidays. He always took Christmas up there with his family.

Briggs's hands started shaking. It could be a coincidence. There were a lot of perfectly suitable targets in the intelligence establishment. There was no reason to believe Shelley had targeted *him*. Rivalry was one thing. Even enmity. But contract murder? Shelley would be flushing his career away—and his life.

Stay calm, Reuben. Get confirmation.

Briggs set the PPD down, opened the lower right drawer in his desk. He pulled out the secure-black phone he kept down there, paired it with the PPD, copied the message, and typed in a number.

He added a 6469 to the beginning of the message—his account ID—and hit send.

Somewhere else in the world—maybe in town, maybe in Minsk—a Russian mercenary named Natalia would get the message and run it against her own set of resources. She would be able to confirm the target, or get close enough that Briggs would be able to decide how to handle things.

THE AFTERNOON WORE him down like a grindstone. It was one thing to pull the strings that resulted in policy decisions that got people killed. It was quite another to be listed for a bounty.

If it was him.

It couldn't really be him. He was only the National Security Advisor. Not important enough to kill. Not like the DNI. Kill the DNI and you could upend the intelligence community for a good week or two, plenty of time to slip something important through the hole you'd just created in the network.

But the National Security Advisor? He served at the pleasure of the President. It wasn't even a congressionally confirmed position. It was his job to translate intel-speak to President-speak, and come at things from a different angle than the establishment wonks. Kill him, and someone else would simply take his place. Briggs might be the best analyst in the country, but he wasn't the only viable candidate, not by a long shot. Removing him wouldn't advance anyone's agenda—it certainly wouldn't change policy.

And he was sure he didn't have any angry husbands (or wives) looking for him. He hadn't slept with anyone that might be vindictive—he was scrupulous about keeping on good terms with current and former lovers, and former wives. That was just a matter of survival in this business.

This contract wasn't anything he needed to worry about, he was sure about that. He saw bounty listings all the time. Whether through local intercepts or through the normal bureaucratic channels, his job kept him in constant contact with the chatter coming out of the private military industry that haunted the borderlands between the North and South American zones. Contract murder was part of the business climate down there—the Persians used it to suborn corruption, the Americans used it to undermine the Persians, and business interests used it to eliminate local competitors who were good enough to be a threat on the open market.

This was more of the same. It would turn out to be someone with a bad investment, or who didn't live up to a bribe. Briggs wasn't on anyone's take, and his investments were all legit, and none of the companies he owned a piece of did business down there. He was careful about that for just this reason.

It was just the paranoia that came with the job tripping him up. Nerves. That was it. He just needed a drink or two to steady them.

And maybe call home to tell his family he'd be late. As soon as he got confirmation, he could take a spinner back home, be there in time to see the kids to bed and have a soulless nightcap with the most recent love of his life.

BY SEVEN O'CLOCK the sun had long since given up its battle with the interminable gray.

The crystal decanter quaked enough in his hands that drops of whisky spilled onto the PPD. One of them lensed the first letters in the word "Bounty" to a ghoulish size. Briggs cursed and set the decanter down, then picked the device up and used his shirt cuff to wick the liquor off before it found a way into the electronics. Manufactured in Panama—common rule of law to one side, Panamanian electronics had a way of failing right when you needed

351 Daniel Sawyer 351

them most.

Briggs was halfway through his sixth tumbler of scotch when the secure phone sounded a gentle tone.

He activated the display.

Job solicited. Target confirmed:
Reuben Briggs

He stared at it.

He blinked, looked away, and stared at it again.

And he laughed.

A loud, mad laugh. As if his impending death set loose something wild deep within his soul. Vindication, or something that tasted like it.

Shelley *had* ordered him dead.

Oh, Briggs couldn't prove it in court. He didn't even have enough evidence to get an indictment. He *might* be able to justify some official surveillance. But if he hadn't been the dick-brained micromanaging shit head that his subordinates took him for, he'd not have known about this dispatch until the bullet hit his brain.

Briggs tossed the PPD on his desk and walked to the window again, weighing his options.

It was a hell of a box to be in, and no mistake. If that bounty got picked up by someone with the clearance, he wouldn't be safe even in the hands of the Secret Service.

And a price that high...

Well, if there was one thing Briggs knew he could depend on, it was the venial nature of public servants. Anyone in debt, anyone with an eye on retirement, anyone with a secret gambling problem was likely to take it—and the list of people fitting that description, and having the proper clearances to pierce even a Secret Service detail, was longer than his arm.

Hell, the list of Secret Service agents fitting that description was as long as his arm, and those were just the ones he knew about. He wasn't willing to indulge in the delusion that he knew them all. He could pick his own detail and still wind up dead.

If a determined commoner could assassinate a President—and the last Presidential assassination had happened only twenty years ago—then a determined insider could get to the National Security Advisor.

But the bounty had just been posted today. Odds were he had a few days to maneuver. A wet boy willing to take this job would want to get away clean. It took time to plan a good op and a clean escape, especially if you were going up against the intel community.

Looking out over the city, Briggs felt like a goose balancing on the slenderest of limbs, waiting for the twig to snap and the hunters to shoot.

If he wanted to survive, he needed to move fast—and he needed to appear perfectly normal. No deviation from previous plans. Not until everything was ready.

Briggs cleared his throat. There was a memo he'd intended to send next week, but he could just as well send it now. Clear the desk. A normal thing to do before the Christmas break.

Computer, begin dictation." He knocked back the full tumbler, nearly choked on the alcohol, recovered from the coughing fit, and poured himself a fresh glass.

From: Reuben Briggs, National Security Advisor, To: Roberto Johanson, President of the United States of North America." He closed his eyes and collected his thoughts. Whoever came after him would want to make it look like an accident. He had time. Not much, but he had time. He just needed to choose his words carefully.

He continued his dictation.

> *Dear Mr. President:*
>
> *Attached you will find the requested analysis of the Mars Governance Treaty.*
>
> *Section 1 deals with the strategic implications of reallocating resources away from fleet renovations in light of the construction of the Persian Destroyer Class (see blue prints and specifications from the DDI in Appendix D). This development threatens our interests closer to Earth and Luna."*

He raised his glass to his lips only to find it empty again. When he picked up the decanter, he found his hands were sweating so much he could barely keep a grip on the thing.

> *Section 2 examines the economics of colonialism and the historic revolutionary window that appears in the fourth generation. We're catching traffic that indicates a growing unrest among the Lunar colonials, as expected. The report details our projections for the timing of revolutionary action on Luna, and suggestions for mitigating it before it creates more pressing geopolitical problems. The Persian situation is also examined for its complicating potential and its parallels to the lead-up to the Asian Nuclear Exchange."*

Could he expose Shelley in time to get the bounty withdrawn? Confront him personally? Blackmail him?

> *Section 3 dissects the economic effects of French and German withdrawal on the ore mining and processing industries. This section also explores the probable amplifying effects of Space Station Nineveh on*

interplanetary traffic in goods, services, labor, and population."

No. Shelley was more likely to kill him personally and arrange a cover-up. The Senator would not stand for being made out a traitor, or a stooge, or a pocket-man. This dispatch was checkmate in their long chess game; Briggs would be dead inside a month, and he wouldn't be able to nail Shelley for it.

How had Shelley connected him to the cold-shouldering?

Johanson. He must have confronted Shelley personally. He was a straightforward man. And Shelley would have connected it to the difficulties with Briggs.

Briggs poured his tumbler of scotch, then set it down on his desk. There was a brochure in the paper tray, for the reef diving expedition he'd been planning to take after the new year, down in the Caribbean. Right before the poker tournament. He'd been looking forward to it ever since the weather turned.

His plans weren't secret. It would be a good place for a hit. Easier to stage an accident out in the middle of the ocean than here in Washington, or up in Plymouth.

He teetered a bit on his feet, from either the stress or the booze. His heart was beating too fast—he'd been jockey-ing a desk for too long and was further out of shape than he'd been in his life so far. But he managed to keep his voice steady for the dictation.

The concluding section uses Nineveh as a case study in private sector investment on the frontier, and examines the argument advanced by the Orbital Dynamics Group that its success is the only practical way to maintain the human expansion out past the asteroid belt. It also details policy recommendations to prevent the Persian situation from escalating, along with projections of the five most likely wartime and peacetime scenarios."

Maybe, just maybe, the Caribbean could be his way out. He could "die" before they had a chance to kill him. A doable job. Even in a constantly-watched world, there were still ways to disappear, if one was careful enough. If one knew the holes in the system.

And Briggs knew all the holes.

But it would have to be convincing. Not even Joanne or the kids could know. If they did, someone might leverage them against him.

Family always made good leverage.

Besides, Joanne would be happy to see him gone—no more fights over how frequently he visited (or didn't).

Finally, in answer to your other question, I've settled on a fishing tour of the West Indies for my vacation. I'll send back some marlin steaks if I get lucky on the troll.

Sincerely.

Computer, correct the dictation for grammar and print me a proof copy collated with the items in the 'Persian-Lunar Tactical 3' directory."

Reuben Briggs walked back to his window and slouched against the wall. The snow-heavy eaves of the building opposite looked like something out of an industrial-era nightmare. He couldn't stand the snow and wet—they always made him feel like a peasant when they cut through his coat.

One way or another, he wouldn't have to deal with the snow after the new year. He might never see the stuff again. That thought cauterized something inside him, and he turned back to his desk as rapidly as his equilibrium would allow.

He took the pack of cards from the corner of the desk and set them on the brochure. He was going to need them.

His flight left for Trinidad a week from Wednesday. If he was going to live to see the Caribbean, he had a lot of work to do.

This ends this sample of
The Briggs Defection
Coming Soon on wherever ebooks and paperbacks are sold

AUTHOR'S NOTE

ONE OF THE benefits of space travel is, I firmly believe, the chance to do things that we can only dream about down here on Earth—chief among them being to soar like a bird.

Not that the idea originates with me. Not by a long shot. I first got my mind opened to the possibilities of true human habitation of space and of other planets the summer I turned nineteen.

During that summer, I found an old battered paperback at a garage sale for ten cents. I had not, in fact, gone to the garage sale actually intending to buy anything. I was just accompanying my then-girlfriend on the only kind of date we could afford. For perspective, this was a summer when I rented floor space in an abandoned building to sleep on, and was in danger of eviction from the abandoned building due to a severe case of unemployability brought on by an acute bout of I'm-too-good-to-work-at-McDonalds-so-to-hell-with-all-of-you.

That dime was, almost literally, the price of a meal (it's amazing what you can do with ramen, and how cheap you can find it when you're truly motivated), and it was more than I could afford, but this book was special, so I managed to bargain it down from a quarter to a dime, and I ate the story instead of the noodles.

Special?

Yes.

The book was *The Menace From Earth* by Robert A.

Heinlein. I'd never heard the title before, but I did know the author. I'd learned about his existence on the day of his death, when my father handed me one of the books Heinlein wrote for kids and said: "Read this."

At the time, I loved fantasy, but hadn't yet fallen in love with science fiction. Heinlein changed that, and permanently. I tore through his catalog as fast as I could find his books, and by the time I moved away to college in those pre-Internet days, I assumed that the twenty books I'd already read constituted his whole bibliography, and I was pretty unhappy about that.

Then I found *The Menace From Earth*, a collection of short novels whose feature title is about a girl who trains tourists in the art of bird-wing flying on the moon, as a way to finance her engineering startup. It was one of a baker's dozen of novels and novelettes that Heinlein wrote for specifically for teenagers (and the only one with a female protagonist), and I still remember huddling in my sleeping bag, reading by candle light (because I couldn't afford a bedside lamp) about the finer points of avionics-in-action as the heroine risked high-speed dives onto hard ground to save the life of a client.

I enjoyed it so much that, when I eventually began writing *The Kabrakan Ascendency*, (my larger series about the world in which *Hadrian's Flight* is set), I threw in "Bob and Ginny's Flying Lessons" as a piece of set dressing, just on a lark.

Little did I know what that small piece of set dressing would do to the broader universe. As of now, it's played a pivotal role in the *Suave Rob* series, now it's front-and-center in *Hadrian's Flight*, and due to the events in this book, I wouldn't be surprised if it showed up in future installments of *The Kabrakan Ascendency* as well.

I suppose it's all sublimation—really, I want to be the one up there on the moon, in a pressurized cave, flying like a bird. Then again, who knows? It is just possible that I'll live long enough to get that chance. If I do, and you do as well, you might just bump into an old, doddering guy in a big set of wings wearing the goofiest grin in the solar system.

You know, now that I really think about it...that dime might have been the best ten cents I ever spent.

J. Daniel Sawyer
Lincoln City, OR
August 2016

ABOUT THE AUTHOR

WHILE *STAR WARS* and *STAR TREK* seeded J. Daniel Sawyer's passion for the unknown, his childhood in academia gave him a deep love of history and an obsession with how the future emerges from the past. This obsession led him through adventures in the film industry, the music industry, venture capital firms in the startup culture of Silicon Valley, and a career creating novels and audiobooks exploring the worlds that assemble themselves in his head.

The author of twenty-four books and innumerable short stories, his travels with bohemians, burners, historians, theologians, and inventors led him eventually to a rural exile where he uses the quiet to write, walk on the beach, and manage a production company that brings innovative stories to the ears of audiences across the world.

www.ingramcontent.com/pod-product-compliance
Lightning Source LLC
Chambersburg PA
CBHW020240200626
46816CB00001BA/55